A ST

Lizzy hea...
foyer, Lizzy listened harder, straining for the sound.
Someone rapped on the door.

Who would call at this hour, in the middle of a storm?
Peering through the windowpane was like staring into a
waterfall.

"Who's out there?"

A long drumroll of thunder cut off the reply. Taking the
precaution of grabbing a cedar cane she kept by the stair, she
unbolted the door. Before she could turn the porcelain knob,
the door swung open.

"Eliza."

The stranger's voice came out of the storm, unexpected
and quiet. Lizzy jumped back, brandishing the cane. "If
you're trying to—to frighten me, you can just get off my
sister's property!"

A man's silhouette filled the doorway. Lizzy could see his
damnable Yankee uniform, but his face was lost in the
gloom. She squeezed the club so hard her fingers went
numb.

"Who are you?"

"Rafe Laffite." He stepped into the foyer and closed the
door. Water flowed off his clothing and across the floor to
Lizzy's bare feet.

"Eliza, I'm not going to hurt you."

His voice, low and deep, wrapped around her like silken
cords, binding her more surely than his caress could have.
She could not force her limbs to propel her away from him.

"Why have you come?" Her vocal cords felt like frayed
hemp.

"To see your face, Eliza." Heat ran through her at his
words, but his knees buckled and he fell against the pilaster.
When Lizzy tried to catch him, his weight crumpled her
onto the staircase.

Diamond

Venita Helton

LEISURE BOOKS   NEW YORK CITY

To my mama and daughter, Joyce and Lindsay. The world shines brighter because you're here. And to you, Devon, my future sports star. Keep working that arm.

A LEISURE BOOK®

September 1998

Published by

Dorchester Publishing Co., Inc.
276 Fifth Avenue
New York, NY 10001

Copyright © 1998 by Venita Helton

ISBN 0-8439-4427-7

The name "Leisure Books" and the stylized "L" with design are trademarks of Dorchester Publishing Co., Inc.

Printed in the United States of America.

Chapter One

Huntsville, Alabama
September 1, 1864

"Mrs. McCord, I presume you've kept count of the number of times you've been hauled in here to answer charges?"

Lizzy McCord was melting under the afternoon sun piercing the windows of the railroad depot. The medieval breastplate she wore over her hooped skirt was as hot as boiler iron. Through the smoke-clogged air, she smelled charred clothing.

Brig. Gen. Seaman Granger leaned back in his chair to take advantage of the only patch of shade in the room, and dragged cigar smoke into his mouth. "Well?"

Lizzy folded her arms. If he was trying to make her feel small, the disastrous afternoon had already accomplished the task. What excuse could she give Rector Bannister for burning down his carriage house? She should have tested her garment-drying machine in her workshop rather than on the Bannisters' wash, but she'd let impatience overrule good sense. As usual.

Her old mammy had told her she'd land in hell someday if she didn't learn patience and humility. It seemed someday was today, humiliation burning in her breast.

"This is the third time, isn't it?" Granger asked.

"Third?"

"Third time you've been charged with public malfeasance."

"Fourth." At his glare, she added, "Sir."

"Fourth." He slapped his quill pen down on the desk. "By the Eternal, what's one more incident?"

He made it sound as though she'd started the fire intentionally. She examined her left hand, burned while beating the flames with a horse blanket. It was paining her now as though she'd dragged it through a brier patch. Her gaze drifted to a locomotive approaching the railyard outside the sooty, flyblown window.

"I asked you a question!"

The dirty old Yankee shopkeeping general was asking her to humiliate herself further . . . or to explode and tell him exactly what she thought of him and his craven bluebellies so he'd have an ironclad excuse to lock her up. She gave him a frosty look.

Granger struck the desk with his fist. "They warned me about Southern women, but, by gum, they never warned me about *you!* I hope I never meet another as fractious!"

Lizzy's hand flew up to slap him, but at the last second she brought it to her own face and brushed away a strand of chestnut brown hair.

"What's this contraption they told me about?" Granger asked. "And how did you manage to set the carriage house afire with the blasted thing?"

Despite her anger, Lizzy answered in the soft, contralto lilt of northern Alabama. "The machine dries clothing, sir. You put wet raiment into the bin and turn the crank, which turns a screw propeller."

"A screw propeller! Like on a steamship?"

"Not that large."

"I gathered that; do I look like a fool? What's its purpose?"

"It injects hot air from the firebox into the tumbling bin. The garments dry within an hour or two. Simple."

"Simple to burn the contents and set the house ablaze!"

"It has some faults, but I believe I can prevent it from happening next time—"

"Next time? There won't be any next time."

"Why, there will so! Of course, I'll have to modify the design a bit. If I add an extra screen to keep out sparks, the machine—"

Granger held up his hands. "I don't want to hear your lunatic scheme. There's a reason everyone calls you Dizzy Lizzy. I, for one, am in complete concordance with their sentiments."

"You just don't understand inventors, sir."

"Oh, I understand inventors, all right. They need to be locked up with all the other madmen running around this rebellious little country of yours. You're proof of that."

"I'm a visionary, General."

"Aye, the wild look in those big blue eyes of yours tells me that. A visionary—bah!"

He leaned back in his chair and contemplated her ensemble. "It would take a visionary to decipher what you're wearing. What, do tell, is that awful contrivance you have over your gown?"

The breastplate had belonged to her father, gotten

9

from a German tinker who'd claimed it once belonged to an archduke of Austria. She was proud of it.

"It's armor," she said.

"I know what it is. What I fail to understand is how you came to be wearing such a ridiculous getup."

"To protect myself."

"Then you knew you were going to start a fire!"

"No! I wore it . . . just in case. Sometimes my experiments go awry."

"Sometimes?" Granger exhaled smoke into her face. "Sometimes, as in that awful, scandalous egg-laying inducer you tried to peddle not long ago!"

"You had no right to lock me up for that," she said.

"I had every right. No decent person would countenance such a thing, tickling a hen's bottom to make it lay. And I haven't forgotten that spring-loaded corset. Why, there was—"

"I told her not to sing in the choir before I had a chance to test it thoroughly."

"—clothing flying everywhere, and right in the middle of church! By heavens, what will it take to make you stop being a thorn in the side of every soldier and citizen in this damned town?"

Lizzy thumped her fists down on the desk and leaned toward him. "How dare you speak of *my* being a thorn in anyone's side when you, personally, are the biggest bramble patch in the state of Alabama, you odious, interloping old greenbrier, you!"

Granger's cigar fell out of his mouth, hit the desk, and rolled onto his lap. With an oath, he swept ashes off his trousers. "See, you've done it again!"

"That was your own clumsiness!"

"Your machinations were at the bottom of it!"

"At least mine make life a little more bearable for

the people of this town—maybe even for your soldiers. Yours cause nothing but heartache!''

''Heartache? Try telling that to Bannister when he sees what you did to his property.''

''I didn't set out to burn down the carriage house, which is more than you can say for the destruction y'all carried to this valley! I wish I had a dollar for every piece of property your bluebellies have burned up!''

The screech of the train pulling into the station drowned out Granger's retort, but Lizzy read his lips. Shocked, she folded her arms and turned her back on him.

Belching steam like a dragon, the locomotive ground to a halt. Behind the tender the doors of a dozen cattle cars slid open and soldiers jumped out. Packs came tumbling after them, and then the gangplanks clanged into place. Horses skittered down and were taken to the watering troughs.

Lizzy trembled with rage. This fresh horde would finish off what little food Huntsville's inhabitants had left. More folks would be thrown into the streets so the Yankees could live in their houses. More white canvas tents would pimple the courthouse square and decent folks' yards. More women and children would suffer. She couldn't stand it.

''God give these swaggering stoats a case of malaria!'' She raised her voice over the stomp of boots on the boardwalk. ''God help Jefferson Davis. God bless the Confederacy. And if it's not asking too much, Lord, help me figure a way to send these cutthroats back up North where they belong!''

''Young woman!'' Granger said. ''Come here at once!''

But her gaze had caught on one officer. Why she'd noticed him in the sea of blue uniforms she couldn't say, but unconsciously she moved close to the window.

Perhaps it was the way he stood, his long, lean form in perfect harmony with his broad shoulders, his easy grace as he motioned to his men, that reminded her of someone.

She could not see his face. He looked eastward, toward the rear of the train, his forage cap pulled low on his brow, his collar-length, tawny hair hiding all but his partial profile, an unkempt beard darkening his jaw. He wore the gold bars of a captain and the blue wool of the North.

It could not be him. And yet . . .

He was twenty paces away, too far to hear, but Lizzy unconsciously raised her fist to knock on the glass. Before she touched it, she snatched away her hand.

He did not turn, but power emanated from him like the cold flash of a diamond. A tilt of his head, a jerk of his thumb sent soldiers rushing to obey some unspoken command.

Deaf to Granger's orders, she stood like a marble pillar, all of her being focused in a recognition that was, at the same time, dread. She didn't want to know, didn't want to believe, wanted more than anything to run away and never return.

At last he turned and started with deliberate tread for the station. Lizzy's chest burned with sudden fire.

It was the man she had once loved.

He had changed, but there was no doubting who he was.

With his bronzed skin stretched across astonishingly high cheekbones, his golden green eyes ranging from the tracks to the depot to each passing soldier, he looked very dangerous.

Willing the dusty, sun-glazed panes of glass to shield her, Lizzy held her breath. He started to pass by; then his cougar's eyes found and held her for an eternity. There was no surprise in his gaze, just recognition. And promise.

And then he smiled, a slow, enigmatic extension of his soul. His fingertips came up, almost brushing the glass. Lizzy sucked in a hot breath of oxygen, waiting with pounding heart for him to release her.

He touched the glass for an instant, then walked on, leaving the marks of his fingers behind. Lizzy recoiled as though she'd been scorched.

The heat was unbearable. She undid the buckles at her sides and cast off the breastplate. Wave after wave of fire crashed against the banks of her awareness. Acid surged into the back of her throat; blood roared in her ears.

She was going to be sick, deathly sick. General Granger's voice came from a long way off; then hands supported her until she slumped onto a chair.

Raphael Dominique Laffite. *Rafe.*

He was not supposed to come back into her life. Long ago she'd given him up for dead. Now, cruel fate had brought this man home in the uniform of a traitor.

The hatred buried long ago rose with grasping fingers for her soul. Years before she had been ready to shoot him on sight. For two cents, she still would.

Chapter Two

The burns on her hand pulsed with every beat of her heart, hot and painful despite the wet rags she'd wrapped around them. She should have asked her sister to tend to her when the Yankees had brought her home last night, but she'd run upstairs to her room, away from Grace's questions. Away from everything but pain.

Barely audible over the wind rattling the shutters, the downstairs clock struck three. Lightning flashed through the louvers and that part of her mind where Rafe Laffite lay.

She tried to focus on the pain in her hand, but all else blurred before his image, bright and powerful as a ray of sunlight, burning through the wall of enmity she'd raised against him so long ago. In her mind's eye he stood at the gates, looking in at her.

"Stop it!"

She sat straight up in bed and grabbed the sides of her head, silencing the whispering in her mind, listening only to the wind in the yew trees, attempting to capture the storm. They were the house's only shield.

A shield was what *she* needed. A shield against Rafe Laffite, against General Granger, against all the Yankees. Against the banishment Granger had threatened her with just before sending her home.

Thunder rolled across the hill and shook the house until the shutters broke open and slammed against the clapboards. Lizzy ran to the window and started to close the shutters. Then, instead, she braced them open with her hands.

Wind as cold as the top of a cloud plowed into her. She stood before the blast, staring up the macadamized western turnpike to Russell Hill. Lightning reached out of the clouds and fingered the breastworks there.

Maybe tonight those bluebellies will get a taste of that hellfire and brimstone Rector Bannister promised them.

Lightning scissored the sky. A solid sheet of rain masked Russell Hill, stormed down the turnpike to pummel the tin roof over her head, and blasted through the window to soak her.

As she struggled to wrest the shutters from the wind that held them open, a thunderbolt dropped out of the storm like a great scythe and hacked the top off a cottonwood tree, flinging it against the house. Lizzy slammed the shutters and ran out into the hall.

"Sister! Hattie Lee! Y'all okay?"

The door at the end of the hall burst open. Grace Fairlove stumbled out holding a candle. She had rags in her hair. Candlewax stained her nightdress. "Merciful heavens, that was a loud crack!" she said. "Have we been hit by lightning?"

"A chunk of the cottonwood hit the house," Lizzy said.

"Oh, Lord!"

15

"Don't get all het up about it; at least it wasn't lightning. Hattie Lee all right?"

"She's asleep—she's got nerves like yours."

"Mine aren't so steady tonight," Lizzy said. "Hush! What was that noise?"

"You're asking what was that noise in the middle of a thunderstorm?" Grace rolled her eyes. "Maybe the broken part of that tree's rubbing the house."

Lizzy moved to the staircase. From where she stood, she could see lightning illuminating the narrow windowpanes on either side of the foyer door.

"There it is again, Sister," Lizzy said, "that tapping sound. Hear it?"

"Lizzy, don't go down there!"

"I'll be back in a minute. Y'all get under the bed. I don't like the sound of that wind; something else might fall on the house."

"You get back up here with us, you hear?"

But Lizzy took hold of the banister. It was cold and wet with humidity. Her foot slipped on the polished oak step.

"I'm going back to Hattie Lee," Grace called to her. "Don't you take too long!"

Blue-white flashes illuminated the foyer. Between crashes of thunder, Lizzy heard the tapping again. Growing careless, she hurried down the staircase. As she stepped into the foyer, the looking glass rattled above the whatnot table. Worried about Grace's figurines, Lizzy steadied the mirror.

Someone rapped on the door.

She flinched. Who would call at this hour, in the middle of a storm? Peering through the windowpane beside the door was like staring into a waterfall.

"Who's out there?"

A long drumroll of thunder cut off the reply. Perhaps

a neighbor was sick and wanted Grace to come. Taking the precaution of grabbing a cedar cane she kept by the stair, she unbolted the door. Before she could turn the porcelain knob, the door swung open.

"Eliza."

The stranger's voice came out of the storm, unexpected and quiet. Lizzy jumped back, brandishing the cane. "If you're trying to—to frighten me, you can just get off my sister's property!"

A man's silhouette filled the doorway. Lizzy could see his Yankee uniform, but his face was lost in the gloom. She squeezed the club so hard her fingers went numb.

"Who are you?"

"Rafe Laffite." He stepped into the foyer and closed the door. Water flowed off his clothing and across the floor to Lizzy's bare feet.

"Eliza, I'm not going to hurt you."

His voice, low and deep, wrapped around her like silken cords, binding her more surely than his caress could have. She could not force her limbs to propel her upstairs.

"Why have you come?" Her vocal cords felt like frayed hemp.

He moved closer. She retreated up onto the bottom step, yet she still had to tilt her head to meet his gaze. In the staccato flashes of lightning his face looked gaunt and forbidding, his eyes shadowy. "By the sacred thunder," he said in French, "you are even more beautiful than I remembered."

"Don't speak so to me!" She should run upstairs and hide with Grace and Hattie Lee, but her feet did not belong to her anymore.

Soaked as he was, he smelled of leather and woodsmoke, sweat and pain. Without touching him, she perceived his trembling. Did he suffer from the rain?

17

She stabbed her forefinger at him, then at the door. "Get out of my sister's house."

Instead of leaving, Rafe Laffite bent closer to her. His breath brushed like hot magnolia leaves against her neck. She had to strain to hear his words over the peals of thunder.

"You need not fear me, Eliza," he said. "I'm not a Yankee."

"Liar," she said. "I saw you come in on the train. And you're wearing a Yankee uniform."

He dropped his hand to the banister, beside hers. Lizzy felt its extreme warmth without touching it. She raised her chin and stared at him through narrowed eyes. "Why have you come?"

"To see your face," he said. Heat ran through her at his words, singed her nerve endings. "To see your face again."

Her knees began to shake. The cane fell from her hand and rolled into the foyer. "You're mad, sir. You must leave. Right now."

Rafe's hand slid across hers, up her arm to her shoulder. Lizzy tried to summon a scream but it would not come. As his fingertips brushed her cheek, she remembered them against the hot glass at the depot.

"You presume too much, sir!"

"It has always . . . been the case," he said. His voice trailed off.

"Rafe! What's wrong with you?"

His knees buckled and he fell against the pilaster. When Lizzy tried to catch him, his weight crumpled her onto the staircase. She managed to roll him halfway off of her lap.

She called his name and tried to shake him awake. He was burning up, his pulse weak and thready. It took all her strength to push him off.

18

"Damn your treacherous hide, Rafe Laffite!" Then she scrambled up, hitched her nightgown above her knees, and dashed upstairs to fetch Grace.

"He sure looks like a Yankee to me, Aunt Lizzy," Hattie Lee said, peering at the man in her aunt's bed. She chewed one of her light brown plaits, then folded her arms across her flat chest. The morning light authenticated her verdict. "Look how filthy he is. Yep, he's a Yankee for sure. A dirty Yankee."

"That's a figure of speech, Hattie Lee." Lizzy wondered why she bothered defending him. "We can't tell about his political persuasion from the dirt under his fingernails."

"Bet he's got it more places than under his nails."

"That's enough!" Lizzy didn't want to think about Rafe's naked body under the quilt. She had seen enough of it last night to satisfy any lingering curiosity over whether he had changed during the years.

And he *had* changed. Besides a horrific, suppurating wound over his left hipbone, the obvious source of his sickness, he bore other scars. Each was a testament to a violent past, a warrior's history carved in human flesh.

She smoothed the covers over his chest, remembering the diagonal slash of white from his left collarbone to his navel that could only have come from a sword. The round scars on either aspect of his right thigh must have come from a musket ball.

"Dirty, dirty, dirty old Yankee boy," Hattie Lee said.

"He's a Louisianan, honey."

Hattie Lee's eyebrows shot up. "Shame on him, then, double-crossing his birth land!" With authority based on ten years of life experience, she returned to her former theme. "Bet he's got Bragg's bodyguards, too; all dirty Yankees does."

"Hush, Hattie Lee. It's bad enough we've got to care for him without you going on about lice. And quit using that soldier talk. Your mother hates it."

Hattie Lee caught one of the bedposts, rocked back on her heels, and swayed from side to side. "I recommend we fight under the black flag, all the same."

"More of that talk! You've got to quit loafing around downtown—I don't understand a word you say anymore!"

"We got to dust him with sulfur powders," the child explained. "Ma'll have a fit if vermin infest the house."

Lizzy dipped a washrag into the ceramic washbasin, wrung it out, then folded it across Laffite's forehead. She hadn't seen any lice on her patient, but it paid to be careful. "Go on over to Spotswood's then," she said, "and get him to put up some powders, if he's got any. Tell him to add it to my bill."

"And a peppermint stick?"

"I doubt he's been able to hide candy from those thieving Yanks downtown, but if he's got one, you may have it."

Before Hattie Lee could bolt, Lizzy called her back. Biting her lip, she looked down at the unconscious man for a second, then, feeling slightly foolish, she squeezed Hattie Lee's hand. "Don't tell anybody we're keeping him, honey."

"Not even the Yankees?"

"Especially not the Yankees. Mr. Laffite may have been telling the truth about what he is . . . or at least, what he is not. Mum's the word."

"Mum's my bond!" Hattie Lee's crinolines caused her skirts to swing into the door frame as she skidded into the hall. Her slippered feet made pounding noises down the steps; then the front door slammed and the house fell quiet.

20

Instead of sitting down in the rocker beside the bed, Lizzy looped her arm around one of the footposts and stood watching the rise and fall of Rafe Laffite's chest. He didn't look well at all—his skin gray, his eyes sunken, each rapid breath a rattle. The large, muscular hands splayed at his sides looked waxen and cold, the veins flattened under the skin.

"How did you pretend to be well at the depot yesterday?" she asked, more of herself than of him.

Maybe he'd had to . . . maybe he'd told her the truth. It wouldn't be the first time a soldier had donned an enemy's uniform for a secret purpose. "By the look of you, your disguise didn't do much good," she said.

Someone had wounded him . . . or had it been an accident? Perhaps he was a Yankee, after all, and had only come back for Grace's doctoring skills.

"You're dying, Raphael Laffite," Lizzy said in a small, hard voice.

She felt neither pain nor pleasure. Nothing. Again she said it, and this time a wintry cold stabbed her spine. She squeezed her eyes shut.

"Lizzy, you ought to be minding Mr. Laffite instead of sleeping on the job."

Lizzy's sister bustled into the room. Grace removed the wet rag, then gently laid her hand on Rafe's brow. "What if he was to stop breathing while your thoughts were elsewhere?"

"I reckon he'd die, sister," Lizzy said. "Folks generally do when they quit breathing. Wouldn't matter where my thoughts were."

"I declare, such an ugly humor you're in! The least you can do is give the poor man some comfort."

Lizzy took the washrag and immersed it in the basin. "That's what I've been doing since he broke in last night. He doesn't know a thing about it. I don't believe we're going to save him no matter what we do. That wound of his is septic; a blind mule can see that.''

"You just move aside then, Crosspatch. Go on and sleep away the day. Don't put yourself out."

"I'll stay."

"No, you won't. I won't have such talk in front of a sick man. After the harm he brought our family, I don't want him here any more than you do, but I'll be switched before I'll stand by and watch him die."

"I wasn't going to let him die!"

"Weren't you?"

Angry words sprang into Lizzy's throat, but she choked them down like a cold lump of corn bread. She couldn't win an argument with her sister.

Ever since her husband's capture at Stone's River, Grace had been as temperamental as a jackass with a load of gunpowder in its belly. "Go get a pail of hot water and some towels," Grace said. She began rolling up her sleeves. "Go on, get it."

"What for?"

"What for? If he's going to stay in my house, he's going to be clean, that's what for."

"Hattie Lee's already gone to the apothecary for sulfur powders," Lizzy said.

"Who told her to do that? He needs soap, not sulfur. Besides, I can tolerate the smell of an unwashed man a sight better than sulfur powders!"

Lizzy went downstairs. The windlass she'd rigged last night was still in place, the hemp line running from the top newel post to the foot of the steps. The stretcher was lashed to it. Without it, they could have never gotten Rafe Laffite upstairs.

When Lizzy came back with water and towels, Grace rose from the rocker and flicked back the quilt to bare her patient to the waist. "Such sores and bruises!"

Grace said. "Comes from lack of food and proper hy-
geine. I'm no palm reader, but it looks to me like this
man's been on campaign for a long time."

"Seven years," Lizzy said. She couldn't take her eyes
off his scars.

"Are you just going to stand there staring, or do I get
some help?"

"I'm helping. I brought soap."

"Then lather a rag. It's time to change that dressing,
too."

Lizzy twisted her fingers. "It's not that easy, Grace.
I—I don't want to touch him."

"Honey, sex is the farthest thing from his mind."

"Grace!"

The older woman reached across the bed and caught
Lizzy's wrists. "He's our patient now, no matter what
he was to you in the past. Maybe if we're kind to him,
God will put it into the heart of some Yankee woman
to nurse my poor William up in that prison."

"You heap a load of brimstone on my head when you
say things like that." Lizzy released a long sigh. "All
right, I'll help."

"I never expected anything else."

"Just don't expect me to wash his . . . nether
regions."

"We'll start north of there and see what we shall
see."

Lizzy lifted her gaze to the ceiling. "I have no intention of seeing anything."

"You might find yourself pleasantly surprised, being
a widow woman and all." The swish of the washrag in
the basin didn't quite drown out her words. Lizzy shot
her a glare.

Tentatively, Lizzy began to scrub Rafe's chest. She
felt the whorls of his hair as his skin became slick and

wet. The sensation forced a hundred memories. Once more his torrid caresses overpowered her reason, immersing her in guilty pleasures. Perceiving her own trembling, she tried to think loftier thoughts, blushing all the while at the knowing look in her sister's eyes.

"Maybe you'd better shave him," Grace said at last. "I don't remember him wearing a beard—I don't believe he wants to wear it now. You know where to find William's shaving cup."

Lizzy fled. In Grace's room, she caught the edge of the washstand and stood looking into her glassy reflection. Her eyes were wild, hunted. Scarlet stained her cheeks. She dragged oxygen into her lungs and let it out slowly. *Calm. Be calm, drat it! He means nothing to you anymore.*

But when she began to shave him a few minutes later, a sense of intimacy more powerful than passion rushed upon her. From the deep clefts in his cheeks to the planes of his jaw and chin, each contour of his face was known to her. She could shave him with her eyes closed, relying on memory alone to guide her hands. Again and again she glanced at his face, afraid he sensed her thoughts in his sleep.

His mouth, grim even in repose, beckoned hers. Unconsciously she wet her lips as she shaved off his mustache. As she worked the blade over his throat, she had to pause several times to still the dangerous trembling of her hand.

Through it all the man did not awaken, although she could see by his fleeting grimaces he felt pain. She winced for him when Grace cut away the linen bindings to uncloak the angry wound over his left hip.

"That's dreadful." Lizzy had to turn away. "Was he shot?"

"Stabbed, more like," Grace said, "and not recently.

24

Looks like he was attacked with a bayonet or something. Imagine that.''

"I'd rather not."

When Grace probed the injury, Rafe groaned and shifted. Instinctively Lizzy took his hand, then let go as if she'd touched a hot stove.

"This is worse than I thought," Grace said. "I couldn't see how bad off he was when I dressed that wound last night. See the ugly streaks reaching for his belly and leg? It's gone purulent. We'll have to drain it."

Drain it. The words shivered up and down Lizzy's spine. She was no good with surgery, and never had been. She even had to sit down when Hattie Lee pulled a tooth.

"I suppose . . . I suppose you'll need my help?" Lizzy asked.

"We sure can't summon the Yankee surgeon after what Mr. Laffite told you last night, can we?"

"I'm tempted to do precisely that. Just because he denies being a Yankee doesn't make it so." But what if he'd told the truth? What if he had dressed as a Yankee to escape detection? Maybe he'd escaped prison. Or maybe he had come back to spy on the Federals.

A spy! If that were true, then he was not a traitor to the cause but an answer to the prayer she'd offered at the depot. With him, she might deal the Yankees a blow. Her heart began to hammer with an emotion she could not name. "How can I help, Grace?"

He could hear their voices fading in and out. He knew the authoritative tones belonged to Grace Fairlove. Eliza's voice was a dulcet purr, wrapping around him like the soft brush of a cat's tail, drawing him upward from the deep, cold well of death.

And then silence cocooned him again. He was suspended on a strand of spider's silk so close to death that its weight wrapped around his spine and dragged him deeper under. With the last of his strength he reached for life.

"Help me tie him to the bedposts, Lizzy. I don't know how he'll react when I cut him. . . ."

"I don't think I can stand to watch."

"Hold it in the brazier until the blade glows red. . . . Yes, like that."

"Sweet Jesus, don't let him feel this. . . . I'm ready, Grace; here's the knife. . . . Oh, Jesus, don't let me faint."

Pain. Agonizing, white-hot pain reached deep into his soul to engulf him in scalding hell. Screams of pain stuck inside his throat, unvoiced. Muscles bunched, tearing at the bonds; his back arched to the sky—hopeless animal rage, consuming pain.

"Hold him, Lizzy! I'll cut him too deep if he does that again! Sweet mercy, lie on his chest if you have to, but hold him still!"

He heard Eliza's voice from an eternity away. Soft skin caressed his cheeks. Cool hands stroked him, quieting the spasms, quenching the fire.

"Rafe, don't move. . . . Rafe, I'm here. Please don't move. We have to make you well . . ."

The well. He was falling into it. Panic set in. Blackness was closing over his head. His frantic hands found no purchase. He was falling, falling into the black water far below. He was drowning . . . dying . . .

Chapter Three

The tang of hot metal singed his nostrils.

A slice of yellow light widened as he pushed open the lantern slide. The metal made a sharp screech.

He was inside Emperor Maximilian's treasure vault. There, beyond the pearls and emeralds, beyond the golden headdresses of kings long vanished from the Mexican pyramids, the great diamond slept in its glass case, its fires dormant, its heart as cold as a reptile under a mountain. He stared at it.

For an instant it seemed the diamond waited; then the jewel inhaled the light, smashed it, and hurled the pieces over him like rainbow fish scales. He winced, feeling cold and hot at the same time. Diamond fever. A cold sickness.

Testing each copper tile with the toe of his boot before setting his weight upon it, he started toward the case. He sensed a tile dip and withdrew his foot. He glanced

27

at the dark cavities that stared at him from the walls like the sockets of a skull.

He felt himself stiffen and throb, as he always did when he faced extreme danger. Ten feet to go. The diamond was as big as life, its center glowing with a strange, bluish red light. His heel brushed a different tile.

The sockets crackled like a rattlesnake's tail and hissed with shooting spears. Too late, he dove toward the diamond case. A spear gashed him high in the left flank and he crashed to the floor. Pain seared through him from stomach to knee.

He grabbed the shaft with both hands and wrenched it free, releasing a crimson snake of blood. Quickly, he tore a makeshift bandage from his clothing and bound the wound. Then, angry and afraid, he smashed the glass case with the spear.

Fire seemed to burst from the diamond as though to burn him, yet when he reached in and wrapped his fingers around it, the gem was as cold as ice. He thrust it into his jacket.

The palace gong began to clang, louder and louder until the cupboards shook and jewels cascaded to the floor. He heard boots thunder in the gallery.

Throwing himself out of the vault, he forced himself to sprint into the shadow of the staircase and yanked open a trapdoor. Like a wounded cougar he disappeared, into the labyrinth below the palace.

Below, as he tried to tend to the gash in his thigh, he felt the diamond cold against his skin, pulsing with the rise and fall of his chest as though drawing his breath into itself. The diamond had claimed a piece of him now, like the memory of Eliza McCord.

Fine black shadows enfolded the bed. Like the hands of a ghostly lover, the tattered lace canopy fluttered in the breeze. Flames glinted on a framed ornament made of Lizzy's hair that hung on the wall, and danced in a looking glass. Through half-closed lids Rafe Laffite surveyed his surroundings.

His gaze stopped. For a long moment he lay still, letting the sight perfuse his soul like a draft of nectar.

She slept in the rocking chair, her slender hands limp on the armrests, one foot tucked under the opposite knee. Her shining brown hair cascaded over her bosom. Her silk dressing gown shimmered like a butterfly's wing.

Rafe scarcely allowed himself to breathe. He could not imagine where he was or how he had come to be here, nor could he fully believe that Eliza sat beside him, her fine-boned face as serene as an angel's, virtually unchanged by time.

Perhaps he was dreaming again. How often during his arduous flight from Mexico he had conjured just such an image! He hardly dared credit the evidence of his eyes.

Snippets of memory came and went. The smell of train smoke filled his nostrils and vanished. For an instant he heard the curses of men packed in a cattle car. His body swayed as the train lurched around a mountain and dropped into the black mouth of a tunnel.

How long had he lain in bed? From the stiffness of his muscles and the hunger in his belly, it must have been more than a day.

A sound recalled him. Instantly wary, he rolled his head to the right and found her watching him. She didn't recoil when he met her gaze, but the suspicion in her deep, sea blue eyes made him cautious.

Knowing she would consider French too intimate, he spoke to her in English. French was the language of love she no longer wanted to hear him speak—he had discovered that in the foyer. "You're awake, then."

For a moment she did not reply; then her voice came like a caress. "I was about to say the same of you. You've slept long enough."

"It seems so."

"I would say that a week *is* so."

"A week?" What sort of madness was this? He was disoriented, but not enough to believe that he had slept for a week.

"You've been very ill," she said. "We were afraid— I mean, *Grace* was afraid—you were not going to wake."

Rafe closed his eyes and thought back. Images glimmered at the edges. In his weakened state, he could not suppress a shudder. "I was ... drowning in a well, Eliza. You called me back."

"I did nothing of the kind!"

She uncurled from the rocker and leaned forward, her spine stiff as a poker, her hands gripping the arms of the chair so hard her knuckles turned white. "Grace called you back," she said, shivering with anger. "Grace saved your life, d'you hear? I had nothing to do with it. Nothing!"

Her wrath penetrated his viscera like a spear. Gritting his teeth, he willed himself to contain his suffering in the presence of this woman who so clearly hated him. "Tender Mrs. Fairlove my thanks, then," he said when he had control of his pain.

"You may tender it yourself, when you see her."

"And when will that be?"

"At first rooster-crow when it's her turn to nurse you. Oh!"

Rafe guessed she hadn't meant to reveal her role as his night nurse. He burned to ask her if she'd been at his side every night for a week, but instead he cleared his throat and looked out the window. "I'm sorry I've put you and

30

your sister to so much trouble, Eliza. I wouldn't have come had there been another way.''

"That I believe.''

He turned his head to consider her. This time she gave a little jump. He knew he was looking at her too hard, that his need was too apparent, that she was on the verge of walking out. Why had he come? He tried to tell himself it was because of his mission, yet in his heart he knew better. It would not do to admit the truth.

"I know you despise me, Eliza.''

"Laws, what a very odd conclusion! How ever did you reach it?''

Rafe dragged air into his lungs and let it out in a long sigh. His wound ached with the effort of breathing, but not half as much as his heart ached. "I've come to tell you I'm sorry.''

She half stood as if to leave the room, then settled back into the chair. Ice crackled in her tone. "Save your breath, Raphael Laffite—you'll not find forgiveness in this world or the next. And I highly doubt that you came back just to say you're sorry.''

"I wish I could deny that charge. Truth is, I started back twice after Charlie's death—''

"Don't speak of my husband!''

"—to accept whatever blame you cared to heap upon me.''

"You shut up, d'you hear?'' Her face was white as milk, her eyes haunted.

"I turned back both times.'' He retreated into himself for a moment, considering his words. "This time, I had no choice but to come.''

She clasped her arms under her bosom and leaned forward, eyes riveted on his face, body rocking to and fro. "No choice? Then there is something you want of me. Now we come to your reason for being here. It

31

seems I haven't sacrificed enough for you."

Guilt buffeted him. He could bear the remorse—God knew he'd experienced enough of it since Charlie's death—but what he had to do next didn't sit well with him. If it weren't for the Confederacy, he would dig up the diamond and go.

Perhaps he should tell her about the stolen diamond, but he was too damned cautious to trust her. She would learn the whole truth when and if she needed to know. Somehow he had to elicit her help without revealing his mission . . . or his feelings for her. One hint of that, and she would cast him off forever.

Before he could frame a satisfactory answer, she said, "I presume you want money. Well, you're too late; your Yankee friends either burned or stole everything I owned. They got my money when they seized the bank, so go to them if you want it."

"I don't want your greenbacks, Eliza, and no Yankee alive is my friend!"

"Are you a spy, then?" Suspicion burned like blue fire in her eyes. There was something else there, too, but Rafe couldn't tell what.

"Never mind, I should have known better," she said. "Just go away, Rafe Laffite. Whatever you want me to do, I can't. I won't. Not for you."

"Eliza."

He had not meant to let her name roll off his tongue as though he were making love to her; the seductive, vibrating timbre flowed spontaneously from his breast. He saw the pulse leap in her throat, her eyes mist over. His heart quickened in answer, just like the old days.

She jumped up so quickly the chair bit plaster from the wall. "Stop it! You're dead to me—there's nothing between us!"

Before he could stop himself, he reached for her hand.

She pulled back, hissing like a cat. Rage shimmered in her eyes.

"Eliza, curb your ire. I meant you no harm."

"You've harmed me enough already. You're nothing but a pirate, like your grandfather!"

"Pirate? No, Eliza, a patriot."

"Patriot is no sobriquet for a man who loves only his own cause!"

"It's the Confederacy I'm thinking of."

Lizzy clapped her hands over her ears. "You go to the devil, Rafe Laffite! Return to him straightaway, and this time, don't come back!"

"Eliza!" But then she was gone, slamming the door behind her with a force that rattled the mirror and shook the canopy over the bed.

"*Sacrebleu,* she hasn't changed a mite!" Rafe shifted and instantly regretted it when pain shot through his side and down his left leg. He swore again as he lifted the quilt to see what was wrong. He was naked as a foal, his only covering a thick white dressing around his middle. "Lord, what have those women been up to?"

Gingerly he lifted the edge of the dressing and tried to inspect his wound. There seemed to be a poultice under the bandage. It felt warm and wet, like a glob of mud. He worked his fingers down to shift it.

"Mr. Laffite, if you please!"

Grace Fairlove stood in the doorway, her right hand clenched on the porcelain knob, her left holding a steaming teakettle. Rafe could see a frown creasing her forehead, and on her lips was the determined pout he remembered.

The passage of seven years had not aged her much—a few gray hairs, a bosom that dipped a little closer to her waist—otherwise she looked the same. Despite the early hour, she was dressed as though ready to go to town, her morning gown of green, starched cotton buttoned to the throat, her hoops blooming around her.

"Kindly remove your hand from the dressing, sir, before you dislodge it!"

"I would do just that, ma'am." He withdrew his hand and pulled the covers over his stomach. "Eliza tells me I owe you my life. For what it's worth, thanks."

"Your thanks is worth even less than your life, Mr. Laffite."

She pushed the door shut, moved to his side, and with the impersonality of a field surgeon, checked his skin for fever, looked into his eyes, and felt the pulse in his neck, arms, and feet. Swiftly she unwrapped the bandages.

"How does it look?"

"Lie back and be still, Mr. Laffite! That hole in your side has just begun to heal. Jump around like that and you'll break it open again."

"I must be about."

"Not with that wound open to the air, you won't. Now you just simmer down while I dress it."

Rafe lay back on the pillow but tilted his head to see his wound. It looked better than the last time he'd tried to tend it, but it stung like a cauldronful of ants.

Grace dropped a handful of dried leaves into the washbasin, then added boiling water until a pungent aroma filled the room. She spooned the mixture onto a square of muslin and folded it into fours.

"Weevil fodder?" Rafe asked, only half in jest. As ravenous as he felt right now, he'd be happy to eat boiled uniform buttons.

"A poultice. I set Lizzy to preparing your breakfast." She lifted it with tongs. Rafe could feel its heat from a foot away.

"Easy with that," he said. "You ought to let it cool."

34

"Don't move. There!"

Rafe jammed his fingers into the mattress and held on. For perhaps ten seconds he battled an impulse to scream; then the agony lessened until numbness ruled his entire left side. "What did you put in that pouch? Popskull and hot coals?"

"I'll thank you not to use your vulgar soldier terms in my house, Mr. Laffite."

"My apologies, Mrs. Fairlove."

"If you understood herbs, you wouldn't be in such terrible shape. Yours isn't the first life I've had to save with wormwood and bloodroot."

"Sounds lethal."

"Putrefaction is lethal, sir. My herbs aren't." She helped him sit up, then wrapped muslin bandages over the poultice. "Mixed with crushed flaxseed, they're the best thing I know to draw poison and cleanse the blood. They kill pain, too."

"And the man along with it, I think."

Grace knotted the dressing with violence, wringing a gasp from Rafe. She let him fall back on the pillow. "If I had wanted to kill you, you'd have been dead these seven days past instead of afflicting me and my household with your offensive language and equally offensive presence."

"I'll remove myself this very evening."

"You'll do nothing of the kind, and we'll settle something right now, sir. You're here because you fell senseless after breaking into my house. I was all for summoning the Yankees until Lizzy mentioned that incredible disclaimer of yours."

"What disclaimer?"

"That you're not a galvanized Yankee."

He was surprised to hear her use soldier talk. "I'm no convert to their cause."

35

"I'll reserve judgment on that score. It's time for the truth. Out with it."

"You know the truth. You wouldn't be asking if there were any doubt in your mind."

Grace's aspect did not change, but a smidgen of ice melted from her tone. "I'd like my ears to hear it, all the same."

"I'm not a damn—pardon me, ma'am—I'm not a Yankee."

Lighter blue than Lizzy's, her eyes bored into his for a long moment. At last she nodded. "The matter's settled, then. I did right to keep you."

"I'm in your debt."

"Yes, you are." Her gaze intensified until Rafe was certain she could see exactly what was in his mind. The idea did not give him solace. "You're deep in my debt, and my intuition tells me that you intend to repay me tenfold."

"Indeed I do."

"I'm not talking about money. You came back to Huntsville masquerading as a Doodle for a reason. Care to discuss it?"

"No. Not at present." Rafe knew better than to lower his guard, even to the woman who'd saved his life. He looked for safer ground. "Do they know I'm here?"

"If you mean the Yankees, the answer is no. We've kept quiet."

"Thanks."

"I don't want your thanks. . . . How were you wounded?"

"That's another thing I don't care to discuss, ma'am. Anyway, I'm starved."

She frowned. "Of course, how forgetful of me. I'll go see if the grits are done. You've had nothing this week but dove broth and dandelion tea, a spoonful at a

36

time when you roused up enough not to choke.''

*Shadow soup and puffweed coffee . . . So that's how
they kept me alive.* Why had they done it, considering
their hatred?

Hand on the doorknob, Grace glanced over her shoulder. ''Don't try to get up. You haven't much strength
and, as you've probably noticed, even less to wear.''

In the murky light of dawn, Lizzy chopped weeds
from a row of greens with a fury that showered clods of
dirt over her dressing gown.

''Isn't it awfully early to be gardening?'' Grace called
from the back door.

Lizzy glanced up but did not reply. Her sister picked
her way through the dewy grass, fetched a cane basket,
then settled her hoops over a gardening stool. Lizzy continued to chop the hard red earth as if mining solid rock.

When the sun showed a golden rim over the mountains to the east, Grace said, ''We're going to have to
help him.''

Lizzy lost her rhythm, so she moved farther down the
row and hacked a clump of grass from the turnip greens.

''He can't do it alone, honey.''

Lizzy threw down the hoe and cocked her fists on her
hips. ''Do what alone? Just what does that rogue require?''

''He hasn't told me yet.''

Lizzy laughed, brittle as a dry stalk of cotton. ''He
won't, either. Not the truth, anyway. Plans like his
shrivel up and die in the light of truth.''

''What do you know about his plans?''

''Why, nothing at all,'' Lizzy said. ''When I asked
what he wanted, it was plain as day he was fixing
to lie.''

"I've got a feeling that man doesn't lie . . . unless he has to."

"He told you something?"

"Not a word."

"Oh, and I've got a pink-checked mule to sell you! He raved for two days after we drained that abscess. A man doesn't come crawling back after seven years, ask for help, then refuse to give particulars."

"He was vague, but I think he's here for a good reason, and as loyal confederationists we've got to render whatever aid he requires."

"*You* render it," Lizzy said. "My loyalty doesn't extend to him."

"Think about the Confederacy."

"My stars, sister, that's all I've done since this war began! Don't you dare lecture me on duty!"

"And don't you speak to me in that tone, after all I've done for you!" Grace struggled to get up. Instead of giving her a hand, Lizzy stepped across the rows on her way out of the garden.

"Without me," Grace said, "you'd be camped across the river in Lacey's Spring right now, with Yankees stopping you from returning!"

"I'd sooner be there!" Lizzy said. "If it weren't for Hattie Lee, I'd as lief pack a trunk and go this minute."

"One word from me to Granger and there won't be even that much delay!"

Lizzy froze in her tracks. "What do you mean?"

"What's the use keeping it from you any longer? Didn't you wonder why the Yankees failed to haul you off after you burned down the carriage house? I talked General Granger into letting you stay on."

"How?"

"By telling him about your equipment."

"You mean my scientific instruments?" Lizzy felt as if she'd just fallen through the barn roof.

"I had to keep you from being banished. I appealed to his covetousness. He agreed to auction off your paraphernalia and use the proceeds to remedy the Bannisters' losses."

"Since when do Yankees cover secessionists' losses?"

"Be reasonable, Lizzy. Our carriage house is full of the most useless old junk."

"That I use to keep you and Hattie Lee in bread and butter!"

"Pshaw! You like to think so, but since when have your inventions brought us anything but trouble?"

"I like your gratitude!"

"And I like yours! You're just like Pa—eccentric and full of grand delusions about your own worth." Grace threw up her hands. "As for your equipment, Granger will be lucky to get a hundred dollars for it, but it's enough to ransom you."

"*Ransom* me? You've sold me downriver!"

Lizzy turned and ran down the overgrown driveway. Within moments she reached the carriage house, twisted the key in the brass lock, and stumbled inside. She slammed the double doors behind her and leaned against them. Her heart threatened to burst from her ribs.

When would Granger's men come with their wagon to take away the very things that had given her solace and hope through the long years of war? The thundercloud of Yankee avarice overshadowed her soul; the bluebellies would come to steal her heart.

She shook her fist at the rafters. "If they come," she said, "I swear I'll blow them to Canaan!"

Chapter Four

Hattie Lee Fairlove gazed at the Yankee in Aunt Lizzy's bed. Asleep, he seemed frail as a day-old cat. She wasn't supposed to be in his room; Ma had strictly forbidden her. Still, she had waited to disobey for two whole days after the Yankee surfaced from his swoon—that was the day Aunt Lizzy'd had a fight with Ma and locked herself in the carriage house. Hattie Lee felt only a slight pang of guilt.

He didn't look quite so much the dirty Yankee today. Aunt Lizzy's special lye soap had given him a shine to make a preacher proud. "And vermin dead as door-knobs," she whispered regretfully.

She wished Ma would let her dust the Yankee for fleas just once. She still had the half-pound tin of sulfur powders from Spotswood's Apothecary under her bed.

Maybe it wasn't too late. Ma was downtown and Aunt Lizzy was tinkering with something in the carriage house. Dusting him wouldn't take but a minute. Nobody'd know the difference unless they smelled him.

Just to make sure the Yankee was dead asleep, she tiptoed over and breathed on his face. He didn't stir. She studied him critically. He didn't look much more than half-starved anymore—about the same as everybody else in town. "It's my dove soup fattened you up, you old Yank."

Her breath stuck in her throat when his eyes snapped open and fixed on her. He sat up, swung his legs over the edge of the bed, and looked past her through the open doorway with his fingers half-curled over like he wanted to rend something. Hattie Lee jumped out of the way.

"Yank? Where?" He captured her with his scary golden green eyes.

"You, mister. I was talking to you."

"Chri—" Rafe broke off in midswear. The energy seemed to leave him all at once. With a loud sigh he dropped back onto the bed.

Hattie Lee picked up the quilt he'd dropped and wadded it at his feet. Now that her heart had settled back under her breastbone where it belonged, she looked at him with renewed interest.

He was wearing her father's long white nightshirt, the laces undone to accomodate his wide chest, his dark blond hair visible in the opening. He looked like the prince in one of her picture books. She wondered if Aunt Lizzy thought so, too.

He opened one eye and looked at her. "Who are you, little girl?"

He spoke sort of like an actor she'd seen one time in a play about New Orleans, exotic and Southern all rolled into one. With a name like Laffite, he was bound to be a pirate, but she didn't want to be rude and come straight out and ask him. Instead, she caught her skirt in her fingertips and curtsied.

"Hattie Lee Fairlove," she said. "I already know who you are. I'm not supposed to be talking to you."

"We talked before, when you were younger. You didn't say much. Cried some."

"Then we're not strangers."

"Not by a long stretch."

"Then it's all right to talk to you." She skipped around the bed and settled into the rocking chair. Her feet missed the floor by three inches.

"What day is it, Hattie Lee Fairlove?"

"September tenth."

"Oh. The hour?"

"Half past five." She didn't trust him to understand, so she added, "In the evening. You sure sleep a lot."

"I'm all through with that." He looked down at himself. "Do you know what your mother did with my clothes?"

"Yes, sir. Boiled 'em and put 'em in the attic."

"Boiled them? Did she find anything in the jacket?"

"Just some old letters. She put 'em up."

"Any chance of you going and getting those letters and the uniform for me?"

"You gonna wear your Yankee raiment? Ma'll skin you from crown to sole!"

"Have you told anyone I'm here?"

"Nope."

"Where's your mother?"

"Waiting for commodities at the courthouse square. Granger's parceling out desecrated vegetables to the civilians today."

Rafe smiled. She'd used soldier's slang for the Yankees' nauseating dessicated vegetables. Then he stopped smiling. She was obviously spending too much time with the army of occupation. "Where's your aunt?"

"In the carriage house. Her workshop's in there—we ain't got any horses. She's been working on something for two days, ever since you first waked up. . . . How'd you get bullet holes in your uniform? You get shot?"

"No, I wasn't wearing it then. Some other fellow was."

"Oh." Hattie Lee grimaced. "Did you kill him?"

"Go get me the uniform," he said, "and I'll give you a dollar."

"A bushel of greenbacks wouldn't buy nothing around here, mister. You keep your dollar and I'll get you your suit. Just don't tell Ma who liberated it from the attic."

"My lips are sealed, miss."

"And another thing, Mr. Laffite, you better watch yourself. When I was listening at the door yesterday, I heard Aunt Lizzy say she was going to blow her up some Yankees."

"I'll keep that in mind."

Lizzy set a stitch in the rubberized silk, bit off the thread, and slowly stood up. The dark blue fabric in her lap slid off into the hundreds of yards of silk on the carriage house floor. The place looked like an ocean.

Even empty, the balloon promised wind and heat and tempest. But would the envelope still hold rosin gas after so many years? Would the mildewed shrouds coiled on the wall fall apart the minute she stretched them taut?

"So you still have it, then."

Her heart leaped. A Yankee stood in the doorway. Light spilled over his head and shoulders then flowed into shadow as he shut the door.

"Nobody asked you to break in," she said, trying to distract him from the balloon. "Go away!"

He stepped into a dusty shaft of light.

"Oh, no, you again!" She had intended to be miles away before Rafe was well enough to venture from the house, yet here he was, like a bad dream. "I suppose you think I should be happy to see you."

Rafe Laffite dropped his gaze to her white nightdress. "I'm certainly happy to see *you*."

"That doesn't excuse your effrontery in just walking in here."

"If I'd knocked, you would have moved something heavy in front of the door."

"How right you are."

"I didn't want you to strain your back."

She flicked her hand as though shooing a fly. "I'm sure my health was your only concern. How'd you get through a locked door, anyway?"

"Magician's trick." He held up a slender pick. "Next time, bar the door instead of using the lock."

"Thanks. I'll bar the front door of the house, too, just in case you come calling at three o'clock in the morning again."

Rafe's hand strayed to his side. "I don't remember much about that night."

Lizzy could scarcely remember it, herself. This man didn't resemble the one who'd stumbled in out of the rain. This was a lion, wounded yet able to pounce. His eyes devoured her already.

Suddenly aware of her lack of proper clothing, she brandished the darning needle. "Stay back!"

"You don't need a weapon, Eliza." His voice brushed her like a velvet currycomb.

It was silly to threaten him with a pin. She turned away and placed the needle in her sewing box by the chair. But when she straightened, he stood right behind her. She should have remembered how silently he moved. Strange how much she'd forgotten, only to recall it in the twinkling of an eye. Strange how memories erased time. Strange and terrible.

Rafe's eyes were dark, shuttered windows. No smile softened the stern lines around his mouth. The slow beat in his throat was the only movement Lizzy could discern. She could not bear his gaze: it probed her mind without allowing her the faintest view into his own.

"Why did you come back, Mr. Laffite?"

"I need you—" He stopped, and started again. "I need your help."

"I cannot—I will not—help you."

"Because of your hatred?"

"What better reason than that?"

"Aye, hatred, the best reason of all," he said. "Men die for that reason by the day."

"You, of all people, should know of men dying!"

His hand moved to his side and dwelt there, not to comfort, but to worry the wound. His Creole ancestry was apparent in his formal words. "You cannot discover the depth of my sorrow for what happened to Charlie. No lead line can plumb it."

She raised her hand to his arm, but dropped it before making contact. The ghost of Charles McCord stood between them. "I have no interest in your sorrow." She spoke with measured coldness, yet her lips trembled, threatening to spill the truth.

For an instant she saw pained bewilderment in his eyes, the look of a man suddenly pierced by an arrow. A rebellious sense of gladness bubbled deep inside her. She had the power to wound him, to avenge herself. After seven bitter years, she could look upon him and laugh. She tried it, briefly, then caught her bottom lip as the note surged out of control.

She saw her husband standing between them, wearing

that uncertain smile that said, *I don't belong.* The giddiness left her. "What a terrible thing, not belonging."

"You belong, Eliza."

"No." She jerked her head, rebuffing him. "I need neither condolence nor reassurance from you."

"Since you cannot accept my apologies, I have only one thing to offer you."

"And what is that?"

"More pain."

His words hung between them, caught in the web of Lizzy's astonishment. "You are quite mad, sir."

He stepped in and took her by the shoulders. He did not kiss her, and Lizzy did not fight. They stood thus for a moment; then Rafe entwined his hand in her hair and pulled her head back.

Lizzy quivered under the golden green lamps of his eyes. He was a big, hungry animal, starved and cruelly treated. A savagery burned within him that she had not discerned in his younger days, but now she knew it had always been just under the surface, growing and awaiting the chance to spring.

"What do you want, Rafe Laffite?"

"You, Eliza." He lowered his face to hers.

Chapter Five

She couldn't move. He bound her with passion deeper than thought and reason. Time rolled back until it ceased to exist, leaving only fire and light and waiting flesh. And then his lips touched hers.

In that moment she knew this was not the man who'd taken her on countless summer nights, who'd lain with her under the old magnolia until dawn. He was a mercenary using her for his own gain. His lovemaking was a deception, even as it had been the night he'd planted his seed in her belly and destroyed her life.

She twisted out of his grasp and fled across the room, stumbled over the silk envelope, and stopped at the wall to stand with feet and hands braced against the boards behind her.

"Go, drat you!"

"No, Eliza. We've played this game of running from each other too many times. This time we cannot run—

we will not run. Not from each other. Not from our duty.''

"Duty? What do you know of duty—you, who haven't a selfless bone in your body?"

"I told you before, I'm a patriot. So are you. Which is why you'll help me."

"Help you do what?"

"Get to Richmond."

"Richmond!" Lizzy's stomach muscles clenched as from a physical blow. "How can I, with the Union's tentacles all over the South?"

Rafe inclined his head toward the gondola.

At last she knew his secret. If he wanted to get there badly enough to risk his life in the balloon, he must be a spy.

"The prevailing winds blow east," Rafe said. "We'll ride them as far as they'll take us, then find another means to finish the journey northward."

"You're crazy," she said, but her thoughts chased each other like squirrels around a tree.

How would Granger react if she told him there was a spy in his camp? Might he lift his order of banishment? Would he let her keep her instruments, and continue selling her inventions? Perhaps she didn't have to run away after all.

Judas. Now where had that thought come from? She wasn't a traitor. "I—I wouldn't take you to church in my balloon!"

"How long till she's ready to fly, Eliza?"

"Your ears must be stopped with wax—I told you I won't help."

"You'll help. If not for me, then for the Confederacy."

"That argument again? You've already failed with that one."

Diamond

Instead of replying, he squatted down and folded silk between his thumb and forefinger. Lizzy's gaze settled on the nape of his neck. He looked so vulnerable there. She looked away.

How could she betray him? *Because he killed Charles, dammit. And because of the baby. Don't forget them.*

Yet, didn't she pray every night for a chance to strike at the Yankees? Perhaps the Lord intended her to use Rafe as a sword. Or perhaps it was only a vain wish of her heart to be near him.

"Remember the last time we met in a barn, Eliza?" His voice flowed into her ears like warm honey. "Remember?"

Yes, she remembered. While the horses slept in their stalls, he had made love to her in her black carriage. That night he swore never to leave her.

"I . . . don't recall."

"You choose not to."

"We all make choices . . . and promises," she said. "Some of us choose not to keep them."

"Some of us are fools, Eliza." Eyes burning bright, he watched her from his crouched position. Even from across the room, she could see the throbbing of his throat, a sinewy play replicated in his hands kneading the silk. His hands looked capable of lovemaking . . . or killing.

She broke contact with the wall and balled her fists. "You should not have come back. Not after breaking your promise."

"You asked me to leave."

"As though I had any choice!"

"There is always a choice."

"Like the one you made when you gambled away my

49

father's money.'' She would focus on that. He would never know about the baby.

His eyes took on the deep green hue of shadows in a lake. ''If it'll help your wounded sentiments, I'll ask you to forgive me once more.''

''It's God's place to forgive, not mine.''

''And if it were yours?''

''I would consign your soul to the devil.''

''It was so consigned years ago, when I lost you.''

She whirled around and hit the wall with her fist. No, she wouldn't cry. Not for this man. Never again. If there were any justice in the world, he would be moldering in the ground. But the image hurt too much. She dug her nails into the healing burn on her left hand in an effort to wrench her mental anguish into physical pain.

The hairs prickled on the back of her neck. He was behind her, she knew. She felt passion flow like milk from a bruised honeysuckle vine, warm and intoxicating. From deep inside her being came an outflow of yearning she did not even try to understand. Her body knew, and that was enough.

Before she could restrain herself, she turned to meet him, to catch his sleeves in her fingers, to feel the fiery strength of his arms. This time she did not object when his mouth came down to claim hers. Trembling, she opened her mouth to his tongue.

So long. Sweet mercy, so long since this man had kissed her. So long since she'd craved the press of his body and abandoned herself to desire. She let him slide her closer against him, let his arms fasten around her shoulders and waist, let him mold his hand to her hip. She knew what would come next . . . they had started like this just yesterday, in the barn.

Yesterday? No. Seven years ago yesterday. She was caught in a fragile illusion, a compression of time that had no reality or substance. There were too many yesterdays between them, lonely yesterdays without solace. Angry yesterdays without forgiveness.

He was looking at her. She remembered now that he never closed his eyes when they kissed. For a moment more he kissed her, then pushed her to arm's length and held her still. His face became expressionless, as though he'd drawn his passion into a box and closed the lid.

She concealed her own emotion. Rage was all mixed up with sexual hunger. "I can't forgive you," she said.

"And yet that look is upon you, Eliza. That faraway look."

He used to say that after we made love. "That's where I should be," she said. "Far away."

He let go of her, reached down and lifted a rumpled bit of silk, let it run through his fingers to the floor. "We'll go there together."

"I don't have room for you."

"You and your father flew together."

"Yes, but we didn't have to take my—" She broke off and stared at the wall.

"What? Your contraptions?"

"There's no use denying my instruments are more important than you."

He didn't flinch. "The Yankees? They're going to take them?"

Lizzy exhaled, defeated. "An auction. Granger doesn't like me very much."

"Foolish man." His smile did not touch his eyes.

"I—I want to kill him. I want to kill them all."

"Do you, Eliza McCord?"

Didn't she? There was dynamite in the loft, left over from her attempts to dislodge the big willow stump down by the creek.

"No," she said. "Sometimes anger gets the best of me and . . ."

"Frightens you," he said. "It always has."

"No."

"You're afraid of your animal side."

"Is it . . . is it so wrong for a civilized person to fear that?"

"We all fear it."

"Even a soldier?" She laid three fingertips against his chest. "Even you?"

Pain vibrated through her hand, plucked the cords of her heart. She withdrew her fingers and hooked them in her skirt. She knew his answer before he spoke.

"I must constantly bridle that portion of my soul," he said.

He was gone, that adventurer who'd ridden off to Mexico. This man felt more, discerned more. But she did not want him to see into her mind, to translate her thoughts before she was fully aware of them, to erode the wall she'd built.

"I won't speak of these things," she said.

He opened his hands in a gesture of release. "You want to save your instruments, and you intend to fly off alone, straight into the Yankees' teeth."

"I've no intention of being eaten."

She looked around her workshop. Brass gauges and old copper tubing, cogwheels, tools, thermometers, and instruments without names dangled from hooks, as though a steam engine had blown to bits and splattered against the walls. "Every piece is precious," she said. "I don't expect you to understand any more than anyone else in this town—you never did before."

"I understand more than you realize, Eliza. I do now; I did then. But even without me, you can't carry this much weight. You'll never get off the ground." Before she could argue, he said, "Pick what you need most and we'll bury the rest until the end of the war."

"Bury my equipment? I'd sooner bury myself. Besides, nothing's changed between us. I've no reason to help you. Now I'll thank you to get out. I've work to do."

"I'll come back later," he said. "Don't bar the door."

"You won't find it open."

"I won't find it locked." He melted away, leaving her to the silence of her own soul.

Why should she take him? It was now the middle of the night, yet she still chased that squirrel round and round the tree. She owed him nothing. He had already torn out her heart. Surely that was enough tribute.

The basket was too dangerous, anyway. There were holes in the floor and the cane was crumbly. She had tried to repair the worst spots, but even after several hours' soaking, the replacement cane remained brittle, its little teeth rasping her hands when she wove it into the basket. She planned to lay a thin wooden panel over the basket floor, but would the sides be strong enough?

Besides, where was she to obtain rosin gas? When her father was alive, they'd gotten it from the gas company by Big Spring. Now, with the plant in Yankee hands, she couldn't stroll in, borrow a nozzle, and inflate the envelope. Still, the answer would come. Matters of science always did.

She wished she could find the answer to Rafe as readily. What was he hiding? What was so important about Richmond? There were other ways to deliver messages to President Davis. What secret made him hazard his life?

His blasted French-Creole secretiveness had ever been

his curse . . . and his pride. *When your family makes its living from piracy and smuggling, a certain amount of lockjaw is to be expected,* he'd once told her.

Still, he would have to prove this one last sacrifice was worth it. Because he was asking her to bury the very things that made her who she was. She wasn't like everybody else. The people she knew wanted to stick to the old ways, to look backward instead of forward. Their myopic vision was losing them the war.

She tightened her grip on the gondola rail and felt the cane crackle. If she didn't help him, would the South lose more men? Did Rafe hold the key to something that might help them win? *It's time to look forward, Eliza.*

They'd need good wind and a heavy sprinkling of God's grace to come nigh enough to Richmond for Rafe to do whatever it was he'd vowed to do. She didn't think they'd have that much luck.

Still, she would look forward—with her eyes fully open. This time, she would not lose her soul to Rafe Laffite. Never again. She would crash the balloon rather than let it happen.

Chapter Six

The soldiers crowding the platform gave the huge, red-haired Frenchman who stepped off the train a wide berth. He did not appear to notice. His light blue eyes, soft and innocent as a cherub's, glowed above his crushed nose.

Leaning one massive hand against a pillar, he watched his two companions, a Mexican captain and a Frenchman, lead their horses from a boxcar. He glanced at his seven American army escorts, his smile as charming and vacant as a sidewalk café in winter.

Huntsville. His sentiments did not lean toward cedar-covered hills and clear streams. The tall, yellow-brick depot did not impress him, nor did the large, Greek Revival homes. To Louis DeCoeur, one town was like another.

Only this one held his quarry. His nostrils flared wide. The diamond was here. He could smell it.

"Mr. DeCoeur, I'll take you around to see General

Granger now. They tell me he's here, inspecting the prisoners."

DeCoeur's head swung toward the orderly, a fresh-faced kid unaffected by the hot, dusty train ride from Memphis. "Then it's his lucky day, *mon ami*."

With a tread incongruous in such a bear of a man, DeCoeur padded around to the front of the station and ducked through the green double doors. Wary of the sudden gloom, he paused to let his eyes adjust.

Twenty soldiers loafed in the pews of the waiting room. A guard stood just inside the telegraph office to the left, from whence issued the staccato clatter of the telegraph machine. At the top of a steep flight of stairs, he detected two more guards. There was an unpleasant smell in the air. *Prison*.

Thirty seconds later, General Granger came downstairs with two lieutenants. He bowed to DeCoeur, who returned a deeper bow with the grace of a French courtier. "Sorry to keep you waiting," Granger said. "Pleased to make your acquaintance."

"But the pleasure is mine, monsieur general. May I tender the good wishes of His Most Serene Highness, Emperor Ferdinand Maximilian of Mexico, whose humble emissary I am?"

"Your servant, sir." Granger indicated a chair by his desk. "Care to sit?"

DeCoeur's smile illuminated the room. "Sit, General? On a behind chafed by saddles and train berths for six weeks?"

"A walk on the grounds, then. Orderly, whiskey and cigars."

Glasses and cigars in hand, they walked across the grass to the roundhouse. Granger showed him around the army encampment and opened a warehouse door to display cotton bales stacked to the roof. When he turned, he found DeCoeur's eyes fastened upon him. The pupils were nearly gone, transformed into strange blue mirrors. Despite the heat, Granger shivered.

"Your telegram indicated you're searching for a Confederate agent," Granger said a bit more loudly than he'd intended.

"*Oui*. He is here."

"We haven't found him."

"Perhaps you do not know where to look, monsieur."

Granger scowled. "Just why is the government of Mexico interested in this man?"

DeCoeur's shoulders lifted and fell in a shrug. "The emperor has his reasons. His country is engaged in civil war, too."

"You're saying there's some connection between our troubles?"

"Perhaps. It is not always given to lesser men to know."

"If the security of the United States is threatened, it is very much my business. Now just what has this Rebel agent done? And if he's found, why should I turn him over to Mexico?"

"The emperor believes your cooperation will mutually benefit our countries."

"In what way?"

"This man came to Mexico as a Confederate emissary, but it did not take long to discover that he is a saboteur. Not a nice man to run free in this little village you occupy. Your depot, for instance . . ."

"What about it?"

"He is an expert with explosives."

Granger caught the implication at once. If anything happened during his watch, his career would go up in flames. "What makes you think he's here?"

"How does a man know anything? He thinks, he fol-

57

lows his nose, his instinct. That is how I know."

"You followed your nose all the way from Mexico City?"

"I followed the stench of bodies, monsieur. First, those of the emperor's French and Mexican troops, then Americans. He uses men for explosives drills. Like a fiend he blows off an arm, then a leg. . . . When I found them, they were no longer alive."

"God help us." Battle was one thing, deliberate torture and murder quite another.

"The emperor, of course, has authorized a handsome payment for the killer's extradition to Mexico City."

"We'll find and shoot him here, by thunder!"

"Relations between our governments have been strained for a long time, monsieur. I presume your Congress still wishes the emperor to cede part of Mexico to the United States?"

"I'm a soldier, not a politician. I'm not privy to the whims of Washington."

"Nevertheless, the emperor believes now is the time for such negotiations."

"Because the Mexican people hate him, and he needs American support," Granger snapped.

DeCoeur's smile slipped. Granger knew that as an agent of a puppet empire, DeCoeur had neither say nor jurisdiction in the fate of the saboteur.

"Tell me all you know of this Rebel," Granger said. "Once we find him, we can come to an understanding."

"We'll walk and talk," said DeCoeur, and led the general down the path.

"Mr. Jack's over at the boardinghouse," Hattie Lee said over dinner that evening. "He sold every bit of his whiskey last night, so I reckon he's gonna visit the widow awhile before he starts back to Lynchburg."

58

Grace choked on her corn bread. Rafe patted her on the back while Lizzy whispered in her niece's ear, "For heaven's sake, honey, you know how your mama feels about you spying around! Don't breathe another word."

"Who's Mr. Jack?" Rafe asked.

"Shh," Lizzy said. Told this morning of their travel plans, Grace was wound as tightly as a clock spring. Any additional pressure might make her fly apart.

Grace rounded on her daughter. "Just how did you find out such a thing, young lady?"

"Why, everybody in town knows, 'cept the stupid Yankees."

"I don't care what they know! How did *you* find out about that whiskey smuggler?"

"Heard him talking over at Littleton's coffeehouse."

Grace slapped her napkin down beside her plate. "You were in that—that saloon!"

"I didn't go inside, Ma."

"Who's Mr. Jack?" Rafe repeated.

"Jack Daniel, drat him!" Grace said. "That young reprobate from Lynchburg."

"What's wrong with him?"

"He bought a Lutheran preacher's distillery five years ago. He was only thirteen," Lizzy said. "Sister thinks it's scandalous."

"He ought to be in the army," Grace said, "instead of smuggling spirits down here!"

"He's fighting his own war," Lizzy said. "He's poison ivy to Granger—and anybody that makes that old coot itch is sweet balm to my mind!"

Rafe tapped his chin. "Interesting sort of fellow."

"Interesting to the devil," Grace said, frowning at Hattie Lee. "Don't grin like he's a hero!"

"Mr. Jack hauls his whiskey all the way from Lynchburg in a rickety old freight wagon," Lizzy said. "The

Yankees almost got him a time or two, but he takes folks' minds off the war.''

"He gets the menfolk squashmolished," Hattie Lee said.

"Soldier slang!" Grace said. "One more word out of you, and I'll blister your heinie with a hickory switch!"

Hattie Lee looked shamefaced but none too frightened. Rafe's wink started her giggling.

"If your father were here, you wouldn't be slinking around town like a little muskrat, finding out things a child your age has no business knowing. What am I going to do with you?"

"Leave her alone, sister," Lizzy said. "She's just naturally curious, that's all."

"I'm going to be a newspaperwoman," Hattie Lee said.

"Oh, eat your dinner!"

"Yes, ma'am."

Lizzy helped the child to more corn bread and turnip greens. She tried not to look at Rafe, but she felt him watching her. He didn't know she'd decided to help him. He could dangle on tenterhooks until the last minute.

When Grace went to the stove for more sassafras tea, Hattie Lee said, "Mr. Laffite, how come you know Ma and Aunt Lizzy?"

Teapot in hand, Grace snapped around. "Didn't I tell you to hush up? Go cut me a switch!"

But Rafe got up and went to Grace. "Allow me," he said, and took the pot from her hand. Ignoring her suspicious look, he seated her, then poured tea all around and set the pot back on the stove. He went to stand behind his chair, and set his hands on the backrest. Grace folded her arms and shook her head, glowering.

"Your pardon, Mrs. Fairlove, but maybe she's got a

right to know, seeing as how she intends to be a news-paperwoman.''

"I think we've already read enough about you and Lizzy in the papers, Mr. Laffite, without Hattie Lee laying a pen to them! There was quite a write-up in the *Huntsville Democrat* when you left town.''

Lizzy buried her face in her teacup. Had Rafe read any of the articles? Considering how spiteful folks had felt toward him, someone might have mailed him a copy. Her own were yellowing in a trunk in the attic.

"I'm fixing to blow up with bewilderment!" Hattie Lee said.

"I heard of a child in Shreveport once, who exploded with bewilderment," Rafe said, settling into his chair. "Made quite a mess.''

"I don't find that one bit amusing," Grace said. "I'll thank you not to speak so over dinner!''

"My apologies, ma'am, but Hattie Lee's old enough to hear a few things. After all, she's kept her lips sealed tighter than a white-oak barrel about my being here. Is it right to keep her ignorant of what's over and done with?''

Lizzy scowled at him. He returned her a look as hard as stone. In his mind, Lizzy was certain, the past wasn't over and done with any more than it was in hers. "There's nothing to be gained by discussing it, Rafe.''

"I met your aunt on the courthouse square in September of 1856," Rafe said.

Lizzy wanted to stop up her ears, to drive away the memory of the tall, golden man looking down on her from the porch of the Northern Bank. With the wind tossing his hair around his chiseled face, he looked as though he'd just stepped out of the mighty column beside him.

"She was loading her donkey with junk she'd bartered from a tinker."

"It—it wasn't junk," Lizzy said.

"So she said when I asked what she wanted with it. Said she built useful things out of other folks' sculch."

"I didn't use any such soldier talk. I called it 'rejectamenta.'"

"That's a made-up word, too, Lizzy," Grace said. "You always thought it sounded better than 'junk.' Talk about making a silk purse out of a sow's ear!"

"Your aunt didn't look like she'd been eating persimmons, as she does right now," Rafe said, dropping his voice.

Lizzy knew he was just trying to get her goat . . . he'd gotten it, too, bells and cart included. Trying to think of a retort, she raised her cup and stared into it.

"Her eyes twinkled so much like stars I could hardly tell what color blue they were."

"You're going to spoil our digestion," Grace said.

Lizzy jumped up and began to clear away the dishes. Unabashed, Rafe raised his voice over the rattle of plates and cups.

"When I asked what her name was, she said, 'Jack Sprat.'"

"But that was the name of her little mule!" Hattie Lee cried. "How come you called yourself by his name, Aunt Lizzy?"

"Mr. Laffite's pulling your leg, honey."

Hattie Lee turned her brown eyes on Rafe. "Turn it loose, sir."

"All right. She told me, 'Eliza Anton-John.' Prettiest name I ever heard. Next thing I knew, I was stacking copper tubes, broken ceramic pots, pig iron, and other rejectamenta onto poor old Jack Sprat's back until all you could see were his ears and tail."

Lizzy dried a cup. She could still see Rafe shucking off his white linen tailcoat and tossing it over the courthouse's iron fence. His shoulders were square and powerful, those of a man who worked the fields. When he rolled up his sleeves and began to load the mule, his arms were as dark brown as his face. His breeches fit him snugly, tapering into tall, polished boots. He was a sight as he bent and straightened, handling the heaviest objects with ease.

And when he'd finished, it seemed only natural to ask him to take a sarsaparilla at Spotswood's Apothecary. After all, the day was hot and dusty, and he'd worked up quite a sweat helping a stranger. The smile that suddenly lit his handsome face devastated her. At that moment, he'd stepped into her life and ruined it.

"—and when I saw her again a week later, she was with her father—your grandfather—Mark Anton-John. I asked him if I could call on her, and he gave me leave."

"If only he'd foreseen the future," Lizzy said, "he would've run you out of town on a rail." A soapy cup slipped from her hand and smashed in the dishpan. She gave a gasp and began to pick out the pieces.

Rafe was suddenly there, reaching into the water, his hand sliding over hers. "Let me—you'll cut yourself."

She pulled her hand away, but stayed close enough to feel the heat of his body. Biting her lip, she watched his hands. The porcelain fragments looked very white in his palm, like magnolia petals. She remembered looking up into the magnolia tree the night they—

"Throw them into the dustbin," she said, and stepped away. Hattie Lee and Grace were looking at her like a moth under glass.

Rafe returned to the table and sat down. "Your aunt had never received a gentleman caller from New Orleans before, even though your grandfather sent his cotton down there.''

"You were a cotton broker?'' Hattie Lee gazed in perplexity at his Federal uniform.

"Cotton was the reason for Mr. Laffite's trip," Grace said. "Cotton and a visit to his lawyer friend, Charlie McCord. Charlie knew all the planters from Tennessee to New Orleans."

Why did they have to bring Charles into the conversation? Poor Charles, with his high hopes... Lizzy could almost feel his presence in the room. She glanced back at Rafe. Silent now, he was drawing patterns on the tablecloth with his knife. It was a habit of his when engaged in worrisome thought.

"My Uncle Charles died in Mexico," Hattie Lee said.

"I know, honey," Rafe said. Tears glittered in his eyes as he met Lizzy's gaze.

Grace cleared her throat. "That's one topic we *won't* get into, Mr. Laffite."

"I still don't see why you were here," Hattie Lee said. "You could've brokered our cotton once it got down to New Orleans. We can't float our cotton anywhere now, not since them stinking, dirty old Yankees blockaded us. How come you was here?''

"Mr. Laffite was an opportunist, Hattie Lee," Lizzy said. "He knew his elder brother was going to inherit the family plantations, and Mr. Laffite didn't care to stay on and manage them as he'd been doing for his father."

"I was as much a slave as the black wretches toiling in the fields," Rafe said. "Cotton brokering was a way out."

"And mercenary soldiering was a way out of cotton brokerage," Lizzy said, throwing her words at him like spears. "Mr. Laffite wanted to go off and fight other men's wars, but his father begged him not to. The old man didn't want him to turn into a pirate like his grand-father.''

"Military school prepares a man for war," Rafe said. "And what my grandfather did brings no shame to me."

Lizzy felt as if they were alone in the room, resuming a battle after a long cease-fire. She picked up a plate and shoved it into the cupboard. She ignored the sound of splintering china.

"Cotton brokering didn't ignite Mr. Laffite's blood," she said, "even though he did as his father asked. But he was rebellious enough to come to Alabama. He figured if he had to lead a settled life, he'd do it far from New Orleans. Besides, here he'd find it easier to disappear once he'd ruined folks' lives!"

"Lizzy, that's enough!" Grace said. "I'll not have this sort of talk under my roof. Haven't we endured enough of it these last years?"

Lizzy threw down the dishrag. She felt Rafe's anger simmering across the room. If only he'd let it out! If only he'd give Grace an excuse to throw him into the street. She couldn't understand why her sister put up with him—it was their father the rogue had hurt. Their father's bank account, and her heart.

"Some strange soldiers came in on the train this evening," Hattie Lee said.

"You've been hanging around the depot again!" Grace shouted.

"But Ma, these were *real* strange soldiers."

"They're all strange, honey," Lizzy said. She gestured at Rafe's blue uniform to include him in the insult. "Yankees are foreigners."

"These weren't Yankees."

Rafe placed his forearms on the table and leaned forward with an intensity that set Hattie Lee back in her chair. "Who were they?"

"Dunno. Them Yankee soldiers called 'em *frogs*."

Rafe slammed his hands down.

"Frogs?" Lizzy said, looking at Rafe. "That's a strange insult."

"Their uniforms—buff-colored trousers and dark green jackets, lots of gold buttons?"

"Yes, sir, how'd you know? One of 'em had swirly gold fancywork on his sleeves, and a red collar like a vicar's."

Rafe came slowly to his feet, his hand to his wounded side. "French Lancers. They're here."

Lizzy stared at him, sensing that suddenly everything had changed. The past didn't matter compared to this nameless, present peril. Were French Lancers fighting for the Yankees, then? In just what sort of mission was Rafe involved?

"These Frenchmen, did you hear anything they said?"

"No, sir."

"How about the Yankees? Hear anything?"

Hattie Lee shook her head. "Just heard 'em say, 'Froggie went a-courting, hop hop hop,' when the soldiers went to use the privy. And they cussed the red-haired man behind his back."

Rafe closed his eyes and caught the edge of the table. His sudden pallor made him look as though he were suffering a relapse.

"Rafe, are you ill? Should you lie down?" Lizzy asked.

She suddenly found herself staring into the most frightening pair of eyes she'd ever seen. Malevolence glittered there, dark and purposeful. She was glad the table stood between her and the man.

"Excuse me," he said. With a curt bow, he pushed

his chair out of the way and stalked from the room. For a second or two the room was silent.

"Well, what are you waiting for?" Grace said. "Go after him!"

"Why should I?"

"Because he's in danger and you're still in love with him!"

"You're crazy." But Lizzy shoved back her chair and hurried outside.

He was a gray ghost in the dusk. Lizzy ran until she was a step behind. He acted as though she were not there. "Are you going to tell me what you're all het up about?"

Laffite reached the carriage house. "Give me the key."

Annoyed, yet fearing the shadows, she found the key in her reticule. "Here."

Rafe unlocked the door and pulled her inside. "Light the lantern."

Lizzy felt around in the darkness for the wooden matchbox. She scraped a match against the wall and, raising the lantern's glass globe, lit the wick.

Rafe went to examine the gondola. "Did you finish it?"

"Does it look like it?"

He didn't answer, but prodded the sides.

"What do those Frenchmen have to do with you?" She stalked across the room and caught him by the jacket. "Well?"

"That's something you don't need to know, Eliza."

"Don't need to know? You rush out here like your tail's on fire and I don't need to know? Let me tell you something, Mr. Laffite," she said, jabbing his breast with her forefinger, "if I don't find out, you don't fly. Period. To heck with your mission."

67

His countenance darkened. Lizzy cocked her fists on her hips. "You can't intimidate me, Rafe Laffite, so you might as well start explaining."

"I'll explain what you need to know when the time comes."

"You'll do it now, or I'll fly that balloon out of Huntsville with my instruments aboard instead of you." To add muscle, she said, "Dammit."

"Stubborn woman." Fighting some inner battle, he kneaded the gondola rail with his hands. Finally he said, "All right, then. It seems I didn't shake off my pursuers. Those are Maximilian's boys. They followed me from Mexico."

"*Mexico?* You're still a mercenary, then! You made us think you'd been fighting Yankees! You're nothing but a hired killer, still running around with Juarez!"

"No! Not since our war broke out, Eliza."

"Then why were you in Mexico instead of fighting for the cause?"

"I *was* fighting, until I got shot and sabered at Chickamauga. I don't suppose you missed the scars?"

Lizzy flushed. He knew she'd seen him naked when she cared for him. "If you were so wounded, how'd you end up in Mexico?"

"President Davis sent me there to recuperate. I can't tell you more than that."

"Aren't you full of secrets. That hole in your side we patched up, how'd you get it?"

"A nasty encounter with a spear."

"Oh. Did those Lancers following you do it?"

"No . . . It happened before I left Mexico."

How had he traveled all the way from Mexico with a wound like that? By rights, he should be dead. He had the constitution of a granite mountain. "You'd better tell me why they're chasing you. You can't expect me to take all these risks without knowing even a particle of the wherefore.''

Rafe heaved a sigh. ''I found out some secrets the president needs to know. It'd put you in danger if I told you—no, don't start yelling again, Eliza. I've already told you more than prudence dictates.''

Lizzy went to stand behind a chair. ''I don't see how they found you.''

''They're like bloodhounds.''

Or wolves. If they had tracked him all the way from Mexico, it was only a matter of time until they found him here. Her mind leaped ahead. Hattie Lee and Grace were in danger as long as he was present. Shaken, she met his gaze. Understanding surged between them, sharp and quick as lightning.

''We've got to get out of here tonight,'' she said.

''Yes. Morning might be too late. You should've let me help you with this balloon today.''

''I don't see where you'd have been any help.'' A thought struck her. ''Oh, my Lord!''

Rafe looked from her to the balloon. ''The gas,'' he said in sudden comprehension. ''How do you get it to the balloon?''

''We have to get the *balloon* to the *gas*. And even if we could slip past the guards at the gasworks, I don't have a wagon to transport all this. The Yankees stole my wagon and mule.''

Rafe vented a soft but heartfelt curse and paced the floor for a minute or two, hands on hips. As Lizzy regarded the taut line of his shoulders, his long legs and powerful arms, her thoughts drifted from danger into paths of phantom pleasure.

She used to lie upon him, caressing his back with her breasts and hands until he gave into her need and rolled her over. Now, as then, she could feel his heated pillar in her loins, purging all other desires, its flame unquenched by her wetness.

"Eliza." The soft purr of her name on his lips made her seek his eyes; she saw her own ardor mirrored there. She knew she was revealing too much, that in that moment her passion stood naked to the very man she was sworn to hate. Too late she moved to the worktable and turned her back to him.

As yesterday, she sensed rather than heard him move close behind her. She stood trembling, waiting to feel his hands on her body. That he had caused her husband's death she did not contemplate; she was too hot to feel shame. That would come later.

"Touch me, Rafe," she said low. "Please . . . touch me."

Chapter Seven

His fingers brushed her shoulders, then drifted down her sleeves to her bare forearms. This time he would not stop; she would not ask him to. She wanted him to remember their passion as clearly as she did, to desire her all over again. Already she felt him surge against her hips.

"You don't want this, Eliza," he said.

His voice was thick, harsh, yet she heard it catch. He took her by the jaw and turned her head until she looked up at him. Like a cougar's at twilight, his eyes glowed with mesmerizing force. They burned her, held her in a grip she dared not break. Lizzy heard a moan escape her throat—the sound of surrender.

"You'll hate me for it," he said.

"I . . . I hate you already," she said. She did not want to think right now. She needed him; that was enough.

"It isn't enough," he said. Had she spoken aloud? "Not for you, Eliza. We learned that lesson before."

Venita Helton

His fingers left her face and he stepped back. Lizzy
caught the edge of the table and hung on, drawing air
into her lungs as though she'd run a great distance.
Shame squeezed her heart.

He didn't apologize or make any excuse, but crossed
to the gondola and stared into it. Lizzy wanted to slap
his face. Only the knowledge of her own sexual culpa-
bility held her back.

"Jack Daniel's got a team," Rafe said.

Her temper rose another degree. He acted as though
nothing had happened between them. "So?"

"You said he hauls whiskey in a freight wagon."

"Yes." Had he been thinking of the damned wagon
while he made love to her?

"Where's the boardinghouse Hattie Lee talked
about?"

So, he had been studying the problem the entire time!
"Eliza?"

"Southwest of the public square," she said, and
folded her arms across her chest. She made herself speak
as though to a stranger. "One of the larger houses."

Rafe looked at her then—a long, deliberate stare that
raised blood to her cheeks. She forced herself to stare
back. "Describe it, Eliza, so I don't have to go knocking
on doors, announcing my intentions to the enemy."

She could send him over to the Williamses. There was
a whole squad of Yankees quartered in their house.
"It's—it's over a mile from here," she said at last.
"Think you can walk that far?"

She saw his hand stray to his wound, then drop. He'd
rather be hanged than admit weakness, the mule. She
said, "It's a big white house on Gates—I don't suppose
you remember the street after all these years?"

"I remember." He went over and opened the door.
"While I'm gone, get food and water to last a week.

72

You'll have to leave your science equipment."

"The heck I will!" she said, but he was already outside. She hurried after him. He was gone, melted into the warm darkness of the yard. How could a wounded man move so fast?

She leaned against the doorpost, stared up at the stars, and stilled her thoughts. The constellations rode the sky like diamond chariots and horses, wheeling and curvetting in one vast, eternal round. *Tonight I'll ride with them.* Her heart began to thud. *Rafe will stand in the chariot beside me.*

Jack Daniel stood in the doorway. In the darkness behind him, his mules jingled their harness and stamped. He whisked off his slouch hat and swept her a bow. "Miz McCord, powerful glad to meet you."

"Won't you come inside, Mr. Jack?" She stepped aside for him to enter the workshop. Rafe came in behind him and shut the door.

Although barely five-foot-two, the whiskey smuggler carried himself like a big man. Not even his baggy frock coat could disguise muscles like baling wire. And despite his youth, his beard was as full as a grown man's. Lizzy looked for the devil-may-care light in his eyes she'd heard was there. Talk was, if Jack Daniel ever settled down to raise a family, half the women from here to Lynchburg would turn out in black for the wedding. He looked pretty harmless, though. Not like she'd expected.

"I hope y'all didn't have any trouble," Lizzy said. "The Yankee patrols—"

"Showed not a whisker," Rafe said. "Jack's got plenty of experience getting past pickets."

Jack Daniel laughed. "Been avoiding Yankees nigh on two years, ma'am. Ain't been caught yet; don't intend to start. Now let's see what you got."

"Over here. Ever seen a balloon, Mr. Jack?"

"Seen you and your pappy fly at the fair up in Franklin County about ten years back. I wasn't but a tadpole then; Ma wouldn't let me take a ride." Jack Daniel peered into the basket, then went over and looked at the silk envelope piled on the floor. "You still advertise artificial limbs?"

"You've got some memory, recalling a thing like that. Sign's on that wall by the ladder."

" 'Universal Joint and Artificial Limb Company, J. W. Weston, New York,' " Jack read off of a long metal sign bent and crusted with rust. "Yep, that's the one I remember. It was nailed onto the bottom of the basket where everybody could read it from way up."

"That's right, we used to—"

Rafe let out a low whistle. He was gazing into the basket, shaking his head. "I asked for necessities. There won't be room to stand, you've got it packed so full."

"There's enough room." She wasn't about to leave *everything* behind. The wooden valise she'd squeezed in contained scientific instruments. "I don't see how we're going to get past the Yankees, anyway. We'll look like a circus wagon. You know they'll stop us, Rafe Laffite, and if they don't shoot us on the spot, they'll throw us in jail."

Jack Daniel screwed on his hat. "Just hang on to your tail feathers and leave this to me."

"We're wasting time," Rafe said. "Get the wagon, Jack." He shuttered the lantern and opened the double doors.

A few minutes later, whispering, sawing at the reins, Jack backed the wagon into the workshop. Rafe pushed past the heads of the two mules and shut the doors, then went around to unload a heap of hay and fence posts from the wagon.

"This's how I keep Yankees from figuring out about my whiskey," Jack said. "I cover the kegs with side meat and throw this mess over-top it. When I hit town around midnight, nobody gives me a second look."

"And then you sell the popskull to the grocery shops, and the sides to the butcher." Hattie Lee emerged from under the table. Her father's old boots stuck out from the hem of her nightdress like steamboat prows. She dipped a curtsy.

"Hattie Lee, you little possum, you're supposed to be inside, asleep in your bed! How'd you get past your mama?" Lizzy demanded.

"I snuck out the back door. Ma was in the parlor, reading her Bible and praying for you."

Lizzy flushed. Only an hour ago, Grace had tried to make her change her mind about flying. She hadn't reckoned on Lizzy choosing such a foolhardy method to help Rafe. Now she was praying.

"I just wanted to watch, Aunt Lizzy," Hattie Lee said. "Thought maybe you'd let me come with you, after all."

"We've been through all that, honey, and made our good-byes." Lizzy squatted down and folded her in her arms. "I want you to run back to the house and make sure and lock the door. Tell your mama I'll be all right."

"Soon as you leave, I will." Hattie Lee began to shake.

"Don't, honey. I can't bear it if you cry," Lizzy said.

"And I can't bear for you to go."

"It won't be for long. I'll be back before the month is out." Maybe it wasn't a fib.

She glanced at Rafe, who was lifting the gondola into the wagon. How could she get him to Richmond when she wasn't even sure they could get out of Huntsville alive?

Stroking her niece's back, she watched Rafe and Jack attempt to carry the balloon. Altogether weighing just under six hundred pounds, the unwieldy mass kept slithering to the ground. "Stuff's heavy as a barrel of whiskey," Jack Daniel said, struggling with his end. "And slick as an inside-out cow womb. What's it made of, Miz McCord?"

"Silk," Lizzy said. She kissed Hattie Lee, then rose and pulled the child against her hip. "Daddy treated it with a solution of turpentine and gutta-percha—crude rubber—to keep the rosin gas from seeping out."

"Her father was an inventor," Rafe said.

His words coming in bursts as he staggered with the balloon, Jack Daniel said, "He ever distill whiskey?"

"No. He didn't want his faculties all fumed up."

"Folks called him a mad scientist," Rafe said. He struggled to keep a wave of silk from crashing to the floor. "He was always into something."

"I don't see where you've got room to call anyone else mad, Mr. Laffite," Lizzy said. "From where I sit, it's your intellect that's half a bubble off the plumb!"

"I never said your father was mad."

Dragging Hattie Lee along by the hand, Lizzy marched over and jabbed her finger at a thick skein of rope on the wall. "If y'all weren't in such a blazing hurry, maybe y'all would've thought to bind the balloon with its own lines first. See, collar and shrouds. Daddy and I always bound it, then slung it up with that block and tackle."

Rafe looked up at a steamboat pulley dangling from a rafter. "Thunderation, if I'm not blind," he said. "Let it fall, Jack."

"Reckon we won't bust a gut, after all."

Ten minutes later, the wagon sat shuddering under the weight of the balloon. "Hope it don't break!" Hattie Lee said.

"It won't." Jack Daniel gave the wagon a pat. "I've hauled whiskey a lot heavier than that little parcel there. This cart's got heavy-gauge springs."

Rafe added eight bags of sand, each weighing twenty-five pounds. Then he and Jack covered everything with canvas, hay, and fence posts.

"What do you use to fill the balloon, Eliza?" Rafe asked.

Lizzy got a rubber-and-horsehair hosepipe out of a trunk and held it against her breast like a coiled snake. "We won't get to use it, Rafe. They'll catch us the minute we get near the Gas Light Company."

"Just bring it, honey," Rafe said.

She slowly extended the hosepipe. As he reached for it, his fingers brushed hers. The contact galvanized her hand to the coil. "Eliza, let go."

But she only clamped down harder. She didn't want to give him the last piece of equipment, but she couldn't stop him from using it to draw her almost to his chest. Sensual energy flowed between them like hot lava. She felt her knees weaken, her breath quicken.

"We aren't alone, honey," he said low.

It took a second for his words to penetrate. Ashamed, she released the hosepipe and stepped back. She'd lowered her defenses not once, but twice, on the same day. Charles McCord must be rolling in his grave.

"Get in there under the canvas," Rafe said. "Quick now! I'll ride up front with Jack. Don't make a sound."

"We'll never get past the guards. We'll wind up in jail."

"Then I'll bust you out, Aunt Lizzy," Hattie Lee said.

Lizzy broke away from Rafe and pressed Hattie Lee's

face to her shoulder. "Oh, baby, who's going to look after you and your mama while I'm away?"

"Don't you worry about us none—we got cornmeal and greens to last us all winter."

"I'm not worried about y'all eating, honey." She didn't want to say she was afraid the Lancers would show up at the door. "Just stay inside and tell your mama to load the squirrel gun."

"Yes, ma'am. I got the cedar cane under my bed already." Hattie Lee lowered her voice. "You go on and show 'em what you're made of, Aunt Lizzy. Nobody'll laugh at you this time, not even them bluetick Yankees. You go on and help Mr. Rafe get to Richmond."

Lizzy's pulse leaped. Hattie Lee wasn't supposed to know their destination. "Don't you tell a soul where I've gone, d'you hear?"

"Mum's my bond." Hattie Lee pressed her lips together, but tears rolled down her cheeks.

Lizzy struggled to keep her voice even. "Obey your mama, honey. Stay out of trouble, and I'll bring you back all the peppermint sticks in Virginia!" Before she could change her mind, she stood up and gave Rafe her hand. His expression told her he'd been watching. Fresh tears stung her eyes. "For pity's sake, Rafe, let's go!"

He lifted her into the wagon. Just before the canvas dropped over her head, Lizzy gazed into Hattie Lee's brown eyes. She wondered if she would ever look into them again.

Chapter Eight

Jack drove the team straight down the macadamized road to Lincoln Street. Slouched over the reins, he whistled between his teeth. This was the last place Rafe wanted to be, perched in plain view of Yankees. His backbone tingled like the first pains of a bullet wound. He wished he had a gun.

"Take the alley," Laffite said. "Less chance of being spotted."

"Hell, I didn't get where I am today by being a wallflower. A fellow's got to be brash."

"Brash or dead, one follows the other."

Jack let out a cackle and slapped Rafe's knee. "You're a good one to preach, old man, considering what you're fixing to do with that balloon back there."

"Shut that trap of yours."

"I know what I'm doing; this ain't my first time in town."

Rafe stiffened, his gaze targeting the deep shadow of

Cumberland Presbyterian Church. ''We've got company.''

''I don't see nothing—''

''Halt!'' The challenge rang out of the darkness. ''Who goes there?''

''Captain LaVert,'' Rafe said, pulling a name that matched his Creole accent out of the air. ''This civilian's got requisitions for the quartermaster.''

''Just hold it right there.'' The sentry moved into the road and unshuttered his lantern.

Rafe knew him instantly; he'd sat beside him in the cattle car all the way from Memphis. If the Yankee recognized him and remembered he'd gone by a different name, his mission was going to suffer one hell of a complication. He resisted the urge to pull his kepi down over his eyes. After all, he'd been bearded and as brown as dirt on the train.

''What do you want, soldier?'' Rafe asked, low and cold.

''Sir, I got orders to check all wagons.''

''What for?''

''Rebels, Captain.''

''You got a townful of them already,'' Jack Daniel said, and spat over the side.

The Yankee thrust out his jaw. ''Maybe you've got some more in your wagon, boy.''

Rafe jabbed his thumb at the junk in the wagon bed. ''You're right. We'll just haul these Rebel fence posts straight to Granger and let him lock 'em up.''

''C'mon, sir, don't give me a bad time. Orders is orders.'' Holding the lantern high, the sentry poked the hay with his bayonet. ''What's Quartermaster want with this lot?''

''He aims to grind up them fence posts and add 'em

to the pork ration,'' Jack Daniel said. ''Probably improve that weevil-fodder Cookie dishes up.''

''You better watch your mouth, boy.''

As the Yankee approached the corner where Lizzy was hidden, Rafe slid his hand into the top of his boot and withdrew a knife. *Don't move, Eliza.*

''Maybe you got something under this junk,'' the Yankee said, holding the tip of his bayonet over Lizzy's hiding place. ''Maybe even a Rebel spy.''

''If I don't have a drink I'm gonna bust!'' Jack Daniel said. ''I'll splatter from here to Lynchburg.'' He reached under the seat and hauled out a greenware jug. Uncorking it, he noisily took a swig and belched.

''What's that you got there, boy?''

''Just a drop of Tennessee's finest sippin' whiskey. It ain't for the dadblamed quartermaster, so don't go jabbing your bayonet in it.'' He handed the jug to Rafe.

The sentry moved closer. ''Lemme have a snort.''

Jack looked at Rafe. The Yankee looked at Rafe, too. ''Just one, sir.''

''There's a regulation against sentries drinking the ardent.''

''Thought he wanted to check the wagon, anyway,'' Jack said.

''That's what he said. You're on duty, soldier.''

The sentry propped his rifle against the wagon. ''Sir, my watch just ended.''

''What a coincidence,'' Rafe said, and handed him the jug.

Two minutes later, the jug considerably lighter, they got under way again. Neither man spoke. Rafe's stomach felt as though he'd pickled it in Jack Daniel's whiskey. *Rebel spy.* Dammit, DeCoeur must have told Granger about him. Now he had the Union Army to run from, too.

Jack turned right onto Eustis Street. Guided by the

spire of the Church of the Nativity, he reached the next corner and steered the mules around the wrought-iron fence into the churchyard. The shadow of the Gothic building covered them.

Rafe jerked the canvas off Lizzy. She emerged hot and dusty, her hair spilling from its pins. He helped her to the grass. "All right, Eliza?"

But she just looked at the church and shook her head. "It's got gas lamps," she said. "And it's the only church the Yankees haven't turned into a stable. I should've thought of it."

"It was Jack's suggestion. I didn't even know the church was here. They must've built it while I was gone."

But Lizzy tightened her lips in disgust. She'd worried herself sick thinking Rafe and Jack were going to drive straight up to the Gas Light Company and get shot.

"You might've told me what you had in mind, Rafe Laffite. Daddy and I always used the company. That's why the church didn't occur to me."

"Nobody's blaming you."

He moved close to her, his tall, shadowy form gathering the night. The sudden gleam of his teeth warned her to be careful while, paradoxically, urging her nearer. "You're brave, Eliza," he said. "Braver than any woman I've ever known. Don't lose heart."

Transfixed, she stared up at him. She knew she was inviting his kiss, but for the life of her, she couldn't move away. Her feet seemed molded of lead. Rafe lowered his head until he looked straight into her eyes. "By heaven, you're beautiful."

She backed away and bumped into Jack Daniel coming around the tailgate. "Whoa!" he said hoarsely, catching her shoulders. "Wait till the wedding, sugar."

Lizzy shook him off. In the darkness she couldn't see

Rafe glare at the whiskey distiller, but she sensed his anger. "Let's get busy before somebody comes," she said. "We've got hours of work ahead of us."

In silence the men unloaded the gondola and set it near the fence, on the windward side of the yard. Lizzy attached shroud lines to the caning at each corner of the basket.

The balloon made a loud *thunk!* when the men pushed it off the wagon. For half a minute the conspirators waited for someone to investigate the noise, but when the street remained quiet, they spread the envelope in the gondola's lee. It filled the yard.

Lizzy chewed her lip, considering the mass of silk. There wasn't enough space to launch. The balloon might crash into the church or be gashed to ribbons on the spiked fence. Reluctantly, she connected the hosepipe to a valve in the mouth of the balloon.

"Rafe, I'm not sure about this," Lizzy said. "We don't have room. I might get you killed."

But Rafe handed her an unlighted lantern and started unreeling hosepipe. Halfway to the northwest tower, he turned back and caught her hand. She jerked free as soon as they reached the sanctuary door.

"Don't haul me around like a rag on a string, Mr. Laffite!"

"You didn't think I was going to let you stand around in the dark with that sawed-off little ladies' man, did you?"

"I thought you might."

"Not on your tintype!"

"Jealous, Rafe? You've more to worry about than that. Didn't you hear what I said about the balloon?"

"You won't crash us, Eliza. I've got confidence."

"But I haven't flown in years!" Lizzy's throat began

to ache from yelling at him in a whisper. "Don't you understand?"

"It'll come back to you the minute we're airborne."

"You're insane, do you understand that?"

"It was your idea to skip town in the balloon, honey, remember? You just didn't plan on carrying me. Now hush while I break into church."

It took him less than a minute to pick the lock and slip inside. Before she followed him, Lizzy propped open the door with a stick to keep it from mashing the hosepipe

The nave was as black as a mausoleum. Rafe whispered, "Where's the nearest lamp?"

"Behind the back row on the right—oh, my!" She'd bashed her knee on a pew. "I can't see half an inch!"

"Stand still, then."

She sensed him move away. Without him, the darkness chilled her. She gripped the back of the pew and listened for his step. There was no sound. "Rafe, where are you?"

"Here's the lamp." His whisper came from several yards away. "Thunderation, I've got to light the lantern to figure out how to work the valve. Hope nobody spots the damn light."

"Stop swearing in church!"

"I'll try." This time his whisper came from right beside her, making her jump. "Hold the lantern up so I can light it."

Lizzy heard a match scrape twice before it flared. From the sharply pitched vault, down the curved timbers to the exquisite stained-glass windows, the sanctuary burst into colored haloes. In the chancel, three lancet windows formed glittering jewels.

"Good God almighty—" Rafe said, then glanced at Lizzy before finishing, "is here."

"And wondering why we are," Lizzy said. This was Rector Bannister's church. Did God recall she'd burned down the good man's carriage house? Her stomach settled into a ball of lead. "Let's—let's get on with it."

"That's what we're here for, honey." Rafe dragged the hosepipe to the gas fixture, lifted off the glass shade, and fumbled with the valve.

"Let me," Lizzy said. "You've never been mechanically minded."

The coupling wouldn't fit. Lizzy's pulse climbed as she struggled to force the connection. Every sound made her start. The Yankees might be just outside, sneaking up on them. Jack Daniel might be in their clutches already. "Dammit," she said, glaring at Rafe.

His left eyebrow lifted fractionally. "I'll go check the gondola. Maybe I'll find something useful in the junk you brought."

"Instruments, you mean!"

But now there was only darkness where he had been. Left alone in the thin lanternlight, she wanted to run after him, but how would it look? He'd think she was a 'fraidy-cat. Still, what if he didn't come back? What if she went to check on him and found General Granger standing there? What if the French Lancers got him?

Stop it! What was the matter with her, acting like a boll weevil straddling a hot coal? She made herself look at the altar.

Brocade. Filigree cloth. Candlesticks in heavy sconces. Symbols of divine power. God didn't take kindly to somebody burning down His servant's carriage house, she was sure. She'd heard enough sermons to know how He punished the wicked. Folks claimed there were people buried under the very floor where she stood. Hattie Lee said they came out at night and dragged the wicked through the floorboards.

85

"I found a scrap of gutta-percha—Eliza, don't shout."

"Don't sneak up on me like that!" She snatched the rubber strip out of his hand. "Is everything all right out there?"

"Still as death."

"Don't use that expression." Her hands shook as she tried to mend the coupling. Rafe reclaimed the gutta-percha and quickly sealed the connection.

"There, fixed. Let's see if it works." He twisted a knob on the lamp until gas began to hiss through the hosepipe. "Let's go watch the elephant take shape."

He put out the lantern before leaving the church. Just outside the door, he said, "Jack tied the mules to the magnolia tree."

Fog had settled into the yard. Although Lizzy couldn't see the mule team, she could make out the big tree twenty yards away. "Where's Jack?"

"Over there on the right, squatting by the balloon."

She couldn't see him, either. Rafe could probe the darkness like a cat. Keeping her comparative blindness a secret, she set off across the grass and stumbled over Jack Daniel.

"Whoa there, sugar. Where's that man of yours?"

"He's not my man, and he's right there."

"He's as much there as a haunt," Jack said. "Hope he don't jump out of the shadders and holler 'Boo!' "

Lizzy looked over her shoulder. Rafe was nowhere in sight. Goose bumps rose on her skin. The way he came and went without a sound was unnatural. He was too silent. Too deadly.

"Damn thing ain't doing nothing," Jack said, and kicked the balloon.

"Don't do that! It takes hours to fill. If the wind picks up, we'll have to hold it, because if it rolls into the prongs on that fence there won't be enough left for a braid rug.''

''Maybe we ought to let the mules stand on it,'' Jack said.

''Very funny, Mr. Jack.'' She wished Rafe would surface. If the Yankees came, she wanted him on the front line.

The balloon moved a little, brushed by the wind. Lizzy hurried windward and caught a shroud. Jack Daniel caught another. ''How's a body control this thing once it's aloft, Miz McCord?''

''When the wind takes hold there's not much you can do.''

''Then how the hell—excuse my swearing, ma'am— how the hell does that man of yours reckon on getting to Richmond?''

''He's not my man, and he's used to being obeyed. He thinks he'll order the balloon around.''

''I got a feeling he's in for a surprise,'' Jack Daniel said. ''Pardon my saying so, but you and this here contraption got a lot in common.''

''Are you calling me stubborn, Mr. Jack?''

''Just a little wayward, ma'am.''

Not wayward enough. Wasn't she doing exactly what Rafe wanted? In all the years she'd known him, she had defied his wishes only once. She hadn't waited for him to come back.

Charles would still be alive if she'd listened to Rafe. He would have continued his law practice instead of marrying her and being pulled into a plantation too large and ill-suited to his abilities, a plantation that drained him emotionally and financially until, desperate, he'd followed Rafe Laffite to Mexico.

Her husband wasn't meant to be a mercenary. He was a scholar, with a scholar's precarious foothold on the earth. Adventuring didn't come naturally to such a man. He didn't last long in the world of sabers and civil strife.

But it was Rafe, not her, who had led him adventuring. Rafe who made it look like the end to his financial woes. Rafe who made him think he could accomplish the impossible. Rafe who led her husband away to death.

Suddenly alive, the balloon shuddered. Its center expanding like a bubble, it rolled on the grass. Sparks crackled and danced across it like lightning bugs.

"What the hell?" Jack Daniel stepped back in alarm.

"Static electricity," Lizzy said. "Friction causes it. If we were using hydrogen instead of rosin gas, the balloon could explode."

Jack Daniel whistled. "Damn."

"Be very quiet," Rafe said from immediately behind them.

Lizzy nearly jumped out of her skin. Whirling, she tried to smack his face, but he caught her wrist, pressed his fingers against her mouth, and pulled her against him.

"Yankees," he whispered. "They're coming up the street."

Chapter Nine

Footsteps tramped in the fog beyond the fence. The balloon was half-full, growing larger by the minute, rolling gently to and fro despite their grip on the shrouds. If the Yankees chanced to look into the churchyard they might see it through the fog.

Rafe's big hands moved to Lizzy's shoulders, urging her to the ground. Holding a line, she crouched beside the balloon. At any moment she expected to see the orange flash of gunfire. Jack Daniel hunkered down beside her.

The team. Would fog and the drooping branches of the magnolia hide the wagon? What if one of the mules stamped or brayed? Her hair stood on end.

"A song, boys!" a voice rang out. " 'All Quiet Along the Potomac Tonight.' " Immediately a tempest of male voices echoed the rhythm of the march.

His musket falls slack—his face, dark and grim,

Grows gentle with memories tender,
As he mutters a prayer for the children asleep,
And their mother—"May heaven defend her!"
The moon seems to shine as brightly as then—
That night, when the love yet unspoken
Leaped up to his lips, and when low murmured vows
Were pledged, to be ever unbroken.

The notes merged with the fog into a ghostly aria, beautiful and painful to hear. Lizzy lowered her face and closed her eyes, but the words reverberated in her marrow, evoking emotion impossible to quell.

The song belonged to Rafe and her, an expression of what should have been. Each sentence sharpened her regret. She sensed his warmth beside her and longed for him to reach out to her, to comfort the girl she had been . . . and the woman she'd become.

Hark! was the night wind that rustles the leaves!
Was it the moonlight so wondrously flashing?
It looked like a rifle! "Ha, Mary, good-bye!"
And his lifeblood is ebbing and 'plashing.
"All quiet along the Potomac tonight,"
No sound save the rush of the river;
While soft falls the dew on the face of the dead,
"The Picket's" off duty forever.

The song melted into the wind and died. Tears streamed down Lizzy's cheeks. Refusing Rafe's hand, she rose and looked into the darkness where the soldiers had disappeared. They'd sung Charles's dirge—it wasn't about Rafe and her. Charles's death eternally separated them. The vows were broken.

She brushed away her tears before meeting Rafe's gaze. His eyes were shadowed, his mouth drawn with

90

pain. For an instant she wondered if he shared her thoughts, if his heart, too, ached with regret. It was too late for that. She was honor-bound to fly him as far as she could. After that, she could leave. There would never be another meeting.

He touched her arm. "Eliza, I—"

"Don't." She pulled back. Fog swirled in a spectral dance between them.

He dropped his hand. "How long till the balloon lifts?"

"Two hours, I think." She turned away and busied herself with the shrouds. She could feel his gaze on her back.

"Them Yankees is canny as a dead coon-dog," Jack Daniel said. "Ain't none of 'em got half an eyeball or they'd have seen this rascal."

"They'll get another chance when she rises," Rafe said. "We're not out of the woods yet."

Not out of the woods at all, Lizzy thought. Even if they succeeded in escaping Huntsville, she could not escape Rafe. She would be stuck in the gondola with him. Alone.

Gradually their surroundings began to turn gray. Three-quarters full, the balloon rose like an inverted hoopskirt above the gondola, shifting with every puff of wind. They had to constantly work the shrouds to keep it off the fence and away from the brick church. The night dissipated until only fog covered them in the naked whiteness of dawn.

"Somebody comes by here, we'll have the devil's own time explaining what the hell we're doing," Jack Daniel said.

"Mr. Laffite's wearing a Yankee uniform. We'll tell them we're Union Balloon Corps."

"Yeah, they'll believe that." Daniel poured acid into

his whisper. "That damn sentry said they was hunting a Rebel spy. Reckon they'll throw us in jail and give the balloon to the blamed signal corps, for real."

Gradually the envelope quit sloshing back and forth and grew taut, rising high and proud as a deep blue thundercloud. Lifted a foot off the ground, the gondola pulled at its tethers.

"It's time, Eliza, wouldn't you say?"

"It's time." The leviathan was as tall as the church roof: the entire yard lay shadowed beneath it. Would she be able to handle it after all these years?

As the early light warmed the brick walls so close by, wind buffeted the crown of the balloon. The shrouds creaked as the bag oscillated. Lizzy disconnected the hosepipe and closed the valvecock while Rafe went into the church. He came back after a minute, coiling the hosepipe around his elbow and hand.

"Stow it in the basket," Lizzy said. "We might need it later." She hated to think under what grave circumstance. She had never flown more than twenty miles from town. Difficulties that she didn't care to imagine might lie ahead.

She circled the balloon. Would the patches hold? Would the shrouds? Where would they find more rosin gas if they needed it?

"Time to go, Eliza. It's getting to be broad daylight." Rafe took her by the elbow.

"Mr. Jack, wait until I'm aboard, then loose the tethers one at a time, catty-corner so's not to spill us. Can you do it?"

"Slicker'n a frog's heinie on a greased skillet, Miz McCord."

As though she were mounting a horse, Lizzy placed both hands on the gondola rail and slung her leg over. As she eased her other leg up, Rafe's hands encircled her waist and lifted her like a child. She submitted until her feet touched the shifting bottom of the basket.

"I could have managed, thank you," she said.

"I've no doubt about that, Eliza, but maybe you want to adjust your skirt."

Her skirt and petticoats were caught on the rail, her pantaloons in plain view. She started to snatch her garments loose, then remembered the fragile condition of the wicker. In the bare second she hesitated, Rafe asked, "Need my help?"

"No!" Despite her care, caning cracked as the fabric came free. She dropped her skirts and looked up.

Rafe's attention was elsewhere, but it was plain to see by the crinkles around his eyes that he'd been looking, all right. Biting her tongue, she moved aft and gestured at him to climb in. He clambered aboard, catching the sides when the basket canted under his weight.

"Take it easy; you won't fall out." Lizzy was surprised at him. His jauntiness was gone. Was he afraid? She hadn't thought him capable of it. If he was nervous this close to the ground, how would he feel a thousand feet up? She began to feel better.

"Loose the tethers, Mr. Jack," Lizzy said in a firm voice.

In a few minutes she would know the freedom of flight once more; she would fly heavenward and touch the wind. It didn't matter that Rafe would be there to share it. A mighty wave of joy surged into her heart.

Rafe leaned out to shake Jack Daniel's hand. "Thanks, Daniel. You've done the Confederacy a great service. Now cut us loose and get the hell out of here."

"See to your own backside, Laffite—ain't nobody can catch mine. Here, you might need this. That pigsticker of yours ain't no good when shooting starts." He handed Rafe a pistol with a barrel nearly twelve inches long. "One of my slaves, Uncle Nearly, made that thing for me. See you give it back sometime."

"You can count on it."

Daniel handed over his cartridge belt. "And see you get that little lady to Richmond in one piece." He tipped his hat to Lizzy. "When you get back this way, Miz McCord, maybe you'll give me leave to pay you court."

"Maybe I will, Mr. Jack," she said, and almost laughed at the expression on Rafe's face. He was jealous, all right, and she didn't care. She was anxious to fly the straining balloon. "Hurry now!"

Jack Daniel freed the first bowline knot. One corner of the basket lifted sharply, spilling Rafe into Lizzy.

"Hold on or you'll eat grass before we're fairly launched," she said. "Embarrassing thing for a would-be aeronaut."

Daniel loosed the opposite tether and the gondola leveled off. Then he released the last two knots and danced back.

Like a quail flushed out of tall grass, the balloon leaped skyward and heeled sharply toward the magnolia. The mules brayed in alarm.

"You're gonna crash!" Jack Daniel screamed.

Lizzy grabbed the crown line and pulled with all her strength, warping the crown. The balloon careened toward the church. The gondola scraped branches as it swung. Lizzy lost her grip on the line and fell to the floor.

Rafe grabbed the crown line and pulled on it as he'd seen Lizzy do. The balloon struck the church with teeth-jarring force, then shot straight up, bouncing off the bricks.

Rafe watched the ground drop away until Jack Daniel's wagon became a child's toy. For a sickening moment the balloon veered toward the steeple, then capriciously bobbed up and over.

"Fire and copperheads, I feel like I've just fallen off a bridge!"

"Let go of the line," Lizzy said as she hauled herself to her feet. "We're clear of the air turbulence created by the building."

"I thought that steeple was going to stab us."

"It didn't, though, and we've no more obstacles to worry about for a while. Nothing in Huntsville reaches as high as that steeple."

"Nothing but a damned Yankee artillery burst. God help us if we drift over Echoll's Hill."

"We're heading that way now," she said.

Rafe struck the basket with his fist. "Damn the wind!"

"Don't be an old woman, Rafe."

Danger sharpened her excitement now as it had in the old days. Nothing could stop her. She was a bird without wings carried along by her own weightlessness. Yankee shells could no sooner pierce her than poke a hole in a cloud. She let out a whoop.

Rafe covered her mouth. "For the love of God, Eliza, would you kindly keep still? It's as quiet as death up here; they'll hear us coming a mile away!"

Lizzy slapped away his hand. Chastened only slightly, she endeavored to keep her voice to a whisper. "Light as a feather, soft as a cloud, we'll fly like a birdie o'er Twickenham Town!"

"If I didn't know better, I'd swear you were drunk," Rafe said, but a smile spread across his face.

Lizzy's delirium left her. She stared up into eyes gone warm as smoked amber above a smile like the pearly inside of a mussel shell. She could almost feel the heat of his lips on hers, the strength of his arms around her.

She caught her breath and turned away, staring down into the fog. Roofs and treetops punctured the haze, and to the east, beyond Echoll's Hill, she saw some tall markers in Maple Hill Cemetery. Here and there she saw patches of ground that fog didn't cover at all. Unfortunately, Echoll's Hill was one of those patches. Soldiers were visible.

They drifted across the hill at five hundred feet—close enough to see the insignia on an artillery captain's collar and to smell ramrod bread. Conversations on the ground were unnaturally loud, as if the soldiers were standing five feet away.

"Skyugle on down to the mess, Private, and get me some coffee."

"They got nothing but seed-tick coffee, sir—boys say Cookie's brewing it out of okra pods. He ran out of parched corn."

"Hell, my digestion can't abide that muck."

The balloon drifted with the smoke. Lizzy's stomach churned. If anyone should look up and see the balloon . . .

"Hey, Sarge, would you look at that!"

Lizzy's heart dropped into her toes. Her throat constricted around a small sound of fright. Rafe reached over and gripped her hand until no blood was left in her fingers. Why didn't he get out the pistol? At any moment the Yankees would start shooting. Lizzy felt very naked and earthbound, like a bird stripped of its feathers and left in the dirt. How many bullets would pierce the bubble before it plummeted to earth?

She saw three men running toward a gun emplacement. "They're going to shoot us down, Rafe!"

Chapter Ten

"They're going to turn the cannon on us!"

"Shh, Eliza. Look."

Raising a cheer that rattled the balloon, soldiers from all over the hill rushed to the battery. Beside the cannon, two dogs fought in a haze of dust and fur. The excited crowd didn't look up. The balloon drifted into the fog swaddling the eastern slope.

"Lord, I thought my heart would stop when they started hollering," Lizzy said.

Rafe shook his head. "We were straight overhead and not one of 'em saw us. What an army."

"Well, coming out of the fog from so high up, I'm not surprised."

"We weren't that high, honey. Mr. Lincoln would set them to polishing their eyeballs if he knew."

"Folks don't look higher than their own noses. Daddy and I used to sneak right up on farmers and scare the daylights out of them. You should see the cloud a sack of flour makes when it hits the ground from fifty feet up.''

Rafe chuckled. ''Those farmers ever try to shoot you down?''

''They were too busy coughing.''

''Now that you mention it, I remember your daddy speaking of it in a letter. He was in a mood to talk about the old days.''

''A letter? When did y'all ever correspond?''

A muscle vibrated in Rafe's cheek. ''When I was in Mexico, Eliza.''

Her face burned. Daddy hadn't told her . . . he'd never spoken of the man who'd almost become his son-in-law. Yet he'd written to him.

Had he told Rafe about the baby? She looked at Rafe, a quick glance that told her nothing. Had he known and refused to come back? Is that why Daddy had arranged her marriage to Charles?

A woman needs a steady sort of man. Young Charles will be good to you, Daddy had said. Nothing about Rafe Laffite.

She took a deep breath. ''What else did he tell you?''

''Little else.'' His eyes narrowed slightly, reading her face. ''You expected—what?''

''Nothing. Nothing at all. I'm just surprised he wrote after what happened. The—the cotton deal, I mean.''

Unable to meet his gaze a moment longer, she turned her back. Not far below, stone monuments jutted out of the mist. Maple Hill Cemetery. Rafe wouldn't get any more out of her than he would a person sleeping under one of those rocks.

The balloon shuddered and began to rotate. Somewhere in the fog her father slept. What would he think if he could see her companion?

I've forgiven him. The words echoed in her skull and

spine. Expecting to find Rafe behind her, she moved sharply aside.

But Rafe was on the other side of the gondola, watching the ground. Not so much as a wisp of his tawny hair moved, yet a feeling of warmth embraced her—warmth with substance, like hands. *Ridiculous!* The fog was tricking her mind. She crouched down and busied herself with the instruments in her wooden valise. Science was her refuge. It always had been.

Careful not to drop it over the side, she mounted a brass gimbal arm to the rail, then connected a three-foot-long brass barometer inscribed with a numbered scale. The gimbal let the tube sway with the balloon.

"I guess you've seen a barometer before," she said at last. If she didn't break the silence, she feared she might hear strange voices again. "But I bet you didn't know you can calculate altitude with one."

Rafe didn't take his eyes off the clouds below. "I never considered the matter."

"No? The French Balloon Corps started using them a century ago."

"Then I'm a hundred years behind the times."

"Maybe not that far out-of-date." Lizzy made a minute adjustment to the brass tube.

"You want the barometer to jostle around like that?"

"It's not jostling," she said, surprised. He'd seemed more interested in what was going on outside the basket. "See that gimbal?"

His swift glance told her he knew the term.

"Without it, any violent maneuvering of the balloon would force the mercury to the top of the tube and break the glass."

"Violent maneuvering?" Rafe tilted his head toward the balloon's underbelly. "Suppose we'll do any more? That business at the church nearly slew me."

"I thought you looked a mite fearful back there."

"I don't deny it. I never thought I'd go flying around like a pigeon."

"You don't look like a pigeon," she said. "More like a hawk with ruffled feathers."

"Ruffled, am I?" he asked, but he watched the barometer as though expecting the mercury to shoot out the top.

His disquietude ought to make her feel in control. Drat it, she *was* in control. The giant bag of gas bearing them along was proof of that. She found her thermometer and mounted it next to the barometer. Backed with ivory and calibrated in tenths of degrees, the instrument's slender column of mercury clung to the lowest mark. It might take a quarter of an hour to adjust.

"Got a compass in that bag of tricks, Eliza?"

"Of course." She showed it to him. Her father's initials on the silver case linked it to the past. Cupping it, she held it against her belly to take a reading.

The needle quivered north-northeast. Somewhere in the fog lay a ridge of mountains they had to cross, but how close? At their present altitude they could run into a tree . . . perhaps even a mountain. Her palms went clammy.

"Empty that ballast bag there," she said. "I'll do this one."

Brown sand streamed behind the basket. The balloon jolted, clawed for height. Lizzy had to bend her knees to keep her balance. As they gained altitude, the rising sun glowed through the fog. Lizzy grabbed a pair of green spectacles from the case and stared through them into the void.

"You look like a june bug," Rafe said, moving beside her. "Your father used to go into the field with those things on his nose."

Why couldn't he be more forgetful? She didn't want to share memories. There were certain things she wished they'd both forget . . . like the touch of naked skin.

Blushing, she bent to check the barometer. The mercury was rising like the blood in her cheeks. She pressed her hands to her face in an effort to control her flush. Rafe would guess her thoughts.

"Eliza—"

"Don't! I mean, don't talk now. I've got to calculate our altitude."

"How close are we to the mountain?"

"I'm not sure." She was calmer now. "I wish this blasted fog would clear."

"It's our shield."

"It's soup. It blinds Yankee eyes and mine, too. I must have been out of my mind to take off in it!"

Rafe touched her hand. She did not withdraw, but let his fingers rest upon hers. "We're rising, Eliza. We've got time."

Warmed by the sun, the gas was expanding, lightening the balloon. She pulled her hand from under his. "I hope the wind off the ridge gives us more lift."

Rafe leaned back against the gondola and smiled in a way that sent another barrage of heat into her cheeks. Drat it, they weren't undertaking this venture for personal reasons—she wouldn't let her emotions trip her up. She didn't smile back.

"Behind those spectacles your eyes are blue as desert turquoise," he said. His voice sounded as though he were making love. "I saw stones that color in Mexico. I bought every one I could find."

Her spine tingled. He was tantalizing her, preying on the desire she was unable to conceal. "You bring up Mexico every chance you get," she said. "I don't care to hear about it."

"You need to know what happened there."

"If you're trying to salve your conscience, you might as well save your breath. I won't forgive you, Rafe Laffite. Your fine word-portraits led Charles off to his death. You made him think Mexico held the answer to all our problems."

"I thought it did," he said. "I didn't lead him there to die."

"Didn't you? I think you studied King David."

His eyes flashed golden green, dangerous and beautiful as a predator's. "What's a dead king have to do with me?"

"His story parallels yours, that's what. He sent Uriah off to war so he'd get killed and David could have his wife."

Rafe snorted. "So now you're Bathsheba and I'm the king of Israel. Did you sniff a little rosin gas while the balloon was filling?"

In an eruption of rage she jumped at him. Her sudden movement made the basket heel over like a sailboat. Thrown into Rafe's chest, for a dizzying eternity she looked over his shoulder straight down at the clouds. Screaming, she clawed for Rafe, for the shrouds, for anything at all, and caught only air.

Off-balance himself, Rafe grabbed a shroud with one hand and Lizzy with the other. Yanking the line, he lunged for the basket's high side, carrying her with him. Like a raft on the high seas, the basket dropped into the trough, then tilted in the opposite direction. Lizzy grabbed the wicker as Rafe fought to keep from flying overboard.

"Hold on!" Rafe threw her to the floor and sprawled on top of her.

Gasping for breath, they lay where they had fallen until the basket bobbed to a level plane. Then Rafe rolled over and seized her in hands like iron, holding her wrists on either side of her head, his chest hard against her breasts. His face was terrible to see.

"You wild little copperhead snake, you nearly killed us!"

"It wasn't meant to be a duet!"

"No? Then you'd best pick another method the next time you try to kill me."

"How about I shoot the top of your head off with Jack Daniel's pistol?"

"How about I lay you across my lap and beat the crawfish out of you?"

"How about you go straight to the devil!"

"I'm with her now!"

Before Lizzy could retort she heard a thin shout. Rafe sprang up and glared over the side. *"Sacrebleu!"*

"What is it? Who's shouting?" Lizzy joined him at the rail.

The fog was breaking up, uncovering patches of land. On a burned-out plantation far below, doll-sized Union soldiers ran around. "What're they yelling?" Lizzy demanded.

"I can't tell, but they're sure excited about something. Can you think of any reason besides us?"

"Are they likely to start shooting?"

"We won't know that until the balls start flying. Keep your head down."

"That'll do a lot of good! The floor's not ironclad and neither was the balloon last time I checked."

Rafe inflated his lungs and bawled at the soldiers: "Union Balloon Corps! Don't shoot!"

"As if they can hear you."

"Have you got a better idea? Seems they're mounting up to chase us—see those toy horses down there?"

Lizzy could see tiny puffs of dust around the

horsemen. More shouting drifted skyward. Then the cavalry streamed after them. "Union Balloon Corps!" Lizzy screamed over the side. "We're one of y'all!"

"You can keep yelling, but it won't take them long to figure out we're the enemy," Rafe said. "They'll just send someone back to town to make sure the balloon corps isn't operating around here."

But Lizzy had another worry. She could see Chapman Mountain ahead, a vast green bulk swirled with fog. She wasn't sure they were high enough to clear its peak. "Empty two more sandbags," she said. "We've got to get more altitude. Maybe we'll cross the saddleback."

As Rafe emptied another bag, the balloon leaped as though pulled by a string. Lizzy checked the barometer. "The mercury's rising the way I like it, and we've got stronger winds up here."

"The horses are dropping back," Rafe said.

"What's flashing up on Chapman Mountain?"

Rafe looked forward, and cursed. "Heliograph, and right in our path." A string of flashes answered from close to town. Rafe swore again.

"Signal mirrors," Lizzy said. Her heart felt like lead. "Can you read it?"

"The signalman on the mountain just sent off a query to the next post. They'll relay the answer to headquarters. And if the boys chasing us know Morse code, they'll start shooting any minute now."

"So will whoever's on the mountain," Lizzy said.

"Maybe not; he just passes the word. Let's drop ballast and see if we can get out of range, anyway." But before he could untie the sandbag, mirrors twinkled again. He went still, watching.

For half a minute sunlight danced back and forth across the valley. "No Union activity in area," Rafe

translated. "Shoot down balloon and bring in aeronauts."

"Lord help us," Lizzy said.

Rafe yanked the strings on two sandbags. The balloon
jolted, rising toward the saddleback at a sharp angle.
Trees reached for the basket.

The first shot came from a stand of cedars halfway
up the slope. Lizzy saw an orange flash just before the
thunderclap reached her ears. She winced but didn't
duck.

Rafe pulled out Jack Daniel's pistol and checked the
load. Lizzy gritted her teeth. Flying wasn't something
he understood. Battle was. He snapped the ramrod into
its holder beneath the barrel. Not yet close enough for
his pistol to be accurate, he was close enough to take
aim and wait.

"Can you see the cavalry?" he asked.

"No. Too many trees, but I think we outran them."

The rifle flared again. This time one of the shrouds
sang like a plucked harpsichord. Fibers unraveled but
the line didn't break. "Any ideas?" Rafe asked.

"I can't get much more altitude right now."

"We're sitting ducks, then. He's still out of this peashooter's range."

"You ought to try shooting back, anyway," Lizzy
said. "That peashooter's got the longest barrel I ever
saw. Maybe its range is long, too."

"We'll try it." Rafe sighted carefully down the barrel
and squeezed the trigger. With a deafening roar, a
tongue of fire shot out of the muzzle. Thunder rolled off
the mountain and down the valley.

"If that Yankee's dead, it's my fault," Lizzy whispered. Sickened, she caught the rail.

Half a second later, a fist-size hole appeared in the
basket just beside her hand. Chaff flew into her eyes.

She felt a tug on her skirt before the rifle report reached her ears. Afraid the balloon had been hit, she grabbed the shrouds and leaned out.

"Get back in here before you fall or get shot," Rafe said with a growl.

"You stick to your job and leave me to mine!" Hiking up her skirts, she started to climb up on the rail. "I've got to see if we've been punctured."

Rafe caught her by the waist and pushed her down on the floor. "Stay there."

Another shot rang out. Rafe fired back. Lizzy couldn't tell if the balloon was hit or not, but the shooting made her mad. "Dadblast you, Yankee!" she hollered. "You're not going to ruin my balloon!"

"Keep your head down!"

"Not until I see that Yankee laid out like a dead polecat on one of those boulders!"

"Thunderation," Rafe said. He rammed home a ball and leaned over the side, searching for movement. The boulders and trees were too thick to see through.

The shot came without warning, sharp and close. Rafe jerked away, his face bloody. Lizzy let out a scream and caught him as he staggered.

"Oh, dear God, dear God!" she cried. "He's head-shot!"

But when she grabbed her petticoats to use for bandages, he caught her hand. "Help me up, honey."

"But—but your head!"

"My head's fine—it's this damned hand." He held it up. A splinter of cane as long and thin as a butter knife protruded from his palm—driven in at an angle when the .54-caliber rifle ball hit the gondola.

Lizzy cried out in horror. Her head reeled and her vision darkened. "I've—I've got to bandage it."

"Bandage it later. I've got a Yank to kill."

Using Lizzy's shoulder for leverage, he clambered to his feet and peered over the side. The rifle cracked again. The shooter appeared from behind a big rock, his face turned up to watch them as he reloaded. Laffite took aim and fired. The soldier disappeared, but Lizzy couldn't tell if he'd been hit or had just ducked his head. Clamping the gun under his left arm, Rafe struggled with a paper cartridge. Blood made his fingers slip.

"Let me, Rafe." Lizzy couldn't look at his hand. "I'll reload."

"Hurry then. I doubt I killed that bushwhacker."

"It doesn't matter—we've left him behind. His friends, too, from the looks of it."

By the time she'd reloaded and handed back the pistol, they were soaring over the eastern ridge. Rafe shoved the pistol into his belt, then looked at his hand.

The skin on his palm puckered over the ridge of cane. "I need some cloth, honey."

Lizzy tore a strip off her petticoat. "That cane's got to come out."

"I know." Turning to screen his hand from her, he braced his elbows on the rail, wrapped the cloth around the splinter, and pulled. The cane stuck fast. Sweat trickled down his face as he tried again. Finally, his right hand slipped and crashed against the basket. "Must be stuck into bone."

"Do you want me to—to—" Lizzy couldn't go on. Spots danced before her eyes, and her knees shook until her legs could hardly support her. If only Grace were here. Grace would know what to do. She'd take his hand like this and grasp the cane like so and—

The splinter was so slippery she could hardly hang on to it. Blood trickled along her arms all the way to her elbows. Sobs racked her throat.

"Brace your foot against my thigh, Eliza. You've got

107

to tug with all your might while I pull in the other direction.''

''My sweet Lord Jesus, I'm going to be sick!''

''Just don't stop.''

The cane burst free. Blood spurted across the front of her dress. She turned and vomited over the side.

Rafe clapped the rag over his hand and sagged against the basket. ''You all right, honey?''

''Does it look like I'm all right?'' Shuddering, she sat down on the floor and hung her head between her knees.

''We'll make a doctor of you yet,'' he said.

''Laws, don't even talk about it. . . . Has it stopped bleeding?''

''As long as I hold it. When you feel better, you can bind this bandage tighter.''

''I don't think I can stand to look at it again.''

But what had Grace told her about puncture wounds? Lockjaw? Anxiety goaded her to his side. ''Take that bandage off,'' she said. ''We've got to bleed the wound before it does you harm.''

''It's bled enough, and it's a scratch, anyway,'' he said. ''Bind it up and forget about it.''

''Drat it, this time you'll do as *I* say!''

''If it humors you, then.'' He lifted the bandage. ''Satisfied?''

''Not yet.'' She grabbed his hand and squeezed until blood rained to earth.

''You still like holding my hand, I see.''

''Stop mocking me. What good will it do to fly you all the way to Richmond if your jaws are too locked up to speak to the president once you get there?''

''That's a point I hadn't considered.''

''You ought to think about yourself once in a while.'' She remembered his helpless body stretched on her bed, the battle scars stark against his feverish skin. How

108

many times he must have been close to death over the years, and with no family to tend him!

Her guilt was like a wedding cake layered with regret for things done and undone. She had to blink back tears as she squeezed the poisoned blood from his strong, tanned hand.

When will you drain the poisonous anger from your heart, child? You've carried it for too long.

Startled, Lizzy let go and stepped back. Rafe had not spoken, yet from whom could the voice have come? Warmth enfolded her as it had over the cemetery a little while ago, when she'd first heard the voice. Was Charles's ghost here? Or her father's?

Perhaps she was taking leave of her senses; it happened to folks under strain. Rafe was the worst strain of her life. "We—we need antiseptic." She knelt to search her valise.

The warmth was making her dizzy. She shut her eyes for a moment and massaged her forehead.

"You look like you're about to faint, honey," Rafe said, squatting down to look at her. His mouth tensed with pain and worry. "Lie down for a minute."

"No." She found a copper flask and pulled the stopper with her teeth.

"What's that?"

She spat out the cork. "Turpentine. Hold still."

Rafe caught his breath when she poured turpentine into the wound. "Must be one of Mrs. Fairlove's remedies," he said through gritted teeth. "She knows how to torture a man."

"I guess I do, too." Avoiding his eyes, she began to wrap his hand.

"You know better than anyone else, Eliza."

Her hands went still on the dressing. "Torture works both ways. You're a master of it yourself."

His eyes glowed amber, then deepened. Lizzy felt as
though they were pulling her into a dark ravine. Within
its depths she sensed losses and returnings . . . wordless
voices speaking out of the dust for her ears alone. Cotton
fields and heavy books . . . sabers and cannons . . . blood
and glory rolled into one. And then silence. Regret. A
face turning homeward at last.

She saw a woman through his eyes, long limbed . . .
hair the color of ripe chestnuts. Eyes burning like turquoise stones under a Mexican sun. Hands with long,
caressing fingers . . . ripe breasts . . . building the fires
. . . coming up through the mist in a climactic shout . . .
Eliza, my love.

"Stop!" She backed as far from him as she could.
"No one should look into another's mind! Why did you
take me into yours?"

"You belong there. You dwell there."

"You're mad! Your pain has made you so!" Her
voice dropped. "Your guilt has."

"I can't resurrect Charlie."

"You resurrected his ghost when you came back!"

"I can lay it to rest, too. I can set your heart at
peace."

"No one can do that." She would not let Rafe fill
that black space in her heart. She wouldn't let him use
his power. What was his to give was his to take away.
She couldn't bear to lose him again. Better that she live
the rest of her days without love.

Devastation rolled through her soul. Unable to abide
the anguish leaping in his eyes, she clenched her teeth
and turned her face away. Better that he had never come
back from Mexico. What was she to do with the prodigal
now?

Chapter Eleven

"He is a prodigal son returning then, our little thief," Louis DeCoeur said. With a strange mixture of innocence and malevolence, his blue eyes danced across the cliff behind Big Spring before resting upon the Mexican captain.

Hidalgo La Peña started to cross himself, then thought better of it and dropped his hand to his side. La Peña wished he had persuaded the third member of their team, the French captain, Jean-Claude Geraud, to tell DeCoeur what they'd learned that morning.

"He is not really a prodigal, señor, for he is no native son of Huntsville, but a Louisianan," La Peña answered in Spanish. "A man of New Orleans."

"Then why does he come here?"

"There is a woman . . . he used to bed her."

DeCoeur's laugh rumbled off the cliff like thunder. "He beds her again, you think? He uses the big diamond, maybe, to aid his lovemaking?"

111

La Peña flushed. He was a decent man, a soldier loyal to Mexico. Despite his dislike for the foreigner Maximilian on his country's throne, he would pursue the stolen treasure to the ends of the earth as the emperor commanded. But this vulgar Frenchman outraged his soul. Squaring his shoulders against the fabric of his dark-green uniform, the captain said, ''It is not certain he is here, Señor DeCoeur. No one has actually seen him. But the apothecary claims someone is ill at the home of this woman—'' He drew a scrap of paper from his breast and consulted it for a moment. ''Grace Fairlove.''

''She is Major Laffite's lover?''

''Not her, but her sister, Eliza McCord. This McCord woman has lived with her sister since our Union *compadres* burned her plantation.''

''Eliza McCord.'' DeCoeur let the name roll off his tongue, savoring it. The name was not feminine—not to French tastes—but it contained a measure of strength he'd come to associate with Americans.

''They dress their women with manly names,'' he said, ''but a woman is as easily broken as a man. Where do we find this Rebel woman? This whore of a traitor to the emperor?''

The captain hesitated to name her address. He wanted the man who'd stolen the diamond—he wanted the *diamond*—but he knew DeCoeur wouldn't stop once the treasure was in his grasp. He would take revenge.

He looked at DeCoeur's hands. The nails were long and sharp as a bear's. Hands for mauling. If La Peña impeded this man, he would not return to his wife and children waiting in Mexico City. ''She lives north of town,'' Hidalgo said. ''The turnpike runs past her house.''

Below his crushed nose, DeCoeur's smile glowed unnaturally. This time Hidalgo could not help crossing his breast. DeCoeur's smile stretched wider. "Let us fetch Captain Geraud and go find this woman and the man she hides."

La Peña had chased Laffite for many hundreds of miles and would not be sorry to kill the bastard, but he feared DeCoeur's plans for the two women. He stalled for time. "We should tell General Granger of our intentions."

"That ass is too stupid to guess the true purpose of our visit. Leave him to his slumber."

"He is not asleep. There was some excitement at dawn about a signal corps balloon. He has been in the telegraph office all morning."

"Then leave him to his tapping," DeCoeur said softly.

"Perhaps we should take breakfast first. If the spy truly is here and his wound festers, we need not rush our plans."

"We'll go now," DeCoeur said. Narrowed to slits, his eyes glittered like the cold water bubbling out of the spring behind him. A chill shook La Peña's spine.

"I will call our escort." Perhaps their American escort would temper DeCoeur's heavy hand.

Hattie Lee was building a dam across the creek to hold the mudsliders and banded watersnake she'd caught that morning. The turtles were in her ma's washtub and the snake was wriggling in a burlap sack. Every once in a while his head poked the burlap.

Afraid she'd blab about the balloon, Ma had forbidden her to go into town and nose around. Being forbidden only made her wilder to go. "Shucks, I wouldn't tell nobody," Hattie Lee told the snake. "They could tear my teeth plumb out of their sockets and string them for a necklace and I wouldn't tell.''

The ghoulish picture sent shivers of delight up and down her spine, but of course, even Yankees wouldn't do anything that awful. Nobody in their right mind would. Aunt Lizzy's secret was safe.

Fast hoofbeats echoed on the turnpike. Holding her dripping skirts in one hand, Hattie Lee dug her toes into the steep clay bank and scrambled to the top. She hid behind a snarl of blackberries.

She saw seven Yankee soldiers; then the ugly red-headed man from the depot came tearing up behind them, dwarfing his black gelding. Behind him galloped the two Lancers, resplendent in their foreign uniforms, their horses high-steppers with nostrils flared. Hattie Lee wondered where they were going.

She looked down into the creek. The turtles would be hunky-dory in the washtub, but the way that old snake was writhing, he'd be out and on his way down the creek to the Tennessee River before she got back. Slithering down the slope, she grabbed the sack and started back up. She'd have to remember to leave the snake by the kitchen door before she went inside. Ma didn't take kindly to scary things.

The soldiers fanned out around the Fairlove home. One of them ran to the carriage house and broke in. It was empty. He saw hoofprints and the marks of wagon wheels in the dust. He dipped his fingers into a pile of dung near the door. No more than twelve hours old.

Louis DeCoeur reined in by the front door and dismounted with a grace uncommon in a man of his contours. When he flung the reins to a young soldier, the gelding bared its teeth and whickered, stamping its hooves until dust flew as high as the eaves.

114

"Hold him steady, *mon ami*, and I will make you a fine present when this job is finished."

Flexing his fingers like a child preparing to play with a new toy, DeCoeur smiled at the soldiers. "If the bastard runs outside, shoot him in the legs."

La Peña and Geraud followed him up the steps to the green door. DeCoeur caressed a brass door knocker shaped like the head of a snarling lion. "These little Confederate women should give brass to their cause," DeCoeur said. "Such greed, to keep pretties when their country needs cannon." Forcing three fingers into the ring, he yanked the knocker from the door in a shower of splinters.

DeCoeur slowly turned the knob. One of the soldiers sneezed, a noise like a musket shot. The door burst open. Grace Fairlove stood there, her blue eyes blazing.

"What do you want?" Her gaze dropped to the door knocker. "Why, you—"

DeCoeur smacked her in the face with the lion. Grace fell back into the foyer and struck her head on a whatnot cabinet. A porcelain shepherdess crashed onto the floor beside her.

"Where is he, madame?" DeCoeur said in French as soft as talcum powder.

La Peña caught DeCoeur's arm. "We will look upstairs. There is no need for this violence—"

DeCoeur brushed him off like a gnat. "Where is the incestuous son of a dog?"

Rising to her elbows, Grace scooted away until she fetched up against the wall. Although her lip bled and her left eye was swelling shut, she flashed him a rebellious look. "I don't know who you're talking about!"

"Her courage will be her death," La Peña whispered to Geraud. He gestured at the soldiers crowding into the foyer. "Go upstairs! For the love of the saints, find the spy!"

Three Federals thundered up to the bedrooms. Crashing and shouting, they dashed from room to room, tipping furniture and emptying wardrobes. Others went into the kitchen and overturned the stove.

"You will not find him in the stove!" La Peña shouted. He stormed into the kitchen. Someone in the parlor smashed the clock.

"Where is he?" DeCoeur demanded of Grace. "Where is the man?"

She edged along the wall. DeCoeur stalked her like a cat, feinting first right, then left, his smile all the more terrifying for its veneer of kindness. Again and again he thrust the brass knocker toward her face.

Captain Geraud spoke up in rapid French. "Monsieur, perhaps if you will allow Geraud to question the madame, we will learn the answer to this riddle."

DeCoeur turned on him like a grizzly, his head swinging from side to side. "You would interfere with me, Geraud? You know better than I how to deal with a woman?"

"No one knows better than you, monsieur."

Suddenly DeCoeur threw back his head and laughed. "But you are more fitted for this one, my handsome young friend. Take the wench."

Geraud squatted on his heels in front of Grace, reached into his blouse, and brought out a white handkerchief edged in lace. With great deliberation he patted the blood from her lips. "There now, madame," he said in accented English. "No one will hurt you. Geraud, he will take care of you."

She did not respond. DeCoeur moved to block the doorway.

"What is your name, please?" Geraud asked.

She switched her gaze back and forth, searching for an escape route, but found nothing but the enemy. "Grace," she said at last. "Grace Fairlove."

"And where is Madame McCord?"

Grace clamped her lips and shook her head. DeCoeur's breathing filled the room, harsh, fast with excitement. "Make her tell you," DeCoeur said. "Or I will."

"She's—she's across the river," Grace said, "carrying food to the Bannister family."

Geraud lifted his black brows and looked up at the redheaded man. DeCoeur's smile came and went like quicksilver. He spoke two words in French—fierce, guttural words.

"Monsieur DeCoeur, he thinks you are lying, madame," Geraud said. "You see, we talked to the apothecary only this morning—Spotswood, I think he calls himself."

"Spotswood was drunk. He—he didn't know what he was saying!"

"He was as sober as a vicar. He told us all about this Rebel staying at your house."

"You're lying!"

"His name is Major Rafe Laffite."

The last bit of color drained from Grace's face. "I've never heard of him!"

Geraud's voice hardened. "The wound in his side, madame—you tended it."

"No!"

"Geraud cannot help you if you will not be truthful." Shaking his head, he stood up and moved aside.

DeCoeur's shadow fell across Grace. "The wound, it was caused by a spear, madame. You tended it."

"I did no such thing!"

DeCoeur smiled with the kindness of an uncle. "Perhaps your memory falters—we must prod it. Geraud, a stick.''

Geraud went outside, then returned with a hickory branch stripped of leaves. DeCoeur began sharpening one end with his sheath knife. ''You will dance, madame, as you have never danced before,'' DeCoeur said in a singsong voice. ''Come, let us dance.''

Grace screamed.

Hattie Lee rounded a clump of locust trees and stopped dead in her tracks. The soldiers were at her house! There were only four in the yard, so the others must be inside. It could only mean one thing: they'd figured out Mr. Laffite was here.

Her hand tightened on the burlap sack. If they were in the house, then her mother was in danger. The look she'd seen in the redheaded man's eyes was as cold as a canebrake rattler's. One way or another, he aimed to get what he wanted. Hattie Lee aimed to stop him.

But how? What could she do against armed men? How could she reach the house without being seen? Except for a few cleared patches, bushes and honeysuckle vines crawled across her yard to the house. Along the foundation, jasmine foamed like green waves.

She looked at the horses a Yankee boy was holding by the front porch. He wasn't paying much attention, just picking his nose and gaping through the doorway. Except for the soldier boy, the outside Yankees were drifting toward the carriage house, pointing at the ground and talking a mile a minute.

''Drat it!'' Hattie Lee said. She'd spent half an hour last night dragging a bush around the backyard to erase the wagon tracks. But the way the Yankees were carrying on, she reckoned she'd missed some.

That didn't matter right now. Ma did. Towing the sack

behind her, she crept across the yard. The open spots between the bushes scared her a little, but nobody yelled out when she darted across. At last she secreted herself in the jasmine. There was a sort of pathway under the vines that led along the foundation to the front porch. Taking care not to disturb the bushes and alert the Yankee boy, she crept up the path.

Somebody screamed inside the house. Hattie Lee gave a jerk that rattled the bushes. They were hurting Ma. Grace screamed again, louder this time. It was all Hattie Lee could do not to bolt out of cover and into the house. But if she did, they'd catch her, too.

Through the vines she could see the horses' legs but not the Yankee boy's. She untied the sack but held its mouth shut. Before she could lose courage, she squeezed through the vines and surfaced right under the nose of the big black gelding. She had the sack open and the snake out before the horse could react to her sudden appearance.

The snake let out a mighty hiss and curved its neck into an *S*, its jaws snapping open. The gelding screamed and reared, forefeet pedaling by Hattie Lee's ears. She jumped at the other horses and shoved the snake right into their faces. They panicked and bolted.

"What the hell's going on?"

It was the Yankee boy coming back out of the house! He'd been inside watching Ma get beaten up! With a shriek of rage, Hattie Lee thrust the snake into his face. The reptile surged out of her hands and disappeared down his shirtfront.

Hattie Lee sprang into the bushes as the youth began screaming and jumping. Yankees streamed out the front door and ran after the horses galloping down the turnpike.

Hattie Lee jumped onto the porch and into the foyer,

119

straight into the arms of the redheaded man. With a great laugh, he swung her up into the air like a sack of turnip greens and caught her on the way back down.

"And it is another little Rebel, Jean-Claude, who rushes to our need!" he said. "Perhaps you do not need to use the stick just yet, unless this child is as stubborn as her mother."

"I won't tell you a derned thing!"

"Hattie Lee!"

Ma's skirts were torn and her crinolines heaped on the floor. One of the lancers was holding her from behind, laughing at her frantic struggles. There was blood on her lip.

"Let go of my ma!"

DeCoeur slammed Hattie Lee into a rocking chair. When she tried to jump up, he planted his forefinger upon her breastbone with a force that knocked the wind out of her and rammed the chair into the wall.

"You will stay, little cherub. Louis DeCoeur, he has a game to play with you."

Chapter Twelve

Blood pounding through his veins, Rafe wrenched himself out of a nightmare. Sprawled against the side of the gondola, his swollen hand throbbing with every beat of his heart, he looked for Lizzy, found her asleep, then jumped up, looking for a threat outside the balloon.

He could see no one on the sunset-stained earth, just the shadow of the balloon sliding across the farmland two hundred feet below. There was no bear with a human face, no Yankee lookouts, no flashing heliographs. No reason for the tortured sounds he'd heard in his dream.

Indeed, the silence was almost unnatural. Because the balloon drifted at the speed of the air currents, there was no wind noise to fill the emptiness.

He wiped sweat from his eyes, then unbuttoned his blue coat and cast it aside. His gray flannel shirt was so clammy he shucked it over his head and tossed it onto the rail. He pulled his suspenders back over his shoulders.

Judging by the sun's position over the mountain ridge to the west, he knew he'd been asleep for hours, sent into shock by his injury. Nightmares, he knew from experience, haunted the wounded. Still, he couldn't shake off the horror. Tuned to a soldier's pitch, instinct told him Louis DeCoeur was still tracking him. The hairs on the back of his neck rose, brushing the fine web between reason and intuition. Danger lay beyond the clouds . . . he wished he could tell from where.

The compass needle quivered northeast of their original heading. The narrow valley below looked vaguely familiar. If he had to guess, he'd say they were somewhere in the Paint Rock Valley, but things looked different from the air, more two-dimensional, like a portrait.

He should've stolen some charts. He'd have to lay his hands on some at the earliest opportunity. That would probably come, he told himself, when the balloon sprang a leak and plummeted to the ground.

Lizzy was still asleep, her hands splayed on the thin quilt. Alarmed by her stillness, he sank to his knees to listen for her breathing, to touch her to make sure she was really there.

Unguarded and innocent in sleep, her expression gradually eased his soul. She still had on those ridiculous green spectacles, and while the sight made him smile, it also tugged his heartstrings. People used to call her eccentric for setting store by such doodads. He thought they made her seem like a little girl.

No, not a girl anymore. Tempered by toil and care, hunger and the privations of war, her thin face shone with more strength and beauty than in her younger years. The passage of time had not snuffed the flame burning within her. It was the flame of life . . . the fire of passion.

He wanted to believe she still loved him. From the clues she'd given him, it was a deep, secret kind of love held tight in her soul, buried like a lump of gold in the heart of a mountain and guarded jealously, rebuffing his attempts to mine it.

"Do not fear love, darling one," he whispered in French.

He pulled his knees up to let his forearms rest upon them. The throbbing of his wound didn't matter. Right now, his heart ached more.

He thought back to the moment he first had seen her. Had he known what sorrow he would bring her, he would've gone back into the bank and closed the huge bronze door.

But he'd touched her and his heart was lost. And after courting her for months, he'd taken her into his arms. He should have married her first. There was a time and a place to take a virgin—on her wedding night, in her husband's house. Not out under the stars with an old magnolia standing sentinel.

But that night when they walked down to the river, flowers fell from the magnolia—waxy white blossoms smelling of summer and heat and desire. Like the passion bending Eliza's body to his, gusts of wind shook the limbs, cutting a swirling fog of flowers free, filling his nostrils with their wild heated scent.

Night after night they met under the tree, and in the carriage house, and even in her bedroom when they could slip past her Mammy's watchful eye. Each meeting whetted his desire for more. For all their skill, none of the women of New Orleans had ever matched the fierce abandonment of Eliza's untutored young body. Her cries still echoed in his ears.

With a curse, Rafe reined in his thoughts. The reckless part of him strained the seams of his trousers, throbbing and burning until he could hardly bear to live inside his own skin. He stood.

The sun touched the horizon. Tattered clouds rushed over the ground like rabbits to a thicket. He checked the barometer to confirm what he'd already guessed. The balloon was sinking. "Eliza."

His voice sounded loud in the stillness. He couldn't get used to that silence. Flying was nothing like riding a horse, where the wind crashed against his eardrums and tangled his hair and flung his coat out behind.

Flying was both stillness and movement, a dance of cloud and air and mist of rain, a rendering of colors on the broad canvas of the earth. Flying was a thin veneer of wood beneath his feet, with nothing beneath the wood but a sense of pressure, as though the air itself had strength.

A verse he'd learned as a child popped into his mind: *"And he shall give his angels charge over thee, lest thou dash thy foot against a stone."*

An angel had charge of him, he thought. She'd come back into his life to bear him over the perilous world. For the first time in many years, he felt close to peace.

He should have married her before going off to Mexico the first time. No matter that he'd intended to redeem his honor; he could have stopped her from becoming another man's wife. Through the long years of separation he'd never stopped loving her. It was Eliza who'd drawn him from the brink of death each time he was wounded.

He'd come close to returning to her once or twice. When Alabama went to war, he'd come back from Mexico to ride with Joe Wheeler. Once, he'd been close enough to Huntsville to get a furlough . . . but somehow he couldn't convince himself she'd welcome him back.

He picked up his uniform jacket and felt the letters hidden in the lining. He didn't know why he'd saved them. There were only three, each burning with anger and bitterness. Two she'd sent him right after he left town, then nothing until after Charlie's death.

Perhaps the letters were why he'd accepted President Davis's decision to send him back to Mexico City after he was wounded at Chickamauga.

She'd brought him home again, though. She'd walked across the continent beside him. At least his fevered mind had told him so. He would not have made it without that grand illusion.

"I suffer for want of you," he said. "Eliza, how I've missed you!"

He knelt again and pushed hair off her forehead. At his touch, her lips opened in a sigh, but her eyes remained shut fast against the fading light. She did not stir when he removed her spectacles and tucked them into the wooden valise.

"Won't you wake?" Unconsciously, he pitched his voice too low for her to hear. He did not want to break the spell. Lowering his face until his mouth hovered just above hers, he inhaled the fragrance reminiscent of clouds and sunlight that clung to her lips. Her dark lashes trembled but she did not open her eyes.

He kissed her then, and saw her eyes open, then close as if she couldn't shake off sleep, yet the manner of her kiss changed until he knew, beyond a doubt, that she was awake. Her arms slipped around his neck.

"My angel."

He buried his hands in her hair. Through her dark, shimmering tresses his bandage shone like a trophy to her courage. He knew what it had cost her, who used to faint at the sight of blood, to doctor his hand. "My brave, beautiful angel,'' he said in French.

"I'm not so brave," she said, answering in the same tongue. "And I'm certainly no angel."

"Only an angel can carry a man into the sky."

"You're light-headed," she said. "And any aeronaut can do it."

He rolled onto his back and pulled her onto his bare chest. She caught hold of his suspender as though to control him.

"Only an angel can drop a man to his knees and make him beg for her kiss," he said.

"You're begging, Rafe?" she asked in a voice as soft as the glow in her eyes.

She seemed vulnerable, ready to listen to words of love, ready to put the past to rest. He drew her head down to his. "I'm begging."

"You shouldn't, Rafe," she whispered, but even so, she didn't pull back. "The balloon—"

"Has flown itself without our help for several hours. It will stay up a little longer. Kiss me, Eliza."

"I don't want to kiss you . . . it hurts when I do."

"And where does it hurt?"

"In here." She touched her breast.

"Then I will be more gentle."

"It's not that—you know what I mean."

She wanted to flee; he could feel it in her muscles. He trailed the fingers of his good hand along her lower back and felt her quiver.

"My love hurts you?" he asked. She tried to roll off him but he did not relax his grip.

"Don't speak of love to me, Rafe Laffite. I know your kind of love."

"You knew its fledlging form. You knew me when I was a wanderer, when I couldn't still my restlessness."

"And you're not restless now?" she asked. "Look at

you—look at the clouds. Your feet aren't exactly anchored in solid rock, you know.''

"They will be . . . as long as yours are anchored beside them.''

"I wish I could believe that. Once upon a time, I did.''

"This is no fairy tale.''

"You've changed, then, without the benefit of some wizard's magic?''

"The magic is within you.'' He caressed her spine. "I don't wish to live the rest of my life alone.''

"Then why didn't you come back a long time ago?''

He spoke quietly, his throat tight with emotion. "By the time I realized my error, you were married. Charlie sent me a letter. How could I have come back?''

"I don't know! I don't know!'' Lizzy shook her head and moaned. "Daddy didn't mind so much about the money you lost . . . not half as much as he minded the pain of my losing you! You shouldn't have left me.''

He folded her close against him, holding her head to his shoulder, feeling her tears on his neck. The speeches he'd rehearsed over the years faded like dew on a summer morning.

Honor. It was a word graven in his heart, but there was another five-letter word written there, too. *Pride*. To his mind, the words had always meant the same thing, but now, looking at himself through this woman's eyes, he detected a difference. Which nuance had driven him to seek his fortune in Mexico?

He raised her face. The tears shimmering in her eyes pained his heart. "Leaving you is not something I shall ever forgive myself for, Eliza. Never. I know what I did to you—to your family. I threw your father's cotton crop away, speculating with Yankees.''

"Daddy said no one could have predicted the panic

of fifty-seven,'' she said. ''He thought it was a good idea, too, sending cotton straight to northern mills instead of to England. He didn't blame you for the crash.''

''The fact remains that I lost his money. I tried to restore my honor—and his capital—but there's no defense for the method I chose. I can only say I'm not the man who went adventuring.''

''Who are you, then? You still demand my all. You still offer nothing but—how did you say it the other day? Pain. You offer me more pain.''

Rafe drew a sharp breath. ''I cause pain because there is no help for it—for now. Don't you see? We've got to see this mission through . . . but afterward . . . I offer you joy afterward.''

''I'll do what I can for the cause—you know that— but the joy you promise surely can't erase the pain . . . can it?''

''No more than it can erase my scars. No, what's done is done. All I can do is beg for the chance to prove myself to you . . . to give you the love you deserve.''

''I can't do that to Charles.''

Rafe shook his head. ''He's dead. You can do nothing to him, good or evil.''

''Don't talk that way!''

Was there a quaver of guilt in her voice? Hadn't she loved Charlie a whit, then? Charlie, who'd been so patently a slave to her, and who'd crucified himself with guilt for following Rafe to Mexico? Perhaps it wouldn't be so difficult to exorcise his ghost and reclaim her love. But he couldn't do it by force.

''The balloon's sinking,'' he said, and made himself let her go.

She gave him a long, searching look, then rolled off him and climbed to her feet. Rafe joined her at the rail.

A hundred feet below, trees reached for them. As they

Diamond

sailed over a farm pond, Rafe saw the indigo balloon burning in the orange fire of sunset. The gondola looked tiny. "Are we losing the gas, Eliza?"

She seemed relieved to speak of something else. "No. It compresses as the balloon cools, so we don't get as much lift. Daddy chose dark blue silk and coated it with a special formulation of gutta-percha for a reason."

"So it won't leak?"

"Yes, but there's more. Because of its special properties, it collects much more heat than an ordinary balloon and creates more lift. Of course, we sink in the evening."

"Will we crash?"

"We won't even touch the ground."

"Good. Richmond's a long walk."

"I don't think we'll get as far as Richmond," Lizzy said. "The prevailing winds won't carry us that far north . . . not unless there's a storm, and I don't want that!"

"Just get us as far as you can, Eliza; that's all I ask."

Lizzy fixed her gaze on the hills ahead. "Are you going to tell me what this is all about?"

He touched her cheek. "Soon."

She tossed her head, breaking the contact. "I don't think you'll ever tell."

"I'll have to. I gave you my word."

"We could go around and around on that," she said, "but I don't feel like fighting anymore."

He knew her better than to believe she'd given up. Marrying Charlie McCord was the last time she'd bent her will to someone else's, he suspected. If anyone but her father had asked her to marry Charlie, she would not—

He drew himself up short. In all fairness, he couldn't judge what she would have done. She had her own mind. Maybe she'd wanted to marry Charlie. Maybe she'd

129

needed someone steady after what he, Rafe, had put her through.

Maybe she had loved Charlie. Perhaps she still loved him, and Rafe Laffite was a conceited old rooster to believe he might possess her secret heart. People changed a lot in seven years. Eliza was no longer the innocent girl she'd been, but a woman who knew her own mind.

She had been married. She had stood before an altar of God with someone else . . . slept in his bed, even. Felt the hot thrust of his body.

A familiar, choking wave of jealousy rose in his throat. He seized the rail and squeezed until his injured hand began to ache. Cursing softly, he released the cane and kneaded his palm.

"You're in pain, Rafe."

"It's nothing to worry about." He didn't look at her.

She laid her hand on his forearm. "We have to land. I'll see to that wound when we're on the ground."

"Land? I thought we couldn't."

"I never said that. We're going to drop anchor like a pirate ship."

Rafe bent an incredulous glance on her until she unhooked the kedge anchor and line from the basket.

"I wondered what that was for," he said.

He didn't want to stop for the night, to look across a campfire at her shapely form, to wonder if she still thought of Charlie when she lay down to sleep. "I didn't know you'd planned to land."

"Since I've never flown this far before, I have to make up the rules as we go. We need to cook supper."

"I'll throw out the anchor."

"Your hand—"

"Doesn't need to be pampered." After making fast

the anchor-rope, he began to pay out the coiled line to lower the anchor. "Any tree will do?"

Lizzy nodded. "Be prepared for a jolt. I don't want you flying out."

"I've had a bit of experience hanging on for dear life," he said. "Watch yourself."

The anchor dropped nearer and nearer the ground. Rafe estimated their speed at hardly more than walking pace, but as the anchor swept over the treetops, it seemed they were moving faster.

The anchor crashed into the slender boughs of a hickory tree and ripped loose a storm of leaves. Swinging like a pendulum gone mad, the gondola bumped and bounced until the anchor tore free and sailed toward another tree.

"Drop it lower, Rafe! Catch that sycamore—we need a *big* tree."

"This is like trying to hook an alligator. Bite it, boy!"

The anchor snagged on a thick white limb, shredding bark and tearing off leaves the size of a man's hand. The balloon kept going for several yards, then stopped with a jerk that threw Lizzy to her knees.

Immediately the line snapped back, taking the balloon with it. For half a minute the craft oscillated back and forth. Rafe reeled in line until the balloon hovered fifteen feet above the treetop.

"Now what?" he asked. "Can you shinny down the rope into the tree?"

"No. That's what this is for." She pulled a rope ladder out of a burlap bag, fastened the top rung to the basket, then threw it over the side into the branches. "Boarders, away!"

Rafe whistled. "A buccaneer lass, ye be," he said in a Barbary Coast accent.

"Here then, ye landlubber, take the food sack and we'll climb down."

"Let me go first." Rafe tied the sack over his shoulder and jammed his flannel shirt into his waistband. When he climbed over the rail onto the ladder, the hemp rungs gave under his weight and squeezed his injured hand. Blood seeped through the bandage. His fingers swelled and his forearm trembled until he had to let go and continue down one-handed.

He descended five rungs before calling to Lizzy. "Come, I'll catch you if you fall."

"You watch your own self—I won't fall."

But when she tried to put her leg over the side, her skirts twisted around and got in the way. Searching for the ladder, she swung her foot back and forth. Rafe reached up to try to place her foot. With her skirts hampering her, she was in danger of falling. As they struggled, the balloon shifted with the wind and jerked the ladder until Lizzy let out a screech of fright.

"That dress has got to come off," Rafe said.

"What!"

"Come—out of it. You can put it back on when you're safe on the ground."

"And have you looking at me?"

"I won't look. At least, I'll try not to look at anything but your feet."

"I'll bet." She got back into the balloon.

Lizzy knew it went against propriety and good sense to take off her clothes in front of Rafe. She was very much aware of the sexual energy flowing between them.

"He can remember he's a gentleman," she muttered as she unbuttoned her dress. "And I, a lady. Nothing will happen."

Finally, dressed in pantaloons and a camisole, clutching her dress under her arm, Lizzy climbed out of the basket.

"*Sacrebleu!*"

"If you're looking up, I swear I'll kill you, Rafe Laffite!"

"I'm not looking; don't fret."

"Easy for you to say."

"I'll catch you if you fall."

The breeze tugged at the ladder, and with every step the balloon jolted just enough to scare her. She glanced down and saw the top of Rafe's head several rungs below. When her toes brushed his shoulder, he seized her ankle and placed her foot on the rung. She felt him plant a kiss on the inside of her ankle.

"Confound you, Rafe, you *are* looking!" She glared down at him. "You just keep on going, you dratted thing!"

"No, we'll go together. The ladder's hung on some branches down there, and I want you close. Climb down to me."

"I won't do it!"

He hooked his forearm through the rung and smiled up at her. "I guess we'll just hang here all night, then."

"Damn you, Rafe!"

"You've already confounded and dratted me. Quit damning me and come down here." He leaned back to open a space between himself and the ladder.

"I can't remember when I've detested you more!" she said, but she climbed down anyway. She heard him suck in his breath as her thigh brushed his jaw along the way. The ladder trembled in her hands.

"Come on, honey," he said. "Come to me."

Tossed by the wind, her hair wrapped around them as she lowered herself into his arms. She could feel his

133

rigid flesh press between her buttocks. She bit her lip and tried to ignore the stimulation.

"We'd best descend before I lose my strength," Rafe said. "Come with me, Delilah."

"I thought you didn't like biblical comparisons," she said in a shaky voice.

"This one fits. I haven't been the same since you sheared off my beard."

"Uncovering your face didn't lessen your strength."

Her attempt to sound harsh failed. Erotic awareness flowed between them until Lizzy forgot she was dangling from a thread forty feet above the ground.

"Kiss me, Rafe," she said, looking up at him over her shoulder.

"You always close your eyes when I kiss you," he said. "Dangerous, considering."

"You'll just have to hold me, then."

"Like this?" Hooking his arms through the ladder, he enclosed her breasts in his hands and pulled her firmly against him, parted her lips with his tongue, and kissed her.

Lizzy felt naked on the ladder, her body locked to his in the eternal tie between man and woman. Her breath came hot and fast, and an ache spread between her thighs.

Rafe pulled back to look at her. "Come, Eliza, quickly."

Together they descended into the heavy foliage of the sycamore. It was murky in the tree, the leaves screening the sunset. When they could descend no farther on the ladder, Rafe helped her onto a thick branch, then climbed over to the anchor and tied the line to the tree.

By the time he'd finished, Lizzy was halfway down the smooth white limbs. Rafe caught up with her and passed by, jumped the last seven or eight feet onto a thick carpet of ferns, and smiled up at her. She hesitated on the branch above him.

She had climbed this far, convinced she would give herself to him as soon as she reached the ground, but now, alone with him in the darkening woods, her fears returned. What guarantee did she have that things would be any different? She had trusted him once; she would be foolish to do so again. The kiss she had begged a few minutes before was madness, her emotion born of danger and exhaustion.

"Come, Eliza."

"I'll—I'll break my leg." She wondered if she could spend all night huddled on the tree branch, just out of reach.

Suddenly his hands closed around her ankles and tugged until she dropped forward. He caught her waist and let her slide down his body until her feet touched the ferns. When she tried to disengage, he tightened his arms around her. If his hand hurt him, he gave no indication of it.

"I won't let you go," he said. "Not now. Not ever."

"It'll soon be too dark to see," she said, pushing against his naked chest with her hands. "We've got to start a fire or the mosquitoes will eat us alive."

"I could eat *you* alive."

He was as insistent as the rush of deep water. Like the confluence of two rivers, their separate pasts converged into a single present. Every moment had led to this.

She stopped pushing and let her hands go still, drawing sensation through her fingertips, feeling him perfuse every nerve ending.

He was a wild animal, this big, strapping soldier, his sinewy body marked by the teeth of battle. Suddenly she wanted to leave her mark on him as well, to bite and

Venita Helton

tear and love him with the savagery of a lioness. To
swallow him and make him part of her.

She hooked her fingers in his suspenders and, holding
him with her eyes, drew his hips to hers. "I want you
again, Rafe."

Chapter Thirteen

Wrapped in the fading aura of sunset, Rafe stared down at her. With his fingertips he caressed her lips. She kissed his fingers. When he slipped his hands down to her wrists, she tightened her grip on his suspenders.

"Eliza, are you sure?"

"I wouldn't do this if I weren't."

She pulled the suspenders off his shoulders and slid them down his arms. Then she unbuttoned his trousers and dragged them down to bare his stomach. The wound over his hip had healed dark red, but it was not the scar that interested her now.

Like a spear jutting from a thicket, he prodded her belly. She could see veins pulse with every beat of his heart. When he reached for the ribbon on her camisole, she stepped back a little and shook her head. "No, not yet," she said. "Let me touch you first."

"Only if I kiss you while you do it."

She melted into the fire of his lips. He tasted like the

earth, salty and alive, hungry and giving at the same instant. She took him in her hands. He was as hard as stone, yet alive as the silken petals of a magnolia. She stroked him up and down, flicked her thumb over him, kneaded him with her fingertips. Touching him made her ache and tremble.

At last he threw back his head and groaned. She felt him catch fire in her hands, leaping and pulsing against her palms until she could hardly hold him.

"Catch the tree limb, Rafe," she said. "Hold tight. Let me do this to you."

"You're torturing me, honey."

"You won't die, I promise."

With his trousers locked around his knees and his body shuddering under her ministrations, he caught the branch overhead with his good hand and cradled her head with the other. Against the glimmering nightfall his muscles seemed cut from dark granite.

"You look like Atlas," Lizzy said. "Atlas holding up the world."

"You are my world."

"We'll see." She licked his left collarbone from shoulder to breastbone. Twisting the branch until the tree shook, he called her name. "Eliza! By the powers, I'll not abide this another moment!"

She made no protest when he untied the camisole ribbon and pushed the straps to her elbows. Her breasts rose proud and swollen with desire. He cupped them in his hands and brought her nipples to his mouth, sucking until she ground her hips against him.

"Rafe, take me now. Please, take me now!"

He tore off her camisole and flung it aside. Eyes burning, he rolled her nipples between his fingers. "I'll eat you alive first."

"Don't tantalize me so!"

138

"And I thought it was I who was tempted," he said. "Come, lie with me."

He lowered her into the ferns and, with his trousers still at midthigh, knelt between her legs and untied the ribbon holding her pantaloons. She squirmed every time his warm fingers touched her.

"Put your arms over your head," he said.

She reached back and took hold of the ferns. Rafe leaned over her, opened her hands, and licked her palms. The erotic feel of his tongue penetrated every nerve. Growing wet with heat, she bolted against his naked body again and again.

He kissed her inner wrists, then nibbled his way to her breasts. Letting go of the ferns, she molded his buttocks to her hands and pulled him hard against her. "It's like it used to be," she said.

Rising to his knees, he stripped off her pantaloons, then stretched on top of her. He did not enter her yet, but licked her throat. Glorying in the feel of his body hair and hot flesh, she writhed against him.

"Do you want me, Eliza?" His voice was hoarse, demanding. "Do you?"

"Yes, just like the first time!"

He slid his hands down her flanks, pulled her thighs wide apart, and pressed against her softness, gazing at her like a wildcat about to mate—ferocious, merciless in his need.

"Please, Rafe."

"Take me, then," he said. With a powerful lunge of his hips he engaged her.

Lightning! She felt struck by lightning on a hot summer's night. Bolts of lightning plunged deep inside her body. Laws, she couldn't hold back. She didn't want it slow. She wanted it fast, again and again and again.

"Just like it used to be," Rafe said against her throat.

She couldn't reply. She was a volcano. Fire licked her insides. She opened her mouth to the white-hot caress of his tongue. She wanted all of him.

But just when she sensed his moment, he went still inside her. She felt him throbbing inside her tight, burning wetness. He was holding back, waiting for her. Tilting her hips, she induced him to kneel between her thighs. He grasped her knees and raised her even higher, until she clasped the small of his back with her feet and began to circle her hips.

"Good . . . good God almighty, you're so good," Rafe said. He grasped the mounds of her buttocks and rocked her hard, teaching her a rhythm all his own. Wave after fiery wave rolled through her belly. She screamed when he finally surged out of control, until white lava filled her and burst over them both.

At last she settled to earth, bringing him with her. Breathing hard, she lay staring into his eyes, which glittered like stars in the darkness. Night pressed in from the woods.

"You still have the power, honey," Rafe whispered. "I'm clay in your hands."

"You'll never be clay in anyone's hands, pirate. I know better than to try to shape you."

He kissed her temple—the lightest brush of his lips. "Your fingerprints are all over me; they never disappeared. . . ."

"Did you try to erase them?" She had to ask, though she feared the answer.

"I tried," he said at last. "But only after I heard you'd married."

She didn't want to think of Charles right now. His image had grown indistinct, like a tintype blurred at the edges. It seemed that he'd never really existed . . . that he was part of a past she had not lived, but read of in a book.

"Did you love him, Eliza?"

His words came like moth wings to a fading candle, yet she heard a flutter of anger. Did he blame her for marrying his friend? Or was he simply jealous that she might have loved someone else? Should she say Charles McCord had never owned her love?

Yet how could she? Only a cold woman could lie in her husband's arms and feel no devotion. Her feelings for Charles had not been like the dance Rafe had led her—there could be only one love like that—but he was the man her father had chosen for her.

How could she pretend that Charles had never mattered, when he'd done all he could to save both her reputation and the plantation? Her brother-in-law, William Fairlove, hadn't wanted responsibility for the burdensome farm . . . or for the baby.

The baby. She didn't want to remember the long, feverish days and nights when she'd called for a child born too early to survive . . . Rafe's child.

"Did you love him, Eliza?" Rafe asked.

Love him? How could she not love him, tiny and blue as he was, helpless as a bird in her arms?

"Of course I loved him," she said. "More than my own life."

She heard him draw a sharp breath. Then he rolled off of her and moved into the shadow of the trees. She heard his suspenders snap against his naked chest.

She sat up and tried to see him, but he was a part of the trees. "What's wrong? Where are you going?"

"I should've scrounged up some wood while it was daylight."

"Wait, I wasn't talking about Charl—"

"The mosquitoes have found us. I suggest you get dressed."

"Rafe!"

There was only silence. She knew he'd melted into the woods. Feeling very tired, she began searching on her hands and knees for her clothing. The wind died, leaving heat as oppressive as the sadness in her soul.

It took her a while to find her pantaloons. Her camisole was gone. It wouldn't have covered her anyway, she thought, since he'd torn it. She found her gown by the sycamore. Awkward in the dark, she struggled to dress. Her fingers felt like wooden spoons trying to poke the mussel-shell buttons into the holes down the front. She didn't bother pulling on her petticoats. It was too much effort.

Rafe had never had trouble dressing her after a long night on the riverbank. He should be here now.

With a sigh, she sat against the tree trunk to wait. Cicadas made a loud *Scree-Scree-Scree* in the branches, and over the din she heard animals scrabbling in the undergrowth. Try as she might, she couldn't hear Rafe.

It was as dark as a cave. There was no moon yet. She sensed the balloon rocking on its tether like some great, chained beast. Pulling her thighs to her chest, she rested her forehead on her knees and held herself very tightly, as though she could squeeze hard enough to snap the cords around her heart.

After their storm of lovemaking, why hadn't he stayed to listen to her? He hadn't given her a chance to explain about the baby. He was too proud, that man, just like his father. *Pride is the bane of the Laffites,* he'd said long ago, in a rare moment of self-revelation. *I'm cursed with a bushel of it.*

Pride had driven him from her arms in 1857. Tonight,

it had done so again. Pride was his weakness, his Achilles' heel. It would be his downfall.

But what of her own pride? Had she really intended to tell him about his child? Wasn't she seven years too late to make that disclosure? If she'd listened to her father and written to Rafe as soon as she'd learned she was pregnant, things might have been different now. Damned foolishness, pride.

If she told him now, how would he react? Their parting just now had proved their relationship still too tenuous, too bitter. He wouldn't understand. He might even accuse her of playing with his feelings, of raining brimstone on his head. He might not believe her.

Her breath hissed between her teeth like steam escaping a boiler. She had to clamp her teeth on her wrist to stifle a cry. It wouldn't help to blow up; he would only close her off. She didn't want that. If angry outbursts were the cure to her problem, she would have been healed long ago. This time she had to think with her head, not her heart.

And yet, how to tell him? How to admit she'd been too full of pride to tell him he was to be a father, and then, afterward, that his child had died? It had been, and still was, his right to know. A man was entitled to grieve.

And why should he mourn a loss he never knew? she thought to herself. Disgusted, she shook her head and sighed. "Drat it, I'll drive myself crazy if I don't stop this!"

"No one accuses you of madness, Eliza McCord. Kindly don't credit yourself with it."

She caught her breath. Rafe was close enough for her to see his glittering eyes. She heard him drop some wood; then he moved away and began to clear leaves from the ground. When he spoke again, his tone was as distant as a stranger's.

"Your neighbors used to call you 'Dizzy Lizzy,'" he said, "but it seemed more a term of endearment than a pronouncement on your sanity."

"I didn't take it that way." She pushed herself to her feet. In spite of her intention to use her brain instead of her emotions, anger simmered in her breast. "And I still don't."

"They're still laughing, then?"

"I don't care to discuss it." Opening the bag of food, she groped for a sulfur match. "Here."

He struck it on his boot. Before long, he had a small campfire going. In its light, his naked torso shone as though some alchemist had fashioned him of molten gold.

"Do we cook over it," he finally asked, "or just look at it?"

She threw the bag at him. "Make your own corn pone, Rafe Laffite. I'm sleeping in the balloon tonight."

"The devil you are!"

"The devil I am!" She jumped for the tree limb. He was on her in two bounds, his good hand imprisoning one of her wrists.

"Let go of me," she said, "or I'll scratch your eyes out!"

"You'll sleep on the ground where I can watch you."

"Why? Afraid I'll fly off and leave you?" She hurled the taunt like a brick.

"Do I have reason to fear?"

"Since the moment I saw you all those years ago, but you were too inflated with self-importance to notice!"

"I didn't see you trying to run," he said. "In fact, you were anxious to buy me a drink."

"You call sarsaparilla a drink? Why, it was the closest thing to milk I could feed a cub like you."

Rafe let go of her wrist, and, with a meaningful smile,

dropped his gaze to her body. "You didn't waste much time graduating me to solid food, though, did you?"

She slapped his face. Piercing as a rifle shot, the sound startled the night creatures. The woods went silent. For a long, still moment, Lizzy faced him. Rafe didn't touch his cheek, but looked into her eyes with a coldness that froze her marrow.

She held her breath. This was not the Rafe Laffite she'd loved scarcely an hour ago. She had seen this look in the eyes of the Yankee men who'd burned her plantation and terrified her Negroes. It was the primal, hungry look of a man who had forgotten who he was, whose past was so full of violence and destruction that he remembered no other way to be. The soul of a savage stared out of his eyes.

And yet, she sensed that the savagery wasn't directed at her. The slap had been the catalyst. He raged against something else. "Rafe, what have you done to yourself?" she cried. "What drives you to such ferocity? What's happened to you?"

He did not speak, but gradually the chill left his eyes. Perhaps he would tell her exactly what they were doing out here in the middle of nowhere. Maybe he would tell her what had changed him into this strange, haunted man.

But his eyes darkened as though a veil had been drawn between their minds. He stepped back and bowed. "I apologize for my ungentlemanly remarks. You don't need to sleep in the gondola, Eliza. I won't bother you again."

She lifted her hand in appeal. "Rafe—"

Turning away, he went to kneel by the fire. Without looking at her again, he made a batter of cornmeal, salt, and water, pressed it onto a stick, and propped it over the flames.

145

One arm wrapped around a tree branch, she stood watching him. The cicadas began *scree*ing again, but she did not share their peace. Her heart beat too fast and tears quivered just beneath her lids. If only she could roll back the minutes and erase their lovemaking. If only she could return to the days before Rafe had come back into her life!

And yet, what would have happened to her? She wasn't sure she could've escaped Huntsville without him. General Granger would have captured her and the balloon, taken her instruments, and banished her to the squalid refugee camp at Lacey's Spring.

"Come and eat, Eliza."

She flinched, not expecting his voice. She could not read his expression.

"It's good," he said, showing her the corn bread. "Palatable, anyway."

Giving him a wide berth, she circled the fire and settled onto her heels. He passed her the stick. The bread was hot and crumbly. After a few minutes, she noticed that Rafe wasn't eating. He'd given her the entire portion.

"You're hungry, too," she said. "Here, have some."

"No." He passed her the tin canteen. "Drink. Weevil fodder won't go down without water."

It tasted like a swamp, but she drank till she was full, then handed back the canteen. "Thanks."

"Don't mention it." Lying back on his elbows, he looked up at the rising moon.

Lizzy gazed at him from under her lashes. His moonlit face glowed like the Tennessee River, silvery smooth on the surface, deep and dangerous underneath. He was as perilous to her soul as a snag to a steamboat. Her pulse quickened.

"You warm enough?" he asked, not looking at her.

146

"Too warm," she said. Afraid she'd betrayed her interest in him, she blushed and stared at her hands.

By the big blue firmament, she was acting like a schoolgirl instead of a woman married and widowed! A woman her age should know better than to believe first love never died. Rafe's interest in her was sexual, pure and simple. Real love would've brought him back after Charles died. He had used her as a sexual convenience tonight. Well, she'd used him, as well. She'd needed intimacy, needed it badly after so many years of loneliness.

There wouldn't be any more of that nonsense. Tonight's encounter was the last.

Perhaps it was time to restate her stance: they were allies only for as long as it took them to get to Richmond. After that, they would go their separate ways. She never wanted him to touch her life again. It was over.

When she lifted her head to speak, his bandage drew her gaze. There was a dark stain on the cloth. Blood. "We ought to tend that," she said. Her attempt to sound brisk faltered.

He tilted his head. "It'll tend itself."

"It'll set up gangrene and kill you."

He dropped his chin onto his chest and stared at her. "Seems you've learned a lot of doctoring, Eliza McCord. Strange. You used to run from the sight of blood. Couldn't even be on the plantation when your damn slave butcher killed a hog."

His tone was purposely cruel, his vulgarity a whiplash. She wasn't going to take it.

"Hogs and men are different," she said. "*Some* of them, anyway."

"I deserved that, I guess."

"You did, and I don't want to fight anymore. May I see your wound?"

147

"There's a creek half a mile from here. I'll go wash it out, if it'll give you peace."

"Washing it won't help. It needs a poultice."

"Like your sister's hellfire-and-brimstone decoctions? I won't have it."

"Why, Rafe Laffite," she said, "I do believe you're just the least bit chicken-livered."

"Only when it comes to pain—my own, that is."

"You'll feel a lot worse when your whole arm swells up like a hog bladder and we have to find somebody to saw it off. I know for a fact I can't do it. We'll have to find a butcher."

"Chri—" He clamped his teeth shut on the oath. After a moment he said, "All right then, Mrs. McCord, do your worst."

Lizzy flicked a stick out of the fire and snuffed it out. Using a rock for a pestle and a flat stone for a mortar, she ground the charcoal to powder. "Take off that bandage and throw it in the fire," she said. "I'll tear you a new one."

She retrieved her petticoats from the shadows and tore strips from the already ragged hem. Then, a few drops at a time, she poured water into the mortar to form thick, black charcoal paste. She came around the fire and squatted by Rafe. Wordlessly he held out his wounded hand.

It felt very warm. Concerned, she touched his other hand to test the difference.

"Is it going to fall off, Eliza McCord?"

"Not yet." She inspected his palm. The wound had closed but the flesh was puffy. "You've been using it too much."

"There were certain things I needed to touch," he said suggestively. He met her angry glare with a solemn expression. "Like the ladder . . . and the tree . . . and wood for the fire."

"I know what you meant." She could smell his male scent and feel his warmth. The combination sent a powerful signal to her brain. "Don't move; I've got to tend this."

"No one's moving but you."

It was true. Her hands were shaking. Rafe was as quiet as a sleeping cat. She slathered charcoal paste on his wound and started binding it.

"I'll buy you a new petticoat when we get to Richmond," Rafe said.

"I don't accept personal gifts from men."

"It won't be a gift, Eliza McCord. I owe it to you."

"Why do you keep calling me 'Eliza McCord'? What do you mean by it?"

His teeth flashed in a smile bereft of amusement. "It's your name, isn't it?"

"You know it is! You're sharpening an ax on it. Why?"

His eyes smoldered like two embers. "Maybe to remind myself that you belong to another man."

Belong to another man. Not *belonged*. Did Charles's ghost haunt Rafe? No, she knew better than that . . . it was Rafe's memory that used to haunt Charles.

Avoiding his gaze, she hurried to finish bandaging him. Then she went back to her side of the fire and lay down. Dew soaked through her dress; she wished she'd brought the quilt from the gondola. She eased a little closer to the fire and closed her eyes.

"Will the balloon rise in the morning?" Rafe asked.

His tone was too quiet, she thought, to have come from any real concern. She wished he'd go talk to a tree.

"Eliza?"

149

"The gas will expand as the balloon warms. She'll rise."

"I guess you learned that from overnight trips with your father."

"We never made any."

He pushed himself to one elbow. "So for all you know, that thing might deflate tonight and leave us stranded."

"It might."

And if it did, he could go on to Richmond without her, since her usefulness was tied to the balloon. He could go on with his adventuring and never know what she was just realizing herself—that she'd never get over him.

But what if he'd made himself a father tonight? She shuddered as though splashed by ice water. Surely God wouldn't let her conceive again. She couldn't bear for things to get worse than they were already.

It was a long time before she dozed off. She dreamed of a little boy with tawny hair and eyes as golden green as those across the fire.

Chapter Fourteen

Birds chirped through the trees. Near the canebrake at the north edge of the clearing, a groundhog stuffed bamboo shoots into its mouth. Lizzy woke up and looked around in confusion. Instead of the fine lace over her bed, a dark canopy of leaves swayed in the slight breeze, and when she turned her head, in place of her bedroom window she saw embers glowing in a shallow depression. All at once she remembered where she was.

But why was she wrapped in the quilt? Last night she'd gone to sleep uncovered, yet this morning she was cocooned in patchwork. Rafe must have scaled the sycamore after she'd drifted off. He'd gone to considerable trouble for her.

Since it was still too dim to see much, she didn't look around at him. Besides, she was afraid he was awake. After last night's encounter, she didn't want to face him for a while.

Rafe Laffite was like a hurricane—a creature of tremendous power and a quiet, almost fragile center. Perhaps his soldiering had damaged more than his body. She suspected that he'd locked the horrors of war inside himself in a misguided attempt to shelter her. Maybe that was why he'd reacted so oddly last night when they'd spoken of Charles.

Soon, she knew, she would have to ask him about Charles's death. She remembered almost word for word the letter Rafe had sent her more than five years ago. In terse sentences he'd offered his condolences, but between the lines of ink she had read his desire to return and comfort her.

She knew he'd longed to wrap his arms around her and share her grief. He'd loved Charles, his lifelong friend. The loss had been Rafe's as much as hers. Perhaps more than hers, she thought in a painful flash of honesty.

Had she assuaged her own guilt by blaming him for Charles's death? Financial trouble alone had not driven her husband to Mexico, yet she couldn't admit she'd been party to his desperation. She'd tried to be a good wife. She'd tried to love him. Of course she had.

Tried to love him by hating Rafe. But Charles had not believed her when she called Rafe a man without honor, with ice water for blood; her husband's troubled face still burned like a brand in her memory. Laws, what sort of love had she thought to establish on a footing of misery?

The past was best kept locked in her heart's deepest cellar. Someday she'd take it out bit by bit, examining each guilty piece until, perhaps, she might forgive herself. Maybe Charles would forgive her, too. And Rafe. She could start by telling him about his child.

Before she could change her mind, she sat up and looked across the fire. He was gone, not even a grass blade pressed down where he'd made his bed. He must have been gone all night.

She jumped to her feet, spooking the birds. The groundhog scampered into the canebrake. Rafe was nowhere in sight. From where she stood under the branches she couldn't see the balloon. Afraid it had either deflated or flown off, she kicked aside the quilt and ran a few yards. Had Rafe taken it?

Creaking at its tether, its deep-blue sides polished by the rising sun, the windcraft hovered over the sycamore. Lizzy's knees went wobbly with relief. ''Rafe,'' she called. ''Rafe! Are you up there?''

When his head did not appear over the gondola, she moved into the trees where he'd gone for firewood last night. The vegetation was very thick. Muscadine, honeysuckle, and wisteria vines crawled into the trees like spiderwebs. Lizzy jumped when a pair of tufted titmice scolded her from a vine, then flew off into the gloom. Folks said the big-eyed birds were an evil omen.

''Rafe!'' She called his name a bit louder. ''Where are you?''

The thorny branches of a locust tree caught her skirts. As she moved deeper into the woods, the vines gave way to a carpet of ferns, poison ivy, and dead leaves. As she scrambled over a fallen oak tree, she smelled moldering fungi. She just missed stepping on a copperhead curled beside the log. The viper hissed and slithered under a rhododendron.

Slipping down a bank to a shallow stream, she looked for Rafe's tracks in the mud but discovered only the small prints of deer and raccoons. She cupped water in her hands and drank. Tasting of leaf mold, the water was as cool as a spring.

''What's he playing at?'' she demanded of the silent, dawn-dappled woods.

He hadn't left her—the tethered balloon proved that—but it was just like him to drag her off on this insane mission, then make her hang around in the woods while he took a pleasant nature walk! She was starving to death, angry, and not a little frightened. With a petulant kick she sent a pinecone rolling into the stream.

The pinecone swirled away. Lizzy knew exactly how it felt to be pulled into a current, to drift along with little control over her direction. She wasn't really mistress of the balloon—it listened to the wind. Since Rafe's advent, she'd had a like amount of control over her personal life. "Aggravating hurricane of a man!"

She didn't feel the least bit guilty anymore. It would serve Rafe Laffite right if she never told him about the baby. He probably wouldn't care, anyway. He was a gambler and a philanderer. He'd probably had a dozen women down in Mexico.

Becoming angrier by the second, she stripped off her clothes and plunged into the stream. It was cold enough to freeze butter, just what she needed to cool her rage. She should have taken a cold bath right after climbing out of the balloon last night. What wild notion had induced her to act like some love-starved grass widow? People made jokes about women who acted as she had.

"You'll catch the ague if you stay in there much longer, Eliza."

Lizzy jerked around and covered herself with her arms. Rafe was standing on the bank a few yards away, gazing into the treetops. He was wearing his full Yankee uniform. The sight of it dismayed her nearly as much as the man wearing it.

"You're no gentleman, Rafe Laffite, to peep at a lady in the bath!"

"I'm not peeping."

"You were!"

154

He glanced sidelong at her. "Briefly. You never know what you'll run across in the woods. I had to be sure it was you, not some haunt."

"How long have you been standing there?"

"Long enough."

"Turn your back!"

He spread his arms and, with exaggerated care, about-faced. "I'll watch for Yankees."

"Yankees?" She froze halfway out of the water. In a whisper she asked, "See any?"

"No." He leaned up against a black gum tree, plucked off a twig, and began to clean his teeth. After a pause he said, "But you never know when they'll come calling."

His casual manner did not wholly disguise the warning. Lizzy hurried out of the water and dressed. "Where have you been?" she demanded, still in a whisper. "I looked all over—Wait, don't turn around! I haven't finished dressing! Where have you been?"

Rafe sighed and resumed his stance against the tree. "I was out getting breakfast. I didn't expect to come back and find you gone."

"You didn't expect me to lie in all morning, worrying myself to a nubbin over you?" The instant she said it, she could have bitten off her tongue. Rafe looked at her over his shoulder. A slow smile warmed his features.

"Thank you," he said. "It sounds trite, but I was unaware you cared."

"I don't. I just—I just thought maybe your wound had made you feverish and you'd wandered off or something."

"Is that so?"

"Yes." She clamped her lips shut on the lie. Why couldn't she admit she was afraid to be alone, that she depended on him?

Venita Helton

That was the *last* thing she would admit. She mustn't forget who needed whom. He didn't know the first thing about piloting the balloon. He didn't know how to avoid a thunderstorm, or when to drop ballast, or how to warp the crown to make minor adjustments in direction. And he certainly didn't know how to use her cherished instruments. As simple a device as the compass was probably a mystery to him.

Head down, she stalked past him, but after taking several steps she realized he wasn't following. "Aren't you coming back to camp?" she asked.

"Yes." He jerked his thumb to the right. "It's that way."

"Oh." Lizzy reversed course. This time she let him lead. He didn't need a compass.

Lizzy almost walked straight into camp, but Rafe caught her arm and held her at the edge of the woods. With the intensity of a hunter he surveyed the camp, then silently moved away until he could see the balloon. At last he was satisfied. "Right, now we'll eat."

Breakfast was already prepared, Lizzy soon discovered. Cornmeal hoecakes steamed on a flat rock in the coals, while meat sizzled on a spit. "Meat?" Lizzy asked. "What is it?"

"Quail. I heard him whistle after we landed last night, so I set a snare for him. All I had to do was collect him this morning. There's not much to the little cock, I'm afraid."

"There's enough." Lizzy took a piece. "Mmm. You can't imagine how long it's been since I've tasted meat."

Rafe reached for a hoecake, heaped it with quail, and passed it to her. "Here."

"But there won't be any for you."

"There's corn bread."

"Yes, well, I feel guilty eating all this."

"Keep it, honey. You're too skinny."

You ought to know, she thought, recollecting last night. He was looking at her now as if he could see straight through her clothes. Blushing, she covered her embarrassment with a sharp retort. "You're not exactly fat, either. Hattie Lee said you favored a starved alley cat. She wanted to feed you milk and sugar, but we didn't have any."

"I got by pretty well on broth and dandelion tea."

Lizzy looked away. "We almost lost you."

For a moment Rafe did not reply. Then he leaned forward and pushed back the hair fallen into her face. "Why, Eliza McCord, I believe those are tears swimming in your big blue eyes."

"I got smoke in them," she said, and pushed his hand away.

"Maybe you should sit upwind." He looked immensely proud of himself.

She changed the subject. "How's your hand?"

"Getting by."

"Are you going to show me?"

"Best to keep it wrapped up. The air might poison it."

"I suppose." Doctors said there was effluvium in moist countryside like this. Although Grace Fairlove didn't hold with the theory that poisonous air caused infection, Lizzy had enough faith in doctors to believe their notions. Rafe obviously did, too.

Still, she felt bad doing nothing. Ever since he had come to her in the storm, wounded and near death, she'd felt responsible for his life. Strange to feel so about a full-grown man, especially one she'd despised for so long. It was rather frightening. It created a bond that had nothing to do with the distant past and everything to do with the present . . . and the future. Maybe what the Cherokees said was true: "When you save the life of a man, he is yours forever. And you are his."

Hesitantly she touched his bandaged hand. "Rafe?"

"Yes?"

She swallowed. There was much she wanted to say, but the words wouldn't come. Not with him looking at her out of those lustrous eyes. He didn't disguise the need that spoke louder than the drumming of her own heart. Her tongue stuck to the roof of her mouth.

What should she tell him if she managed to unstick the words? That she loved him? Laws, no. She'd been a fool once; she'd be a bigger fool to repeat history. There would be other differences of opinion strong enough to divide them all over again.

She felt his right hand close over hers. The look in his eyes was as tender as cotton flowers. There were harsh lines around his mouth, those of a man enduring pain, yet his lips invited her kiss, and the warmth of his breath on her face excited an answering warmth deep down inside her.

No, please don't do this to me again.

"Speak to me, Eliza."

She answered him with a shake of her head.

"I ache," he said.

"Your—your hand?"

"No. In here." He touched his chest.

"I can't help your pain. Not that kind." Her words grated past vocal cords gone rusty with tears. Abruptly she stood.

With the swiftness of a cat he followed her, his handsome face turned down to hers. The softness was gone from his eyes, replaced by heated wanting. His voice bore a ragged edge. "Don't run, darling."

Raising her hands, she took two steps backward and

said, "If your wound pains you, I'll tend it, but I'll be dashed before I'll tend anything else!"

His face closed down like a hurricane turning inward, forcing his anger into his quiet inner eye. Even so, Lizzy felt the winds of his displeasure.

"Let's go," he said.

Although he spoke almost too quietly to hear, his words rushed upon her in a wave of sexuality. Alive to the warning, she shoved the remaining hoecakes into the sack and hastened to the sycamore. She didn't know whether to start climbing or to run off into the woods. In the end, she stood watching him.

For several seconds Rafe stood with his back to her, his hands clenched at his sides, his head hanging low. Then with great vehemence he kicked dirt over the fire until it was out.

His movements calmer now, he spread dry leaves over the site, then moved around the clearing, making certain they'd left nothing to betray them. He cursed when he reached into a wild rose vine and pricked his hand. Lizzy saw a flash of white, and then he thrust whatever he had found into his jacket. Was it her torn camisole, and if so, what did he intend to do with it? Keep it as a trophy?

Let him go on with his explorations; she had a tree to climb. She stretched on tiptoe for the branch. She wasn't sure she could pull herself up, but she didn't want to ask Rafe's help, didn't want to feel his hands. Didn't want to give him control.

"Catch the bough," he said from behind her.

"I can do it myself—oh!"

He swept her with dizzying suddenness onto his shoulder, then lifted her to the branch until she straddled it like a horse.

"Let go! I can manage without you!"

"Suit yourself."

But when she tried to drag her skirts down over her pantaloons, she lost her balance and started to fall. Like a mountain lion he leaped onto the branch beside her, locked one arm around her waist, and pulled her to a standing position. His eyes were not at all kind.

"Maybe I ought to take that damned dress off you."

"Do it and I'll slap your face!"

"I've no designs on your virtue. You can't climb in those clothes."

"You watch me!" Resentment obliterating her clumsiness, she leaped out of his arms and began to climb like a squirrel. Each time her skirts caught and threw her off-balance, she yanked them free and kept going. She didn't hesitate when a branch snapped off under her foot.

Rafe's curse echoed as the limb crashed down. Lizzy didn't spare him a glance. Determined to beat him, she hauled herself to the rope ladder and breathlessly struggled to untie the knots securing it to the tree. Maybe she'd fly off without him.

"Allow me." Rafe stepped onto an adjacent branch and swiftly freed the ladder, put his foot on the bottom rung, and steadied its sides. "After you, Eliza McCord."

With him holding the ladder, she knew she couldn't help but touch him when she started to climb. After what had just happened on the ground, touching him was the last thing she wanted. She'd have to pretend not to notice.

Making certain not to touch his hands, she seized the ladder and stepped onto the second rung. Rafe kept the ladder steady, but she was uncomfortably aware of his hot, muscular body on the other side of the ropes. She stepped up to the second rung. Now they were face-to-face.

For an instant too long she stared at him through the

ladder. White as ivory, his teeth gleamed in a mocking smile. His face might have been cast from stone but for the burning light in his eyes. "You hesitate. Shall I carry you on my back?"

"You surely won't!" Lizzy caught the next rung. As she'd feared, she swung into Rafe. She tried to climb faster, but with aching slowness her breasts dragged up his chest and her thighs thrust against him. She heard his breathing change, and the hard bulge she felt between his thighs left no doubt about his reaction.

She made herself continue upward, but when she felt his hot breath against her lower belly, she nearly fell off the ladder. Looking down, she discovered his mouth only inches away. Lizzy could not suppress an image of him lifting her skirt, locking his arms around her buttocks to pull her softness through the rungs, giving her the sort of tongue-lashing she craved. The vision made her wet.

Mercy, this was terrible. He surely sensed what was going on in her mind—her shuddering reaction made it clear. In another moment he would oblige her. "Damn you, Rafe Laffite!" she said, and hurried on before her wishes became reality. She heard him chuckle.

At last she was clear of him, but the ladder began to bounce now that she was above his restraining hands. In the treetop the leaves were very thick, yet as insubstantial as cobwebs; one misstep would plunge her through them. She missed Rafe's hard body.

But when her head cleared the treetop, she forgot her fear. Perched on an endless coverlet of green-pocketed fog, the rolling country looked dense enough to walk on, like a shirred blanket stretched upon the ground.

Above her the sleek bowl of balloon disappeared into the firmament, while to the east the sun rode a mountain ridge, its golden light muting the blue-washed slopes. It was like being inside a watercolor painting, except the air had movement, and from all around her the sounds of life rose and fell in a melodic whisper.

The magic helped her ascend through the last few yards of air. She eased into the swaying basket and, looking over the side, discovered Rafe had filled the ballast bags. He'd been busy last night.

The balloon dipped, then slowly began to rise. A few seconds later, his hair burnished by sunlight, Rafe appeared in the crown of the sycamore. As the balloon lifted him clear, he looked up at her.

Those flashing eyes alarmed her—she didn't want him coming any nearer. Though dangling on the end of the ladder, he was in control, holding her already, vowing not to let her go. She had saved his life and now she belonged to him. Her hands closed on the basket rail.

Ignoring the treetops swirling past his feet, he climbed toward her with the same silent fluidity with which he walked the ground. Once more the image of being stalked by a cougar sprang to her mind.

Balance the load, she told herself, a frail excuse to break eye contact, but enough to loosen her fingers on the rail. She moved to the opposite side. *Think like an aeronaut.* Wind eddies caught and spun the balloon, causing the shrouds to rub the silk envelope. There were clouds to the east, but nothing that looked dangerous. She checked the barometer.

She felt not the slightest jolt when Rafe climbed aboard. It was uncanny. "What are you, Rafe Laffite?"

He paused, then began hauling in the ladder. Lizzy knew he had heard her; she could sense his displeasure. No, not displeasure. Awareness like a galvanic charge. She felt it leap from his skin to her own, from his brain to hers. She didn't question him again.

162

What would happen on this long day's journey? Her compass wouldn't give her the reading she sought. No instrument in existence could tell her the thoughts in the mind of Rafe Laffite.

She would have to find out the hard way. She just hoped she could live with the answer.

Chapter Fifteen

Perched on the front seat, Hattie Lee Fairlove rode in the railcar just behind the tender. She blinked against the black clouds pouring through the window from the huge smokestack, and squirmed in her seat.

"I wish you'd move over some," she said to Captain Geraud, who sat next to her on the worn red velveteen bench. "I'm smushed flat as a june bug."

"You *are* a little june bug," Geraud said in barely understandable English. He stroked Hattie Lee's cheek with his knuckles. "Perhaps I will take you home to play with."

"I ain't nobody's play-pretty," Hattie Lee said, and jammed her elbow into Geraud's side.

"Geraud, you will not toy with the girl-child," DeCoeur said in French.

He knocked several charts from his lap as he reached across the aisle to tap Geraud's knee with the calipers he'd been using; then, with a twist of his head, he in-

164

dicated the Union soldiers overflowing the seats behind them. Hattie Lee wondered what he meant by it. She wished she'd listened when Aunt Lizzy had tried to teach her French.

"There are too many Americans watching for you to play your little games, even with a Rebel," DeCoeur said. "Leave her alone."

Hattie Lee pressed her nose to the window. Leaves blurred past, then disappeared when the train clattered onto a trestle. Down on the river, a group of Federals waved and shouted from the deck of a shallow-draft gunboat. The train riders hung out the windows and hollered back until Hattie Lee felt like she was standing inside an iron drum while somebody banged on it with a cow's leg. She stuffed her fingers into her ears and shifted her gaze to DeCoeur.

Rolling his charts one by one and tucking them under his arm, Louis DeCoeur got out of his seat, stooped through the doorway onto the front platform, and gestured to Hidalgo La Peña to join him. Hidalgo walked so slowly that Hattie Lee judged he was reluctant to follow.

Why had DeCoeur brought her on this crazy chase? She was a hostage, she supposed, but what good could she do them? The train surely couldn't catch up with Aunt Lizzy's balloon. Besides, how could DeCoeur guess where the balloon was? Still, she knew a hunter when she saw one: DeCoeur would catch his prey or die trying.

If she were to escape, she'd foil DeCoeur's plans to use her. All her captors needed to do was take their eyes off her for one minute and she'd disappear like a rabbit into blackberry briers. And as for getting lost in the wilds of Alabama, why, all she had to do was follow the railroad track and watch out for Yankees.

"Where are we?" she asked Geraud.

"Far from your home."

"Well, salt my mule and fry him in hog fat, if that ain't a big surprise!"

Geraud raised his brows. "The mam'selle wishes me to do what to her mule?"

"Never mind—where are y'all taking me?"

"It is not for a little one to know."

"Ha! You ain't telling 'cause you don't know! Mr. Louis don't trust you with secrets."

The Frenchman shrugged. "Perhaps not."

Scowling, Hattie Lee clapped her arms over her chest and sat back in the seat. If Geraud wouldn't tell her, she'd have to spy it out. Trouble was, they usually spoke French—even the Mexican man did.

Behind her, one of the Yankees coughed and spat on the floor. Hattie Lee swiveled around and stared at him. He winked, his bristly jaw widening in a grin. She didn't smile back. It wasn't part of her plan.

The soldier's grin faltered. Then he stuck his hand in his blouse and felt around. At first Hattie Lee thought he was chasing fleas, but after a moment, he held out a broken stick of sassafras candy. Blue fluffs of wool stuck to the sweet, but Hattie Lee solemnly took it. She let a dimple form in her cheek. The soldier's grin swelled.

Divide and conquer, that was what Aunt Lizzy had told her to do one time when a herd of boys picked on her. These soldiers were a mite bigger than schoolboys, but she reckoned they thought along the same lines.

On the platform, DeCoeur was smoking a cigar. Hattie Lee saw him hand one to the Mexican Lancer. "Bet he don't offer *you* cigars," she said.

Geraud frowned. "And what makes the mam'selle believe such a thing, eh?"

Wrinkling her nose, Hattie Lee sniffed the sleeve of

166

his dark green uniform. " 'Cause if you smoked, you wouldn't stink so bad. Cigars sorta cover up the smell.''

His dark eyes brightened. "The little one needs a strap across her backside, *non?*"

"Just telling the truth like I learnt in Sunday school," Hattie Lee said, casting her gaze down and smoothing her dress over her knees. She waited until she sensed him return to his brooding. "Don't you worry none. Mr. Louis and that other fellow stink real bad, too, even with them cigars. They probably don't notice you at all." Steepling her hands over her nose, she slouched away from him in the seat.

Muttering, Geraud yanked open the gold frog at his throat and loosened his collar.

"Sure do look friendly with their heads together, puffing them big fat cigars," Hattie Lee said. "Reckon what they're talking about?"

"It is none of your concern. Go to sleep!"

Hattie Lee leaned back and shut her eyes. She let her head sway to the rhythm of the train. After a while her mouth fell open. She snored gently. Since she could feel Geraud watching her, she tried not to let her eyes move around beneath her lids. After a few minutes, she felt him steal out of his seat and heard the door open. Wind and smoke rushed in.

Hattie Lee opened her eyes a crack. Geraud was with the others on the platform. All three were looking at the mountain of wood heaped in the tender. She scrunched around, peered over the seat at the Yankee, and bent upon him her sweetest, gap-toothed smile, the one that formed dimples in both cheeks. "Thank you for that sassafras candy, Colonel."

"It wasn't much," the soldier said. "And I ain't a colonel."

"Oh. Major?"

"No, corporal. Corporal Spears," he said, but his chest puffed up like a carp left out of water too long. "I'm one of your escorts."

Since the Yankees all looked the same in their blue uniforms this was news to her, but she pretended she already knew. She jerked her thumb at the Lancers. "After them foreigners, you don't seem half bad, even if you are a Yankee."

Spears laughed. "They giving you trouble?"

"Uh-huh. I don't understand half the things they say. Maybe you can help me."

"I don't know any French."

"It wasn't French I heard that black-headed one speak," she said. "It was plain old ugliness, I think, but I couldn't make it all out. What's it mean when they call your mama a fancy lady?"

Spears gave an embarrassed chuckle and rubbed the back of his neck. "Now don't you pay no mind to what they say about your ma. I'm sure she's got a fine reputation, even if she ain't got a steady man around."

"They didn't say it about *my* mama."

He quit massaging his neck. The grin faded slowly from his lips. "Whose mother did they say it about?"

"Yours," Hattie Lee said.

Spears stared at the foreigners through narrowed eyes. "What else did them Frogs say?"

"Well, they said y'all execute so many flanking movements your underwear's done outflanked itself. Don't know what they mean by that, either." Everybody knew soldiers turned their underdrawers inside out to escape lice.

"They say anything else?"

"Before or after they called y'all sheet-slitters' sons?"

"After."

"I don't want to get you mad, Colonel."

"I ain't planning to get mad at you. What'd they say?"

"Well, they said any Yankee stationed in Huntsville was a shirker, and he only joined up to get old Mr. Lincoln's bounty fund. Said he couldn't fight worth a— You sure you want to hear the rest, Colonel?"

"Corporal. And yeah, more than anything."

"All right then, but I hope you don't get het up about swear words. Ma sure does." She dropped her voice. "They said y'all couldn't fight worth a dog-tail damn, anyhow. Said one French Lancer with his arms and legs cut off and his eyeballs hid under a cot could whup fifteen Yankees in his sleep, and still have enough strength left over to raze Washington city and carry off the women."

"They did, eh?"

Hattie Lee nodded once, decisively. "Course, they was just joshing. They didn't mean all that . . . even if they did say they wanted to shuck you and the rest of our escort."

"They want to get rid of us?"

Hattie Lee held up her hands. "Don't look at me—I just heard what I heard. I don't know what they're whispering about out there. Probably the weather." She turned around and stuck her candy in her mouth. From the whispers behind her, she knew Spears was talking to his companions.

"The engineer, he says we will be in Bridgeport this evening," Louis DeCoeur said, squinting against the billowing smoke. "There we will learn whether we follow the right track. Perhaps someone has telegraphed word of Laffite's position."

"And if not?" La Peña asked.

"Then I will decide our course."

La Peña knew it was time to speak on behalf of the people of Mexico. "It seems to me, señor," he said, "that our best course is to hasten to Richmond. There we can speak to the Confederate president and tender to him our plight. I am sure he will return the diamond to us as soon as Laffite—"

"And what makes you think he'll turn over a diamond worth more than his whole country? It is a stone with which to rule the world!"

"And you have wished to rule the world for years, have you not?" La Peña said, shaking with rage. "Ever since that scheme you hatched in Pensacola, with the Rebel submarine."

"I bid you be silent, *mon ami*," Louis DeCoeur said. His pupils gaped like ebony holes.

But La Peña was incensed. "You play first one side, and then the other, but always you play for Louis DeCoeur! The diamond—you want it for yourself!"

"Shh, do not speak so to him," Geraud said, laying his hand on the Mexican's arm.

"Why should I not? It is the truth! This DeCoeur the emperor coddles worked for the British—and the Confederacy—just three years ago. He made General Bragg a torpedo, and developed a submarine propelled by its own power!"

DeCoeur's facial muscles rippled like disturbed water in a pond. The end of his cigar smoldered dangerously close to his fingers, but he did not appear to notice the heat.

"You see the scars on his face, his crushed nose?" La Peña said, pointing. "Those are not the only marks of perfidy he bears. Beneath his shirt are scarred and twisted muscles—remnants of a fiery explosion no human should have lived through! I tell you, Geraud,

DeCoeur is not as other men. He is a devil, a master of treachery, a—''

DeCoeur's left hand closed around the Lancer's throat and lifted him off the ground. La Peña fought to get free, but his struggles were no more effective than a rat's against a grizzly.

''Go on, little man,'' DeCoeur said, ''tell Jean-Claude about the treacherous Joshua Langdon, who stole my beautiful submarine and broke her apart.''

La Peña heard himself make a strangling noise. His kicks were too feeble to save him, his hands as disjointed as broken chicken wings. DeCoeur's iron fingers were crushing his trachea, cutting off his air. The roar of an ocean sounded in his ears. He couldn't hear the soldiers anymore. Were they watching him strangle?

''Tell him about the flames of hell lighting Pensacola Bay that night!'' DeCoeur said. ''Tell him about the agonizing rack of fire old Louis lay in. Here, you must feel it!''

The glowing cigar end streaked toward his left eye. Flaming pain seized his brow bone and slammed his eyelid shut. Uttering a tortured scream, the Mexican broke the vise on his throat, fell to the platform and rolled perilously close to the edge. DeCoeur smoked his cigar and watched.

Gripping the platform rail, his Adam's apple bouncing, Jean-Claude Geraud stared at his companion. The soldiers sat in the car in silence, their faces reflecting Geraud's horror. Hattie Lee sat frozen, her hands over her mouth.

''Get up,'' DeCoeur said, prodding La Peña with the toe of his boot. ''I missed your eye. The damned Americans are watching. The honor of the Lancers is at stake.''

La Peña struggled to his knees. One hand covering

his eye, he crawled into the railroad car. After a few seconds, Spears and another soldier caught him under the armpits and dragged him to the backseat to bathe the burn.

Hattie Lee remained on the front seat, staring at DeCoeur and Geraud as though they were rattlesnakes. She knew she would scream if she uncovered her mouth, so she remained exactly as she was. Only when her eyes began to smart did she dare blink.

What kind of monsters were they? She had to get out of here. There was no longer a question of dividing and conquering her captors. Besides, after what the Yankees had just witnessed, they were either against DeCoeur or they weren't. If his own men weren't safe from him, how could the Yankees enjoy a moment's rest?

Before long, the train was bound to pull into a depot. If the Yankees hadn't burned the station at Bridgeport, the engineer would be sure to stop to take on water. Until then, she must do nothing to attract DeCoeur's attention. La Peña's wounding made her want to vomit, or faint, or both. If DeCoeur would do it to his own man, he would do it to her.

As if discerning her thoughts, DeCoeur looked straight at her and smiled. There was nothing human in his eyes. Hattie Lee shook with fear.

And then, as she always did in emergencies, she thought of her mother's face. Ma's oft-repeated advice rang in her mind: *When you're scared and miserable, Hattie Lee, think about someone besides yourself. You can be sure there's somebody a lot more needy than you. Ask the good Lord Jesus to help you be strong for them . . . set your spirit at peace by helping another.*

She made herself think of Aunt Lizzy and Rafe Laffite. They were counting on her to be brave, to do nothing that would make it easier for DeCoeur to catch them.

Whatever business Mr. Rafe was engaged in, it was bound to affect the Confederacy. And if it affected the army, it was bound to affect her daddy, too.

As she stared into DeCoeur's eyes, she thought of how her daddy needed her to be strong. He was rotting in prison somewhere. Mr. Rafe Laffite was going to Richmond to talk to the president. Maybe his words would help Daddy get free.

A shadow fell over her. DeCoeur's bulk filled her view. His lips stretched tight in a smile. "Mademoiselle Fairlove, I am sure you have much to tell Uncle Louis," he said. "You are hiding things, my naughty little one. Tell me where your aunt is flying."

Hattie Lee could not force her vocal cords to deny the charge. When she tried to shake her head, the muscles of her neck froze solid. She could only sit while the dreadful smile loomed nearer and nearer.

Chapter Sixteen

They were flying at less than three thousand feet when Lizzy spotted a flash in the rolling greensward behind them. Before she could tell what it was, the world turned to milk. "Be ready with that spyglass when we come out of the cloud," Lizzy said in a voice that shook like a dry reed. "I think we've been spotted."

"Thunder!" From his position forward, Rafe spun toward her. He had a brass spyglass in his hand, discovered early that morning in the bottom of Lizzy's valise. "Where are they?"

"Southwest."

"What'd you see?"

"Only a flash before we went into the cloud, but it must've been from another heliograph. I can't think of anything else that bright."

For half a minute they waited in the thick, white silence. Lizzy shifted her weight to her left leg, subtly closing the gap between Rafe and her. She wished he would touch her, reassure her, but there was nothing to do but wait.

Suddenly the cloud shredded as though run through a cotton comber. Rafe snapped the glass to his eye. Bright blasts of Morse code pierced the mountain crest. He swung the glass east and saw lightning flash there, as well.

"They've spotted us, all right," he said.

"What're they saying?"

"They're arguing."

"Arguing?" Lizzy practically danced with anxiety. "What about?"

"Whether to shoot us down or not."

"Oh, dear God!"

"You can thank God they're fussing and not firing . . . so far," Rafe said. "They'd have a hard time hitting us at this altitude. Still, I wonder why the vacillation?"

"Don't question providence—it's bad luck."

"You're superstitious, Eliza."

"Maybe, but haven't we got enough problems without you asking why we're *not* getting shot at?"

Rafe didn't answer. He brought the glass around to the left, then winced and jerked his head away before looking again. Lizzy caught his sleeve. "What did you see?"

"The inside of a rifle barrel."

"Just one?" She said, knowing it was too much to hope for.

"Afraid not." Then, almost to himself, he said, "More pressure on the trigger, boys, and the suspense is over."

"Will you kindly not encourage them!"

"They don't require much encouragement."

Lizzy leaned over the side. Without the spyglass she couldn't see the soldiers, but the glittering play of mirrors pierced her eyes like a broken bottle. Fear bunched up inside her, brought her close to Rafe, locked her hands around his right bicep.

"It's okay, baby," he said low, but his gaze held fast to the mirrors.

With his hair tousled around his dark face, his profile set and waiting with a hunger she could feel, he looked predatory, capable of meting out death. Her pulse throbbed with a violence she couldn't wholly blame on danger. She craved him; it was as simple and as complicated as that. Even now, with her life in jeopardy, she could not stifle the need welling up inside her. Maybe the jeopardy made her want him more; she couldn't tell.

She tightened her grip and felt his muscles turn to iron. Heat soaked through his sleeve, entered her fingertips and coursed through her veins. Warmth spread through her loins and gathered in her belly like a lump of molten thunder.

"What are you thinking?" Rafe asked. He did not relinquish the spyglass.

Did he sense her thoughts? Was it necessary to tell him? She ought to tell him, now, before they died. She ought to tell him that she loved him still, that she'd never wanted anything so much as him. She ought to.

But not yet. In another minute they might fly out of the Yankees' range and then she would have told all. She couldn't give him that much power over her. She couldn't bare the secret, not yet. Maybe not ever, because if she did, it might be the end of the fragile hope she'd hidden even from herself. To love Rafe and not be loved again by him . . . No, her mind recoiled from the thought.

There was honor, after all. And humiliation.

"What're you thinking?" he asked her, but again he did not look at her.

Her brain whirled. Then she pointed at the flashes. "That I feel like a child who doesn't know her letters."

He lowered the spyglass then, and took her measure in a long, appraising stare. Sexuality flowed from him as it had last night when he'd held her high above the ground. "You don't look like a six-year-old, Eliza McCord," he said in a gravelly whisper.

She swallowed hard. "I feel like one, unable to read those messages." *Lord, I'm babbling; that's not what I'm feeling at all!* And then, because she had to hide the secret, she said, "Tell me what they're saying. What're they planning?"

"My grandfather used to say it's best not to know the depth of the water until it's already up to your neck."

"You believe that?"

His eyes smoldered like bits of amber as he gazed into the far distance. He looked like a man reaching for his own death.

Laws, what a ghastly thought! Rafe didn't seek death . . . any more than any mercenary sought it. But those eyes saw things she couldn't. *He has the sight, Lizzy,* her father used to say. *Be very careful of him. He is ancient inside, I think. Such men want more than you or I can give.*

She hadn't believed him. Back then, it was only important that Rafe saw her. She did not question what filled his mind's eye. He was her vagabond prince . . . and a Delta villain.

Such men want more than you or I can give. . . . If her seven-years-past innocence had not been enough, how much less she had to offer him now, this bruised, defiant creature she had become. And how much less he could offer her. There was no hope of reclaiming lost trust.

Maybe the yearning sensuality between them was an

illusion, too, and always had been. Would she spend the rest of her life chasing love as inconsequential as the wind?

Crack! Smoke bloomed upon the grass.

"That's it, then," Rafe muttered, and slapped the spyglass into her hand.

Jack Daniel's pistol materialized in his fist. Resting the long barrel on the rail, he took aim. Before he could shoot, smoke wisped like dandelion puffs all over the ground.

"They're shooting, Rafe!"

"Why didn't that occur to me?" he said, and fired back. With sure movements he reloaded the piece, fired, and reloaded again. "Good thing they don't have a cannon."

"Don't even think it; they'll wheel one out!"

"I'm glad you aren't superstitious."

She ripped open a ballast bag and let dirt fly on the wind. The balloon gained only a few feet. "We must be trapped beneath a layer of cold air."

"Empty more bags, then," Rafe said. "Don't make your head a target."

When she'd dumped two more without the reduced weight having any effect on the balloon, she gripped the shrouds and yelled, "Rise! Go into the cloud bank!"

"Pray for more wind," Rafe said. "We're slower than a one-winged vulture. I ought to get out and push."

"Maybe, but we're drifting away from them."

"They're mounting up to chase us," he said.

"Cavalry!"

"If we can make those clouds, we'll lose them."

Rafe shot at the lead horseman but succeeded only in snapping a branch off a tree. "Damn, I'm shooting like my grandmother." Ripping open a paper cartridge with his teeth, he poured gunpowder into the muzzle, rammed

178

in a ball, and snapped off another shot. "Damn again! I might as well sit in Granny Loire's rocking chair and knock down flies with a peashooter."

Lizzy looked at him in disbelief. Was that a smile pulling one corner of his lips? "You're—you're actually enjoying this, I think!"

"And you're not?" he said as he reloaded.

"You're just a little bit touched!"

"It keeps me from getting too scared."

"What, the madness or the enjoyment?"

"There isn't much difference from where I'm sitting, honey." He pulled the trigger.

At that instant, the windcraft drifted into heavy clouds and the sound of gunfire became muted. "The fools are wasting powder," Rafe said.

"But even a fool can crash the balloon if he's lucky."

"Keep praying for stronger winds, then. I can walk this fast."

"That I'd like to see."

"It's not so impossible," he said.

Lizzy almost believed him. There was something ethereal in drifting across the sky with a man whose calmness belied the circumstances. Perhaps he could walk the cottony fastness . . . perhaps no bullet could touch him.

But when her gaze fell upon his bandaged hand the exhilaration disappeared. He was a man of flesh and blood. She had seen him injured twice. The third time would be his death. Not even a warrior cheated the devil forever. But maybe *she* could. The devil hadn't reckoned on her bringing a bit of brimstone. She dumped her valise upside down and pawed through the debris.

"What're you looking for?"

"Shh—keep your voice down," Lizzy said. "It's peculiar how sound carries. Don't give them a reference point to shoot at through these clouds.''

''Just what are you trying to locate?''

''Something to throw.''

''Empty more ballast on their heads, then.''

''There's got to be something here I can use for a bomb!''

Rafe looked at her strangely. ''What do you know about bombs, Eliza McCord?''

''Enough to know that lighting this kerosene and throwing in some black powder would come in handy right now!'' She held up the copper kerosene flask. ''Think of the bang!''

''I didn't think you knew explosives.''

''You've forgotten more about me than you ever knew.''

''I knew you had a passion for inventing things,'' Rafe said, ''not for taking life.''

Lizzy snapped up her head. She could barely see him through the vapor. ''You're a fine one to preach about taking life, Rafe Laffite! Which of the two of us kills for money?''

He answered in a voice redolent of wind through a canebrake. ''Though you believe I relish spilling a man's lifeblood, I've never killed without purpose.''

''You never killed at all, when I knew you!''

''That was a lifetime ago.''

''*Our* lifetime ago.''

''Yes, our lifetime.'' Oblivious to his wounded hand, he caught the rail and squeezed until the cane groaned. ''And you can't live with how I've altered.''

Lizzy hurled the copper flask back into the valise, then jumped up and whirled away to stare into the cloud. Through clenched teeth she said, ''The change that's come over you is evil.''

"War influences a man like the moon the ocean tides."

"You cannot blame your guilt on forces outside yourself!"

"No, someday I'll stand alone before the Great Judge to answer for my deeds. I will not apologize. War or no war, as long as I'm alive, the control is mine."

"Ha! It *was* yours, before you threw in your lot with the devil. God won't give you another chance."

"Aren't you the fiery little Calvinist."

"I guess I know which of us is going to hell."

He gripped her by the shoulders and spun her around, forcing her gaze up to his handsome, angry face. Down-curved yet sensuous, his lips could give pain or pleasure with equal ease. The paradox did not frighten her: in the grip of this raging lion, she wouldn't beg for mercy. He could devour her and drop dead with the effort of digestion.

"You are not the girl you were, Eliza, any more than I am the man I was."

"I am not on trial here—I haven't become a mercenary!"

"You have always been a mercenary, lining your pockets with money from your failed inventions."

"Why, you!" She tried to slap his face, but he dragged her right arm behind her back, and when she followed through with a left hook, he caught her with the hand holding the pistol. She felt the cold steel barrel press her forearm.

"Let go of me, you Louisiana swamp fox!" she said.

She tried to butt his chin, but he crushed her to his chest and held her while she writhed and kicked. Losing strength, she stopped fighting at last. Radiating fire and ice, Rafe said, "Damned if you aren't as savage as I, Eliza. Admit it."

"No!"

"Then be cold, if you can."

She saw his intent and tried to lunge free, but his mouth claimed hers. With his tongue he wrested open her lips, then, letting go of her wrists, he encircled her with his arms. She tried to push him away, but his arms were steel shackles.

Slipping one arm down to her waist, he ground her pelvis into his until she could feel every blazing inch of him. Her clothing could not protect her; fire started between her thighs. She moaned as he kissed and fondled her in a licentious rhythm.

The cultured Louisianan who had bound her heart with silken tethers so long ago was now an unholy, ruinous master. There was no gentleness in him—a fierce storm of wanting had obliterated that side of his character. He was a warrior, a throbbing mass of muscle and bone. Such men did not wait for the prize to come; they rushed to take it, to consume it like wine from a broken cask before it could escape into the ground.

She jerked her head aside, freeing her mouth. He did not release her body. "You cannot hide your wildness, Miss Eliza," he said. "I feel it pulsing here."

He dragged up her skirts and found her softness. She could hear his breath coming in short, harsh stabs. It was delicious torment, a maelstrom of rage and passion and pride. Fighting her own desire to let him suck her into the whirlpool, Lizzy arched away from him, but the movement only brought her pelvis against his hardness.

"Have you forgotten the soldiers?" she asked, breathless.

"They can't find us in the clouds. No one can find us. You're alone with me."

He caught the back of her neck and forced her upright

against him. "Look at me, Eliza. See yourself in my eyes. See your own savagery."

But Lizzy saw only his. She felt his pulse racing against her own heart. In a few seconds he would press her down and have his way with her. She couldn't stop him; her body didn't want him to stop. His touch pushed her over the edge . . . yet she was not a mindless animal obeying instinct. She would not give in to nature.

"Your—your father would grieve for you, if he knew what you've become," she said. "The spirit of the Rafe Laffite he sired doesn't fit your skin."

Tongues of fire leaped in his eyes. For a moment his lips compressed, and then the lines around his mouth deepened in a cruel smile. Inside her pantaloons, his thumb pressed her most sensitive place.

In a storm of sexual anguish she cried, "You're a pirate cut from the cloth of your grandfather!"

"I've done things a hundred times worse than Dominique Youx Laffite," he said. The look on his face revealed he was not yet through with such things.

"Let go of me!" she cried. "So help me, I'll flay you like a channel-cat and be dratted before I'll be sorry about it!"

"Flay me, Eliza," he said. "Don't be sorry." He dragged her face close and tongued the corners of her lips. The contact seared her like a torch. He bore her to the floor of the basket.

"You want me, Eliza."

"No!"

And then, glaring into his hot golden green eyes, she saw her plantation house on fire. Brandishing her father's saber, she charged down the steps, but before she could strike the Yankee horseman, he kicked the blade out of her hand. She fought with all her might, but his hands closed on her with bruising strength. Vanquished

183

in the dirt of her front yard, she could help neither herself nor her servants. An orgy of gunfire and coarse laughter punctuated the screams of the Negro women. It seemed demons ravished them. She screamed.

"Eliza! Hold, girl, I won't hurt you—Eliza!" The voice came close and deep, slicing through the nightmare. "Be still, my darling."

She couldn't fight anymore. She had no power, none at all. Everything she loved was gone . . . they had left her not a shred of dignity.

"Come, darling, let me hold you," Rafe said. "Eliza, my love, my love, forgive me."

Rafe had not raped her—that much she was able to separate from the terrible memory. His face was taut with anguish and regret, his long fingers reaching to stroke her cheeks.

"I want you to kill them," she said low. She captured his jaw in her hands. "D'you hear?"

"I'll try."

"Don't just try; do it!" She felt a little mad and didn't care.

"The soldiers won't get you, *ma chérie*." He brushed back her hair. "I called up bad memories. I would take them away if I could."

"Kill them!"

"They're gone, Eliza. Long gone, probably killed in battle already."

"I want to see their bones." She knew she was talking crazy, but she couldn't help it. For two years she'd tried to suppress the memory of that dreadful day, but every so often it leaped out of the shadows. She had plenty of reason to hate the North. Plenty of reason to fight.

"Let me up, Rafe."

He lifted her to the rail. Below, the mists were a thick

curtain against the Yankee riflemen, as if nature hid them until they could strike back.

"I'm not afraid," she repeated.

"I have never seen you afraid, Eliza," he said in French. "Raging like a trapped swan is not fear."

"You know what they did to me," she said, and glared at him over her shoulder. "There, I'm soiled, and you know it now."

His eyes narrowed and a muscle rippled in his jaw. He looked as though he wanted to eat raw flesh. There, he despised her.

"I'm a fallen woman, Rafe Laffite!"

"Don't ever say that again. There is nothing unclean about you—I won't hear such talk! What those bastards did was wrong. What I did was wrong, making you remember. The shame is mine, not yours."

She hardly knew what to say. "But it's the mark of Cain upon a woman."

"Who says so?"

"I've seen enough shamed women to know what I'm talking about—isn't Huntsville occupied by white-trash Yankees?"

"Has someone laid blame at your door, Eliza?"

"I never told a soul."

"Then you've carried the burden by yourself all this time."

"Yes," she said. Impulsively, she lifted her fingers to the angry muscle in his cheek, felt the tremor run through her body.

"If I ever find out they're alive," he said, "I'll kill them with my own two hands."

She believed him. He emanated power even in repose. His worn jacket could not hide his tense, waiting sinews; when they sprang to life, it would be without sound or warning. Woe be to the Yankee in his path.

185

It was enough that he had promised vengeance. Whether or not he did it suddenly didn't matter. "Let us speak no more of it," she said.

Like a fire banked for the night, the anger faded from his eyes. He took her by the hands. "I have much to say to you."

"This isn't the time."

"And when will it come?" His eyes turned a depthless shade of green; his lips parted as though to release a cascade of passion.

He snatched her breath when he looked at her like that. Did he love her, or was it another illusion? He did not blame her for being ravished, but how might he react to the other memory, the one she'd hidden until it was as much a part of her as the nails on her hands?

It was his right to know about his child, yet was it her right to purge her soul at the cost of his peace? After such a space of time, might the confession anger him? It was a question she couldn't answer.

Pulling her hands out of his grip, she stared into cold, white wilderness as desolate as the bottom of her soul.

Chapter Seventeen

She looked like a lost spirit standing apart from him, her slender hands curled loosely over the rail to keep her from floating away. Almost colorless in the fog, her hair flowed around cheeks gone pale as ivory. Clouds veiled her eyes.

Rafe recognized that withdrawn look. She did not want to hear what he had to say, and he could not press her to listen, not after the inner tumult he'd wrought.

When she sighed and touched her forehead, he took her elbow. "Are you ill?"

She pulled her arm away. "No."

Seeking inspiration, he frowned up at the balloon. No help there—the thing was a symbol of all Eliza had done for him. In return, he'd forced her to relive memories best left dead. No hangman could have twisted a stouter rope than he'd done of his own words and actions. She wouldn't forgive him this time.

Sliding his bandaged hand up one of the rough hemp

shrouds, he leaned his head against it. He had engaged her help in order to complete his mission; he had not intended to become involved with her again.

But that was before he'd looked into her eyes and seen the confusion of love lingering in her soul. That sweet aura had wrenched his heart, tied his mind into knots, rent his control. She was like a magnolia flower in a storm, fragile and brave, hard to break, but not impossibly hard. *God forgive me for bruising her.*

His hand throbbed. Instinctively he tightened his grip on the shroud, as a younger version of his hand used to grasp the rosary while he made confession. Would Eliza ever let him do penance?

No more outbursts of passion, he decided. No more promises easily made and easily broken. And the next time she wanted to throw kerosene bombs at Yankee shooters, he'd keep his damned mouth shut instead of climbing into the pulpit to preach her a sermon. Who was he to disapprove of her tactics? As she had so painfully reminded him, *he* was the mercenary. At least, he had been.

"Why is that man chasing us, Rafe? Why?" she asked. "I want the whole truth. I've had my fill of evasions."

"I stole something he wants, Eliza."

"What?" The word was ragged, torn from her throat. "You told me you'd discovered information—not stolen some *thing*. I knew this trip was a charade—that you've used me!"

"No. I didn't steal for my own gain. If I had, I wouldn't have involved you."

Nostrils flaring, she tossed her head and folded her arms. "Indeed? Then why?"

"I have something Davis needs to help us win the war."

"You stole something from Mexico?"

"Yes."

"I fail to see how anything of theirs can help us whip the Yankees. I can imagine a few things that would help *you,* though, like money. Did you steal the emperor's golden crown?"

Rafe clamped his teeth together and looked into the cloud. In his mind, the mists congealed into the treasure vault beneath Maximilian's palace. Gold lay in jaundiced heaps next to the diamond glittering in the glass case.

By the shadow of death, he couldn't bring himself to tell her the truth: he had observed enough of human nature to know what Moctezuma's diamond could do. The thing had power over the mind; it made itself the end and object of existence. Even the great Maximilian had languished over the stone buried in his vault. The diamond had possessed him.

Locks are to keep honest folk honest, he thought. If I lock away the truth, Eliza will never know of the diamond's existence. She'll never burn with covetousness.

With the back of his hand he wiped dampness off his forehead. He noticed that his hand shook slightly, as it sometimes did when he thought too much on the diamond. It was dangerous to take his mind off his mission and focus on the stone itself. He was not immune to greed.

Sometimes he wondered how, when the time came, he was going to hand over a diamond nearly six inches long whose brilliance outdid the noonday sun. Since he had nearly gotten killed taking it from the vault, his blood was on it. Didn't that give him claim?

"Blast my eyes!" he swore, and struck the rail with his fist. He was burning with diamond fever . . . again. Somehow he had to get the priceless stone to Davis, hand it over, and walk away. He was a soldier, he reminded himself sternly. His job was fighting Yankees, not stealing diamonds that could wipe out hordes of people at one blow. He did not want the evil thing.

Feeling Eliza's hand on his arm, he looked around. Her face was so pale it was almost transparent, yet her eyes sparked steel blue. "You're going to tell me if we have gold on board, Rafe Laffite, or I'll jerk open the valve and crash the balloon," she said. "Don't think I won't!"

He suddenly felt better. Angry as she was, her eyes shone with a promise brighter than any diamond. They were warmer, too. He could wrap his soul in them. "You don't need to crash us—you've already brought me down to earth."

"Well?"

"It's not gold, Eliza," he said. He couldn't take a chance on her developing gold fever and demanding to see it. "It's a . . . book."

"Oh, no," she said with a shake of her head. "You can't make me believe that Frenchman would chase after you for a book."

"He would for this one." This time, the lie fell easily from his tongue. "It's his journal, filled with details on his latest weapon."

"A scientific journal?" A wave of acquisitiveness swept the cynicism from her features. "Give me!"

Thunderation, now he'd done it. He could see that to get her hands on a new invention, she would gladly forgo diamonds and gold. "I can't give it to you."

"I don't want to keep it—just look at it!"

"Sorry. No one gets a peep at it but Jeff Davis."

"I suppose he'll have to pay for a peep. You're a mercenary, Rafe Laffite."

"Not anymore."

"I don't believe you."

"I told you before—I stopped soldiering for money when Alabama seceded from the Union. I left Juárez and came back to fight for Joe Wheeler."

"But then you went back to Mexico, and I suppose you're still getting army pay."

"Irregularly, and in worthless greenbacks, honey. I use them to start fires."

"Maybe so, but it seems mighty odd to me that a man fighting for the Confederacy wound up south of the border again. Maybe you needed to supplement your greenbacks with gold."

"You're too cynical. Davis needed a diplomat who spoke French and Spanish, and who wasn't above spying for him."

"That sounds like your horse and bridle, all right. Especially the spying part."

Rafe let that go. If she wanted to hurl barbs at him, let her. He deserved it. Perhaps when she ran out of ammunition they could . . . Hell, they could what? Regain lost trust? Not after what she'd been through. Not after the rape. In a roundabout way, she probably blamed him for it.

Even with that aside, what about her profession of love for Charlie McCord? Had she thought of him while they made love last night? Rafe felt his jaw muscles clench. Jealousy. God, he despised its grip. He'd rather take a sword thrust.

"What's so important about Mexico?" she asked. "I thought they had their own national war to contend with."

"That's exactly why Maximilian would like to woo Lincoln!"

He didn't want to talk about the war. He wanted to question her on their own private duel. To lay some ghosts to rest.

191

"Folks say he'd like to woo Davis," she said, speaking in a rush. Was she trying to repel any foray into the past?

"Folks are hoping for miracles," he said. Maybe the time for truth would come later. "It's Davis who's tried to cozy up to Maximilian ever since the bastard took the throne."

"Nothing's wrong with that—we need an ally."

"It won't be Maximilian," he said. "His power belongs to the king of France—he's Napoleon's puppet, and Napoleon sides with Lincoln."

"Maybe Juarez and his people will kill him. They hate him enough."

"It won't be in time to help our cause."

"You don't know that. You don't have a crystal ball."

Rafe's thoughts flicked to the big crystal hidden beneath their feet. He wished he could lift the false floor to make sure it was all right. Even in its flat steel box, it might have been destroyed by a minié ball.

"I don't need a crystal ball to discern the lay of the land, Eliza. The end is near."

"For us?" She arched her brows and tilted her chin. "Seems that President Davis didn't pick the right diplomat—he should have picked one with more faith."

"I wish faith were all it took to curry the favor of a king." Watching her through narrowed lids, he folded his arms across his chest and leaned back against the gondola. "They require harder currency."

"Mercenary talk again! Maximilian ought to see that our cause is just. I don't understand why he's throwing in his lot with the Yankees."

"It's in his interest to keep us fighting," he said. "You realize that France took over Mexico because the States were too torn apart to stop her."

192

"But why help Lincoln win?"

"Because Benito Juárez, the rightful president, wants to get rid of Maximilian and the French army. Since the emperor is outnumbered and the Confederacy can't spare him so much as a broken-down mule, he's got no reason to bargain with us. He needs the North."

"What would the Yankees gain?"

"Land. Maximilian's promising them chunks of California. . . . And DeCoeur's invention."

She frowned and looked off into space. "What's in the book, Rafe?" she asked at length. "What is this thing Louis DeCoeur invented?"

"If I tell you, will you stop asking to see it?"

"Yes."

He looked into her wide, solemn eyes. He suspected she had her fingers crossed behind her back. "DeCoeur is a madman."

"So I guessed."

"You know only the half of it. He used to brag at court that someone killed him once, but then he rose from the flames like Lucifer's dragon."

"That's horrible. Where did he get such a notion?"

"From real life, I suppose. Shortly after the war started, he was in Pensacola working on a submarine and self-propelled torpedoes for General Bragg."

"He was working for *our* side?"

"Actually, he was engaged by a British cartel. Anyway, a Yankee spy got into the dry dock one night and blew it up. DeCoeur was inside. He's scarred from the neck down. Burns."

"It sounds like a monster story."

"It is." He dropped his voice. "DeCoeur told Maximilian he's an avenging angel sent to breathe fire onto the earth."

"And this weapon he conceived, is it the means?"

"Yes—a bomb. He figures if he follows through on Maximilian's scheme to trade its secret to the North, he'll become commander of the Union forces. He'll get to kill and be adored for it, and Maximilian will have the reinforcements he wants."

"Great balls of eternal fire! No wonder you're so anxious to keep that book—but what about DeCoeur? Even without notes, an inventor ought to be able to reproduce his own work. You should be chasing DeCoeur."

"I'll get him, honey."

She studied him for a few seconds. Rafe sensed her wariness. She wasn't fooled, not completely. She knew he hadn't told her all. "Seems with a weapon like that," she said, "Maximilian doesn't need anyone's help."

"He needs an army to use it, Eliza. Even with a hundred bombs, he doesn't have the manpower to put down the revolt."

"Does the bomb actually exist," she asked, "or did DeCoeur just draw the plans?"

"It exists." Rafe gripped the rail. This part was absolutely true. Everything he was telling her was true, except for the book. "He tested it on some Mexican patriots . . . you don't want to hear about it."

"No, but I want to know what's in that book. Torpedoes chained in rivers don't work half the time—this bomb might not be as bad as you fear."

"This one is used on dry land, and it's full of white phosphorus," Rafe said, "an extremely unstable compound. Heat it much over ninety degrees and it blows sky-high. DeCoeur has to encapsulate it in iron and continually pour water over the casing to keep it cool."

"Not a very practical weapon," she said, making a dismissive gesture with her hand. "You'd blow up your own men."

"So far, he hasn't. As I said, he tries it out on peasants. . . . Phosphorus eats into the skin like lye. You can't get it off.''

She fell silent, though Rafe could sense her battling both revulsion and scientific curiosity. Curiosity won out. ''So how does he set it off? By fuse?''

He had hoped she wouldn't ask that question. ''A detonator,'' he said carefully. ''Long range. No fuse.''

''Ha! There's no such thing.''

Rafe looked over the side. The cloud was beginning to break up. Through the mist he could see patches of mountainside and a railroad cross-hatching. No sign of Yankees.

What if Grant got hold of DeCoeur's white phosphorus bombs? Or, perhaps worse than Grant, the barbarous General Sherman, who had cut a swath of destruction from Vicksburg to Meridianville before Nathan Bedford Forrest stopped him?

Great gods, what *if* Sherman got the weapon? On September second, only a week ago, the bastard had taken Atlanta. If the rumors were true, he was raping Georgia as he had Mississippi. Rafe could imagine him seizing upon DeCoeur's weapon with delight. He must not let DeCoeur reclaim the diamond!

''How does it work?'' she asked.

''DeCoeur has a cast-iron box with mirrors inside. In the center he positions a special . . . crystal. Sunlight penetrates a hole in the top of the box. The crystal gathers the light. I don't pretend to know how, but the mirrors and the crystal produce a single beam that strikes the bomb laid dozens of yards away.''

''Poppycock! Why, it would take a diamond, a huge one, to make a beam of light.'' She shook her head. ''No, no, not even a diamond could do that. You'd have a thousand rays, not one, even with the help of mirrors. Preposterous.''

Good, he'd skirted that obstacle. She'd seized on the truth and discarded it. "Still, I must get the plans to Davis," he said. "Sherman might've cut off Richmond already."

"We've got to try and get some news."

"Tonight, then, when we land."

"Rafe, I think you've gone to a lot of trouble for nothing—this detonator business is incredible," she said. "DeCoeur must have been pulling Maximilian's leg, proposing such an invention. You let him pull yours, too."

"Even without the detonator, there's the phosphorus."

"Yes."

"Knowing how to control it would give the South a powerful weapon," he said.

"A terrible one." He saw her eyes go smoke gray, and alarm cloud her features. "Throw that book away, Rafe!"

He looked into the distance. Moctezuma's diamond with its bloodred center seemed to pulsate through the soles of his feet, as though DeCoeur's own heart quickened it. He should have left it buried in Eliza's garden, where he'd hidden it before breaking into her house that fateful night. *It's not a book,* he wanted to say. A book would be easier to throw away, to forget. Not so the diamond.

And not so his memory. Once he read something, it was emblazoned on his brain like a tintype. Taking advantage of a secretary's carelessness, he had seen DeCoeur's diagrams. Not only did he have to turn over the diamond, but the knowledge of how to use it.

DeCoeur was still after him; he sensed it in his gut. This business of tracking the balloon by heliograph could only have originated with DeCoeur. It was a race to Richmond. If Rafe arrived first, the South would own the key to the most deadly device conceived by man. One slip, and he and Eliza would be dead, and the diamond back in evil hands.

"If there really is such a weapon, what man alive could resist the lure of total power?" she whispered. "Can Jefferson Davis, do you think?"

He smoothed her hair in a vaguely comforting gesture. "The Confederacy doesn't want total power, honey. We just want to be left to choose our own way without these Yankee tyrants ramming their will down our gullets."

"But what's to stop us from treating the Yankees the way they've treated us?" She put her hands over her eyes and shook her head. "I can't believe I'm thinking this way! I hate them—why should I want to fight fair?"

"Honor, honey. You can't blot out your nature."

"I shouldn't care about honor after what's happened to me and my family—after what's happened to my country. I shouldn't! But, dear God, I'm so tired. There's got to be an end to all this. . . . I'm tired of fighting." She dropped her head against his chest as if it were too heavy to hold up any longer. He put his arms around her.

Throw away the diamond, Rafe.

The words came out of the cloud. Half expecting to see a ghost, he stared into the filmy muffler. He felt very damp and cold.

Don't open Pandora's box. Was he going mad?

You'll be responsible for millions of tortured souls. The voice was familiar, still, and small. It reminded him of Charlie McCord's. He cursed his conscience, his imagination. "I *am* going mad!"

"I thought you wanted it that way," Lizzy said without looking at him. "It keeps you from getting scared, right?"

"I'm scared, Eliza," he said, and this time she looked up at him, wide-eyed.

"What are you afraid of—the Yankees? They'll never find us in this fog."

No, it wasn't Yankees. It was his damned sense of responsibility waging war on his soldierly instinct.

"What do you fear?" she asked.

He needed to speak French again, the language his family spoke at home, to make sense of his own convoluted feelings. He needed to feel like Rafe Laffite again, to climb out of this strange soldier suit and back into his own skin. He looked into her eyes, saw her pupils dilate, and noticed the swift pulsing in her temples. Her slight intake of breath did not escape him. Tightening his arms around her, he molded her breasts to his chest. His loins stirred.

"I used to hunt alligators in the swamps around New Orleans," he said in French as soft as the whisper of clouds. "At night, you wait and wait by a black sinkhole with your lantern shuttered and your ears wide open to the slightest sound."

"That's the way I've slept since the Yankees invaded Huntsville," she answered quietly in English. Her eyes lost color, turning gray and hard as flint. "It's a terrible way to live."

"Yes, it tries the spirit." He traced her spine with his fingers.

"You were speaking of alligators."

Her lips were so close, so warm and tantalizing. He felt his body throb against her. "You sit in the pirogue with your line baited with raw meat, waiting for a very long time. Sometimes you think there is no alligator there, that you'll pole home and sleep. At that instant, the water boils and the monster explodes."

"Because you struck him with the pole and woke him

up.'' She looked down at the clouds uneasily. "It was a mistake to move.''

"Yes. While he sleeps, there is no danger. Awaken him, and—''

"—you have the fight of your life on your hands, with no one to blame but yourself. You should have left the alligator alone in the first place,'' she said. "Buy your meat at the butcher's like civilized people do.''

She'd purposely mistaken his meaning. "Is there civility in war? I haven't seen it.''

"Because there is none,'' she said. "Still, you're afraid of waking the alligator.''

"Yes. There are horrors down in that black sinkhole I would rather not arouse. I'm afraid of what will happen when we reach the president and show him the bait.''

"Bait! Great storms of brimstone, you're not a traitor, are you?'' she cried. "Is all this to trap Jefferson Davis?''

"You know me better than that, Eliza McCord.''

"You said 'bait.' It sounded like a trick.''

"I was still thinking about alligators, I guess.'' He fell silent for a moment; then his voice came like the brush of a light breeze, stirring the curls on her forehead. "I had not given much thought to the consequences until now. The more I contemplate handing over the . . . book, the more I hesitate.''

"I guess I'm not the only one who feels the prick of honor,'' Lizzy said in a small voice, as if the admission hurt her.

"Honor sometimes comes in fits and starts.''

"Is there something more you haven't told me? Are you holding back?''

He hesitated the barest fraction of an instant. "No.''

"You're fibbing—you've got something else.''

"If I do, you don't need to know it.''

199

She struck his chest. "There it is again—I don't need to know! What if I yank that valve open and let the balloon fall out of the sky? Would *you* need to know you were about to splatter like a watermelon?"

"It's for your own good."

"When are you going to stop treating me like a half-witted child?"

"When you learn to let well enough alone."

"That'll be the day I give up trying to understand you," she said, and pushed him until he let her go. "By heaven, it won't be long!"

Switching to English, he said, "I don't mean to hurt you, Eliza, no matter how it seems. This is not about you. I've set out to kill a bull alligator with a penknife; if I fail to kill him with the first blow, he'll rip me to shreds."

"You're ripping me to shreds, not trusting me. It's plain as day I'm only useful as long as I have something you want. I don't need a gypsy to read tea leaves in my cup—if I crash the balloon, you'll go off and leave me." She stamped her foot. "Anything for your secret mission!"

"By the Eternal's eye, how can you say something you do not believe?"

"I do believe it! I do!"

He snatched her to him. "Eliza, darling, you know I love you. You know it."

"Stop it! I don't want to hear it!"

"Yes, you do. You want to hear me say it again and again, until it bores through that brick wall between us."

"I wish there *were* a wall between us!"

With his thumbs he caught the angle of her jaw and lifted her face. "Listen to me, love."

"I can't hear you!"

"Your heart hears me."

"It's deaf and I'm blind. I can't see you!" she said, and squeezed her eyes shut.

Rafe kissed her lids. "You do not need to see me to feel my love." Easing his wounded hand down her spine, he massaged her lower back. "I'll give you joy if you'll receive it."

"You can't give me joy without trust."

"I trust my life to you."

"You're holding something back."

"What, my soul? Take it!" He let go of her and ripped open his jacket and shirt all the way to the navel. "Take it."

"I . . . don't . . . want it," she said.

"You deceive yourself."

"Then we'll both play the deceiver, won't we?"

"I want you," he said. "I will not pretend indifference anymore. Not after last night."

"Last night didn't happen!"

"We'll start over tonight, then."

"No, we won't. We're not going to anchor tonight."

"The balloon will sink."

"Not that far. We can fly all night at a low altitude."

"We'll crash into a mountain in the darkness."

Scowling, she turned away. Rafe lifted his gaze to a red-tailed hawk darting through the clouds. Wheeling, soaring, gliding, the bird exulted in its freedom. He would not give Eliza her freedom. . . . He had endured too many years without her to lose her again. When they got to Richmond, it would be the beginning, not the end.

He slipped his arms around her and pulled her close.

Chapter Eighteen

Lizzy wished she could think of a way to stay aloft all night, but as the sun dipped toward the horizon and the gas molecules contracted, the balloon shed altitude like a goose molted feathers. Judging by the half-inch depression of mercury in the barometer, they were within three hundred feet of the ground. If they kept flying they'd lose another hundred during the night, a hazardous loss in hilly terrain. They'd plaster a cliff.

"I wish I knew where we are," she said, examining the compass. "This thing's worthless without a chart."

"We just might be able to remedy that," Rafe said. "Look!"

Three columns of pale gray smoke leaned over a distant hill. "Soldiers?" Lizzy asked.

"It's a camp."

"Yes, but whose side? If they're ours, you'll get arrested the minute you show up wearing that Yankee uniform, and if they're Yankees, we can't just walk in and ask to borrow their maps.''

''Why not?''

''Why not? Are you mad?''

He grinned and took the compass. ''We'll get a bearing on that camp and then we'll see.''

''The man *is* mad,'' Lizzy said, looking heavenward.

''It's been my experience that the Lord protects madmen and dumb animals,'' he said as he sighted along the needle. He snapped the silver lid shut. ''We should pass within two miles of them if the wind doesn't shift.''

''What happens if they spot us?''

''I doubt they will. It's getting too dim to see much, the foliage is too thick, and their minds will be on supper now, anyway.''

Since they had eaten nothing since breakfast, Lizzy was thinking about supper, too, but suddenly she wasn't hungry. At any moment she expected to face another storm of bullets. It didn't take a scientist to figure out the odds against them: one of these times, a Yankee ball would bring them down.

''How can you be so casual about all this?'' she asked.

With his muscular arms folded loosely across his chest, Rafe looked as calm as a cat on a hearthstone. But when he turned his face toward her, she saw he was not indifferent at all. That look was in his eyes again— watchful, confident, cruel. He knew what he wanted and exactly how to go about getting it. All other considerations were secondary.

''Somebody's going to die tonight,'' Lizzy said, shivering.

His lips twisted slightly, as if tasting a bitter acorn. ''Does the idea disturb you?''

"Yes."

"Because it might be us?"

"Us, or somebody down there we've never laid eyes on before. I feel sick."

A look of mingled respect and sadness came into his eyes. "You've seen the elephant, Eliza. It's not romantic, is it?"

"I don't understand."

"You've seen battle—*been* in battle."

She lifted her shoulders in a helpless gesture. "Strange way to fight, from a balloon."

"Easier than from the ground . . . but I suppose you guessed that already. From up here, you cannot see them die."

She dragged air into her lungs and let it out slowly. "I don't want to kill anyone. I don't want *you* to kill anyone." She didn't. The anger that had burned so fiercely in her breast now flickered low, and not even the memory of rape could rekindle it. She was sad and very tired.

"I thought I wanted to see all Yankees dead, Rafe, but I've got no stomach for it anymore. Our whole way of life is gone; nothing we can do will bring it back."

He looked toward the smoke. "I am not interested in retrieving the past, honey," he said, "but in preserving what little we still have. We stand to lose all. *All.* If the Union wins, there won't be a free man the length and breadth of the South. And win she certainly will, if Louis DeCoeur gives Lincoln the bomb."

Lizzy shivered again. This time Rafe noticed, and, snapping open the quilt, wrapped it around her. His hands lingered on her shoulders while his eyes searched hers.

He frightened her. No, his *words* frightened her, she amended, trying to ignore the hot impulses transmitted by his touch. Lowering her eyes, she clasped the quilt tightly around herself. Rafe heaved a soft groan and looked over the side.

As the balloon reached down for the trees, he picked up the anchor, moved aft, and let the line uncoil from his hands. The anchor swung back and forth, lower and lower, its shanks biting treetops. Branches broke and sailed off into space, the gondola bumped and swayed, and wind rushed over the aeronauts as the balloon ceased to move at wind speed.

At last the anchor caught in an immensely tall poplar, sending a flurry of tulip-shaped leaves onto the ground far below. "I don't think that anchor's secure," Lizzy said. "See, it's sliding over the branch. You'd better try to pull it back up."

"I have another idea."

"Don't!" Lizzy said, but it was too late.

Rafe shinnied over the side, hooked one leg around the rope, and began to descend. He knew that if the anchor suddenly pulled free, he might lose his grip and fall; even if he held on, the balloon would drag him along like a marionette until he crashed into a tree.

Ten feet more and he'd enter the treetop. A wind gust tugged the balloon and swayed the tree, but Rafe let himself down until his foot touched leaves.

Crack! The branch broke, the anchor ripped loose, and the balloon took off like a wild horse. Hands clamped to the rope and legs pedaling thin air, Rafe tore out of the tree. He saw the ground rush past in a swirling kaleidoscope of green and black. He was going to crash into another tree. A broken bough aimed at his belly.

It was going to impale him. Half a second from impact, he relaxed his grip and let the rope slide through his hands like a flame. Below him, tree limbs spread like the staves of a parasol; if he struck them at this speed, he would break straight through to the ground.

The anchor was sliding toward him. He clamped down on the rope with all his might; his feet slammed into the iron shanks. A slave to Rafe's sudden stop, the balloon dipped and swung him through the foliage.

He hit the tree trunk a glancing blow. Dazed, he fell onto a branch and with burning hands whipped the line around a limb to secure the balloon. As he sank onto the branch, he noted with surprise that the broken bough he'd avoided was scarcely twenty feet overhead. It had seemed he had fallen hundreds of feet.

"Rafe!" Lizzy's voice came from far away. The leaves hid her and the balloon.

"I'm all right, honey." Feeling something sticky on his palms, he rubbed them down his pant legs, then yelped in pain. He held them up. The bandage was torn off his injured hand. Rope burns blazed on both palms.

"Rafe Laffite! Are you alive?" Fifteen feet overhead, Lizzy appeared on the end of the rope ladder, her tucked-in skirts foaming over the waistband of her pantaloons. Her eyes were wide with alarm.

"Bolts and shackles, Eliza!" he exclaimed, jumping up. "Why didn't you wait for me to fetch you?"

"What, so you could throw me into the tree like you did yourself?" She rapidly descended and stopped beside him. "You shortened my life by two years, you impatient old pickled mule!"

"I'll make it up to you, pet."

"I'll settle for your promise not to do anything else so heroically foolish."

"It will take a kiss to seal that bargain."

Lizzy's smile faded, but cobalt sparks radiated through her irises. Rafe's knees turned to water. "Not even a kiss seals a pact with a wasp-stung fool," she said. "The minute I turn my back, you'll be up to your old tricks again."

"It's what you most admire about me, not so?"

"No," Lizzy said. This time there was no banter in her voice. "*This* is what I most admire." She curved her arms around his neck and pulled his face down to hers. He hesitated only an instant before he began to kiss her, tasting and teasing, his tongue roaming her mouth.

Using the tree trunk behind him for balance, he bent his arms around her waist and pulled her against him. The wind tilted the branches, shook the tree, and whipped up the grass a hundred feet below, yet the danger only heightened his arousal.

She drew back slightly and looked up at him like an animal trapped in a net of its own making. He saw her flick the tip of her tongue between her lips, drawing his kiss into her mouth.

"You are beautiful, Eliza," he whispered. He kissed her again, keeping his eyes half-open. Compelled to explore her every reaction, he couldn't bear not to watch.

"*You're* beautiful, Rafe," she murmured in a spate of emotion.

She had never seen such beauty in a man; he wore his soul in his deep golden green eyes, and shared it in the warmth flowing through his fingertips into her veins. "What a beautiful man you are!"

A muscle throbbed in his cheek and his eyes misted over; then he kissed her again, tenderly but with deep sentience, a lingering motion of love. She let him pull her deep into his embrace, her body coming alive with the pulsating power of him. As his hands drifted down to her hips, he rocked her slowly back and forth, a foretaste and a promise of the loving to come.

He was hard and young and strong. She loved him—

there was no use denying it. She'd thought her heart would stop when he fell into the tree. She could not bear to lose him again.

They parted in silent, mutual accord and began to descend the tree. Rafe was ever near, supporting, assisting, hovering like a guardian angel. Not even the dizzying height could shake Lizzy's confidence. Rafe wouldn't let her fall, let the wind blow as it willed.

The unspoken need between them overrode all other desires, so that when they reached the bottom of the big trunk it was inevitable that they came together, warm and willing, naked in the glowing twilight.

"Do you want me, Eliza?" Rafe asked, and then, "Yes, I think you do."

Chapter Nineteen

Her breath coming in sharp, quick stabs, Lizzy rubbed against him until his respiration grew ragged and he could not restrain the thrusting motions of his hips.

"Are you ready?" he asked, caressing her inner thighs until she grew wet. "You madden me, woman."

No, he wasn't mad; she was. Gripped by a power mightier than reason, she gave herself up. She wanted him, he wanted her, and the past faded away as if it had never existed. There was nothing but the present, nothing but this man, nothing but his pillar holding up the earth.

"Yes, by the great blue, I'm ready!" She rolled on top of him, then down, down onto the thing she craved. Her voice rose to the treetops in a song of consummation, of victory and desire.

"Eliza, my sweet Eliza," he said. "Oh, Cupid's mercy!"

Lizzy arched her spine and let her head fall back,

thrusting her breasts toward his face. Rafe seized them in his torn hands and brought first one, then the other to his mouth, sucking until she begged him to stop. Then, mounding her breasts, he buried his face in the deep cleft between them.

"My beautiful . . . naked . . . Eliza," he said. "I want to blaze a trail all the way down to your belly." Clasping the soft roundness of her buttocks, he began to withdraw.

"No, no!" She rained kisses over his neck and chest. "Don't stop!"

"Just for a little while. I want to taste your honey."

He pulled her up until she rested on her hands and knees, open to his quest. Skillfully, artfully, he titillated her with tongue and lips and teeth, nibbling and licking, guiding her shuddering movements with a firm clasp on her hips.

Lizzy felt as though he were draining her last drop of nectar. She was a flower spread open to the probing tongue of a hornet, her petals quivering with each deep thrust. Husky and unlike her own, her voice seemed to come from a long way off.

"You are mine, Eliza," he said. "This is mine."

Rolling her onto her back, taking her mouth in a red-hot kiss, he sheathed himself. Firm and swollen with passion, he pressed against her, their bodies audibly colliding in frenzied passion. Opening her mouth to his kiss, Lizzy wrapped her arms and legs around him and returned thrust for thrust in a wild torrent of lovemaking. For a long time they coupled with the violence of animals in the forest leaves.

At last Rafe's long body went rigid, and with a mighty cry he opened the floodgates of desire. Lizzy was transported, drowned by wave after wave of wet heat. Her throat aflame, she seized the juncture of his neck and shoulder in her teeth to muffle her screams.

Instead of fading, the ache between her thighs crescendoed; like an unbroken filly she bucked and thrashed, seeking freedom from the heat yet plunging deeper upon it. Rafe held her hips in his strong hands and urged her on.

''Come on, baby, let it go,'' he said hoarsely. ''Don't stop. . . . By Juno, you ought to see yourself! Beautiful! Yes, that's it . . . go on, darling, ride it. It's yours . . . make it work for you.''

Lizzy tried to call his name but she could only gasp and cry out. He was so hard and long and strong . . . she wanted to tell him what he did to her, wanted to beg him to do it always. *Don't ever stop, Rafe. Please, don't ever stop.*

His golden fire burned her to her very core, stripping away all illusion. She knew she had never fooled him, that all these years he must have known she craved him. His eyes could look through miles of wilderness and forest and see into the very bedroom in which she slept. Those eyes had watched her writhe, dream-locked with the man she could never forget.

A white-hot bubble rose from the soles of her feet, consuming inch by inch her belly, breasts, and face, until all at once it burst, filling brain and body with blazes of color and heat. Her body convulsing, she drank his kiss like a flaming draft.

She could not open her eyes. For a long time she lay scarcely conscious of the world, her being entwined with his.

''You broke me, Eliza,'' Rafe said low, stroking her jaw.

She forced her lids open and tried to smile, but tears slid down her cheeks and wet his fingers. ''I broke you? It seems the other way around.''

"You broke my will," he said. "What will you ask of me? Name it and it's yours."

"Anything?"

"Even the moon."

"Are you a genie from the *Arabian Nights* to promise me the moon?" She wanted to laugh and cry—she was not the only one who had lost her senses to the love-spell. "Perhaps you should leave it up there."

"If I can figure out a way to unhook it from the sky, it's yours."

Lizzy glided her fingers over his satiny shoulder and deepened her voice. "I believe, O great genie, that your powers have landed me in the middle of a strange and exotic tale."

"You're telling the tale, my young Scheherazade."

"Am I then?" She rolled up on one elbow, leaned over, and kissed him lingeringly. Then she jumped to her feet. "It's getting dark!"

"The better to ravish you, my dear."

"But the maps—the charts!"

Rafe let fly a single long, drawn-out oath, then climbed to his feet. "Eliza, ever the pragmatist!"

"Somebody's got to keep their wits," she said, and stretched up to kiss him under the chin. He tried to catch her but she skipped aside and grabbed her pantaloons. "Fie! A gentleman ought not to look!"

"I thought I was a genie—they always look."

"Only when appearing suddenly out of smoke clouds. The ground's quite clear where you're standing."

"Is that fog I see drifting out of the woods?" he said, and then his tone became serious. "I'll climb back to the balloon and rescue our equipment."

"Naked?"

Rafe looked down at himself. "It beats the Yankee suit."

212

"It sure does, but it's hardly practical. Think of all those sticks and things."

Rafe pulled a face. Wordlessly they dressed each other, then came together for a last kiss.

"Careful, Rafe."

"Always, baby." He swung into the tree and made his way rapidly out of sight.

Lizzy sat down to wait and hugged her knees to her chest. She swatted a mosquito on her ankle. Still shivering with the remnants of sexual excitement, she had only to breathe to detect his scent in her nostrils. It was the ragged, hot taste of summer passion. She remembered it well.

This time neither had admitted loving the other. The hidden love had bubbled over during their moments of passion when it was impossible to hide anything, yet when the deed was over they had fenced carefully, using jests as foils.

A pang of guilt darted through her. They could not continue to couple like beasts of the field, whispering no words of commitment, and making no pledge. It wasn't right. And yet who was it who feared commitment? Not Rafe. He would have taken her to the altar years ago if she hadn't cast him off. She was the one holding back. She was the one afraid of the future.

Now was not the time to dwell on distant tomorrows. She and Rafe were going off to steal the Yankees' charts, if Yankees they were and if they had charts to steal. She wasn't sure of either, and she wasn't at all sure they could find the encampment.

With night nearly upon them and the camp some two miles off, they stood a good chance of getting lost in the dark. What if they couldn't find the Yankees, and then couldn't find their way back to the balloon?

Rafe surely knew what he was doing. If he could

213

make it all the way from Mexico with nothing but the shirt on his back while a pack of mad dogs snapped at his heels, it would be child's play to find the Yankee camp in pitch-blackness.

"Eliza."

She nearly jumped out of her skin. He was there beside her, his eyes glowing in the twilight. "I wish you'd stop slipping up on me like that—my heart can't take it! How do you do it, anyway?"

"It's an old habit," he said, shrugging as if it was something learned so long ago that he was surprised at her amazement.

"It's a bad habit." She dropped her voice and smiled halfheartedly. "I believe in ghosts, I guess you know by now."

"I know. Maybe I won't say anything next time, just kiss you on the back of the neck so you'll know I am real."

"Rafe!"

"Ghosts don't have lips," he said. "At least, not ones you can feel."

"I wish you'd stop. I've got chilblains on my feet."

"Maybe they need massaging," he said suggestively, but he reached down to take her hand, instead, and raised her. "I begrudge the night. It's getting too dark to see you."

"And too dark to find those Yankees."

"I'll find them."

"You're not leaving me all alone!"

"I can't risk your breaking an ankle or something in the dark."

"What about *your* ankle?"

"I'll be all right."

"I'm going with you." She caught him by the wrist and raised herself on tiptoe, trying to see into his shadowed face. "Suppose a Yankee were to sneak up on me? You saw how easy it is!"

"You're trying to outmaneuver me."

"I'll succeed, too, Rafe Laffite, because you know if you don't let me come along, I'll sneak after you."

"You're a bad woman, Eliza McCord."

"Which is exactly what you like about me."

"Exactly. Come here and let me see how bad you are."

It was several minutes before he stopped kissing her. Lizzy gave a little moan when his lips left hers and he moved back a pace. She couldn't see the passion etching his features, but she'd felt the hammer blows of his heart and knew he wanted her again.

"You win, honey. Come on, and stick close."

He started into the woods. The moon had not risen yet and the darkness was complete except for the sparks of lightning bugs. It seemed they would crash into a tree sooner or later, but Rafe, guided by a sense Lizzy didn't share, walked along steadily. She couldn't hear the sound of his footsteps. By comparison, hers sounded like the tread of a horse. "How're we going to sneak into their camp?"

"We're not sneaking. I'll find a convenient place to stash you, then walk right into camp."

"You'll be arrested!"

"Nope—I'll tell them I'm a messenger from Sherman in Atlanta. I've got documents to prove it."

"What if they spot the fakes? They might torture you or something. Haven't you heard General Sherman's maxim: 'War is cruelty, and you cannot refine it'?"

"Hush, we'll run into pickets pretty soon."

"If we're going the right way."

"We are," he said with certainty. "If we're challenged, I want you to drop down and hide in the undergrowth. Stay there until I come back. I don't want these bluecoats to see you—they may have gotten word to watch out for us.''

''What if they're not bluecoats? One look at that uniform and a Confederate'll shoot you!''

''If they're Confederates, I'll tell them the whole story.'' He didn't sound at all worried, which worried Lizzy. Squeezing her hand, he continued into the blackness. Lizzy stumbled over a root and nearly fell.

''Where'd you get that uniform, anyway?'' she whispered.

''Off a dead Yankee.''

''Laws! That bullet hole in the breast—did you put it there?''

''You think I would kill to get a uniform?''

''I don't know what you'd do—you're not exactly the man I remember.''

''I'm not a murderer, either.''

''I didn't say you were.''

''Eliza.''

''What?''

''Kindly hush up now.''

''It's not so easy, with the woods as dark as the bottom of a spring cave. I have to talk.''

''And I have to leave you here by this hackberry tree.''

''How do you know it's a hackberry? I can't even see a tree!''

He placed her hand on misshapen, tortured bark. Even in the dark the hackberry was unmistakable, a mass of injury and deformity. Lizzy didn't want to stay near it. ''I won't say another word, Rafe. Just take me a little farther.''

She took a death grip on his hand and stayed close behind him, but even the warmth of his back could not dam the river of alarm in her soul. The night was sinister and alive with millions of spirits; the weight of an ocean pressed down on her shoulders. Or was it the weight of unseen hands?

She was moving almost as soundlessly as Rafe, her feet detouring around roots and twigs, finding soft ground like a hunted animal taking on fear-born instinct. Silence was her only shield.

A stick snapped in the blackness. Lizzy's heart bounded against her back teeth. Before she could make a sound, Rafe pushed her to the ground and whispered, "Don't move."

If only she were armed! She felt around on the spongy ground until she located a stick.

"God's nightshirt, where'd you come from?" A rifle hammer clicked. Lizzy couldn't see the owner of the voice so close by. Rafe's foot pressed between her shoulder blades.

"I came from Atlanta. I have a dispatch for your commander."

"Just sit tight a minute, and bear in mind I got you covered."

Lizzy heard a scrape; then a match flared five feet away. Rafe stood between her and the light. Hoping the tangled vines and plants would further obscure her shape, she pressed her face into the dirt.

"Captain, huh?" the picket said, viewing Rafe in the scant seconds before the match went out. He didn't realize Rafe's quick eyes had sized him up, as well. "Willie Sherman's well off enough he can use captains for messengers?"

"I was the only one stupid enough to volunteer," Rafe said. "The rest of them wanted to stay in Atlanta, raising hell and sampling the fare."

"Any women left, Captain?"

217

"A few fancy ladies."

"Business good?" the soldier asked with a chuckle.

"Booming, but I haven't time to stand around jawing about it. Who's your commander?"

There was a short silence. Lizzy held her breath, imagining the long rifle pointed at Rafe's middle. Even in the dark, the soldier couldn't miss—he had struck a match to be sure of Rafe's position.

"I asked who your commander was."

"What the devil? Where'd you go, sir?"

"Over here, Corporal." Rafe's voice came from several yards beyond the picket.

"Dammit, sir, you can't move until I tell you to move! I got to check you out, first."

"Either you show me to your commander or I'll go myself and report you for dereliction of duty," Rafe said. "This is no cotillion; I'm too damn tired to dance with you all night."

The soldier struck a second match. Rafe was already moving ahead of him toward the camp. "Wait up, sir! You can't go down there without an escort!"

Lizzy let out her breath. The stick was still clenched in her hand, her fingers wrapped around it so tightly she couldn't let go. She stood up and with careful steps began to follow the dancing match glow. Lightning bugs flitted across her path and fizzled out in the woods, but she kept her gaze on the match.

She was crawling over a log when the match went out. From ahead there was no sound but the chirring hum and screech of insects. Should she sit tight and wait for Rafe or try to follow him in the dark? The insects grew louder, locusts shrilled a deafening cadence, and filmy things brushed her face.

Ghosts. They haunted woods like these. Her old mammy used to tell her stories about them when she was small. Maybe it was their shrouds she felt brushing her. "Dear God!" she exclaimed under her breath. The stick dropped from her fingers with a dry, powdery thump. Losing her nerve, she jumped off the log and sped blindly after Rafe. She could see the match again. She ran after it as fast as she dared.

She followed it straight into a curtain of long, fibrous wisteria vines. She'd been following a lightning bug! Or was it a ghost's lantern? She tore loose and took off again. The matches were everywhere, dancing and floating in black space. Briers tore her clothes and scratched her shoulders.

She couldn't stop, not with the woods full of haunts. She had to keep going even if it meant stumbling straight into the Yankee camp and finishing out the war in prison. Even that was better than the nameless horror clutching and clutching. . . .

The ground disappeared beneath her feet. For a second she thought ghosts had lifted her into the air. Then with a mighty splash she came down in a stream. As she struggled to get up, cold mud closed over her hands and sucked at her legs.

She heard something plop into the water nearby. Then came a second plop, the long, heavy sound of snakes dropping off a branch. She felt the water moving, lapping her thighs. The snakes were coming after her.

Chapter Twenty

Rafe walked into the camp with the Yankee picket dogging his heels. Golden puddles of fire shimmered between scores of white tents pitched among the trees. In the quiet time between supper and the sounding of taps, soldiers played cards and harmonicas. Others sat side by side yet solitary, writing to loved ones far away.

Infantry, Rafe thought. A veteran outfit from the looks of it. There weren't a hundred tents in the whole camp, a sure sign of a regiment that had gone to hell and crawled back with just a tithe of its number.

Rafe slowed his pace to let the picket catch up. In the firelight, the soldier's eyes glittered like a muskrat's, small and ornery. Greasy strips of hair decorated the perimeter of his kepi. He was caked with grime from his forage jacket collar to the creases of his half boots.

"Thisaway to the commandant's quarters," he said.

A large tent with Union colors draped from a pole stood close to the trees. Through its open doorway Rafe glimpsed a man at a folding desk. He dipped his quill into a pot of ink by his right elbow and resumed writing.

A grandfatherly man in white whiskers and a blue frock coat, its epaulettes glinting with silver eagles, paced behind the scrivener, dictating short, sharp sentences, occasionally pausing to watch his words scratched down.

The picket moved to the doorway and thumped his rifle butt on the ground. The colonel looked around. Rafe saw that the grandfatherly impression the man had conveyed was false; there was cold blue steel in his eyes and cruel cuts beside his mouth and nose.

"Yes, what is it? Who is this man?" His voice was as cold as his stare.

"He appeared in the woods, Colonel Williams, sir. Says he gots a dispatch from General Sherman."

Williams took Rafe's measure. Rafe was aware that his appearance—hair awry, cheeks bearded, clothes torn—made him look as though he'd been on the march a long time. Exactly the effect he wanted.

"Come in here, Captain."

Rafe ducked his head to enter the tent, and snapped to attention. The picket remained outside.

"Have you got a name?" Williams asked.

"McLeod, sir. Benjamin McLeod. Twentieth Corps."

Williams switched his gaze to his scribe's lettering. For half a minute he remained silent. Rafe felt a rivulet of sweat trickle down his spine. His stomach growled loudly in the silence.

The colonel fired a glance at Rafe's middle. His query came like a rifle volley: "How long have you been traveling?"

"Three days, sir."

"Where's your horse?"

"Broke her leg crossing a creek."

"You shot her, I suppose." Again his gaze flashed to Rafe's belly.

Rafe forced a weary smile. "Sorry, Colonel, I should have taken it out when I walked into camp." Easing his hand into his jacket, he brought out Jack Daniel's pistol and dangled it by the trigger guard. "Lost my belt in the creek, too. I was lucky to save the gun."

Williams took it. "This isn't army issue."

"No, sir. It's a homemade Rebel piece. Got it when we stormed Atlanta."

"We were there, too." Williams grimaced as though reliving a wicked memory. "Is it true what they say, that now the shooting's stopped, Sherman's boys have turned the city into a brothel?"

"Er, yes, sir. They're not going hungry or lacking for creature comforts."

Williams stared into his eyes a long minute. Rafe looked back unwaveringly, his posture militarily correct yet relaxed enough to give the impression of tiredness. His stomach growled again.

"Corporal," Williams barked at the picket, "get our guest some supper before he starves to death before our eyes, and give him something stronger than coffee." He turned to his scribe. "Out."

Hurriedly sprinkling sand on the ink and blowing it off, the scribe then gathered the papers and pushed them into the desk. Before he closed the lid, Rafe spotted several rolled documents. Maps?

"Sit down," Williams said, gesturing at the vacated camp stool. He sighted down the pistol barrel. "Where's the dispatch?"

Rafe thrust his hand into his bosom and pulled out a scrap of paper stained with pokeberry juice ink.

"Did you read it?"

"No, sir."

Diamond

"You didn't, eh? Smart young fellow like you?"

"I follow orders, sir. Curiosity's not part of the script."

Williams tossed the pistol on the cot and took the note. He read it without expression. Rafe breathed slowly. In a few seconds he'd learn if he was to be guest of honor at a firing squad.

The picket came back with a tin plate heaped with beans, salt beef, and dessicated vegetables boiled to a sickly yellow paste. He placed a cup of coffee on the desk. "Cookie poured a dram of rotgut in it, sir," he told the colonel.

"By your leave, sir?" Rafe asked.

Williams flicked his hand. "Don't stand on ceremony, soldier. Eat before you fall over."

Rafe started on the spiked coffee. The first sip shot wildfire through his veins. When the colonel wasn't looking, he slipped the beef into his jacket for Lizzy.

"So General Johnston's threatening the interior, is he?" Williams said, staring at the forgery. He crushed the paper. "By gum, I'd like to get my hands around his rebellious neck and squeeze him to death in front of his men!"

"You might get the chance to do that, sir."

"I thought you didn't read this."

"General Sherman briefed me before I left just in case I lost the dispatch. He's mad as sin about Johnston escaping his net, but he doesn't intend to repeat the mistake the Rebel, General Hood, made at Atlanta in sending his force off on a wild-goose chase."

"He'd damned well better keep his mind on the objective," Williams said, "and lay waste to Georgia."

Rafe felt his jaw tighten. So Sherman planned to repeat his Mississippi march of death and destruction, did he? *Hell's bells.* "He hasn't forgotten, sir, but he's

223

afraid that by the time he reaches Augusta, Johnston will have moved into Pennsylvania. If Johnston gets through the Watauga Gap he can move straight up the Cumberlands."

"I'm aware of the topography, Captain McLeod."

"Of course, sir, but as you can see from the dispatch, Sherman wants you and other regiments scattered around the state to stop Johnston."

"My name's not on the dispatch."

"I had orders to give it to you, sir. That's all I know."

Williams tugged his beard and turned a pace or two around the room. Then he shoved a black felt hat trimmed with a gold bugle over his eyes and stalked out of the tent. He didn't trouble to see if Rafe was following.

Rafe glanced at his pistol on the cot, scowled, and left it. As he strode after the colonel, the picket and a dozen soldiers fell into step behind him. He walked on in apparent unconcern.

But his step faltered near the edge of camp. He knew where Williams was leading him now; he should've known the wily old coot wouldn't blindly accept his word.

Looking like a woman in hoopskirts standing on her head, a two-wheeled signal wagon with white canvas sides rested on its tongue. Two signal corpsmen slept beneath it on gutta-percha ground cloths.

"Get up from there," the colonel said.

When they didn't awaken fast enough, he kicked the soles of their boots. They crawled out fast then, cursing, and snapped to pained attention when they saw who'd kicked them. The onlookers laughed.

Rafe didn't smile. He had reason to loathe the U.S. Signal Corps; its own army did not. In his experience, the Yankee fighting men had about as much use for the corps as a hog for a Sunday suit.

"You received any intelligence of a Confederate force near the Watauga Gap?" Williams demanded. Outwardly calm, Rafe waited for the answer he knew would come.

"No, sir."

"Heard anything interesting?"

"Nothing for two days, sir, not since that Rebel balloon sighting."

Rafe turned a poker face toward the colonel now staring at him. "Seems peculiar the signalmen haven't heard the news," Williams said.

"We haven't tapped into a telegraph line for two days, Colonel," one of them said. "Need to get closer to a railroad, if you'll pardon my saying so."

Williams ignored him. He moved a pace closer to Rafe and stared up at him as if he could suck the truth through his teeth. "Your name isn't McLeod."

"It's the name I was born with, Colonel—"

"And you haven't done much of a job disguising that Southern accent of yours."

"We're not all Rebels, sir."

"Shut up! Something about you stinks to heaven and I intend to find out what it is. Corporal, arrest this man!"

"You're making a mistake," Rafe said.

"Am I? We'll sort that out in the morning." He snapped his fingers. "Put him in the stockade."

Rafe almost raised his big fists to the soldiers closing in on him, but reason held him back. He stood no chance against so many. Better to act like an aggrieved innocent until he could escape.

The men laid hold of him and started dragging him off. "Just you look over that dispatch, Colonel," Rafe shouted back at him. "You're bound to discern the truth if you'll just look!"

Colonel Williams snorted like a bull and turned to the signalmen. "In the morning, take a squad and get that flying telegraph of yours set up. Contact Sherman. I want to get to the bottom of this. If McLeod's as full of hish-hash as I think he is, we're going to give the firing squad a little practice right around lunchtime."

The snake hissed. Lizzy jerked her hands out of the mud and surged through the water. The thing was going to get her—it was swimming after her—she knew it! The mud opened beneath her feet and sucked her down. Crying with terror, she fought its grasp until she managed to twist her fingers in the roots of a cottonwood and scramble out of the water.

The woods were silent. There were no snakes, no ghosts, nothing but silence. Even the lightning bugs were gone. She didn't dare stay here by the stream— Rafe wouldn't find her in the dark. She had to find the Yankee camp, had to find Rafe.

For a long time she wandered in the darkness. Just as she was beginning to lose hope, she heard faint singing. She hurried toward the sound until she saw campfires through the trees. She eased to the edge of the trees and dropped to all fours.

Soldiers were everywhere among the tents, roaring the chorus of the loathsome ditty she'd heard to exhaustion in Huntsville. "Down with the traitor, up with the star! Shouting the battle cry of freedom!"

She had to find Rafe. If he left camp without her, she'd never find her way back to the balloon. He'd waste precious time trying to find her, and perhaps get killed. Drat it, why hadn't she stayed put as he'd told her?

Rafe wanted maps. Where would the Yankees keep

them? If she found the maps, she'd find Rafe. She moved along behind the trees until she saw a large sibley tent with a Union flag dangling beside it. She didn't recognize the standard hanging from a second pole, but the limp campaign streamers told her it was a regimental flag. *The regimental commander. Who else would keep maps?*

She didn't see anyone close by, so she crawled out of the undergrowth to the back of the tent and pulled up a tent peg. Through the crack she could see an oil lamp flickering on a field desk, casting grotesque shadows on the walls. The tent was empty, so she enlarged the opening and squeezed inside.

Jack Daniel's pistol glinted up at her like the eye of a dead man. With shaking fingers she lifted it from the cot. Dear God, what had happened to Rafe? Where was he?

"Somebody there?" a voice hollered from outside.

Lizzy dove under the cot just as the tent flaps snapped open. She lay still, grasping the pistol in sweaty palms, her heart hammering in her throat. Would he see her under the cot?

"I could've sworn I heard something in here," he said.

"Maybe it was a rat, sir," came a second voice, higher than the first.

"Aye, a rat. Go on, Corporal, back to your post. I'll call you if I need you." Lizzy heard the flaps swish shut, then a scraping sound. He was tying the flaps shut. She tried to melt into the tent wall at her back. Would the shadows hide her?

As the man moved into the room she saw his shiny Jefferson boots. The cot blocked her view of the upper half of the man, but she saw blue uniform trousers with a light blue stripe down the welt, and the tails of a frock coat.

Dear Lord, if he squats down he'll see me.

The boots turned, paused, then moved to the center pole. Steel shrieked, setting her teeth on edge. The point of a sword swept the ground by the boots.

Cold waves of terror washed over Lizzy. The man knew she was there. He was going to slice her up with the sword. She turned her fist to aim the pistol at his right knee. The throbbing of her heart made the barrel waver.

Suddenly the Yankee rammed the sword into the ground and let go. The blade vibrated like a tuning fork. The boots remained beside it.

Lizzy tightened her finger on the trigger. If he touched the sword again, she'd shoot him in the feet.

The boots moved to the cot and stopped. Lizzy saw the red dust powdering the crevice between the sole and upper. Lampblack and neat's-foot oil vied with the stench of sweat and mildew.

He turned, grinding his heels into the dirt inches from her face. The cot creaked as he settled onto it. The center bulged until it touched Lizzy's head. She battled a powerful urge to raise the pistol and shoot him right in the backside.

She heard a sharp sigh. Then the cot shifted and groaned as he stretched out. She could see the sword still quivering in the ground.

Her jangling thoughts gradually slowed. She could get away after he went to sleep, but she'd come here to find Rafe and the maps. She wouldn't turn tail and run just because the regimental commander had walked in and nearly caught her. If anyone knew where to find Rafe, it would be the man above her.

She waited until his breathing became a snore. Fearing she'd find him awake and staring at her, she eased out just enough to peep over the edge of the cot. He was asleep. She inched out of hiding.

He wasn't frightening at all. With his whiskers splayed upon his chest and his mouth open, he looked like a little old man. She was ashamed of herself for almost shooting him.

"I was wondering when you'd finally crawl out of there."

The steely voice pinned her to the ground. She stared into eyes like frost on a pump handle. There was nothing paternal about him now. Lizzy scuttled away as fast as she could and leveled the pistol at his stomach.

He sat up and swung his feet to the ground. Although he rested his hands on his knees and didn't try to stand, he looked like a lion ready to pounce.

"Stay where you are!" she whispered hoarsely. "Move a muscle and I'll part your hair!"

The man's smile was as cruel as the silver eagles on his shoulders. "Don't threaten me, young woman."

"I'm not threatening, Colonel—I'm promising. There's a sight of difference in the two!"

"You fire that thing and you'll bring the whole camp down on your head," he said. "Now what do you want?"

"Where's Rafe Laffite?"

His smile grew even meaner. "Ah, your traveling companion. We locked him up half an hour ago."

Lizzy tightened her trigger finger. "Locked him up where? Where is he?"

He went on as though he hadn't heard. "You're Dizzy Lizzy McCord, the quaint lady inventor. The entire army's been watching you. You don't think that blue gasball of yours is invisible to the Signal Corps? Poor naive little girl."

"How'd you like to get your brains splattered all over the tent? Now you take me to Major Laffite!" But he folded his arms and looked her up and down, mocking her.

"What are you smilin' at?" she demanded, her accent thick with outrage. "Don't you know better than to smile at a woman with a gun aimed at your head?"

"It's not loaded, Eliza." Rafe stepped into the tent behind her.

She had the satisfaction of seeing the colonel's smile melt like tallow. Rafe sprang at him before he could shout, and pressed the tip of a short artillery sword against his throat.

Rafe looked like he'd been in a fight. His uniform was ripped and his cheek bruised. A broken piece of rope dangled from his left wrist. "Get the maps out of the desk, Eliza. You'll probably find cartridges and balls for that pistol. Load it."

"Don't open that desk, young woman!" Williams said.

Lizzy found the ammunition. She bit off the end of a cartridge, poured in powder, and rammed home the wad and ball. Then she found the maps and unrolled them just enough to see what they were. "Orders of battle and terrain maps. This is what we wanted, Rafe, and then some." Rolling them up, she thrust them under her arm. "You're not smiling anymore, are you, Yankee?"

"Don't talk to him," Rafe said. "Just blow his head off if he tries anything."

"With pleasure," she said, and cocked the weapon. She was surprised at how nasty she felt. Nothing like a loaded gun to fill a body with power.

"There's a soldier outside," the colonel said, although the power was gone from his voice.

Rafe's smile came and went like the twitch of a cougar's tail. "He's asleep, sir."

"Blast and damn his lazy soul!"

"Don't be too hard on him, sir. I didn't give him much choice about sleeping. He'll probably require a compress on his head when he comes to."

Williams folded his arms and worked his jaw muscles. His teeth made a grinding noise.

Rafe found a rope in the field trunk and bound him to the cot. He stuffed rags into his mouth. "Your bugler will sound taps pretty soon, Colonel. You don't have to stand at attention."

Instead of taking the artillery sword, he jerked the colonel's sword from the ground. It was a silver presentation piece, its hilt shaped like a naked woman. "Magnificent. What balance!" He slid it into the scabbard, then secured it at his right hip with the colonel's yellow-fringed sash. "You can have mine in exchange."

"Let's get out of here!" Lizzy uncocked the pistol.

"We were just on our way. Until we meet again, Colonel, may the road rise to meet you."

They slipped out of the tent and ran into the woods. Holding his hand, Lizzy ran behind him for a long time. She heard a bugle in the distance. Rafe didn't slow down.

How would he find the balloon when they seemed to be traveling a different route? It was a mystery, but Lizzy was convinced he'd find it. He'd found her, hadn't he? And they had the maps. A conviction grew in her that Rafe could do anything. Maybe even pull the moon out of the sky.

She was falling head over heels in love with him again, and this time there was nothing she could do about it. She didn't want to do anything about it. *Just*

*love me back, Rafe. Don't let go this time no matter what
I do or say.*

Distant shouts and the bark of a rifle told them the
hunt was on. Lizzy's legs felt stiff as barrel staves, trying
to keep up with Rafe's long stride. He held tightly to
her hand until they reached the tulip poplar. "This is it,
honey. Let me boost you up."

They cast off less than three minutes later. The balloon moved sluggishly away from the treetop and drifted
east. While Rafe watched the ground for Yankees, Lizzy
stared forward, her fingers white as piano keys on the
crown line, prepared to warp the canopy if they slid too
close to a tree. Provided she saw it in time.

"Throw off ballast, Rafe! We've got to go higher."

Rafe emptied all the bags. Ponderous as an elephant,
the balloon bumped into a rising current of air. Pine
needles brushed by a foot below the basket. "Dear Lord,
trees we can handle, just don't let us meet up with a
cliff," Lizzy murmured.

"Sounds like I ought to pray, too, Eliza."

"Do you remember how?"

"Times like these bring back a potent lot of memories."

"Then pray. Pray like your soul depends on it." She
didn't expect him to; he only called on the Lord's name
to preface a curse. She was startled when he began to
pray.

"Thank you, Lord," he said, "for bringing us through
this far. And thank you for this unusual lady. She's like
Elijah flying this chariot. . . . I love her." His amen
reached up through the soles of his feet and resonated
on the warm air.

She wasn't ready to face his declaration. "He—he
probably hasn't heard someone pray from the air since
Elijah dashed off in the wheel of fire," she said.

Moving behind her, Rafe dropped his arms around her waist and lowered his head to the hollow of her shoulder. Lizzy trembled. It was hard to concentrate with Rafe's warm mouth on her. His tongue traced the side of her neck.

"Is that the way to act after communing with the Lord?" she asked.

"It's the only way," he said.

Lizzy gave up the fight and leaned back against him. The balloon floated on. There was no sound from below.

"Look at the stars," Rafe said. "Silver dust on black velvet."

"They look like diamonds to me."

She felt him stiffen, his muscles instantly tense and wary. Fearing they were about to crash, she jerked away and caught the crown line.

"It's all right, honey," he said, catching her hands before she could pull the line. "No danger."

"What's ailing you then?"

"You are," he said in a husky whisper. Turning her to face him, he brought his mouth close to hers. "And you've got the cure."

Through a shimmering golden blue cloud the sun broke over the mountains. Caught in soft whirlpools, the balloon swirled along valleys that switched back and twisted as though undecided where to run.

Watching both the compass and the barometer, Lizzy knelt on the floor. Rafe studied one of the maps, then shot the sun with a sextant he'd stolen from the Yankee signal wagon. After comparing the reading to Lizzy's chronometer and figuring the logarithm in his head, he pointed out their longitude on the map. "If we keep to our present course," he said, frowning, "we'll go right past Chattanooga in an hour or two. Maybe through the middle of town.''

''Isn't it in Yankee hands?''

He didn't answer, just nodded and looked out across the landscape. Here and there, smoke rose from farmhouses nesting on hillsides shorn of trees. Unnaturally loud, a dog's bark sounded as though it came from right beside the balloon. Smells were strangely acute, too: somebody was frying sausage.

Lizzy didn't want to dwell on what might lie over the next mountain. Rafe had that look on his face again, the look that made her gut twist and her fingers itch for a gun. They were going into battle again. She could feel it. Acid trickled into her stomach and burned her throat. If only there were a way to steer the balloon, to drive it so high and far and fast that no Yankee could spot it, let alone shoot at it.

''You'd better eat something,'' Rafe said.

''I'm not hungry.''

''It doesn't matter. Here's some corn bread and beef I got last night.''

''What will you eat?''

''I ate with the colonel, right before he got suspicious and arrested me.''

Rafe wondered if he ought to tell her about the heliograph he'd stolen from the signal wagon. No, she'd cook up some scheme to use it before it was necessary. Her scientific urges were never far away.

He wanted to explore other urges. He hadn't made love to her last night—flying in the dark was too risky—and he intended to remedy the situation soon. She needed to be kissed and loved, often and hard. He planned to make it his life's work.

He could hardly keep his mind on his mission. The diamond dwindled to a worthless piece of glass beside her. It didn't matter that she was covered with dirt and her hair looked as though no boar-bristle brush would ever untangle it again. All he saw was the fiery woman he loved.

Did she love him? He'd been a cad to mention his feelings in vocal prayer last night, and then he'd been too reluctant to follow up when she didn't respond to his gambit. He wondered if she'd stay mad at him forever. Her father had forgiven him; why not her?

She was studying the instruments again, her fingers crumbling the corn bread to chicken feed. Her nervousness sent a pang through his heart. What a good-for-nothing bastard he was to put her in harm's way. There would be a reception committee in Chattanooga; of that he was certain.

He twirled a lock of her hair between his thumb and forefinger and said, "You look like you fell into a creek last night."

"I sort of stumbled through one on my way to find you."

"It happens."

"You didn't have such an easy time of it, either," she said. "You ought to see that bruised cheekbone of yours, and your hair looks like a colony of rats took up residence in it."

"I guess I should've borrowed the colonel's hat while I was collecting things."

"You should have," she said. "You'd look a sight better, even in that awful Yankee uniform you're so fond of."

"You don't mean to be half as ugly as you talk, Eliza."

"If you're trying to rile me, I'm too tired."

"Then you won't try to fight me if I steal a kiss?"

Her smile struck him like a sunbeam through a rain-

cloud. "I'll fight you if you *don't* try, you randy old lion, you."

He knelt beside her and pulled her close, taking her mouth in a deep kiss. It was some time before either glanced up again. When they did, Lizzy breathed a low cry of alarm.

The rugged brow of Lookout Mountain jutted against the sky, its slope plunging to the stark sprawl of Chattanooga. Rafe slitted his eyes. "What a heartbreak to lose that mountain!"

Lizzy bent her hands over the rail as the big mountain came closer and closer, its treeless slopes pockmarked by huge boulders and blackened stumps. The town seemed to float in the silt of the Tennessee River sliding around Moccasin Bend. A thick pall of smoke overhung the scene like the winding sheet of a corpse.

"Do they have cannons up there?" Lizzy asked.

"Right along the ridge. They belonged to our boys before we abandoned the mountain in the battle above the clouds."

"I wish we had more ballast to drop," Lizzy said. They were going to pass less than three miles from the ridge. She dragged on the crown line but the balloon barely altered course. "Do you think they'll shoot at us?"

Rafe didn't respond. On the crest of the mountain a signalman was wigwagging. White with a red square center, the flag was visible for miles. Rafe saw a wigwag answer from a distant hill.

"Can you read it?"

"No," Rafe said. "They're using code."

"That colonel said the whole Union army is watching us." Lizzy raised the spyglass. Her voice cracked as she said, "I can see the cannons."

"They're not going to blast away with the cannons, Eliza."

"No, just rifle fire. Either way, we're dead."

Fulfilling her prophecy, a shot cracked from the town below. In a blaze of anger, Lizzy shook her fist over the side. "Leave us alone, you corn-fed sons of coots!"

"Quit making yourself a target; pull your head back!"

"What difference does it make if I get shot now or later? We can't fly over a whole townful of Yankees!"

"Can you get us to the river?"

"Why can't you just accept fate?" she screamed back.

"I'm not made that way, and neither are you, Eliza McCord. Now give me that line!"

But instead of handing it over, she hauled on the crown line as though she'd roped a steer. "Come on, balloon! Move!"

Rafe caught the line above her hands and added his strength. The balloon revolved, dropped a few feet of altitude, then encountered wind spiraling off the river. The craft switched ninety degrees toward the giant Moccasin Bend. A bullet whistled through the shrouds.

"Come on, baby. Go!" Rafe shouted.

The current swept them along faster, pulling them toward the upper bend of the river. Lizzy didn't know what would happen once they reached it. She and her father had almost drowned in the Tennessee one time when a downdraft had plunged them into it.

Boom!

The aeronauts twisted around to see a puff of smoke bloom on the mountaintop. A noise like a train shook the balloon. Trees exploded on the boot-shaped island in the river.

"I thought you said they wouldn't fire the cannons!"

"I'm as surprised as you are, honey."

237

She ought to jerk the release valve to let off gas. Better they should drop into the Yankees' laps than get shot out of the sky.

"Come on, move!" Rafe said. With all his might he yanked the crown line. It made no difference. Again the cannon thundered, and once more a ball crashed onto the island. Small-arms fire rattled like dried black-eyed peas in a pan.

As the balloon approached the river, the temperature change between land and water created turbulence. Like a cork on a wild ocean, the craft dropped down invisible troughs, then leaped to the crest with a suddenness that dropped Lizzy's stomach into her toes.

Rafe pulled the heliograph out of his jacket and extended the viewing loop from the brass arm. The mirror shot stabs of sunlight everywhere as he jiggled it.

"Where'd you get that? What are you saying? Can they read it? What if nobody understands?" Lizzy demanded. "Why didn't you use it a while ago?"

"Hold your fire," Rafe said, interpreting his message. "We're on a secret mission. Don't shoot."

"They won't believe that!"

"Have they stopped firing?"

"Yes . . ."

"Well, then." He kept flashing the message. "I guess we've confused them."

Gradually the balloon skipped around the muddy banks to the northeast, running away from the river toward the mountains.

At last Chattanooga disappeared, smudged into the mist. Lizzy slid to the floor and shut her eyes. "God's on our side, that's plain. That was some prayer you spoke last night."

"It was your prayer He heard. I'm just a heathen."

"Nobody stays heathen who flies through the middle of a lead hailstorm in a balloon."

Rafe sank down beside her and took her face in his hands. He rocked her head gently from side to side. "Brave heart."

"Brave as a chicken heart."

"A mighty big chicken heart, then."

"Just you keep praying, Rafe Laffite, and maybe we'll get through this little misadventure of yours." She shook her head. "My stars, such trouble for a book!"

Rafe's slight hesitation brought the blight of doubt to her mind. She pulled back.

"Louis DeCoeur's book," Rafe said. "Trouble, yes, but worth every drop of sweat."

"If I sweat much more I'll dry up and float off without the help of this balloon."

"I'd best tie you to a shroud, then."

He'd meant her to take his words lightly, she supposed, but the undercurrent of sensuality made her tingle. It seemed that the worse the peril, the tinglier she became.

"Kiss me, Rafe Laffite," she said, pressing her mouth to his. "Kiss me like you mean it."

"I do mean it, baby." And he did.

As the sun climbed, the winds unfurled, driving the balloon along like a great schooner. Clinging to the shrouds, Lizzy leaned out to gaze up at the great blue sail skimming the clouds.

It seemed impossible that the balloon had survived another Yankee assault, yet there it was, pregnant with rosin gas, riding over the obstacles. It was traveling faster than it had in two days.

Lizzy looked down her nose at Rafe, who was studying the ground through a pair of brass binoculars. "Where did you get those?"

"Same place I got the heliograph. From the United States Signal Corps. Generous bunch."

"I hope you didn't have to kill anybody to get them."

Rafe lowered the glasses and looked at her with faint bemusement. "Was that you I heard last night, threatening to blow the colonel's brains out?"

"I wouldn't have done it."

"Sometimes it's only necessary to threaten to get your way." The creases beside his mouth deepened. "In my case, I didn't even have to threaten. Once I broke out of their pitiful stockade, it wasn't hard to go over to the signal wagon and help myself to their equipment. The boys were asleep."

"Wasn't much sense waking them up just to borrow a few things," Lizzy said.

" 'Help yourself' is their motto."

He returned the glasses to his eyes, but this time he didn't scan the ground. He scanned Lizzy instead, from the tips of her shoes to the top of her head. Grinning, he focused on her breasts. Without her camisole beneath, her thin gown left very little to his imagination.

"You ought to be horsewhipped, Rafe Laffite," she said. "You really are shameless."

"I was just using scientific instruments to broaden my knowledge. I thought you wanted me to show a little more interest in the subject." He lowered the binoculars, his eyes flashing. "But then, I don't need the help of these things to examine your finer points, Eliza."

"You certainly don't—you need spectacles, instead." Lizzy held her filthy skirts away from her. Her left sleeve was gone, torn off last night during their mad dash through the woods. "I look like I've been wallowing with hogs."

"A little soap and water . . . some perfume . . . a little more soap and water . . . In six weeks you'll be good as new."

"At which time you'll be ready for your yearly bath, provided we can round up enough boiling water."

"We've got time—I'm not due till January." He ran his hand down her bare arm, then back up, slipping his warm fingertips under the strip of material over her shoulder. When he let his thumb slide down to the curve of her breast, she rose on her toes and sighed. Very slowly he withdrew his fingers and returned them to her naked arm.

His touch burned like a brand; she could still feel the imprint of his thumb on her breast. His voice—throaty, low, harsh—betrayed his desire. She could see the hungry glint in his eye, yet he did not follow up his advantage. She looked down at his hard fingers lying against her skin.

Dropping her hands to his hips, she pulled his pelvis against hers. "Stay close to me, my golden cougar. Don't leave me ever again."

"I won't, darling."

"Seal it, Rafe. Seal it."

Craving the heat and wetness and fire of him, she met him openmouthed. The past burned away under the lightning stroke of desire. She wanted him fully and completely—no more games, no more fear. Sex and love. Joy. That was what she wanted. That was what he was giving her.

Parrying his tongue thrusts, she teased and tantalized, purposely raising his ardor until she thought her dress would tear under its onslaught.

He let go of her arms and took her hips in his hands, kneading and massaging, kissing. Sensation overpowered her. She forced her hands under his jacket and shirt to his naked back.

Still kissing her, Rafe pulled her skirts up to her waist and grasped the string of her pantaloons. The knot wouldn't budge, so he seized the fabric over her seat and tore it right down the seam.

Lizzy moaned but didn't try to stop him as he enlarged the rent. She unbuttoned his trousers and let them fall to his knees, seized him with both hands, and guided him into her torn pantaloons. Mewls of pleasure quivered in her throat.

Rafe caught an overhead shroud to steady himself, then snatched her into his free arm and lifted her until she straddled his waist. He opened the rent fabric and entered her.

Locking her arms around his neck, she kissed him as though imbibing of the pool of life. Earth and sky merged in dazzling confusion while the man and woman came together in the timeless union of love.

In the distance, the Smoky Mountains rose in a cathedral of green spires overhung with clouds and fire. Bumping and swaying, the fragile balloon drifted toward the fastness.

Unseen by the lovers, sunlight jangled down the mountain slopes in a sparkling chain.

The Yankees were waiting.

Chapter Twenty-one

Watching the trees whip past, Hattie Lee Fairlove stood on the platform behind the coal tender. The clackety-clack of the train wheels mocked her thoughts. "We're gonna catch her . . . we're gonna catch her," the rhythm seemed to say.

"You ain't gonna find her, Mr. Hidalgo," she told the Mexican holding her hand.

La Peña looked down at her out of his good eye— the other was still bandaged—and smiled. "I think you underestimate our abilities, child."

"My underestimation'll make up for your over-estimation, I reckon. My Aunt Lizzy's away up there in the clouds, flying along like a—like a comet. This busted-down old rustbucket cain't catch up with no comet."

"Maybe the comet will crash."

Hattie Lee tried to jerk her hand out of his, but he gripped hers harder. She wished he would let go just long enough for her to jump, because around the curving tracks she saw a steep grade coming up that was bound to slow the train to a crawl. The locomotive wasn't going all that fast, anyway.

"Aunt Lizzy won't crash," she said. "She used to fly all the time with my granddaddy. They flew county fairs and gave rides—called themselves the 'Cloud-Kissing Charioteers.' They were flying when I was just a baby."

"And did you fly, too, little one?"

"No-o. But I'm not no 'fraidy-cat!"

"That I believe. I do not understand why this Aunt Lizzy of yours did not take you up. Surely a woman of her abilities would trust herself to fly her own niece."

"I was too little then, and when Granddaddy died, she didn't fly no more. Sort of broke her heart, that's what Ma says, 'cause she set such store by Granddaddy. They did all sorts of things together."

Hidalgo La Peña did not wish to know about this woman he was sworn to hunt down. Right now, he hunted a name with only a shadowy figure attached. It was not difficult to kill a shadow. But a woman of flesh and blood . . . he did not want her to become real to him. He shied from thinking of Eliza McCord as this child's aunt. He was coming to like his young prisoner.

In spite of himself, he asked, "What did your aunt and your grandfather do together?"

"Why, they invented things. Once they blew up the smokehouse testing some chemical Granddaddy thought would smoke the hams faster. Aunt Lizzy still has a scar on her head from a flying chimney brick—her hair covers it up—but folks said it was the start of all her troubles."

"Troubles?"

"Inventing troubles. They started calling her 'Dizzy Lizzy,' but I don't think it had much to do with the brick.'' Hattie Lee's big brown eyes got even bigger. ''I like Huntsville, but there's a powerful lot of people that'd rather stick to the old ways of doing things. Take corsets, for instance.''

Hidalgo La Peña wasn't sure he had heard correctly. Perhaps it was the noise, or perhaps it was the strange American dialect the child spoke. ''Excuse me, señorita, but *corsets?*''

''Corsets,'' she said with an emphatic nod. ''Aunt Lizzy got thrown in jail over corsets. Of course, that rotten old Yankee commander did it, so you got to consider the source. But folks was shocked, all the same.''

La Peña didn't like his own interest in the child's story: Eliza McCord was taking shape in his mind. He should excuse himself and go back into the car, but somehow he had to know a little more. Raising his brows, he waited for enlightenment.

''She and Granddaddy drew up some plans for a spring-loaded corset,'' Hattie Lee said. ''But then Granddaddy died, so it was a while before Aunt Lizzy got back to inventing. When she did, though, it was a doozy.''

''A doozy?''

''Yep. She said Grandma and the ladies used to fuss about their corsets all the time. It wasn't so bad before the war when there were servants to lace 'em up the back, but once times got hard, ladies had to ask their husbands to help. And you know how few husbands we got left, thanks to General Lee calling 'em all up to the army.''

''They could surrender,'' La Peña said, ''and come back to lace up their ladies.''

''Hmph! Aunt Lizzy wouldn't abide no such talk if she was here. . . . Besides, if folks would adopt her

245

spring-loaded corset, ain't nobody would need a man around."

"Your Aunt Lizzy would take a measure of joy out of life, then." Maybe he did not care about this Southern American woman, after all. "Tell me about this new corset."

"Aunt Lizzy made it out of muslin and cast iron."

"A cast-iron corset? Did she expect the wearer to cook on it?"

"You're not very funny," Hattie Lee said, and flipped her braid at him.

"Please, señorita," La Peña said, giving her hand a squeeze. "I do wish to know about this miraculous invention. Perhaps my wife should have one."

"There's not any more. Not after what happened to Miz Bannister."

"And what was that?"

"Well, it was like this. Miz Bannister said she was gonna curl up and die if she didn't have the first corset Aunt Lizzy produced. She said it was kind of heavy, but heavy was what she needed, what with her waistline and all—ordinary whalebone didn't hold up. Anyway, Aunt Lizzy fitted her out and Miz Bannister went off to church."

"A good place for a pious woman."

"Yes, well, not that day. You see, Miz Bannister has the prettiest voice you ever heard in your life. She's first soprano in the choir—folks say angels shut up for shame when she starts singing, she's so much better than the heavenly choir."

La Peña shot an uneasy look at the cloudy sky. People of his faith did not say such things.

"That Sunday, she made a regular point of stepping out a ways from the choir—I reckon 'cause it'd been so long since she'd had a waistline for anybody to admire.

Anyway, she cut loose with 'Glory bursting from afar,' and then jumped up to a high *C* for the last line.''

La Peña was having trouble following all this. "Did her voice break?"

"Not her voice. Right when she let loose on 'Wide o'er the nations soon will shine,' her front clasp broke and the springs shot the corset apart. Naturally her dress couldn't stand the strain," Hattie Lee said, "and her glory bursted all over the chancel. Aunt Lizzy said even the stained-glass figures in the windows blushed. It was a sight to see."

La Peña chuckled. "And that's when Aunt Lizzy was arrested."

"Wasn't much way to get around it—she told me so herself after all the shoutin' died down. We were sitting in the middle row and she just up and wrapped Miz Bannister in her shawl; then she turned around just as proud as a new brood-hen and said it was all her fault about the corset giving way and nobody ought to be laughing in church, no way. She was a gloryful sight. She held her head up when them Yankees led her off, and everybody stood up and cheered her. I stood on the pew."

The Lancer's mouth tightened and a strange warmth filled his gut. He supposed he would have cheered her, too, had he been there. Such a woman aroused the heart in a man. He could picture her, head up, wrists extended for the iron cuffs, not a drop of self-pity in her eyes. This Eliza McCord was a woman to reckon with.

He glanced into the troop car. Louis DeCoeur was lolling on the backseat, his huge red head pushed against the window glass. Red wine stained his shirtfront and there were sweat marks under his arms. He looked like a bear that had eaten fermented mulberries. The other Frenchman sat up front, his dark head rolling with the train's motion, his mouth open. Holy Mary, he had chosen two fine companions for his quest!

"What's the matter, Mr. Hidalgo?"

"Nothing," he said, forcing a smile. "Let us go back inside. Night will fall soon, and I do not wish you to breathe the air."

Inside the car, La Peña seated Hattie Lee by Corporal Spears, the Yankee she seemed to like, then strode down the aisle to DeCoeur.

"What are your plans for the child?" he demanded.

Like the beat of a vulture's wing, DeCoeur's lips fluttered back from his teeth. "My plans are still the same. We will give Laffite a choice. The diamond for the child."

"And if he refuses?"

The question hung between them. La Peña felt his hair prickle. He was going to have to kill the blackhearted demon.

"I know what is in your mind," DeCoeur said in a voice that La Peña felt through the floorboards. "Better men than you have tried and failed. Throw in your lot with me lest you perish, as well."

"You will not hurt the girl—I will not let you."

"And why would old Uncle Louis hurt the little girl? She is more precious than rubies, that one."

"But not more precious than the diamond."

DeCoeur shrugged. "I would lie to say it was so. But you and I, we have no quarrel. Mine is a good plan, one to ensure the 'demoiselle's safety."

"Then say what it is, curse you!"

"Laffite is close at hand. We will relay him a message by heliograph. He will want to come down."

Want to come down. Hidalgo almost laughed at the sickening irony. What guarantee had they that this Southern American man would value the life of a ragged little girl over a priceless treasure? The diamond was part of Rafe Laffite, purchased with his own blood.

The Mexican leaned into DeCoeur's face. "We will try your plan, señor. But if it fails, you will not touch a single hair on the child's head. This is my oath and bond."

DeCoeur extended his paw. "It is done, *mon ami*. If the trap fails, the child goes free. You have my word."

The explosion came without warning. One minute they were rocking along, lulled by the clatter of the wheels, and the next minute the world was filled with fire, smoke, and earsplitting concussions.

From her seat in front, Hattie Lee saw the locomotive rise like a shiny black monster over the coal tender, then leap off the tracks pulling the cars behind it. She tried to grab on to something, but the world spun sideways. Helpless as a bird in a tornado, she rolled over and over. Men banged into her, crashed down on her head, flailed limbs into her back. She couldn't breathe, couldn't scream, couldn't stop tumbling.

At last the world came to a stop. She couldn't see a thing. There was a suffocating weight on her chest and she couldn't feel her arms and legs. Smoke stung her eyes and burned her nose. All around her she heard moans and screams. The Yankees must've taken her to hell with them. She hoped the devil wouldn't find her. *I ain't no Yankee!* she tried to shout, but she couldn't stretch her lungs enough to make a sound.

Then the terrible weight shifted and her ribs gave such a heave she thought they'd broken to bits. Blessed, smoky air flowed into her lungs and she could see again. She was alive, after all!

Heaped on the ceiling of the upside-down car, the Yankees began squeezing through the windows like weevils into cotton bolls. The train was resting on the steep slope of a ditch. It shook and teetered with the Yankees' panicky movements. At any second the thing might slide to the bottom and mash the roof flat.

And then she saw fire in the trees. Flaming whirlwinds twisted along the grass above the ditch and licked the engine. She could hear the crackle of rifles, too. She tried to drag herself to the window but she couldn't move. Twisting around, she saw Jean-Claude Geraud lying across her legs. His eyes were closed.

"Wake up, you big lump!" Hattie Lee screeched. "I ain't staying in here to roast—wake up!"

Smoke billowed into the car. Hattie Lee was sure the train was on fire. She tried to kick Geraud off her but he was too heavy to budge. She caught the sleeve of a soldier squeezing past her and screamed for help. He shook her off and crawled out the window.

Shots erupted from the woods close by. The Yankees returned fire. Hattie Lee could see shadowy riders among the trees. Rebel yells reverberated through the ditch. Hattie Lee screamed back. On the other side of the ditch a rider galloped by, discharged his pistol, and was gone. Hattie Lee recoiled from a Yankee falling just outside. He had a round hole in his forehead like a third eye.

She was really and truly trapped, with the dead Yankee blocking the window and Geraud pinning her legs. She screamed and screamed, but with the battle raging she might as well have whispered.

Suddenly the body outside rolled down into the ditch and Hidalgo La Peña reached through the window. He grabbed her under the arms and jerked her. Bullets clanged off the car and whined into the night. La Peña climbed back up to the train and forced his upper body into the car.

Its iron wheels curled against the sky like the legs of

a dead june bug, the car rocked on the slope as if it were about to turn over. Hattie Lee exploded up the slope and reached inside to help the Mexican pull Geraud clear. They dragged him down into the ditch.

"Stay here!" La Peña shouted. He ran off into the smoke.

Hattie Lee knew they weren't safe with the train looming over them, but she didn't dare climb out of the ditch into the middle of the firefight. Besides, the grass was burning in front of the train. She threw dirt on the flames that got too close.

At last the Rebel cavalry retreated into the woods and the Yankees put out the fires. La Peña and some Yankees helped Geraud out of the ditch and laid him on a blanket. Hattie Lee dabbed the goose egg on his forehead with a wet rag.

Louis DeCoeur appeared out of the darkness and started bellowing orders at the Yankees.

"Wonder who authorized him to boss them bluebellies around?" Hattie Lee whispered to La Peña. She hoped his bossiness would occupy all his attention and give her a chance to slip into the woods after the cavalry.

"Are you all right, *chica*?"

La Peña was smiling at her. Injured or not, his face was wreathed with kindness. She hoped he wouldn't get into trouble when she ran away. "I reckon I'd be dead without you, Mr. Hidalgo."

"I did not do so much."

"All the same, I'm beholden to you."

DeCoeur stalked over to Geraud and scowled down at him. Geraud's attempt to smile looked pitiful under the huge purple knot on his head. "Why is the Rebel child free to roam, Geraud?" he asked in a voice as deceptively quiet as deep water before a cataract.

251

"She—she is not roaming, monsieur. See, she bathes my head!"

La Peña placed his hand on Hattie Lee's shoulder. "The child is assisting me, señor. She will not flee—will you, little one?"

Hattie Lee looked into his kindly eyes and knew his words were more than a query. They requested her bond. Her heart sank down to her toes.

Once spoken, she couldn't take it back. *My word's my bond.* But the Confederate cavalry was out there somewhere; they might never get this close to her again. She could picture them riding away and leaving her far behind.

"No, sir," she said in a choked voice. "No, sir, I won't run."

Sometimes honor was a stupid thing.

By early morning, the Yankees had gotten reinforcements from Bridgeport. The soldiers had brought forty mules and drovers. Mad or not, Hattie Lee liked the way the early morning light splashed through the trees and over the backs of the mules. They were all sizes and colors, some no bigger than jackasses, others towering draft animals, and each one a lot prettier and well mannered than the army mule skinners cussing them.

"No way can they haul that train back up on the tracks," Hattie Lee said, squeezing Hidalgo La Peña's hand. "Not even with all them boys they brought to help, I betcha five dollars they cain't do it."

La Peña's good eye showed the strain of worry, but he smiled at her. "Do you have five dollars, little princess?"

"No . . . not on me."

"Good. Then we have no bet and my *pesos* are safe."

"I guess." Hattie Lee let go of his hand and sat down on the bank to watch the drama unfold. She still wished

252

he'd bet with her. "All I need is a grubstake."

"Maybe you'll find another taker."

A squad of dirty Yankees shuffled past on the far side of the ditch, grunting and cussing under the weight of the rail they carried on their shoulders. They looked like pallbearers. They were scavenging rails from behind the train to repair the track in front.

One of the pallbearers glanced at Hattie Lee. She scowled when he pushed out his stubbly chin and twisted to sass her over his shoulder. "Bet you're mighty proud of your friends for blowing up the track, ain't you, you Rebel brat?"

"We didn't invite y'all down here to invade our country," she said. "If y'all cain't run with the big dogs, stay under the porch with the fleas!"

"By Pluto, I'd wash your saucy mouth out with lye soap if I wasn't carrying this rail!"

Hattie Lee stood up and shouted, "That'd be a good trick, since you ain't seen a sliver of soap in two years, you buttermilk-faced, walleyed side of moldy fatback!"

The soldier dropped his end of the rail and started into the ditch with murder in his eyes.

Instantly La Peña shoved Hattie Lee behind him and dropped his hand to his sword. Although he did not draw it, his fingertips caressed the hilt like a lover. His stare was all the more frightening for the bandage over his eyes. He looked as if he did not care which of them died.

The Yankee took root in the ditch. He looked up at the angry Mexican and his sword, then back at his companions. They had already gone. "You'd better tell her to keep her trap shut!" he said. "You tell her that, Mex, or I'll carve me a harmonica out of your throat with that pigsticker of yours!"

Then he turned tail and ran. La Peña drew Hattie Lee

into the curve of his arm. "You are going to find your-self in serious difficulty, *chica*, if you do not learn to control your temper."

She plopped down to watch the engineers. They had all kinds of equipment: blocks and tackle, iron poles, great coils of line, even a new cowcatcher. Pounding away in makeshift forges, blacksmiths added to the general noise and confusion.

Louis DeCoeur rushed everywhere, outswearing even the muleskinners. Everyone acted afraid of him, from the officers right down to the privates, but he was getting the work done.

He's a scientist, all right, Hattie Lee thought as he adjusted the tension of a line on a block-and-tackle lashed to a huge tree. The pulleys would make the mules' job easier; without them, the team wouldn't stand a chance. Scores of lines ran through the mule harness and blocks to the locomotive. Soldiers lined up in front of the animals, holding bights of rope.

When all was set to DeCoeur's specifications, he uncoiled a bullwhip and went to the bank ahead of the engine. "Ready! On my command . . . heave!"

His whip cracked like a rifle shot. Men and mules hauled away on the ropes. Heels and hooves dug into the clay, gouged up furrows, threw clods over mule skinners and men.

"More effort!" DeCouer bellowed, cracking the whip.

Hattie Lee's breath caught in her chest. She clasped her hands under her chest and stared until her eyes bugged out. She'd never seen such a terrifying, wonderful show in all her life.

Despite the furious efforts of man and beast, the locomotive didn't budge. Over the shouts and creaking harness the ropes screeched to the breaking point.

DeCoeur roared like a man possessed, his blue eyes bulging from their sockets, his neck veins cording. Hattie Lee crossed her fingers in hopes he'd drop dead.

Snap!

Hattie Lee thought DeCoeur had cracked his bullwhip; then she saw a rope snap free and flail a soldier across the back. The other end lashed a mule's face. The mule fell screaming, blood spurting, legs thrashing up dirt.

Men dropped their ropes and rushed to the fallen soldier. Someone shouted, ''He's cut in half!''

Hattie Lee's legs turned to dumplings, spilling her to the ground. She hid her face in her skirt. Through the roaring in her ears she heard DeCoeur thunder: ''Keep pulling! *Sacrebleu*, do not stop now! Pull, you bedswerving devils!''

Shouting in rage and anguish, the men obeyed. The trees holding the blocks and tackle jolted and shook under the tremendous pressure; drovers mercilessly whipped any mule that balked.

The locomotive stirred, then began moving up the slope like an overturned house. ''Redouble your efforts!'' DeCoeur screamed. ''Harder, you rascals!''

Hattie Lee chewed her knuckles. Against her will her eyes found the dead man, now being bundled out of the way. The wounded mule brayed in agony.

She didn't know if she was about to vomit or faint. She could feel La Peña patting her shoulders; she wanted to bury her head in his chest, but she could only sit frozen while the noise vibrated along the edges of her teeth and rasped her brain. Another rope was sure to break—maybe more. She flashed a look of hatred at Louis DeCoeur—she was sure he didn't care who else died.

The locomotive wheels touched the crossties and

stopped. DeCoeur shouted, "Tie off the lines! 'Tis enough pulling for now. You men—get down there with the poles!"

Dozens of soldiers jogged down the slope and jammed long iron poles against the roof of the locomotive, while others tied cables to various points near the top. They pounded long iron stakes into the ground and bent the cables to them. Hattie Lee guessed that without the cables, inertia would carry the locomotive right on over once the mules pulled it onto the track.

"On my command," DeCoeur said. "Heave!"

Again the mules and soldiers strained at the ropes while the downslope men pushed with the poles. Its rivets screeching and wheels cracking the ties, the engine gradually rose. It hovered at twenty degrees, then thirty, then forty. There it stayed, shuddering, gravity pulling against the towering iron wall. Men gasped and cried. A mule dropped dead, leaving the drover cursing it.

"By the fires of perdition, put your hearts into it!"

A despairing cry went up, officers shouted, drovers struck mules and soldiers alike. The locomotive rose to forty-five degrees, hovered, and rose a degree higher.

With a noise like a thunderclap a tree split halfway up its trunk and crashed onto the soldiers at the far end. Its tackle whipped back into the engine. The sudden loss of tension slewed the rear of the locomotive several feet.

"As your lives depend upon it, heave!"

With the last of their strength they dragged the huge engine onto the track. It toppled toward them several degrees before the cables on the opposite side became taut. Then it clanged down on the rails with a concussion that knocked men into the dirt.

"It's done, *muchacha!*" La Peña cried. He gestured at the railroad cars still in the ditch. "The cars will be an easy matter, compared to the engine!"

"Wonder how many more boys he'll kill, righting the rest of it?" Hattie Lee said, glaring at DeCoeur through her tears. When La Peña didn't reply, she yelled, "Do y'all think chasing my Aunt Lizzy is worth all this death?"

His face turned cold. "The diamond is worth it. Life matters little beside it."

"Does that include your own life, Mr. Hidalgo?"

"My life is nothing."

"Then you must not have no children."

He hesitated. "If I do not get that diamond back to Mexico, my children will not have a father. The emperor has decreed it."

Hattie Lee stared at him in shock. Hidalgo La Peña was a lost man . . . she could see it in his face. Of such men there was no point in begging favors. No point in asking him to leave Aunt Lizzy alone. All she could do was try to delay the inevitable.

Inevitable, because they were going to catch Aunt Lizzy and Mr. Rafe. How she knew, she couldn't tell. Maybe it was the bad feeling in her gut. Maybe it was because of a force she was just beginning to realize. Without even seeing it, she knew the diamond was worth any risk to these men. They'd beaten her mother when she refused to help them. They would do worse to Aunt Lizzy.

Somehow, she had to stop them. It was a tall order for a ten-year-old girl.

Chapter Twenty-two

"Good gracious, the wind is getting bad!" Lizzy had to grab a shroud against the violently jerking balloon. "It's the night wind coming off those mountains—it sets up turbulence when it hits this warm air."

"Anything we can do about it?"

"Nothing but land as soon as we can—hang on!"

The balloon shot upward on a geyser of hot air. Twisting and turning, its sides caving in then snapping open like a luffing sail, the blue envelope swept the gondola after it. Lizzy dropped to her knees and held on. Rafe remained on his feet, though his knuckles grew ivory white on the rail.

"Is this thing about to crash, Eliza?"

"It might—I think the top is trying to curl over. That's a bad sign. Daddy and I crashed into the river when it curled like that."

Rafe leaned out to stare up at the balloon. The envelope was indeed curling. He wondered if the gondola would suddenly become too heavy for it; Lizzy had told him about the displacement of air and how many cubic feet of gas it took to lift them. The distortion might make a difference.

But the balloon continued its upward climb until the tall trees began to look like bushes, then little sprigs of green. Ahead, the face of a mountain frowned a warning: *Stay away, stay away!*

As the air thinned, they began to gasp as though they were running. The air got cold, making every panting breath a swirl of fog. Lizzy wrapped herself in the quilt.

"I think we're out of the worst of it," Rafe said. "Looks like we're starting to descend."

The trees were growing larger again, and he didn't have to drag air into his lungs. Like a tired bird, the balloon settled toward the summit of a mountain. And then he saw something that made him wish for more altitude. A heliograph flashed not three miles distant.

He glanced at Lizzy, but she was unfolding one of the stolen charts. She looked worried enough without being told there were Yankees nearby.

Suddenly she looked up at him. A slow smile warmed her lips, and her clear blue eyes filled with such a potent mixture of love and desire that he nearly forgot his own concerns. He did not smile back, but let his spirit reach out to caress her. Jove, what love he bore her!

As though her lips had turned to porcelain, her smile took on a serious cast. "You're worried, aren't you?"

"Not worried. Concerned."

"Because there are Yankees watching us."

"You knew?"

"They're not being secretive about it, Rafe. I saw their mirrors, and on that hill over there"—she pointed at a distant crag—"somebody's waving a red-and-white flag."

Rafe raised his binoculars and studied the wigwag for half a minute. "Looks like they're hazy on what to do—that's a point on our side."

The balloon bumped another thermal and began to rise again, this time not quite as fast and not as high, but well within rifle range. Now that they were into the mountains, he couldn't see any more signals. Maybe they had left the Yankees behind.

And then, across a narrow valley, he saw a ribbon of blue. He raised his glasses again. "Infantry, may God drench 'em with blackstrap molasses and turpentine!"

Lizzy got out her spyglass and studied the soldiers. "They'll never get here in time, Rafe. We're traveling too fast for them, and just look at that awful terrain they've got to cover. They might as well make camp for the night . . . which is something we're going to have to do, too, I'm afraid."

"Not yet, honey. We'll fly until there's not enough daylight to go by. We can make a night landing."

She shook her head. "Too dangerous. These mountains are lots more tricky than the ones we flew through last night." Before she'd finished speaking, the balloon pitched up and set the basket swinging. "Feel that wind? There's too much change in temperature, what with these gorges and all. We were lucky that curler didn't crash us a while ago!"

Rafe eyed the Yankees. He knew she was right, but the idea of landing within ten miles of Yankees didn't sit well.

"Besides, I've got to answer the call of nature before it gets the best of me," Lizzy said, blushing.

"The chamber pot—"

"I'm not fixing to use the chamber pot in front of you!"

"I'll turn my back."

"No. We've got to land real soon, Rafe, and I mean it."

Rafe sighed. "Let's make another few miles first."

"As soon as we reach the other side of that mountain, we've got to land. I just hope we don't catch any more updrafts!"

"You're something, you know that?"

"I'm determined, I'll allow."

"No shame in that, Eliza McCord. It's gotten you through this far, and it will get you through the rest of it."

"You talk as though you won't be with me, Rafe."

"I'll be with you," he said low. "I'll always be with you."

Lizzy shivered. "The Yankees want to kill you. Louis DeCoeur wants to kill you. I don't think they'll ever leave you alone. You'd better come and hold me, Rafe Laffite. I don't feel determined enough to stand on my own right now."

Rafe pulled her against his chest and looked over the top of her head at the slopes. There was so much ground to cover. So many Yankees to elude. "Don't be afraid, honey," he said. "Don't be afraid. We'll whisper a prayer, and before you know it, we'll be on the ground warming our toes by a fire."

"We can't make a fire tonight. The Yankees'll see it."

"Not if we dig a hole and screen it with branches. Heck, one night down in Mexico, I made a fire a hundred yards from an enemy camp and passed the most restful night cooking their plunder. Never had the first sign of trouble."

"You stole their provisions?"

"By the trainload."

"Well, don't try stealing any tonight! I couldn't bear a repeat of last night."

"I'll get you something to eat," he said. "Don't worry about that."

"Promise not to do anything foolish."

"Cross my heart and hope to die."

Lizzy unfastened his top two buttons and kissed the notch above his breastbone. Instantly aroused, Rafe stroked her hair away from her face. The sight of her lips against his naked skin made him hungry. "We'd best wait till we land this thing, Eliza."

"I have no intention of going any further," she said, but she kissed his chest again.

The balloon bumped over an updraft, jarring her face into his breastbone. She pulled back and rubbed her nose. He chuckled softly. "That will teach you, vixen."

"There's plenty of things I need to learn, Rafe, but that's not one of them." She brushed her lips across his bristly jaw, grimaced, then turned to face the mountain.

Violet sunbeams mottled the slopes and softened the boulders. Here and there, maples draped with autumn colors shimmered between towering hemlock, spruce, and fir trees. Shadows lay long across the ground, cold fingers of darkness. The land was vast and quiet, a silence stretching hundreds of miles. It was hard to believe that human beings might inhabit the slopes. The aeronauts held hands and kept a close, tense watch.

As daylight faded from the sky, the wind dropped, and with it the balloon. Trying to angle toward a stand of spruce, Lizzy caught the crown line and warped the canopy while Rafe prepared the anchor.

"Please be careful tonight, Rafe," she said. "No more jumping into trees! You nearly stopped my heart last time."

"Mine didn't pump so well afterward, either."

But as he prepared to toss the anchor out, his gaze caught on a dark slash in the mountainside. "I believe there's a cave up in the woods there. Let's keep drifting for a minute."

Mindful of Yankees, he let the balloon drift past the large cleft in the rocks. There was no noise and when he sniffed he couldn't smell horses, latrines, or woodsmoke. Leaves carpeted the ground in front of the cave—a sign nobody was using it.

"Safe, do you think?" she asked.

"As a cast-iron cocoon."

He tossed the anchor into a massive fir thirty feet below. The balloon kept moving for several yards, then jerked like a hooked fish and settled into a tug-of-war. Lizzy picked up the ladder and waited for Rafe to haul the balloon closer to the tree. Sweat broke through his jacket, and he grunted like Hercules fighting a monster.

"You're the strongest man I've ever met," she said. "I can't wait to put my hands all over you."

"Let me get us to the ground, tigress, and I'm at your pleasure. There!" He tied off the line and turned to her, a predatory glint in his eye. "Why don't I just eat you up right here?"

"Because you promised me a fire," she said. "I didn't count on finding a cave to go with it. How interesting."

"Not half as interesting as you. Come on, before I explode with anticipation." Brushing her breasts with his forearms, Rafe took the ladder from her and threw it over the side. He hung the Yankee colonel's sword in his sash, then climbed onto the ladder.

Lizzy tossed the quilt into the tree. "Just a minute, Rafe; I've got to find something."

After a few seconds, she handed him a package

wrapped in oilskin. He tucked it under his arm. "What's this, honey?"

"You'll find out later."

Rafe caught her foot and set it on the ladder. From where he stood, her torn pantaloons afforded him a view seen only in his wildest dreams. "You make a strong man weak."

"Quit staring so hard, then," she said. "Next time, I go first."

"Who would be there to catch you?"

"Maybe some other wolf."

"If there is any catching of tasty young morsels to be done, I'm the wolf for the job."

Lizzy scuffed her foot across the top of his head. "That's exactly what I'm hoping for. Keep going, will you, please?"

"Just don't lag behind."

She climbed down past him while he was securing the anchor line. He had to walk the limbs around the trunk to retrieve the quilt. She reached the ground and disappeared behind a rhododendron, so he took his time climbing down. By the time he touched the ground, she was back.

"You climb like a little old lady," she said.

"I don't do this like a little old lady." He embraced and kissed her, his hands ranging down her back.

"I thought you were going to build that fire in the *cave*," she said.

"I'd rather kindle it in you, girl. It burns hotter."

"It does when you twirl that fire stick of yours." Before he could kiss her again, she skipped away. "The cave's back this way, isn't it?"

"The other way," he said, extending his hand. "It's confusing, what with all these trees."

Embarrassed, Lizzy trailed back to him. "With my

sense of direction, I really ought not to be out without a keeper.''

"You don't need a keeper, just a lover.''

"I ought to wear the dratted compass around my neck.''

"Hey, you do the flying and I'll do the tracking. My job requires very little finesse compared to yours.''

She smiled. "You're the only man I know who never builds himself up at my expense.''

"I'm not worth a damn without you, Eliza.''

He caught her hand and led her to the slope. The trees were so thick that from where they stood, the cave was invisible. After climbing for several minutes, he pointed out a ten-foot-wide slash across the hillside. Its mouth opened only a yard at its highest point. To reach it, they would have to climb a scree.

"Wait here a minute—I want to check it first.'' Without slipping or making a sound, Rafe climbed the rock-strewn slope and peered in. After a few seconds, he stooped and went inside. Darkness swallowed him.

Lizzy waited for him to reappear. Feeling eyes on the back of her head, she whipped around to survey the mountainside. Nothing. Again her gaze returned to the cave, only to switch back to the woods. It was getting too dark to see much. Her skin crawled.

The whole Union Army's watching you. You don't think you're invisible, you naive little girl . . . The whole Union Army. . . .

They were out there; she could feel them. She really was naive to think she could escape the hunters. The chill mountain wind ruffled her hair. Goose bumps teased her spine.

From the woods behind her rose a long, deep howl. She was not alone, after all.

Chapter Twenty-three

Lizzy lost her nerve and bolted up the scree. Stones scattered underfoot, tumbling and crashing down the slope. She slipped and cut her right knee, but terror deadened the pain and drove her off again on a mad scramble for handholds.

"Eliza, what's the matter?"

Her diaphragm contracted on a cry of relief when Rafe crawled out of the cave. He hurried down and drew her close. "You're shaking all over. What happened?"

"Where were you?"

"Checking the cave. Are you all right?"

"Fine," Lizzy said more sharply than she'd meant to. "I just got tired of waiting, that's all."

He drew his gun and eyed the woods, methodically checking each tree and shadow.

"There's nobody there, Rafe. I—I heard a wolf. It scared me."

"Let's get into the cave. Watch your head."

Expecting to find only cramped darkness inside, she stooped through the low opening and discovered a large antechamber whose ceiling arched high into the gloom. A pool glistened at the foot of the rear wall. Limestone glowed from a fire flickering in a room off to the left.

"Come, it's warmer in here," Rafe said. He led her through a passageway into a side room.

A fire bloomed in a shallow pit. Beside it, the quilt spread over soft gray dirt. In this room the ceiling dropped low. Limestone deposits corrugated the moist cave walls. Wind blew through a black, narrow crevice in the back wall.

"You've been busy," she said, stooping to warm her hands at the fire. She tried not to look at the quilt.

"Not very. Somebody laid in a good bit of wood." He pointed out a pile of split oak by a boulder.

Tingles walked up and down Lizzy's spine as she glanced from the logs to the crevice in the wall. "Maybe that somebody is in here."

"No, the signs are old."

"They could come back." Should she tell him about her feeling of being watched?

"They'd already be here if they were coming," he said, shrugging. "We're safe for tonight."

"How can you be so certain? Doesn't the cave go back a ways?"

"I examined the tracks—nobody's there." Exhaustion rimmed his eyes and roughened his voice. He tried to smile and gave up.

Lizzy wasn't ready to surrender. It was one thing to sleep under the trees, and another to lie down in a black cave with who-knew-what staring from behind the stalagmites. "What about animal tracks? I'll bet you a Yankee dime there's a bear down in there."

"If there is, we'll have him for dinner."

"Maybe he'll have us. And what about that wolf I heard?"

"It doesn't live here—there'd be sign." He lifted the food bag and handed it across. "If you'll bake us some corn bread, I'll nose around outside for something to eat with it."

"Don't go out there!"

"I'll leave you the pistol."

"What if somebody sneaks up on you?"

Rafe smiled as though he'd just taken a scalp. Winding his fingers around the hilt of his sword, he said, "This pigsticker will make one hell of an incision, Eliza."

"But, Rafe—"

He passed her the pistol and cartridge box, tugged his forelock in a playful salute, and left the chamber. Lizzy started to call after him again, but the plea died in her throat. He was gone and she had work to do. She'd better get hold of herself.

Still, she kept an eye on the dark crevice while she mixed the corn bread and pressed it onto a stick. The aperture compelled her like a mysterious door in a nightmare that beckoned the sleeper out of bed. She wanted to walk through it.

Stop this! She rubbed her forehead with her knuckles, but when she opened her eyes, the sensation was like a kick to the spine. She knew better. Only fools wandered into caves alone.

Picking a flaming brand out of the fire, she rushed past the crevice without looking at it. Back in the antechamber, she stopped at the pool she'd noticed on the way in. It wasn't very wide, hardly more than a puddle. She shucked off her shoes and stuck her big toe in the water. Cold. Cold and dark as the earth.

She jammed the brand between two rocks, then

stripped off her clothes and agitated the water with her toe. She almost stepped in before remembering they needed drinking water. Naked and shivering, she ran back to the chamber, got the canteen, and filled it.

Then she stepped into the cold water.

Her foot met nothing but coldness. Too late she tried to recover her balance. She plunged in over her head and sank into blackness as deep as a grave.

The sinkhole was deep and funnel shaped. Within seconds she was squeezed into a tube so narrow she could hardly kick. Clawing at the slippery rocks, she fell deeper, deeper underwater. Her lungs burned like fire. She was drowning.

Forcing her limbs to stop flailing, she let herself sink down into the pit. The water felt heavy, as though she'd fallen into a freezing vat of molasses. At last her feet touched rock. With all her power she pushed straight up, knifing for the surface, scraping her shoulders and knees. She was losing speed. She had to take a breath. If she opened her mouth she would inhale water.

Torchlight. Air! She grabbed the edge and coughed and coughed, jerking in lungfuls of air. At last she crawled out and curled up next to the torch. It was a long time before she moved.

Idiot! Dizzy Lizzy, indeed. What if Rafe had seen me?

She pulled herself to her knees and bundled up her dirty clothes. Stiff with cold and shock, she hobbled back to the small chamber and crouched by the fire. Waterdrops slid down her spine like melting icicles. Teeth clacking, she dragged the quilt around her and let the fire thaw her out.

She glanced at the crevice. It didn't alarm her anymore, not after the watery pit she'd fallen into. Compared to the sinkhole, the crevice was about as scary as a butter churn.

When she'd thawed enough to move without splintering, she broke the strings on the oilskin package and extracted a wrinkled blue gown with a lace collar as yellow as old parchment. It wasn't a burlap sack, she thought, but it sure wasn't princess raiment.

Pulling it on, she tried to push the mussel-shell buttons through the holes down the back, but her fingers still felt like ice. After buttoning only three or four, she gave up and tied the sash around her waist, arranging the bow over her left hip. Then she combed her wet hair and bent close to the fire to dry it.

"If you aren't the balm of Gilead," Rafe said from behind her.

She straightened and spun around. "When are you going to quit sneaking up on me?"

He was standing just inside the chamber, holding a handful of hickory nuts, some greens, and a squirrel. As he lowered the food to a boulder, a soft whistle escaped his lips. His eyes smoldered like golden embers. His fierce scrutiny embarrassed her.

"My—my hair's all wet," she said.

"You washed it."

"Um, yes."

"It shines like copper."

Self-conscious, she touched it. "You think so?"

"I think you can give my breath back as soon as you're through with it, ma'am."

"Do you—do you like the dress?"

He folded his arms and slowly looked her up and down. A muscle throbbed in his cheek. "For a minute there, I thought I'd walked into the wrong cave."

"Cavemen do it all the time, I think."

In two bounds he crossed the room and caught her hair, pulled her head back over his arm, and bared her throat to his lips. With sensual thoroughness he tasted

270

her from the tip of her chin to the swells of her breasts. "This caveman will never visit the wrong cave," he said, raising his heated gaze. "You're my woman. I want no other."

And then he lowered her to the quilt. It was a long time before they remembered dinner.

He slept at last, his bright head cradled on his arms, his strong, naked body shining like gold. Lizzy propped herself on one elbow to admire him.

"You delicious Apollo," she whispered, stroking his belly with her fingertips. He felt good to touch, his skin sheathing his hard sinews like a velvet glove. "You make the sun rise."

He lit sunbursts inside of her—bright pathways into the deepest structure of her being. He was light and spirit and fire, all things beautiful. He was love.

Love. She should whisper the secret to him, unfold the warmth guarded in her heart, give him the word of acceptance that would move their relationship into a new realm. It was a healing word . . . a forgiving word. "I love you," she said too softly to stir the air. She moved closer to his ear. "I love you." But this time no sound at all came.

Rafe stirred. For a second she thought his eyes would open, but then he settled once more into the arms of exhaustion.

Frowning more at her own lack of nerve than at his failure to awaken, Lizzy tried to make her vocal cords unlock the words again. She couldn't. Not with him sleeping. It wouldn't count if he heard it only in his dreams. She owed him a still, open-eyed moment of honesty.

Later, then. There would be time. Folding the quilt over them both, she laid her arm across his belly, rested her head against his warm side, and tried to sleep.

Wind sighed through the cave like the ululating wail of a child. Water dripped like the ticking of a clock, loud and steady. An ember popped. The wind rose to a shrill whine, rushing through the chamber into the crevice.

Lizzy sat up. The fire was low, the cave washed dark red. As she eased out of the quilt, her shadow danced upon the wall like an elongated ghost. She dressed and pulled on her shoes, then sat on a boulder to watch Rafe sleep. As still and innocent as a boy, he slept on, the taut lines at the corners of his mouth relaxed into a faint smile. She wished she could record his image on tintype. It was rare to find him so unguarded.

Unguarded. With Rafe so dead asleep, it was up to her to keep watch. The small hairs prickled on the back of her neck as she turned her head to look at the black crevice. It beckoned her with the cold imperiousness of a crone's finger. *Come and see,* whispered the wind.

She wasn't afraid; no, she wasn't. Limestone caves honeycombed the mountains around Huntsville. She'd explored them with her father. She'd found flint tools and weapons that once belonged to ancient people. There wasn't anything to fear. There were rare animals in caves—blind crawfish, glowworms, luminous fungi, creatures people never saw. Maybe there was something in this cave of scientific value. Men made reputations exploring places like this. She could use a boost to her reputation.

Only fools wander into caves alone. Always take someone along. Her father had been adamant.

She wouldn't go very far, just peep in for a minute or two. She went to the woodpile and sorted through the logs until she found several pieces of cedar. Stripping the inner bark, she wrapped the papery strands around one end of a stout piece of oak to form a torch head.

"Rafe? Want to come with me?" Her voice whispered back at her from the shadows. When he didn't stir, she said, "I'll be back in a minute."

She lit the torch and tiptoed over to the crevice. Pausing just long enough to take a deep breath, she pushed the torch ahead of her and ducked inside. There wasn't much to see, just a narrow chute not quite as high as her head. The wind rushing into the tunnel from the chamber behind her blew the torch flame almost horizontal. If she hesitated much longer, it would go out.

She had to stoop over to walk. Despite her care, her dress brushed the wet, black-streaked limestone. Water dripped onto her head. She almost turned back, then decided to go on for just a few more minutes. The tunnel would probably end in a blind wall, anyway.

The chute ran as straight and level as a mine shaft for a hundred paces, then bifurcated. Lizzy chose the left fork because it was wider and the floor less muddy. She discovered a dead end within fifteen feet. The right fork slanted down like a ramp. The limestone floor was slick, made more hazardous by small round pockets of water every few yards. Lizzy avoided them, fearing sinkholes.

As she burrowed deeper underground, her torch lit grotesque shapes protruding from the walls. Sculpted by the dripping water of centuries, butterscotch-colored footstools merged into long strands of pulled taffy.

Gradually the tunnel widened and the ceiling rose. Holding the torch high, Lizzy felt her way around a sharp corner and descended a set of crude steps carved, she guessed, by Indians long ago. The tunnel branched into three. Using her torch, she blazed the wall beside the middle passage, then marked the main tunnel so she could find her way back out.

The passage wound down into the earth for a very

long way. Stalactites and waxy knobs of calcite protruded from the ceiling and walls like a sterile, petrified forest. There was no life so deep underground.

She pressed on, touching, feeling, savoring. Her palms became white and slick with calcite. The still, cool air smelled musty, like bottomlands broken to the plow for the first time. Her nostrils quivered at the raw scent of water vapor trapped forever in the earth.

As she came around a corner, her breath departed in rush. She curved her arm around a stalagmite as tall as a man and stared in astonishment.

Her torchlight got lost in the blackness of an immense cathedral room. The fireglow touched what seemed to be castles and dragons, saints and martyrs, comets and rivers and chariots with wings. Yellow-white columns stretched from ceiling to floor like the pipes of an organ. Waterfalls of pure white stone poured soundlessly over frozen cliffs.

Like one in a trance, Lizzy drifted from one incredible formation to another. In wonder she held her torch behind a translucent hedge of straws, which rang like chimes when she tapped them. In the center of the room stood a fortress, built inch by inch over many millenia. On the topmost battlement water still dripped, one drop at a time, patiently adding minute layers of calcium. Michaelangelo himself could not rival what nature had crafted with such careless precision.

There were stone toadstools large enough to sit on. Fragile lily pads floated on impossibly slender columns. Beside a tower, what appeared to be a white chocolate bear guarded a tribe of gnomes. Meringue seemed to drip from the ceiling. Stalagmites touched the fingertips of stalactites, while what looked like the roof of a plantation house was supported by a vast colonnade.

If only her father were with her. How he would marvel! Together they would explore and map the entire cave. Her breast burned with emotion. "Daddy, I miss you so much," she whispered, "my dear old crony."

The cave carried her voice back into the vaults, amplifying and multiplying the sound until the cathedral seemed inhabited by ghosts. Her father was suddenly very close, a warm presence in the cavern. She raised the torch and went on.

She'd never seen anything like this in an Alabama cave. Here, everything was larger, vaster, more intricate, breathtaking in its very age. She could touch the roots of the mountains, feel strength vibrating through them. The earth had a very old spirit.

She thought of Rafe. His was an old spirit, too. Old and strong, forgiving. Enigmatic at times. She wanted to see him again, to touch his face and make passionate love. To say the words stuck too long in her throat. To tell him about the baby they'd made one hot summer night, then lost when the world turned cold. Suddenly, the weight of the mountain pressed down on her. It was time to go.

But when she began to retrace her footsteps, the torch reflected in a silvery pool she'd missed on the way in. A wave of scientific curiosity swept aside her good intentions. Pressing between two columns curved like the spindles of a Queen Anne bed, she eased past a gleaming formation shaped like a statue of the Virgin, and bent over the pool.

For a long time she looked into her own face. Then, more by instinct than sight, she sensed movement deep underwater. She leaned nearer. There was something down there. She knew it. She felt it. There! A flash of white, then gone. She lowered the torch almost to the surface and stared without blinking.

The water trembled. Wavelets lapped the edge of the

pool and wet her hand. She felt a presence looking back at her. Goose bumps tingled along the base of her spine. A blur rose from the deep well. Water rings pulsed across the pool. The creature broke the surface.

Lizzy stared into a dead-white face without eyes. Whiskers jutted from either side of its wide mouth. Black streaks marred its pale, slippery body. She recoiled with a gasp. ''A catfish! A blind one, at that!''

The thing flipped its tail and began to descend into the pool. Lizzy reached into the water but it slipped through her fingers. Intensely curious, she groped along the sides. She detected no algae, no living organism on which the creature could feed.

Shaking water off her hand, she climbed to her feet and gazed into the pool. How did the creature survive in a world without food and light?

Light was what she needed. Her torch wouldn't last much longer. The cedar wrappings were gone and the top of the oak shaft was burning with an unsteady flame.

On her way back to the Queen Anne spindles, she saw a bridge spanning a black moat. She decided to take a quick look. Stepping cautiously onto the stone bridge, she edged her way to the middle and swept the torch low. She couldn't see the bottom of the pit.

The torch sputtered and died to a red ember. Darkness closed down like a clammy hand. Lizzy's heart gave a great bound of fear. Vertigo seized her, drove her to her knees. She could hear water dripping into the pit, a splashing poison of fear. The torch end floated like a ruby in deep space. She couldn't tell how close it was; there was no reference point. In the darkness, there was no up or down.

She blew on the torch until her head spun. Too scared to pray, she focused all her energy on the red tip. If she failed to light it, she'd die down here, blind as the fish. "Please!" she begged the ruby.

A golden ember sparked. She coaxed and wheedled, willing oxygen to feed the tiny flame. The oak flared. Lizzy jumped up and ran to the far end of the bridge.

Stone giants stood in her path, their heads lost in gloom. Lizzy hurried around them to an enormous yellow chandelier hanging almost to the floor. She didn't find beauty in it. She was too far from daylight.

After about a hundred years, she found the tunnel. Without another glance at the cathedral, she scurried into the passage on her way back to Rafe. The torch flickered. Alarmed, she stopped and blew on it until the flame lengthened, then hurried on again. Time was her enemy. She forced her aching legs to run.

The grotto was steeper than she remembered, the formations sharper, less like taffy. She didn't see the strange knobs she'd stroked. Doubt flared within her.

She was in the right tunnel, she was sure. But where was the main passageway? She'd surely come far enough to find the juncture. The walls seemed closer, too. When she brushed around a bend and saw the cave walls squeezed like the eye of a needle, she knew for certain.

She had taken the wrong tunnel.

Nausea bubbled in her throat. If she turned back to the cathedral to try to find the right passage, the torch might go out, leaving her that much deeper underground. This tunnel led upward. Perhaps there was another opening in the mountain! Pressing forward, she squeezed through the eye into a wider passage.

The tunnel branched again. Both led upward. Agonized, Lizzy chose the left. Holding on to the wall, she negotiated a boulder fallen from the ceiling. Although the boulder's soft edges and budding stalagmites revealed it had fallen long ago, Lizzy's scalp prickled as her gaze swept the ceiling. *Stay put*.

A black hole gaped in the wall. Pushing the torch ahead of her, she stepped into a cavern. It was smaller than the cathedral, and instead of earth, it smelled of rotting things. Lizzy edged farther into the chamber and lifted the torch. The ceiling moved.

Bats.

Squeaking like rusty mice, eyes like staring pinpricks, hundreds and thousands of bats quivered on the ceiling. Suddenly they exploded, their wings clapping like leather bellows, brushing and wheeling and swooping furiously about her.

Lizzy dropped flat. Buffeted by small, hairy bodies, she tried to crawl to the entrance. She dropped the torch and it rolled away from her. Weeping, she scrambled after it. Dark creatures about it caught fire, flying off like comets. Scores of others pelted the brand.

"No!" Lizzy screamed, diving at the torch. The screeching rose to a crescendo. Bodies ricocheted off her back like minié balls.

She grabbed the fiery end of the torch, screamed in pain, and dropped it. The torch went out.

She was alone with the bats.

Chapter Twenty-four

Rafe had to stoop as he ran down the tunnel. He carried a torch made of green boughs wrapped in pieces of Lizzy's old gown and smothered with pine pitch. He'd searched everywhere for her, until he'd finally figured out where she'd gone. Now he was sure he was on the right track, for Lizzy's footprints showed wherever limestone yielded to mud.

From time to time he stopped to listen. He heard no sound but his heartbeat. Magnified by the deep chasms, his voice burst back at him a hundred times when he shouted her name.

He shouldn't have shut his eyes. He should have tied her to him. Infernal woman and her scientific wonderment! That same wonderment had gotten her and her father into trouble too many times to count. Now, if he didn't find her soon, it might kill her.

The tunnel forked. Rafe's eyes riveted on the mark

Lizzy had blazed with her torch, and he was off like a tiger on the scent.

Its walls studded with stalactite teeth, the tunnel twisted like a serpent. As Rafe hastened through a narrow spot, a rough edge ripped his sleeve and cut a bloody swath across his arm. He ran faster. The torch flame streaming behind him, he plunged around a corner into the cathedral room. His breath caught in his throat. *Hades' underworld. The old demon was hiding amongst the rocks.*

"Eliza!" His voice rolled through the tortured formations and mocked him a dozen times. He waited for the echoes to fall silent before calling again. Her name trembled in the deep vaults, a futile cry of desolation. There was no answer.

Bounding down the slope, he began to search the labyrinth of stone. Everywhere he found footprints cast in mud and fingerprints molded in calcium salts.

After a ten-minute search he discovered the pool. Drawn by a sense keener than sight, a bloodless catfish rose to the surface and stared at him from a bloated, eyeless face. The creature looked as dead as the lightless hell in which it dwelled. Rafe's gut turned chill. Where was Eliza?

He followed her trail to the stone bridge. Like a gargoyle's maw, the chasm gaped away into blackness. Water gurgled and soughed in its bowels. Her footprints disappeared into the stone, but in the middle of the span he found cold ashes. In them he read her disorientation, her struggle to rekindle the stick, her dangerous flirtation with the fissure. Saul's breath, had she fallen?

Dropping flat, Rafe pressed his torch down into the pit. He could see only ten feet or so. "Eliza!"

No answer. His heart sledgehammering his ribs, he

searched the ashes. There was no soot leading away, no dust to hold her footprints.

"Oh, Lord, let me find her on the other side!" He crossed the bridge. Since the limestone was dry and the formations bone-hard, there was nothing to betray her path. Bending low, Rafe searched several yards into the first three tunnels. No sign.

Ducking under an arch, he discerned a faint track between tall colonnades. As he squatted to look, a distant rumble vibrated the floor, and from deep in the cavern he heard the crash of stone. Echoes rebounded from the walls, hiding their origin in a perplexity of noise.

"Eliza!" Her name rolled back at him. Had she brought down the roof?

He found another track. Had the crash come from this tunnel? There was no cloud of dust, but that could mean he was far from the source. He ascended the steep corridor. Other shafts crisscrossed the narrow passage, and several times he followed footprints into them, but each time the tracks faded and he returned to the main tunnel.

And then the prints disappeared altogether, lost upon stone. Tracking by instinct, Rafe stayed in the main tunnel. His torch was only two-thirds its former size. If he did not find her soon, he'd have to go back to the surface and make another light.

Ahead the corridor compressed to a needle's eye. At the top of the arch, Rafe detected a faint, greasy smudge. Woodsmoke? Squeezing through the eye, he began to run. The tunnel convulsed, turning back on itself only to bend sharply upward. He leaped over a jumble of boulders.

"Eliza! Answer me!" Echoes boomeranged against his eardrums. He stopped to listen. His heart thudded loudly in the silence.

And then, out of the blackness, he heard a distant cry.

Lightning coursed through his being, shoving him forward at a dead run. Vaulting a stone bier, spurning dark, beckoning passages, he rushed after the echo.

"Speak again, Eliza!"

"Help me!"

The sound came from behind him. Quick as a kestrel, he turned and flung himself into a side passage. The scent of dead things saturated his nostrils. Dank, angry air rushed him as a thousand shapes descended. Wings buffeted his face and caromed into the torch flame. He dropped to the cold floor.

"Eliza!"

"Rafe! Bats!"

"I see them—where are you?"

"Here!"

He raised the torch. Boulders and stalagmites encrusted with guano pimpled the floor, and between them were dark pits. "Yell again, honey!"

A screeching swarm of banshees swirled into the torchlight, their eyes bloodred. He heard her scream. Stumbling to a pile of boulders, he found her huddled against a stalagmite, her head buried in her arms. She was clutching a burned stick. The bats flew everywhere. Just as he reached her, the swarm grew frenzied once more. Several struck him and the torch, knocking it from his hand. It went out.

Blackness ruled. Rafe enfolded her in his arms and put his body between her and the bats, shielding her against the stalagmite. "Be very still, Eliza. Don't scream. Don't move."

She huddled against him, sobbing. Holding her against his heart, Rafe covered her ears and rocked her very, very slowly. "Don't be afraid, honey. Shh. They are quieting now. Shh, don't cry."

"They're all over us!"

"No, no. They are going back to the ceiling," he said. "It's cold in these mountains—they're in hibernation. We woke them up, but now they are going back to sleep."

"I hit them with my stick—they tried to bite me!"

Rafe shuddered. Bats carried rabies.

A painful fever of love burned his brain, an overwhelming fear for her life. But aloud he said, "I'm going to get you out of here, Eliza McCord. Do you believe me?"

"Yes."

"Will you follow me?"

"In the dark?"

"In the dark."

He felt her nod against his chest. "Say it, honey."

"I'll do anything you say."

Emotion blocked his reply, and so he stroked her hair for several seconds before he was able to murmur, "We are going to stand up and walk out of here, beloved."

"All right . . . Just don't let go of my hand."

"It's a part of me." He pulled her up. "Stay right behind me. Don't deviate right or left. Straight and narrow all the way."

He felt her place her free hand on his back. The bats were calmer now, but wings swished near the ceiling and squeaks slashed the darkness like exclamation points on a slate.

Rafe opened his eyes so wide his facial muscles ached, but his pupils captured not the slightest glimmer of light. He was totally blind, his eyes as useless as his vanquished torch. Midnight pressed down from every side, tangible and terrifying.

Through the dark ballroom of death he led her a careful dance. Every few seconds he paused, snapped his fingers, listened, and sniffed the air. Then he proceeded with the same cautious tread.

Lizzy's foot brushed a stalagmite coated with dried guano. The encrustation disintegrated with the sound of crumbling bones. She caught her breath on a sob of revulsion.

"Come on, honey. Don't be afraid. Just close your eyes and follow me."

"Close my eyes? I already can't see the hand in front of my face."

"You don't need to," he said. "Let your eyes sleep. There are other guides."

She closed her eyes. Within a few seconds, she felt Rafe's calmness center in her being. A fresh draft of air filled her nostrils, washing away the scent of decay. But when she tried again to see, the shroud of midnight covered her. Her throat tightened with fear.

"Don't stop, Eliza. We're out of the bats' lair."

"How can you tell? Maybe they've just fallen silent. We might be wandering in circles."

"Sniff the air. Listen to our tread."

She listened. Was there a faint echo? Groping with one hand, she touched cold, wet stone.

"If I were to let go of your other hand—which I won't—you would touch the opposite wall," he said. "We're in a tunnel."

"Then we'll end up back in the cathedral! Glory be— we can find our way out of there!"

"We're not in that tunnel. I've chosen another."

It took several seconds for the terrible import of his words to register. "We'll never get out!"

"Shh, honey. As my grandfather, Dominique Laffite, used to say, be tranquil."

"Since when does a pirate tell anyone to be tranquil?"

Rafe took her face in his hands. "*Ma chérie,* do not let fear override hope. Trust me."

"How? It's your fault I'm down here in this hell-hole!" Immediately ashamed of herself, she burst into tears.

"I've gotten you into a rough stretch of water, I know," he said. "I don't blame you for being angry."

"I'm sorry. It's not your fault I wandered down here . . . and I've forgiven you for what happened years ago. I oughtn't act so small."

"You, small? You're a champion, the bravest woman I know. If I were you, I'd never speak to a wooden jackass like me again."

A chuckle shivered through her. "You're not a jack-ass. Not a wooden one, anyway."

"A cast-iron one, then, as you'll see if you bang on my head." He dropped his bantering tone. "If you've forgiven me, you're a better saint than the heavenly host, and I'll spend the rest of my life making it up to you."

"Time's short, I'm afraid."

"A hundred years is too short," he said, "for what I have in mind."

Though trapped in complete darkness, Lizzy felt a wellspring of light bubble inside her. "Maybe you'll show me what you have in mind."

She felt his fingertips in the notch beneath her chin. Breathless, she waited for his kiss. Since she couldn't see him, only the contact of his fingers joined them. It was like standing in the spirit world, waiting for a living soul to call her forth. In him there was life and hope. In him there was no fear of darkness. Whatever happened would happen to them together. As long as he was with her, she thought she could face it.

"Rafe, we'll get out of here, won't we?"

"I don't have the slightest doubt. Are you ready to go on?"

"Yes. Only . . . talk to me as we walk. I don't want to feel alone."

"You'll never be alone, darling. Never, never again." As he began to lead her along, his voice rumbled rich and low. "I'll never repeat the mistake I made seven years ago. No power on earth will ever drag me from your side."

She contained her emotion with an effort. "I'll never thrust you away again, Rafe. I never stopped blaming myself for that."

"Why did you marry him, Eliza?"

Caught by surprise, she stumbled against his back. He steadied her, and for a moment she sensed the touch of his eyes. He did not repeat the question. He did not have to; it hung in the air between them like a balloon. "You don't want to know, Rafe," she said at last. Now wasn't the time to tell him about the baby. He had enough worries.

"Charlie said he had loved you forever."

His voice was as disembodied as her conscience. She didn't like it. She'd spent too many years quashing her guilt over Charles into a ball the size of a pincushion. Did forgiving Rafe mean she had to admit her own sins?

The pins pricked her breast. When Charles had married her, he'd known she still loved Rafe. It was his misfortune, he said, that she'd fallen for his best friend before he could declare himself. He knew she carried Rafe's child. He was her lifeline, he said. He could save her and her father from social ruin. And so, hiding her guilt behind a veil, she'd married him in the Church of the Nativity.

"Why did you marry him, Eliza?"

"I—I didn't think you were ever coming back.

286

Charles and my father were close . . . it seemed like a good match." She heard his sharp intake of air. She'd hurt him again. The gloom was darker than imagination.

"It was a good match, I suppose," he said. "A woman needs a man to care for her."

"He . . . tried."

"Tried, Eliza?" A dangerous note vibrated in his words. "He did not keep you well?"

"Times were hard." She couldn't speak ill of the dead.

"Even after I returned the money?"

"What money?"

"Never mind. You weren't supposed to know about it, anyway."

But she jerked her hand free, cutting herself loose in the dark. Rafe caught her shoulders. "Don't break contact!"

"What money? What wasn't I supposed to know?"

"I guess it won't hurt for you to find out now. The reason I joined Juárez in Mexico was to win enough money to repay your father and the other investors in that cotton deal I brokered. I sent back the money, all of it, plus double the interest."

"Daddy never said anything about it, and neither did Charles!"

"You were married by then, remember?"

"So?"

Rafe's voice purled like deep, slow water. "And how would you have felt, Eliza McCord, to know your former lover was not the unmitigated bastard you thought he was?"

"I never thought that of you."

"I'm glad to know it," he said with a hint of the old mockery, "since your letters stated otherwise."

"I was angry when I wrote them."

"You made that clear." His fingers touched her cheek. "I deserved it."

"Let's not start that again. Daddy always said that words spoken in anger breed seven generations of anger. What's past is past, Rafe, and I won't abide more regrets. Haven't we suffered enough?"

"A lifetime's worth."

"Then tell me the end of the story and let's put it to rest. You'll get no blame from me, I promise."

He led her on a ways before speaking. "Your father died before I'd finished repaying the debt. I sent the balance to Charles, bit by bit, month after month. I swore him to secrecy. He wasn't to tell you."

"He had no trouble honoring that commitment," Lizzy said. Her mouth tasted like acid. She'd known nothing of Rafe's payments. Nothing of his honor. "Once Daddy was dead and Charles and I inherited the plantation, he sealed the books in the vault and changed the combination."

"Then he did as I asked him."

"No! He—he did it for himself, Rafe. He was jealous of you . . . he thought he never measured up."

Rafe said nothing for a moment. "Then why did he join me in Mexico?"

"We were broke. It didn't take him long. The plantation was more than he'd bargained for . . . he thought he could set everything right by imitating you."

Rafe breathed an oath. "And instead he lost his life."

"Yes." She touched his face. "I wronged you more deeply than I imagined. I can't go the rest of my life without telling you I'm sorry. I *am* sorry. Dear God, I feel like I thrust a knife into you!"

He caught her in his arms. "You thrust a knife into my soul every time I see you, every time I hear you, every time I think of you! I've slain myself on the blade of love every hour of the day and night."

"Don't speak like that! How can you love me so after all that happened?"

"Speak forgiveness to your own soul, Eliza," he said. "Then forget all but your love for me, as I have forgotten all but mine for you. Perfect love, all my life I've wanted perfect love. I find it in you."

Tendrils of love entwined Lizzy's heart. It didn't matter that she stood in a primordial night. In her blindness, she saw as she'd never seen before.

"I love you, Rafe Laffite," she said. "I love you forever. Always and forever."

"And I love you, Eliza. You own my soul."

"Make love to me, Rafe. Right here."

It was a long time before they again walked into the darkness.

Chapter Twenty-five

"Come on, Eliza, let's keep moving."

She was becoming weak. Although she didn't complain, her dry, shallow breaths alarmed him. "Don't give up, honey."

He refused to think about his own diminishing strength, the parched, raw feeling in his core, the madness gnawing at his mind. The blackness was beyond imagination. It had breath and power of its own, a creeping aliveness that penetrated his nerve endings and permeated the hollows of his being. It overwhelmed him, sucked his life juices, leached his very bones. With only blackness to see, his vision turned inward to the ghastly predations in his brain.

Consigned to perdition, he was cast by his own sins into a place far from the reach of any but God. It was to God he must turn. But when he tried to pray, his tongue stuck to his teeth and cobwebs laced his throat.

Boulders pressed the air from his lungs. In the Stygian night, devils laughed.

Father in heaven, help me! His mind uttered the desperate cry; he could not force his mouth to move. *Help me save Eliza! Show me the light!*

He had made a terrible mistake choosing this tunnel. She had warned him to go back to the cathedral, but in his arrogance he had gone the other way. *Don't let her die for my folly.*

Keep following the bats.

The thought entered his mind with galvanic force. His every sense excited, Rafe swung his head back and forth like a blind wolf. *Lord, is it You?*

Your feet are on the path. Follow it.

He didn't question the decision. Whether it had come from his own imagination or from a greater source he did not ponder. It felt right. It confirmed his hopes that somehow, some way, he could bring Eliza back to life.

Eagerly he pressed forward, his right hand brushing the clammy wall. At times the tunnel forked, but he continued to follow his instincts. The bats knew the way out. All he had to do was follow the signs they'd left before going into hibernation. The infrequent patches of guano on the tunnel floor had not yet decayed to dirt, and sometimes when he sniffed the air, he detected an elusive scent of vegetation.

He wiped sweat from his face. The air was cold and still. He searched for subtle changes in temperature and movement—a warm gust of air, a change in humidity— anything that would steer him through the maze.

"There's water here, Eliza. I'll get you some." He heard her make a small sound as she slumped against the wall. Scooping water from a puddle, he raised it to her lips. "Drink, honey."

291

"I'm not thirsty."

"Yes, you are. You just don't know it. Come on."

He felt her lips move against his hands. "You know I love you," he said.

"I know." Her voice was faint. "But I'm so tired."

She was shaking like a willow switch. How long since she'd eaten? How many miles had they wandered? "Let me lie down and sleep, Rafe . . . just for a little while."

"No, we've got to go on." If she shut her eyes, she might never wake up. Even now, he could barely feel her breathing. Catching her behind the knees and shoulders, he lifted her, turned into the blackness, and climbed swiftly upward. Like a bat he listened for echoes to guide him around curves and obstacles. He felt at one with the darkness.

And then his footfalls disappeared. He stopped to listen for an echo. Nothing. The echo returned, a faint *thump-thump* rising out of the ground. Somewhere close in front of him lay a deep hole. He took one step back and set his precious burden behind him. "Don't move, Eliza."

Gingerly he moved forward again until his foot touched air instead of stone. He stepped back and clapped his hands. The reverberation came from deep in the ground. "There's a sinkhole in front of us," he said.

She didn't answer for several seconds. "Can we get around it?"

"I'll see. Wait right there."

He began to feel his way along a narrow ledge. He had to inch along sideways, jamming his fingers into every crevice. The rock wall pressed against his spine, forcing him to lean forward, away from his center of gravity. Vertigo washed through his brain with such intensity he thought he was falling. His heart pounded in his ears like a bass drum.

One, two, three steps. Five . . . fifteen . . . sixteen. Sixteen paces. His boot touched solid ground. He was across. Willing the dizziness to fade, he leaned against the wall and took long breaths of clammy air.

"Rafe, where are you? What are you doing?"

"Don't move—I'm coming back."

It wasn't any easier. Despite the cold, sweat poured down his face and stung his eyes. At last he cleared the pit and bent to take her hand.

"We have to cross a ledge, honey. You have to walk sideways. Can you do it?" He felt her trembling. When she didn't answer, he took her by the shoulders, steadying her. "Can you do it?"

"I don't know! How deep is the sinkhole?"

She'd know it if he lied. "Too deep for us to drop into for a stroll."

"My legs are shaky."

He couldn't carry her across the pit. Their fate rested on her. If she wouldn't risk it, he'd have to take her back down into the cathedral to try to find another way out. And that, he knew, was sure death.

"If you can walk sixteen feet," he said, "I'll carry you the rest of the way out of the cave."

"I can do it," she said in a small voice. "Lead me, Rafe."

The next minutes of his life dragged on for ten years. Holding her right hand, he led her step by step across the void. All the while he talked softly to her, urged her to plant her feet, to maintain contact with the wall, to hold her head perfectly still so she wouldn't get dizzy. Pebbles skidded into the darkness and fell for many seconds before the echo came.

At last he reached solid ground. He caught her to him and lifted her clear of the ledge. He didn't set her down, but kissed her passionately. He wanted to get her out of the cave, to cover her with warm quilts, to feed her until she was strong and whole once more.

"Thunderation, I love you!" Then, carried away on a tide of gratitude for their narrow escape, he said, "I've just become a churchgoing man."

"I should've gotten you lost in a cave years ago," she said.

"Maybe. Come on, let's keep going."

But she gripped his hand and held him still. "Wait, I have something to tell you. I had a . . . baby."

He felt as though he'd been hit in the head with an anvil. He exhaled a single word: "When?"

"Five months after you left."

Now he knew why she'd married Charlie so quickly. "It was my baby."

"Yes, Rafe." Her voice sighed like a breeze.

He leaned up against the wall and took her face in his hands. He wished he could see her eyes. "What happened, Eliza? Where's my child?"

Her long silence told him something terrible had happened. Then, sounding strangely resigned, her voice echoed through the vault. "He was born too soon. Not even my sister could save him."

His brain reeled. He could not take it in. This woman he had loved and left had birthed his child. He had fathered a son . . . a son he'd never seen . . . a son too small to abide a big, harsh world. And Eliza hadn't told him. He clenched his teeth on a cry of anguish.

Lizzy clapped her hand over her mouth to stifle a sob. She hadn't expected him to feel so distressed, yet that cry of desolation had sprung from his soul. In that instant she knew he would have returned to her, loved her, comforted her. Dear God, she should have told him. How long she had wandered the wilderness of solitude, when a word would have brought him back!

"I'm sorry, Rafe. I'm so sorry."

He crushed her to him. For a time, he did not speak. Blackness pressed down like a tomb, holding them still, holding them for eternity. "You have nothing to be sorry about," he said. "I'm the one who caused your pain. I could ask your forgiveness, but I wouldn't ask for what I don't deserve."

She touched his cheek and found it wet. "Rafe, dear Rafe, this is the last time we'll speak of regrets. God forgave us both, and we must forgive each other."

"I laid a mountain of sorrow on you."

"I'd gladly take it up again!" She caught his jaw and dragged his face down to hers. With all her being she wanted to see him once more, to look into his eyes and whisper her love. "Our lives are at stake now; my love for you is not. I love you, Rafe. Nothing can change that. If we die down here, we'll die loving each other still. With my last breath I'll whisper your name."

"There won't be any last breath, Eliza McCord," he said. Scooping her into his arms, he charged into the night.

She clung to his neck as he bore her along. Strangely, she was not afraid of falling into a sinkhole. He had the instincts of an animal, his senses fixed in a white-hot shaft that bored through stone and saw green earth. Up and up he climbed, his breath growing ragged and harsh, his muscles iron bands around her. Although she sensed tunnels branching off in all directions, he climbed the steepest one.

A musty scent of leaves merged with the sweat of the man. Then a white slit leaped through the darkness. Crying out, she hid her face against his shoulder. "What is it? What is it, Rafe?"

"Daylight. We made it, honey."

*   *   *

295

"I count three Yankees," Lizzy whispered. "Two sitting beneath the balloon tree, one about ten feet up on that dead branch. He looks like a buzzard, the way he's staring around. Bet he's looking for us."

Since they'd hidden on the hillside directly opposite the top of the fir, they could look down on the Yankees. The balloon was tantalizingly close, less than two hundred feet away. It might as well have been on the moon.

Propped on his elbows, Rafe peered around the waxy boughs of a mountain laurel. There were five other Yankees in the woods below, but none seemed interested in the balloon wobbling above them. They seemed intrigued by the frequent flashes of lightning in the southwest.

Yankees were the last thing Rafe had expected to find after escaping the cave through an opening almost a mile away. Somehow, he'd forgotten they were fugitives and the balloon a gigantic wigwag signaling their position.

"What do we do now?" Lizzy asked. She was smeared with mud, her pretty dress ruined for life, but the glow in her blue eyes made the Yankees seem manageable.

"We'll go down and liberate the balloon, that's what."

She eyed the pistol jammed in his waistband. "If you shoot those boys, you'll rouse up the rest of them."

"I don't intend to use the gun."

"You'll go down there and ask them, pretty-please, to give back our balloon?"

"Something like that." Using the laurel bush for cover, Rafe stood up, opened his jacket, and removed his suspenders. Doubling the straps in his hand, he picked up a rock and fitted it into the makeshift sling.

"Don't tell me," Lizzy said. "David and Goliath?"

"I used to be pretty good with a slingshot when I was twelve."

"Let's hope you still are. How will you keep them from seeing you?"

"From the looks of it, those two under the tree are asleep, and the buzzard's studying them like he's thinking of swooping down for dinner. Besides, he doesn't expect to see anybody up here."

Rafe stepped from behind cover and spun the slingshot over his head. Once, twice, and the rock sprang free. It sliced the air over Lizzy's head before zinging off into the woods. Rafe dropped flat and slithered over to her as fast as a black racer.

"Good gosh almighty!" he whispered. "Are you all right? Did I hit you?"

"Would I be here to tell about it if you had, Rafe Laffite?" she demanded in a fiery whisper. "I thought you said you were good with a slingshot!"

"I was, at age twelve."

"I wish you were twelve now!"

"No, you don't." He splayed his fingers over her buttocks and smiled into her eyes.

She pushed him away. "Stick to business!"

"You are my business," he said, but he moved off and fitted another rock to the sling. "Keep your head down."

"I'll mind my head; you mind your aim, little shepherd-king David." She wound her arms over her head and buried her face in the dirt.

Rafe whirled the slingshot, waited almost until its zenith, and released the rock. It hit the treetop.

"Quit knocking needles down here, Clephus!" yelled one of the Yankees. "You done messed my hat up!"

"I didn't knock down nothing! It was a bird or a squirrel or something, or maybe your brain ain't seated flush with your shoulders!"

Lizzy sighed, rolled onto her back, and looked up at

Rafe. "You've stirred up a nest of hornets, darling. Maybe we ought to go down there and shoot them, after all."

"You don't mean that and you know it. Watch your head."

Rafe picked up a good-size rock and seated it carefully. This time he gave five good spins, stepped into the throw, and let the rock fly. The stone shot straight as a bullet and caught Clephus in the chest. Crowing like a winded rooster, he keeled off the branch and crashed through the foliage to the ground.

"Stay here, Eliza!" Wadding his suspenders in his hand, Rafe dashed downhill. After a few seconds, he reached the cut at the bottom of the slope and dove into the undergrowth. He could hear the Yankees clucking over their friend.

"What'd you go and fall out of the tree for, you dang baboon?" one of them said.

"You done broke your arm, fool. Sarge is gonna be madder'n a rabid dog at you, and I ain't taking no blame!"

Clephus groaned and cursed.

"Reckon we got to bind that arm up for him—What the hell?"

"Just set your guns down nice and easy," Rafe said as he stepped out from behind a tree. He aimed Jack Daniel's pistol at the bigger of the soldiers standing over Clephus. "Don't cause me trouble, boys, and you'll live to tell your grandchildren all about the war."

Their faces registering sick dismay, the Yankees dropped their rifles on the ground. Clephus rolled around in agony. Rafe stepped forward and kicked the rifles aside. "Turn back to back," he told the uninjured pair. "Hold hands."

The short Yankee whispered to his companion, "It's that Rebel spy we been chasing!"

"You ain't gonna get away with this, Reb," the other said. "Sergeant'll have your head on a pike."

"Not my idea of a hat stand," Rafe said. Jamming his pistol into the side of the bigger man, he one-handedly bound their wrists together with his suspenders. "Now sit down."

"Hold it right there, you Rebel mudsill!"

Turning, Rafe came face-to-muzzle with a Remington army revolver. He looked past the bore to the hand clutching the wooden grip, and from there to Clephus's sweating, chalk white face. The soldier's broken arm jerked at his side. "Drop your gun, Reb."

With the Yankee's gun almost touching his forehead, Rafe had no choice. He dropped his pistol into the dirt, raised his hands waist-high, and stared into the Yankee's tortured eyes. "Why don't you let me bind that arm of yours?" Rafe asked.

"Stay where you are!" Clephus's gaze switched to the soldiers. "You two move out from behind the bastard so's I can plug him between the eyes!"

"You'd shoot an unarmed man?" Rafe asked.

"You've caused enough trouble," the Yankee said.

Sweat beaded Clephus's forehead like raindrops on whitewash, and there was a pale green ring around his lips. His trigger finger tightened until its tendons stuck out. Another pound of pressure and the world would explode into red mush. Rafe tensed to spring.

Before he could attack, a loud *crack!* reverberated in the clearing. For an instant he thought Clephus had pulled the trigger and killed him. Then he saw the Yankee stagger forward, pistol barrel rising to the sky, eyes rolling up in his head. He pitched onto the ground beside Rafe.

Legs splayed and hands wrapped around a broken branch, Lizzy stood over the unconscious body. A splintered chunk of oak lay next to Clephus.

"That boy's head will feel like hammered iron when he wakes up," Rafe said. Retrieving both pistols, he pointed them at the Yankees, who promptly left off struggling with their bonds. "Nice work, Mrs. McCord."

But Lizzy dropped down on one knee and palpated the back of Clephus's head. "Did I knock his brains loose, do you think?"

"You're talking about a Yankee, honey. Skull's too thick; brain's too small. He'll be fine. Get his trousers."

"His *trousers?*" But even as she mouthed the words, Lizzy rolled the Yankee onto his back. She had to yank off his boots before she could pull his trousers over his feet.

"Hurry, Eliza, tear me some strips. Let's bind these characters."

Before long the three soldiers lay bound under a rhododendron. "All right, let's get out of here before their friends show up!" Lizzy said.

Rafe bundled the Yankees' rifles and cartridge boxes together with a strip of cloth, slung the load over his left shoulder, and climbed into the tree. He pulled Lizzy up behind him. They released the tether and jumped onto the ladder. The balloon began to sweep over the trees before they'd reached the basket.

"We're in for a storm," Lizzy said. "Look at those clouds!"

Rafe was more interested in the ground. Although he saw no soldiers among the trees, he wasn't optimistic enough to believe they were all in the cave. After checking the loads on the four guns he now possessed, he handed Lizzy a rifle.

"If anybody shows his face, kill him."

Lizzy hardly heard him. The storm wasn't far off. Dark, swirling cloud demons spat fire and lightning. Solid gray walls of rain cloaked the northeast. The wind struck the balloon, distorting its side, forcing it into a skid across the treetops. Lizzy's throat tightened. They were going awfully fast. Usually she could rely on ground effect to carry them up and over slopes, but with the winds so unstable, they could be driven straight into a mountain.

Rafe looked back at the launch site. "Sweet thunderation, now they've seen us!"

Well behind the balloon, three Yankees appeared on a boulder. Fire flashed from their guns but the wind carried away the sound. Lizzy aimed one of the rifles at a blue uniform, but the basket twisted and spoiled her shot. The recoil sent her staggering. The basket clipped a treetop, tore off branches, and lurched like a drunken marine. Lizzy threw her rifle overboard.

"What are you doing?" Rafe hollered.

"Lightening the load! We've got to get altitude or we'll crash into that cliff! See it?"

She threw every loose object she could find overboard, then dumped the contents of the valise onto the floor and threw out the case.

Borne by an obstacle flow of wind, the balloon mounted the cliff. Dead pines poking from the crevices tried to gash the fragile silk envelope sweeping by. Lizzy threw away the second rifle. Bouncing over the boulders, it splintered into a hundred pieces.

The balloon cleared the mountaintop like a buck leaping a fence and continued to rise at a terrible rate. The morning sky became black as night. Lizzy looked over her shoulder. Her vocal cords froze.

A monstrous thunderhead stooped to suck them in. Lizzy saw the balloon disappear into its black maw. Then darkness swallowed her.

Chapter Twenty-six

Like a marionette jerked into the air, the balloon ascended into the cloud so fast that Lizzy and Rafe were knocked off their feet. They lay pressed to the floor, held by invisible hands. Sucking and clawing, the wind battered the balloon out of shape, then yanked it into a blazing firestorm. Thunderous explosions racked the fragile air machine. Rain swamped the basket, obliterating the gondola's lateral stability. It began to rock like a dinghy on a running sea.

Lizzy's gaze fastened on the barometer. Minus twenty-five inches of mercury. They were over eighteen thousand feet high and still climbing. "I've got to vent the gas, Rafe!"

The wind ripped the scream from her throat and hurled it away. Struggling to stand, she reached for the valve, but the gondola canted violently and flung her into Rafe, who seized her in a mighty grip.

"Let go! Let go! I've got to reach the valve!" She

couldn't make him hear her. As the water-filled basket spun out of control, she struggled and screamed, but he wouldn't let go.

The swirling, roaring maelstrom sucked them deep into its core. Hemp began to snap and untwist from the balloon collar. If they lost the harness, the basket would fall out of the sky.

"Let go, Rafe!" In a desperate burst of strength Lizzy broke free and made a grab for the valve, but before she could touch it, sleet blinded her. "Help me vent the gas! We've got to drop out of this storm!"

Understanding at last, Rafe reached up and seized the valve. As he pulled, the envelope began to collapse under the weight of sleet. Pushed by the icy cloud, the balloon raced downward.

"Don't vent the gas!" Lizzy shrieked, realizing their peril. She grabbed Rafe's hand to stop him. "We're out of control—we'll crash!"

"Start bailing water, then!"

He began scooping with his hands but the influx of rain was too rapid. The terrible weight hastened their plunge to earth. If they hit the ground at this speed, they would fold up like a wrecked train.

As anxious now to stay aloft as she had been to land only seconds before, Lizzy bailed as fast as she could. Freezing rain poured into the basket. A single glance at the barometer told her they had less than two thousand feet to go before they crashed. She tore her gaze from the instrument. When the end came, she didn't want to know it.

And then, drawn by invisible forces of the atmosphere, the balloon leaped into the sky. Slave to the vicious cycle of winds, the craft spun and twisted until one of the main sheets snapped. The gondola spilled over forty-five degrees. A cataract of rainwater poured out, sweeping Lizzy along with it.

As she plunged over the side, Rafe caught her by the hem of her dress. Tangling his knee in the lines to keep from falling out, he tried to drag her back. The basket gyrated.

Lizzy clawed raw air. Lightning ripped and tore at her skin. Thunder crashed against her skull and tried to sunder Rafe's grip on her. "Pull me in! Don't let me fall!"

As the gondola swung high, Lizzy sailed like a flyer on the high trapeze. Just at the moment of weightlessness, Rafe yanked her back. They landed against the gondola's lee side.

"Grab the rail!" he yelled. "Hold on, honey, we're going back the other way!"

Lizzy couldn't reach the rail. As the gondola swung through a hundred and eighty degrees, she seized the caning by Rafe's right hand and felt his free arm close around her waist. Burying her fingers in the wicker, she tried to jam her feet through the floor.

The balloon plummeted so fast that Lizzy thought they would hit the ground, but the thunderhead snatched them greedily back into its bosom and hurled them thousands of feet into rain-soaked air almost too thin to breathe.

Rendered translucent by lightning, the blue silk balloon looked as insubstantial as a jellyfish, unable to bear their weight. At any moment it could furl up and tumble out of the sky.

The cloud was an anvil, the lightning a terrible hammer pounding them to oblivion, preparing to cast them into the dirt like a ruined horseshoe. The wind crescendoed to a frenzied screech, shaking the balloon back and forth, warping the envelope first one way and then the other, smashing down the top, flattening the sides. The craft shot up and down, buffeted and pounded and crushed.

And then the balloon burst out of the thunderhead like a marble out of a shooter's hand. Pushed by the leading edge of the cloud, the craft tacked along at a dizzying speed. Lightning reached after it, gilding the silk with gold filigree.

Lizzy and Rafe managed to stand. Far below, mountains hulked under piles of cotton clouds; sharp peaks poked through the mass like clumps of dirt in a cotton picker's sack.

Although Rafe was holding her, Lizzy dared not let go of the basket; the cockeyed way the thing was hanging from the collar let her see more of the earth than she wanted to.

Rafe kissed the top of her head. "Was it only a few hours ago I promised to become a churchgoing man?"

"Yes, it was, and you'd better not have changed your mind."

"Eliza, if there were a church up in these clouds, I'd be in the front pew."

Lizzy laughed through her tears. "I'm surprised we're not sitting in a heavenly choir loft right now, shining our haloes."

"Mine's too tarnished to shine. Besides, God must have bigger plans for us." Rafe wondered if the diamond had survived.

Lizzy looked at the harness, then at the mountains a long way down. "We're hanging by a thread."

"We only broke one sheet—it looks like the rest are all right," Rafe said. "We're secure enough for the time being. I'm afraid your instruments are gone."

Lizzy had already noticed the empty gimbal that had held the barometer. "I'd rather lose the gadgets than our lives."

"I'll buy you a new barometer."

"I don't want a new one." She fingered his bristly cheek. "You know, I don't think I ever want to fly again. This is the last time."

Rafe smiled, a slow, lingering execution of muscles and teeth that made Lizzy's pulse race. "I kind of hoped you'd fly with me one more time, Eliza. A going-away trip. After the wedding."

She couldn't speak. Searching his eyes, she read his determination. Without uttering a word, she joined her lips to his.

But minutes later, they realized the balloon was sinking. There was no way to stop the balloon's plunge. They had nothing left with which to lighten the load.

As the rosin gas poured into the atmosphere from some unseen puncture, the balloon started flapping like a deflated pig bladder. Rocks and trees rushed up to meet them.

"I love you, Eliza."

"And I love you."

She wrapped her arms around his waist and buried her head under his chin. She felt strangely calm, as if she'd known all along that this moment would come.

How would it feel to die? Would they know pain, or would oblivion come to them all in an instant, and then blessed release from the body into the spirit world?

"You're all I ever wanted, Rafe." She kissed the hollow of his throat, savoring his warmth and strength. It might be a long time before resurrection morning. Even so, she thought her spirit would be able to touch his.

"Promise me that if we die, you'll take my hand the second you awaken," she said, leaning back to look into his tawny eyes.

"We won't die, honey."

"Just promise me, Rafe!"

307

"I promise not to let go of you for a single second."

Lizzy heard the crash of tree limbs. The gondola flipped sideways and she felt herself falling like a rag doll, and then she knew no more.

Rafe sat on the ground cradling Lizzy. Twenty-five feet overhead, its silk canopy covering the treetop, the tangled wreckage swayed on the breeze. Giving off a pungent scent, broken pine boughs carpeted the ground.

He gently turned Lizzy's face and studied her cheek for the fifth time in the last two minutes. He had already pressed moss into the gash running from her left ear to her chin. Despite her injury, her eyes twinkled like stars. She gave him a lopsided leer.

"If this cut didn't hurt so much, I'd swear I was dead. Just look at that balloon!"

"Just look at that tree trunk—one side as slick as a snake's belly." Rafe pointed at the boughs lying around them. "I'd hate to think what would have happened if those limbs hadn't slowed us down."

"You ought to be ashamed of yourself, pulling me on top of you when we hit," she said. "You're not a mattress."

"I couldn't think of a better way to soften your fall."

She prodded him in the ribs. "Anything broken?"

"No, thank God, or your gentle touch would finish me off."

She grinned, then winced at the pain in her cheek. "If you're not broken, there's nothing to stop you from making love to me, Rafe Laffite."

But Rafe swung his head up and stared into the trees. His nostrils flaring, he set Lizzy aside and vaulted to his feet.

"What is it?"

"Listen!" he said.

The damp ground shuddered. Hoofbeats! Before the couple could hide, riders poured out of the woods. Rafe stood perfectly still under the thicket of pistols.

"Y'all are under arrest," a lieutenant said, tilting his gray forage cap back on his head. "Put your Yankee hands in the air!"

Chapter Twenty-seven

Outside the surgeon's tent, two soldiers in butternut stood at sloppy parade rest. While one of them cleaned his half boot with his bayonet, the other peered into the tent.

Clutching a threadbare sheet over her bosom, Lizzy glared back at him. She didn't appreciate being stared at like an animal in a cage; the surgeon ought to have kept the tent flaps closed after the examination.

Doc Price was fussing with his instruments at a table behind her. She swiveled on the stool to watch him. She didn't like the look of the knife he was sharpening, and those needles looked big enough to darn a canvas sail.

"How long till the quartermaster brings back my gown, Doctor?"

"Might be hours—he's got to boil and press it." Doc Price tested the edge of his scalpel on his thumb, grunted, and dropped the knife into an enamel tray. Straightening, he stroked his beard and peered at her through his gold-rimmed spectacles. "Your gown looked like you'd run it through a pigsty, Miz McCord."

"I got it dirty in a cave."

"Cave or pigsty, you'll be lucky if it comes clean."

"I didn't ask for maid service. Where's Rafe Laffite?"

Instead of answering, Price poured brown liquid onto a wad of cotton and applied it to her cheek. She flinched, but he made a clucking noise and pressed it to the wound again. "Keep still, young woman. That's a deep gash you've got. Here, you hold the cotton."

The hem of his Confederate-issue frock coat brushed Lizzy's knee, opening the sheet to her hip. She snatched it closed. The curious guard outside cleared his throat. She shot him another glare.

"I'll have to set a stitch or two in that cut," the surgeon said.

"Oh. Do you think it's necessary? Won't it heal by itself?"

"Sure, it'll heal, and you'll have an ugly scar to remember the incident. A few stitches, and within a month you'll hardly be able to see it."

Her gaze flicked to the needles in the tray. She'd rather crash the balloon all over again than feel them pierce her skin.

"I'll give you a drop of absinthe, my dear," Price said in a softer tone. "It's the best I can do for painkiller, since we're out of laudanum."

Without waiting for argument, he threaded a needle with catgut, then poured absinthe from a small, triangular flask into a tin cup. Lizzy shut her eyes. The clink of metal and glass, and the stench of the wormwood-derived absinthe, turned her stomach.

Where was Rafe? She hadn't seen him since they rode into camp and the doctor had whisked her off. She could use his strong arms right now, but she feared he had a lot more worries than her operation.

Lieutenant McElvey, the man who'd captured them, didn't believe Rafe was a Confederate. During the long trip to the army encampment, he had hammered at Rafe's story like a blacksmith on a mule shoe. Rafe couldn't produce a single paper to prove his loyalty. When Lizzy started to burst out with the story of Louis DeCoeur's book, Rafe silenced her with a glance.

What would they do to him? How ironic that the whole Union Army knew exactly who he was and what he was about, while his own people believed him a Yankee spy!

"They shoot spies, don't they?" she asked.

Needle and thread dangling from his fingertips, the surgeon turned around and fastened his gaze on her. "Is he a spy?"

"No."

"Can you prove it?"

"No . . . yes." Softly, earnestly, she poured out the entire tale. At the end of it, the surgeon set his suturing materials on the tray, eyed Lizzy one last time, then strode out of the tent.

Cupping her throbbing cheek in her hand, she stared after him. She wondered if she'd done the right thing.

"Miz McCord, you're free to go now. There's somebody out here that wants to see you," Price said.

Dressed now in her laundered gown, Lizzy ran out of the surgeon's tent. Blinking in the sunlight, she stopped dead in her tracks.

His wide shoulders barred with major's epaulettes, Rafe Laffite stood tall and straight in a Confederate cavalryman's uniform. The golden plume on his hat tossed in the breeze. A silver saber hung by his side. He didn't move, just looked at her out of solemn eyes.

Had she riled him? All of a sudden she was angry. "Rafe Laffite, you didn't expect me to sit still and watch you get shot, did you?"

His mouth quivered. "Remind me not to tell you secrets," he said, then held out his arms.

She rushed into them and caught his jaw, dragging his mouth down to hers. He smelled like soap, and his growth of beard had fallen to the razor. Tingles shot through her system from one end to the other. She didn't care who was looking.

When she finally stopped to draw breath, he gently touched her cheek. "Five stitches," he said. "My poor lamb. Should I beat the hell out of the sawbones?"

"I already did. I kicked his shins every time he stuck me."

"He deserved it." Then, his eyes dancing, he asked, "Want to see the balloon?"

"You got it down?"

"The boys got it down and hauled it here in a wagon."

The balloon was spread upon the grass in a clearing. The basket crouched nearby like a broken-winded mule, its sheets tangled around it like an uncombed mane. "The Yankees shot us down," Rafe said. "It wasn't the storm that crashed us, after all. Just look at those bullet holes."

She slipped off her shoes and stepped onto the silk. Crouching, she pushed her fingers into the holes. Tears stung her eyes.

Rafe looked at her gravely. "Think we can patch it?"

Not wanting him to see her tears, she rubbed her eyes with the back of her hand. "I—I suppose Doc Price would let me have a needle and thread. If we commandeered some poor soul's gutta-percha ground cloth, we could get the cook to melt it down. But how could we refill the balloon? There aren't many gas lamps growing on trees out here.''

"I've worked that out already. Lieutenant McElvey will take us to Jonesboro.''

"And what's in Jonesboro?''

"An iron works. The biggest one in the South.''

"Oh.'' Lizzy's mind raced ahead. She thought she knew what Rafe was concocting, and she liked it not one bit.

"Mix sulfuric acid and iron and what do you get?'' he asked.

She lifted her chin and gazed at him through slitted eyes. "Hydrogen gas.''

He smiled at her as though she were a star pupil reciting Paracelsus' *Theory of Chaos in Metallurgy*. She didn't smile back. Grudgingly she said, "I guess you know that hydrogen outlifts rosin gas by at least thirty percent.''

"I never gave much thought to it,'' he said.

"Yes, you have—I can tell by that look in your eyes. You know more about science than you've admitted.''

Rafe shrugged. "I know that once we fill the bag with hydrogen, we'll float too high for any Yankee to shoot us down.''

"There's another property of hydrogen to consider.''

"I already thought of that,'' he said. "It's unstable.''

"It's *explosive!* Do you know how many French aeronauts have gone down in flames?'' She had to pierce the hide of stubbornness he'd pulled over his brain. "Why do you think Daddy and I never used hydrogen?''

"Look, honey, if Jonesboro had rosin gas we'd use it, but McElvey says they don't.''

Taking his right hand in both of hers, she pressed it

over her heart. "One bullet through the envelope and we'll be done for."

"Would you rather walk to Richmond?"

"I'd rather take the damned train!" she said, throwing off his hand.

"We'll end up doing that, anyway, before all is said and done, but I'd just as soon put it off. Too many Yankees attacking the railroad. I can't afford to get caught now."

"Can you afford to get blown up now? That's your choice!"

A muscle throbbed in his cheek. "I won't ask you to go any farther, Eliza. You can stay in Jonesboro—they say John Morgan's secured the region—and I'll go on alone."

Lizzy pushed her face close to Rafe's and said between her teeth, "That's my balloon, Major Laffite! Nobody flies it without my leave!"

"I'm confiscating it on behalf of the Confederate Army, ma'am. You'll get it back after the war."

"Rafe Laffite, how can you be so pigheaded?" she screamed. From all over the camp, heads lifted in surprise. She didn't temper her voice. "I swore I'd never fly again, but I'm taking back that oath! If you go, I go, or I'll take a hatchet and chop that balloon into so many pieces there won't be enough left to blow your nose on!"

"Did I ever mention you're the most belligerent female I've ever run across?" A smile creased his face.

He'd trapped her. Turning on her heel, she strode off to the surgeon's tent. She had a balloon to patch. Doc Price could sew up something besides skin.

The Pleasant Valley Iron Works in Bumpass Cove, Tennessee, looked like a scene out of hell. Acre upon acre of rusty dirt pushed against pyramids of pig iron. Dust rose from ore-crushing pits, fires blazed in open retorts, and thick, rubiginous smoke shrouded the morning.

Gazing up at a monstrous stone furnace, Lizzy sat against a cottonwood tree by the Nolichucky River. Her eyes burned from smoke and lack of sleep. Since arriving at the ironworks four days ago, she and Rafe had worked like fiends to convert an old retort to hydrogen production.

"Lord, I must have been out of my mind to agree to this."

Maybe she could ask Duff Green, foreman of the ironworks, to take her into Jonesboro. Since the town was a railroad hub, there was a good chance of finding a train bound for Richmond. Surely someone could give her better than even odds on getting past the Yankees.

"Eliza, we're ready to inflate the balloon." Rafe was standing a few feet from the tree.

"One of these days I'm going to stop being surprised when you sneak up on me."

"One of these days I'll remember to make more noise," he said, but the gleam in his eyes promised things that had nothing to do with walking. He came and took her hand, helped her up, then, with his fingertips, lifted her chin and kissed her.

But instead of warmth, cold infused Lizzy's system. With a cry, she threw her arms around his neck. "Rafe, Rafe, please, let's not do this. I've got such a terrible feeling about it—it's too dangerous!"

"Nothing will happen, Eliza," he whispered against her hair. "People have been using hydrogen for years."

"And you know what happens to them sometimes!"

"Honey, if old Thaddeus Lowe's Yankee aeronauts can hang over a battlefield in tethered balloons without getting shot down, we can fly over anything that comes along.''

"You know better than that, Rafe. You saw the holes in the envelope! We've already been shot down. And don't tell me lightning never strikes twice!''

"I don't expect you to come," he said. "You can stay in Jonesboro. There's a boardinghouse just down the hill from young Henry Jackson's place.''

Lizzy gripped him by the epaulettes. "You're not going without me!''

"I don't want to endanger your life further.''

"There are trains, Rafe!''

"I hear the Yankees cut the rail up at Iron Mountain. Telegraph's down, too.''

"If I didn't know better, I'd swear you arranged the whole thing just to get me up in that balloon again.''

Grinning rakishly, Rafe cupped her left breast. "Being alone with you in a balloon has certain advantages, Eliza McCord. It beats the hell out of a train for privacy.''

Smoke drifted across the balloon floating taut and full over the ironworkers gripping the mooring lines. The reddish cast from the furnaces made it look as though it were on fire, and made the men like hellions.

Feeling as though she were entering a Viking funeral barge, Lizzy let Rafe help her into the basket. It took all her willpower to keep her fear hidden inside, away from the curious onlookers.

Rafe climbed into the balloon. The ironworks' owner, R. L. Blair, stood on the platform beside it with a bottle of port and three glasses. He poured for Rafe and Lizzy, then lifted his glass to the balloon.

"To the Confederacy!" His men hollered and stamped.

"To that big ol' gas bag up there!" Laughter mingled with the cheers.

"To the Pleasant Valley Iron Works, and you men who made all this possible!"

Lizzy raised her glass to them, then took a sip. Her hand shook. She hastily lowered the glass.

"To the intrepid Miz Lizzy McCord, and that gallant son of the Confederacy, Major Rafe Laffite!"

The balloon rocked as a hundred men thundered with the voice of Vulcan: "Hoorah! Hoorah to the aeronauts!"

"Cast off the lines!" R. L. Blair shouted, overcome with excitement.

Taken unawares, two of the handlers failed to release their lines. As the other six handlers let go, the balloon leaped convulsively, causing the basket to cant. Making a grab for the rail, Lizzy spilled wine all over her dress. Rafe threw his arm around her.

"Release the lines!" he commanded the tardy handlers.

The balloon lifted through the nightmare glare and smoke of the furnaces until, at six hundred feet, the wind sent it leaping like a buck. For a long time the craft rushed along the current of smoke until, at last, it surged into clear blue air.

Lizzy checked the barometer Mr. Blair had supplied, then studied the wispy clouds. Far below, the balloon's tiny shadow raced across the ground, jumping mountains and gorges. She shivered in the cool air. "We're nearly a mile high, Rafe."

"Yes, and it's a good, steady wind, honey," Rafe said, moving near. His eyes like sunlit bits of amber, his strong face warmed her. "Still mad at me?"

"I ought to be, but instead I feel . . . exhilarated." It was true. For her, flying was a powerful aphrodesiac;

mixed with Rafe Laffite's brand of sexuality, it was explosive. She trembled when he held out his hands.

"Glad you didn't give up flying?"

"Very glad." She flowed into his arms. "Imagine taking a train, when we can have all the world at our feet."

"Rail travel is for lesser mortals."

"You get more conceited with altitude," she said, but thrills of pleasure raced up and down her spine. She slipped her hands down to stroke his hardening flesh. Against his throat she murmured, "You are certainly no lesser mortal, darling."

"How could I be, when I fly with Aphrodite in my arms?" Rafe whispered. "A mile above the earth . . . there's cause to celebrate, I think."

"We've been this high before," she said.

"But celebrated it only once."

"True, and I don't remember celebrating with a man wearing the proper uniform, Major Laffite."

"We've been negligent, I fear."

"It's never too late to repent."

"Never too late, indeed," he said as he began to unbutton her dress.

Much later, he rested his fingertips against her sore cheek. "Does it still hurt?"

"Oh, just awfully," she lied. "Maybe you should give me another of your medical treatments."

"You won't protest?"

"If I did, you could always tie me with the sheets," she said with a wicked chuckle.

Rafe's eyes flashed. "Now that would be quite a scene, Eliza McCord . . . you spread-eagled to the wind, your cute little derriere hanging over the basket while I ravished you."

"Rafe! What are you doing? I was just teasing!"

"Tease me at your peril, young siren!" Laughing like a devil, he stood her up and held her wrists against a line over her head. His hard flesh pushed against her thighs and belly as he rained kisses upon her shoulders.

"Rafe, we're going to fall out!" she said, but he was doing such delightfully naughty things that she couldn't stop giggling. "Is this how birds do it?"

Rising, Rafe kissed her throat until she writhed uncontrollably. "This is how birds of prey do it, honey. Just like this."

Rafe knew they couldn't land that night. Even though the hydrogen cooled with the falling sun, because of its extraordinary lightness the balloon failed to dip much toward earth. The only way to land was to vent gas, and he was damned if he'd do that.

He studied the charts and compass Mr. Blair had given him, shot the sun with the sextant, compared the reading to Blair's pocket watch, then worked out the logarithm. "We're still on course. This balloon isn't coming down, so we'll just trust to luck that this easterly won't deviate much."

"I see a railroad down there," she said. "Sooner or later, we'll have to catch a train. You know this wind isn't going to carry us all the way to Richmond—we're lucky we've gotten this far north."

"If we can just get across the Blue Ridge, I'll be satisfied."

"Something tells me you'll never be satisfied, Rafe Laffite, until you unload the thing you're carrying. And even then, you won't be able to unload it from your mind."

"Been doing a little snooping, honey?"

"Snooping? What are you talking about?"

"Never mind." He raised her hand and kissed it.

"Sometimes my brain is as soft as a cotton-clad steamboat. Sorry."

Lizzy regarded him for a moment in silence. "You thought I went looking for the plans to the bomb."

"I . . . yes. But only for a minute."

"If I had wanted them, they would be in my hands already—it's obvious where they're hidden."

"Now, Eliza—"

But she bored her finger into his breastbone. "Don't you 'now Eliza' me! You're acting as skittish as a sinner at a tent revival, my handsome young Major Laffite, and all for nothing. We agreed I wouldn't look at your moldy old plans because I didn't want to be tempted to use them against the North, myself! I suppose you don't trust me."

"You have every right to be angry," he said.

"Say you acted like a jackass."

"How about if I kiss you, instead?"

"Uh-uh! Say 'I'm a jackass.' "

"You're a jackass."

"Rafe!"

"All right, I'm a jackass, and you're the sweetest filly I ever met. Now what about that kiss?"

"Try and take it!" Lizzy said. Laughing, she charged away from him. Pretending not to be able to catch her, he chased her around the basket. At last he caught and kissed her.

"You're really sorry for doubting me?" she asked.

"As Great Uncle Renato Beluche used to say, 'I am sorrier than the rabbit who jumped into the coon-dogs' kennel,' " he said in French. "Let me make it up to you, Eliza. I know just how to do it."

"And how is that?"

"Relax and see." Laying her on the soft quilts supplied by the ladies of Jonesboro, he obtained her forgiveness.

Later, Lizzy rested her head on his arm and listened to the silence. It was dark now, the only sound the rustle of silk when the balloon bumped air currents. Stars spilled past the canopy like diamonds out of a black velvet bag. Sparkling meteors sliced the sky before the horizon snuffed them out.

Snuggling closer to Rafe, Lizzy pushed her fingers through the hair on his chest, then ran her hand down to the scar on his flank. "I was afraid you were going to die from this."

"I would have, without you and Mrs. Fairlove."

"You never told us how it happened."

Rafe thought back to a dark night in Mexico City, way down under the emperor's palace, to a treasure vault. It was something he did not want to remember. The diamond wouldn't let him forget.

"Are you all right, Rafe?"

"It was just a bad recollection. . . . Nothing to worry about." But he wiped sweat from his face.

"You were so silent. You looked like you saw a ghost. Louis DeCoeur's?"

"I wish his ghost were all I had to contend with. I have a feeling he's not far away."

"How could he possibly catch up with us?"

"By train or horse. Train, more likely. Don't forget, he has the Signal Corps on his side. He probably knows about where we are. Our delay at Jonesboro didn't help us any, either. We've given him ample time to catch up."

"I'd like to get my hands around his throat and fix him good!" Looking like a Valkyrie under the stars, she rose to her knees and pantomimed the threat.

Rafe caught her wrists and snatched her down on top of him. "If you have the misfortune of meeting that ogre face-to-face, Eliza, run like the devil himself was after you!"

"I'll run after I wring his neck like a turkey's."

"Stubborn chit. It's my goal in life to keep you away from him." Letting go of her wrists, he trailed his hands down her back. "I'll keep you all to myself."

"I don't want it any other way," she said. "Will you make love to me again?"

Rafe applied himself to the task.

Chapter Twenty-eight

Rafe seized the rail in his strong hands and squeezed until the cane began to crack, his gaze riveted on a stream of smoke far to the west. His jaw worked as though he were chewing a mouthful of swear words.

"What is it, Rafe?" Lizzy shoved off the quilt and jumped to her feet. Her wrinkled dress swung around her legs as she joined him. Early morning light pierced her eyes. No, it was the slash of a heliograph. "A signal?"

"Yes. And there's a train not too far away." He took her by the shoulders and looked into her eyes a long moment.

She read bleakness in his expression. Chills snaked up and down her spine. What horror had the Yankees concocted for them now? Instinctively she looked up at the balloon. The hydrogen . . .

"Are they fixing to start shooting at us again?"

"No."

There was something else at work here . . . something worse than bullets. "What is it? You've got to tell me!"

He laid his hand over hers. In a voice she scarcely recognized, he said, "They have Hattie Lee."

"Hattie Lee?" Her mind went numb. The child was back in Alabama . . . wasn't she?

"Louis DeCoeur has her."

"Oh, no!" Lizzy caught the rail and sank to her knees. A shriek ripped her vocal cords. "What has he done to her?"

"Nothing—nothing."

"Then why does he have her?"

"He wants to trade her."

"For the book?"

A spasm twisted Rafe's visage. "For the diamond."

Lizzy stared at him in astonishment.

"Maximilian's diamond, Eliza. I stole the thing. It's hidden under your feet."

For several seconds Lizzy couldn't speak or react. Then a wall of anger crashed down on her. Jumping up, she pummeled Rafe's chest. "Liar! You lied to me! Lied to me again! I hate you! I'll hate you for the rest of my life, Rafe Laffite!"

Rafe caught her wrists and pulled her against his chest. "We'll get her back. I won't let him hurt her."

"What about Grace? Does he have my sister, too?"

"They said nothing of your sister."

"He's killed her!" Screeching, Lizzy struggled to free herself, but he slid his arms around her shoulders and held her close.

"The Yankees wouldn't let him hurt Grace; you know they wouldn't."

"Then how did DeCoeur take Hattie Lee?"

"It's a simple thing to steal a child. We'll get her back."

"Get her back from that monster? What fairy tale do you live in?"

"The one where the good guys win. We'll get her back. Believe in me."

"How can I?" Her voice fell to a moan. "How can I ever believe in you again?"

"Because of *this*." Shifting her aside, he lifted one of the floorboards and extracted a metal box. He raised the lid.

The diamond burst before her eyes like a thousand suns, each facet breaking the spectrum and hurling the bands into every corner of the basket. The blue silk bag overhead was a kaleidoscope, Rafe's eyes, jewels.

"This is what DeCoeur is after—nothing else matters to him." He plucked the diamond out of the case and held it up. A peculiar reddish blue light infused the shining icicle.

Speechless, Lizzy could only stare at the thing. Its very beauty was evil incarnate. An image rose from her consciousness: men and nations had died for the stone . . . the life of a little girl meant nothing to it. Hattie Lee was dead as long as the stone lived.

"DeCoeur promises to give us Hattie Lee in exchange for the diamond, Eliza."

"Then give it to him! What does his greed matter compared to my niece's life?"

Rafe stared into her eyes. "This is the key to his white phosphorus bomb. He puts it in the detonator box to concentrate its light. He can explode a bomb from a mile away."

"I don't care about that! I want Hattie Lee!"

"He and Maximilian want to use it against us—they made promises to Ulysses Grant."

"Grant can go to the devil!"

Rafe did not reply. His gaze returned to the stone. A muscle convulsed in his cheek.

Tortured, Lizzy caught his wrist and stared at the diamond. At last she knew why Rafe wanted to get to Richmond, why he *needed* to get there. He wanted to turn the jewel over to President Davis, along with the plans to the bomb. It could save the South.

Dear Lord in heaven, what could she do? Hattie Lee's life for the diamond . . . or the Confederacy's life for the diamond. Weighed in such a balance, what did the life of one child matter?

Rafe had made his choice. She saw it in his eyes, in the grim set of his lips, in the very uniform he wore. He had sworn an oath to the Confederacy. He would keep it.

Burying her face in her hands, Lizzy wept. She wanted to die . . . oh, how she wanted to die.

"I'm giving the cursed thing back." His voice surged through her nerve endings. She raised her head.

Clasping the jewel in his fist, he stood looking down at her. A brilliant corona of sunlight crowned his head, outdoing the clashing glitter of the diamond.

"He'll get his damned rock back, Eliza."

Leaning over the side, he flashed Morse code with the diamond. The heliograph replied. Reaching up, Rafe yanked the vent ring. Hissing, the balloon began to descend.

Chapter Twenty-nine

Dropping fast, the balloon skimmed over a farm hacked out of a hillside. A mule brayed and kicked a pole off of its ramshackle pen, and a hog squealed and ran through the open door into the cabin.

"Does he expect us to meet him at the train?" Lizzy asked. "All those Yankees . . . how can we get away with Hattie Lee after we hand over the diamond? DeCoeur won't keep his end of the bargain!"

"He'll meet us in the woods."

"Where?"

"He'll signal with smoke. I'll have to track him. It's going to take a long time—the train's probably ten miles from here."

He reached up and shut off the gas valve. "I don't want to lose all the hydrogen," he said. "We're going to need this balloon again. We're low enough to snag a tree."

He handed her the diamond, then tossed the anchor

overboard. With a high-pitched whine the line ran over the rail. The anchor swung over four or five trees before crashing into a black walnut.

"Come on, honey, not a moment to lose!" Snatching the compass and a chart, Rafe started down the ladder.

Lizzy climbed into the rough black boughs. Before she was halfway to the ground, the wind picked up and shook the tree. Walnuts encased in heavy green jackets popped off the limbs like grapeshot, striking her head and shoulders. Rafe caught two in the forehead as he tried to shield her.

Once on the ground, Rafe took a compass bearing and hid his pistol in his jacket. "I'll take the diamond, Eliza."

"It's in a safe place." She pushed up her right breast and showed him the diamond outlined through her dress. "Why not let me carry it?"

"You're not coming, that's why."

"I'll be fried for a hush puppy before I'll stay here!"

"And what if I miss DeCoeur in the woods and he comes here to find both of us gone? What do you think he'll do to your niece?"

"Why don't we signal him with smoke and let him come to us?"

"That's what he wanted to do, and I disagreed. He had to compromise. I don't want him killing us and taking the balloon. It's better that I go to him."

"Laws." Biting her lip, Lizzy drew forth the diamond. The thing felt as dead cold as a snake. She tried not to look at it as she placed it in Rafe's palm. His gaze settled on it with an expression she didn't like.

"Rafe, you will find them, won't you? I mean, the diamond . . ." She didn't know how to go on. There was no estimating the worth of that stone, especially when weighed against its military might. She believed in Rafe, yet even the strongest man might be tempted.

He gazed at her for a long time, his golden green eyes deep and clear as a forest spring, guileless, pure, perilous. "Hattie Lee's value goes far beyond this diamond, Eliza McCord," he said low. "Her worth is measured in my love for you. No shiny piece of carbon can approach it. Set your uneasiness aside."

Lizzy came into his arms and poured her relief into a hard embrace. "I'm sorry. Come back to me, Rafe. Bring Hattie Lee."

"That's the only way I'll come back," he said. "And you can be sure it'll be quick."

He kissed her one last time, then turned and vanished into the woods. Lizzy couldn't hear even a whisper of footsteps. She touched her lips with the tip of her tongue. It was as though she'd been kissed by a phantom.

Rafe could see Hattie Lee's braids sticking out from behind a sapling. She was sitting on the ground, her wrists bound to the tree trunk behind her. Her hands looked blue beneath the rough cords. Rafe's gut churned with anger.

Twenty feet away, Louis DeCoeur stood with a Union soldier, eating ramrod bread and salt pork. A fire blazed close to a tulip poplar tree, but neither DeCoeur nor the soldier seemed worried. As Rafe watched, a second soldier threw an armload of pine boughs onto the blaze. A dense cloud of pitch rolled skyward.

Fools. They didn't need to burn down the woods for him to find them. He could have found them even without the smoke.

Tied to a picket line, five army horses stood in patient resignation a dozen yards from the fire. DeCoeur sauntered over and fed a black gelding a handful of corn.

Careful, Rafe warned himself. *Five horses. Two men*

unaccounted for. Where the hell are the Lancers? Traversing the woods with his gaze, Rafe eased through the undergrowth on hands and knees. He slipped behind Hattie Lee and put his hand over her mouth. She jumped and made a small sound of fear.

"Shh, honey. It's your old friend, Rafe. Don't let out a peep." He took his hand away. Hattie Lee didn't look around. She waited like a wet leaf on a windowpane while he untied her hands.

"So, you gray dog, we have you at last!"

He knew Geraud's voice. Rafe didn't try to rise. Hooking his leg back, he caught Geraud around the knees and spilled him onto his rump, then twisted with the speed of a bobcat to jump him. But Jean-Claude Geraud shoved his pistol into Rafe's face and pulled the trigger. The gun went off like a crack of thunder. Rafe jerked convulsively; Hattie Lee let out a scream.

His ears ringing like church bells, Rafe staggered back. Burned powder clogged his nostrils, and a bullet graze stung his left cheek. Geraud cocked his revolver and began to squeeze the trigger. Rafe kicked the gun into the bushes.

Geraud yanked a dagger from his boot. "You will die, thief!"

Rafe dodged the strike. Thrown off-balance, Geraud stumbled forward. Rafe drove his fist into the Lancer's breadbasket. Geraud crashed into the dirt and lay whooping.

Drawing his pistol, Rafe spun to face the Yankees charging his back. "Stop right there, bluebelly!" He aimed at a corporal. The Yankee's eyes flickered. Too late Rafe looked behind him.

Hidalgo La Peña struck him over the right ear with his sword hilt. Rafe crashed senseless to the ground. Hattie Lee rushed at the horses, but Louis DeCoeur snatched her up and tossed her to Corporal Spears.

"Do not let the chit out of your sight," he said. "Perhaps we will need her again."

DeCoeur jammed the toe of his boot into Rafe's rib cage and rolled him over. Like a grizzly snuffling its prey, he squatted down and began going through Rafe's uniform. At first he worked methodically, but when he failed to turn up the diamond his movements became frenzied. At last he tore off Rafe's jacket and shredded it, then subjected his trousers to the same fate. Rafe lay naked on the ground.

DeCoeur rose slowly to his feet. For over a minute he stared at the unconscious man; then, uttering a blasphemy in French, he began kicking him. Again and again his huge boot thudded into Rafe's side. All the while, he uttered terrible oaths.

Finally Hidalgo La Peña caught him by the arm. DeCoeur flung him off, but the Mexican shouted, "Stop, señor! You will kill the *gringo* before we can question him. Slay him and we will never get the diamond!"

DeCoeur's lips drew back from gums gone red as blood; even the whites of his eyes blazed.

"Don't let him hurt Mr. Rafe!" Hattie Lee cried. "Please, Mr. Hidalgo, don't let that man hurt him!"

"Short of killing you, señor," La Peña said, touching the hilt of his sword, "I do not know how to stop you. Do you wish me to go so far?"

DeCoeur's rage blew out like a candle in a thunderstorm. The lightning faded from his eyes and calmness overtook his features. "Come, *mon ami*," he said, "we will not quarrel over the bastard. Geraud can bathe his head, and then he will tell us what we wish to know, eh?"

Laffite moaned. La Peña said, "He will be awake soon, and without Geraud's ministrations. Please re-

member, señor, he will not serve the emperor if he is
dead.''

Louis swept him a bow. "And it is the emperor we
wish to serve, *non?*"

La Peña did not answer, but strode in tight-lipped silence to reclaim Hattie Lee. She ran sobbing into his
arms.

Rafe awakened a few minutes later to find himself
standing naked and bruised, his hands tied to a branch
overhead. He was in a hell of a spot.

Geraud and the two Yankees lounged under a shag-
bark hickory on the other side of the fire. Hattie Lee sat
near them, her head bowed. Hidalgo La Peña knelt beside her, talking too quietly for Rafe to hear. Once, he
glanced up and caught Rafe's eye. It was not a friendly
look.

If he told them where to find the diamond, odds were
that they would kill him, then go and kill Eliza. Poor
little Hattie Lee would die, too.

"So, we meet again, Monsieur Laffite," DeCoeur
said, approaching him. "It has been a long time since
the—how do the Americans say it? The good old days
in Mexico City. Shame on you for leaving without saying good-bye."

Rafe said nothing.

"You are ready to talk now, *mon ami?*" DeCoeur
spoke with false solicitude. Rafe stared him in the eyes
and did not reply.

DeCoeur suddenly caught him by the hair and twisted
his head back. "Perhaps our Southern man does not
comprehend how we extract information. He does not
know our ways, eh, Jean-Claude?"

"I know your ways, DeCoeur," Rafe said. "I saw

your handiwork in Mexico. That dungeon under Maximilian's palace—''

"Is where I would like to have you," Geraud interrupted with a nasty flash of teeth. "But the forest will do as well. Maybe we will make you dance upon a sharp stick to loosen your tongue."

"A pervert's pleasure."

Geraud slapped him across the cheek, tearing his hair from DeCoeur's grip. His eyes wells of death, he began describing the tortures he would inflict if Rafe didn't talk.

Rafe pretended indifference. He knew that clumsy torturers like Geraud terrified their victims into bubbling hysteria to amplify the pain, which would come later. Rafe forced himself not to listen. If he could hold out, Eliza would have a chance to escape. They wouldn't kill him until they knew where to find the diamond.

He glanced at Hattie Lee and the Mexican Lancer. La Peña hovered as if she were his own child. Rafe remembered him from Maximilian's court. He was a man of honor.

DeCoeur struck him in the face. His head snapped back and the world turned to fire. Through the roar in his ears he heard DeCoeur's insane howl of rage: "You son of a whore, you dare to smile? Where is it? Where? What have you done with my beauty?"

DeCoeur hammered him across the knees with a stick until Rafe cried out in anguish; then Geraud boxed his ears and rammed his knee into his privates. His muscles convulsing, Rafe threw up. DeCoeur struck him in the left kidney.

"Where is the balloon?" DeCoeur screamed. "Where is the diamond?"

"Go to hell," Rafe muttered, and spat in his face.

Uttering a blasphemy, DeCoeur hit him on the point

of the chin. Rafe's head crashed back against the tree; the world darkened.

"No! You will not die!" Lumbering to the fire, DeCoeur snatched up a tin cupful of water and splashed it into his face. "Wake up or the next time I will sluice you with fire!"

Groaning, Rafe climbed through layers of pain. The world was a gray, spinning spiderweb; flames seemed to score his chest and head. He spat blood into the dirt.

Grabbing him by the hair, DeCoeur pressed Geraud's dagger to his throat. Rafe felt the fiery kiss of steel. "I will cut your throat, bastard!" DeCoeur was shaking like an oak in a hurricane. His hand slipped on the bloody handle of the knife.

Rafe forced his words. "Do it and you'll never find out where I hid the diamond. I'm the only one on earth who knows where it is."

"Tell me!"

"I will have to show you."

"Liar!" Geraud said. "Do not listen to him, monsieur! He is a slippery one—he seeks to escape us again."

"I know what the Rebel seeks." DeCoeur increased the pressure of the blade. "Tell me where it is, and I will spare your miserable life. I will leave you here with one of the Federals. He will untie you later."

"I'll tell you nothing."

"So, you are extremely brave, a hero. But heroes die in the same agony as cowards, my friend." Releasing Rafe, he stared at Hattie Lee. "But perhaps you are not such a hero, after all. Perhaps you would see the child die in your stead."

"Don't touch her!" Rafe flexed his wrists in a vain attempt to burst the ropes. "As you value your soul, do not touch her."

"I have no soul," DeCoeur said, and suddenly he laughed. "Untie him, Geraud, it will be faster if he leads us. We are taking a little trip into the forest. Bring the girl."

When Rafe stood free, his naked body bathed in sweat and blood, DeCoeur said, "If you act a fool in the tiniest degree, I will let Geraud play with the little girl. We understand these things, we two, *non?*"

Rubbing his swollen wrists, Rafe nodded. With the point of his dagger, Louis DeCoeur lifted Rafe's shredded trousers and swept them into his face. "Your garment, monsieur."

Lizzy heard hoofbeats coming her way. She jumped up, clutching a stick, and waited in an agony of suspense. An old man on a big red mule rode out of the trees and reined in. He stabbed a gnarled finger at the balloon. "What the hell kinda contraption's that, girlie?"

"A—a gas balloon. You alone, sir?"

"No, I ain't. This here's Ol' Bess. Say howdy."

Wonderful. A lunatic. Where the blazes is Rafe?

"I done seed that thing floating across my farm. Didn't know you'd landed her until a while ago, when my granddaughter come and told me about the young feller back down in the woods. Figured y'all were together. Thought I'd come and see if I could find the balloon."

"What young fellow? You mean Rafe Laffite?"

"Don't know his name. Just know my granddaughter says he's in a barrel of trouble."

Lizzy's heart bounded. "What trouble? With Yankees?"

"Yankees and some uniforms she never seed afore."

Lizzy rushed forward and caught the mule's head

rope. "Where are they? What kind of trouble? Is a little girl with them, and a woman?"

"There's a girl-child. That man of yours has got enough trouble without no woman involved. They're riding him nigh buck-naked through the woods."

"Dear Lord! You've got to help me find him!"

"Ain't none of my business," he said.

Lizzy screamed at him, "Those aren't just Yankees out there—those are Frenchmen from Emperor Maximilian's army!"

"Don't know no emperor."

"He's the emperor of Mexico; haven't you ever heard of him? His men are here to make war on us!"

"On who?"

"Us!" Lizzy jerked the mule's rope, trying to turn him. "All of us—North and South!"

"Is that so? I'll be dadblamed afore I let some foreigner on my property. I got boys in the army. They aim to make war on my boys?"

"Unless we stop them."

"Hell, I ain't got a weapon to my name. Done give my squirrel gun to one of the boys when he went off to the fight."

"Got any dynamite sticks on that farm of yours?"

The old man looked surprised. "Hell, yes, I got dynamite. Been blowin' stumps down by the creek."

"Let's go get it."

Chapter Thirty

Horseflies bit Rafe's naked shoulders and back. Riding double behind Cooper Green, one of the Yankees, he had to concentrate on keeping his seat on the mare's sweaty hindquarters, no easy task with his hands tied behind his back.

DeCoeur rode behind him on a big black gelding. Hidalgo La Peña followed, riding with Hattie Lee in front of him on his horse, then Geraud and the second Yankee, Corporal Spears.

"Go around the boulder, Yank," Rafe said when Cooper Green hesitated at a fork in the trail. A boulder as big and sharp as a church spire loomed just ahead.

The Yankee jerked the horse to the right. DeCoeur, swearing under his breath, kicked his gelding until its nose touched the small of Rafe's back. Whickering, the animal bared its teeth.

At that instant the earth heaved in a blinding explosion of dirt and noise. Green's horse screamed and clawed the air. Rafe jumped off and rolled against the boulder. Too slow to escape, the Yankee fell under the horse. His rib cage splintered with the sound of crunching gravel.

"Draw your weapons!" Louis DeCoeur bellowed. "We are under attack!"

Nobody was in a position to fight. Blinded by smoke and debris, the panicky horses carried their riders helplessly into the woods. Only DeCoeur and Hidalgo La Peña managed to control their mounts.

"Stay where you are, American," La Peña ordered Rafe, training his pistol on his breastbone. He held Hattie Lee under one arm.

"Where are they?" DeCoeur screamed in a mixture of French and Spanish. "Where are the swinish cowards?"

"Be silent and listen!" Hidalgo La Peña said. Geraud and Spears came trotting back.

"Who's out there?" DeCoeur demanded of them. "Who attacked me?"

"Damned if I know," Spears said. Then his gaze settled on the mangled body of Cooper Green. With a curse, he rode over and jumped down beside him. He threw a glance of pure hatred at DeCoeur. "Looks to me like you weren't the one getting attacked, anyway."

Louis DeCoeur descended on Rafe and shoved him against the boulder. "Son of a whore, who tried to kill me?"

"You have enemies all over the continent," Rafe said. "I can't keep track of them all."

DeCoeur punched his face, then pressed his pistol into his stomach. "Old Louis, he can shoot you in the gut right now. You would still live long enough to take us to the diamond."

"That's a big gamble," Rafe said. "My tolerance for pain isn't what it used to be."

"Silence!" DeCoeur jabbed hard with the gun. He turned from Rafe to yell at the Yankee corporal. "Leave him!"

"I'm not leaving my buddy!"

"He is not important."

"He's crushed to death," Spears said. "I ain't leaving his body!"

"This is your fault," DeCoeur snapped at Rafe. "Somehow, you have done this thing."

"I wish I could take the credit."

Mouthing an oath, DeCoeur slammed Rafe's shoulder with the butt of his pistol. Rafe twisted just enough to save his collarbone but a bruise began to color his left shoulder. DeCoeur mounted his horse and slewed it at Corporal Spears, who stood his ground to protect his fallen comrade.

"You will ride in front this time," DeCoeur said. "Keep your eyes open."

"Drop dead, Frenchie," Spears said.

DeCoeur leaned out of the saddle, pressed his pistol against the Yankee's forehead, and pulled the trigger. The corporal's head exploded in a pink cloud. He fell over Cooper Green.

Hattie Lee's scream echoed with the gunshot. La Peña pushed her face against his chest and held her there.

Rafe surged toward Louis DeCoeur, but, with his hands tied, he could do nothing. "You're the devil's own kinsman, DeCoeur," he said with a growl. "If it takes me to the end of my days, I'll send you back to hell."

"Hell is wherever I am, *mon ami,*" DeCoeur said, and this time his smile was genuine. "Geraud, I do not think our Major Laffite should ride anymore. Put him on a lead rope and attach him to your horse.''

Geraud tied a fifteen-foot rope to his wrists and attached it to his saddle horn. La Peña watched in silence. Once, he touched the scarred flesh over his eye. De-Coeur handed Geraud a braided leather thong. "Keep the Rebel running. No more delays.''

"What if there are more bombs, monsieur?''

"There will not be, with our major in the lead. His friends do not wish to hurt him.''

"Go, Rebel!'' Geraud said, cracking the whip across Rafe's naked back. "Run!''

Rafe had to run barefoot. He could feel the hot bursts of the horse's nostrils on his back. If he stumbled, the beast would mash him into the ground.

Eliza must have set off the bomb; he'd seen a flash of blue among the trees just before the explosion. *Careful, Eliza. Don't get caught.*

"You are too slow, Rebel. Hurry up!'' Geraud lashed him low on the back, the whip curling around his loins. His lungs burning, Rafe ran faster. The horse moved closer to his heels; its foam stung the wounds on his back.

Rafe flexed his wrists to stretch and untwist his bonds. He could feel the sharp ends of the hemp fibers dig into his flesh. Suddenly he snapped the rope.

He lunged off the path. Too close to stop, the horse began to pass him. Rafe changed direction and slammed into its right flank. Enraged, the horse pivoted. Rafe stumbled and fell.

Geraud spurred the animal into a tight spin. Trapped in the center of the equestrian tornado, Rafe grabbed the horse's mane and pulled Geraud out of the saddle.

Whump! A second explosion rocked the woods. Dirt sprayed the horses and riders. Rafe fell to his knees, blinded.

DeCoeur missed the brunt of the blast. Spying Lizzy through the trees, he bellowed, "Nameless bitch, you'll die this very hour!"

He charged after her, laughing when the ancient mule she tried to mount shook her off and lumbered away. She hitched up her skirts and ran. DeCoeur whooped and fired his revolver. She dove into a stand of cedar.

"You cannot hide from me!" he shouted. "Come out, girl, that I may kill you!"

He spurred his gelding into the trees. Boughs snapped and stung his face, but he mowed them aside with great sweeps of his arms. Soon he burst out on the other side. She was thirty paces ahead, running hard. DeCoeur jammed his spurs into the gelding.

"You do not deserve a bullet, madame! Instead, you will kiss my horse's hooves!" He saw her throw him a terrified glance, and then her arms went up like wings. She screamed, lurched forward, and the earth swallowed her up.

Warned, DeCoeur sawed at the reins, dragging the gelding to its haunches just short of a precipice. He heard a crash behind him.

"Fire and brimstone to you, foreigner," a fierce old voice said, "according to the word of the Lord!"

DeCoeur flung up his arm just in time to deflect a heavy walking stick an old man wielded. The cane struck the gelding's rump instead. Like a stung rabbit the horse leaped toward the cliff. The man unleashed a yell and sprang after him, trying to drive him over, but with a mighty tug DeCoeur turned the horse and charged.

In trying to escape, the old man stumbled into a rho-dodendron bush. He twisted around and raised his walk-ing stick over his head. DeCoeur shot him through the heart.

342

"Git the hell out of my country," he said, still defiant as he sank to his knees. Then he dropped sideways into the bush.

DeCoeur trotted back to the path and snatched Hattie Lee from La Peña. Before the Mexican could reclaim her, he backed away, pressed his revolver to Hattie Lee's temple, and shouted at Rafe, "Give me the diamond or I will put a bullet through her brain!"

"You son of a bitch," Rafe said. "Let that child go!"

DeCoeur stroked Hattie Lee's hair with the pistol. "She is my—how do you Americans say it? My ace in the hole."

"Where's Eliza?"

"At the bottom of a cliff."

White-lipped and cold, Rafe said, "You will die for that."

The Frenchman only laughed. Rafe stepped toward La Peña and said, "You let him take the child, La Peña. DeCoeur will not let you take the diamond back to Mexico."

La Peña said nothing, but his gaze settled on De-Coeur. Hattie Lee whimpered. The Lancer glanced at her, and for an instant his visage softened.

"He wants it for himself," Rafe Laffite said.

"Do not listen to the liar, *mon ami,*" DeCoeur said. "Our plan is as it has always been."

"That diamond will be your death, DeCoeur," Rafe said.

"*Au contraire,* it is your lady's death. Perhaps I will take you to see her body after you give me the diamond. It is a good place to die. Together your bodies can feed the vultures."

Geraud spoke in a rasp like a rusty sawblade. "Tell the Rebel to hand over the stone!"

DeCoeur cocked his revolver and gently rotated the

muzzle against the soft wisps of hair at Hattie Lee's temple. "What is your choice, Major Laffite? Will you claim another death for your conscience?"

Rafe appeared to gauge his chances, then let his shoulders sag. "I'll take you. It's not far."

DeCoeur nudged his horse forward until its teeth almost touched Rafe's forehead. Gripping Hattie Lee like a rag doll, he leaned down and spoke too quietly for the others to hear. "Only I stand between death and the little girl, monsieur. Do as I say, and I will give you the girl. Disobey and, well, perhaps a bullet would be too quick for her."

Rafe turned and walked up the trail. DeCoeur and the Lancers followed slowly.

Grasping at tree roots and vines, Lizzy struggled up the twelve-foot cliff. She clawed her way over the top and lay panting for a minute.

The old man was gone. Had he gotten tired of harassing DeCoeur and gone home to his granddaughter? Maybe he'd gone after the mule.

As she trotted off toward the game trail, she passed a big rhododendron bush decorated with red poison ivy. She didn't see the old man's feet sticking out from under the edge of the bush.

After a few minutes she heard voices. The balloon was close by, just over the next rise. Why was DeCoeur heading for it? If Rafe had given him the diamond, he ought to be on his way back to Mexico. He knew the balloon could fly only east; stealing it would do him no good.

She heard a thin wail. *Hattie Lee!* Lizzy hitched her skirts to her thighs and ran. As she dashed around an umbrella magnolia tree, a king snake curled into a defensive posture on the ground right in front of her. Startled, she crashed into the tree boughs. The two-foot-long leaves curled around her like the winding cloths of a mummy.

By the time she'd fought her way back onto the path, Hidalgo La Peña was there, leveling his pistol at her head. For an instant his eyes brightened as though he'd recognized her. Then he scowled and said, "Your niece waits for you, Señora McCord. Perhaps you will be good enough to set off no more bombs."

"Where's my sister? What did you do to Grace?"

"Nothing. She is safe in her home awaiting the return of the little girl. I warned her against any treachery, and I doubt she would risk the life of her only child, eh? But we are wasting time in conversation. The sooner we finish our business, the sooner you can take your niece home. Now go. I will follow."

Hattie Lee screeched when Lizzy appeared on the path, but when the little girl tried to leap out of De-Coeur's arms, he squeezed her against his side until she lost her breath.

"So you are the man who wars on children!"

Lizzy saw sparks in DeCoeur's eyes. His mouth widened in a humorless grin. He did not reply.

"Gently, Eliza. Have a care how you talk to him," Rafe said.

His low-voiced caution chilled her more than the look on DeCoeur's face. Rafe was twenty paces away, guarded by a French Lancer. In his eyes she read his relief at finding her alive—and his concern that she would not remain so for long.

She saw terror in Hattie Lee's huge brown eyes. Holding herself back like a jockey before the starting gun, she said, "Put her down, sir."

"I will when your lover turns over my property." He

345

looked her over. "You are the little anarchist who makes bombs."

"Let the women go, DeCoeur," Rafe said. "Your business is with me."

"You are in no position to bargain, Major," DeCoeur said. "Now get me my diamond."

"Go, señora, beside your man." La Peña gestured with his gun.

Instead, Lizzy walked to DeCoeur, stared into his face, then caught Hattie Lee's hand. "You'll get your damned rock, Mr. DeCoeur. Now give me the child or I'll—"

DeCoeur slapped her hard across the wrist, breaking her contact with her niece. Hattie Lee let out a shriek. Lizzy stepped back, rubbing her wrist.

"You will *what*, madame?"

"I will kill you."

"Before you try it, Madame McCord, please remember that I need only one hostage."

Rafe caught Lizzy's arm and pulled her into step beside him. "You'll get yourself killed, Eliza. Be quiet now."

"I thought you were going to give him the diamond!"

"He'll get it."

"When?" She glanced over her shoulder. Geraud was riding just behind them.

Very softly Rafe said, "When you see me strike, take Hattie Lee to the balloon. Fly off."

"Without you? I can't."

"Silence!" Geraud said. "Speak again and I will slit your tongues!"

Rafe stopped walking and looked around Geraud's horse at DeCoeur. "Put the child down and I'll show you the hiding place."

DeCoeur dismounted. Pushing Geraud off the trail, he

paced over to Rafe. Abruptly he thrust the child at Lizzy. "Geraud, cover them! Hidalgo, come with me."

Pressing his gun into Rafe's spine, DeCoeur followed Rafe to a gigantic pin oak. Rafe reached high into a crevice, brought out the stone, and lifted it into a tunnel of light piercing the trees.

The prisms cast cold blue darts of fire all over the woods. Lizzy and Hattie Lee gasped in amazement; La Peña crossed himself. Even Geraud lowered his gun, mesmerized.

But DeCoeur snarled like a rabid bear: "Give it to me!"

Louis DeCoeur reached for it. Rafe slashed him across the left cheek with the diamond. DeCoeur's pistol went off with a roar, the ball smashing the trunk by Rafe's hip. Rafe knocked the gun out of his hand and slashed his face again.

DeCoeur grabbed for the blood-slick stone and rammed his knee between Rafe's legs. Twisting to avoid the strike, Rafe didn't see DeCoeur's hands coming up to lock on his throat.

His fingers dug in like steel clamps, crushing muscles and veins together, closing off the air. Rafe pounded with his fists and the diamond, but DeCoeur only dug in and bore him to the ground.

"How does it feel to die, thief?" DeCoeur demanded in French. "*Mon dieu,* but how your eyes bulge, and how black your face is turning! What an ugly picture the gallant Major Laffite presents!"

The pain was incredible, a suffocating pressure against his eardrums like being immersed under a thousand gallons of water. Darkness held him, dragged him deep. He didn't feel the diamond roll from his grasp. He began to dream of a warm bed with Eliza curled against him. He could hear her voice calling . . . calling. Then the pain stopped.

DeCoeur released his death grip on Rafe's throat to pounce upon the priceless jewel rolling in the mud. Seizing the bloody crystal, he kissed its cold blue light. ''My beauty! I have you at last!''

Chapter Thirty-one

The instant Rafe sprang into action, Geraud tried to saber Lizzy. She jerked Hattie Lee behind a tree. Geraud's saber ripped off bark beside her head.

Geraud forced his mount after them in a lethal game of tag. He slashed madly again and again at the tree trunk, amputating limbs and bark.

Lizzy knew if she bolted through the woods, Geraud would ride them down and kill them. All she could do was keep pushing Hattie Lee around the trunk, hoping to tire Geraud's horse.

Thirty feet away, Rafe dragged air into his battered throat and swayed to his feet. Nearby, DeCoeur gazed raptly into the diamond. The Frenchman seemed oblivious to all but the stone.

Hattie Lee screamed, drawing Rafe's attention. Geraud's saber was descending toward Lizzy's raised arms. "No!" Rafe yelled.

La Peña crashed his horse into Geraud's, knocking

Lizzy over a sycamore log. Geraud fell beside her but immediately rolled to his feet, brandishing his saber. Hattie Lee fled.

"Son of a mestizo bitch," Geraud snarled at La Peña, "dismount and fight me!"

"You'll fight me!" Rafe said, slamming into him from the right.

Geraud fell to one knee but retained his sword. Before Rafe could land a kick, he lunged at him, slashing. Rafe gave ground, then snatched up a stick and used it to parry Geraud's powerful blows.

"Only little boys play with sticks!" Geraud said, and with an overhand blow he chopped the stick in half. Instantly he pressed his advantage, his deadly steel slicing close to Rafe's chest, driving him back into a tree. "DeCoeur has the diamond, my Rebel friend. What do you have but death?"

La Peña jumped into the fray, parrying a saber cut meant for Rafe. "Captain Geraud, you are undermatched—perhaps you would care for a better-armed opponent."

The two swordsmen thrust and parried in an ancient, deadly ballet. La Peña moved with controlled grace. Babbling profanities, Geraud began to launch uncoordinated attacks.

Rafe left them and began searching for Lizzy and Hattie Lee. He found Lizzy behind a log, half-senseless.

"Where's Hattie Lee?" he shouted.

Before she could answer, Geraud vented a terrible scream. Rafe twisted in time to see him fall back, blood gushing from his throat. Hidalgo La Peña pivoted toward Rafe and raised his bloody weapon.

"You are my prisoner, Major," he said, but his voice was thin. A bright crimson stain bloomed on the front of his green jacket. "You must stand trial for the theft of the diamond."

"You are hurt, La Peña," Rafe said, and started toward him.

La Peña brandished his blade, and with his free hand, drew his pistol. "Put your hands behind your head! Woman, you will take the rope from my horse and bind him for the trip to Mexico."

A shadow passed over them. Driven on a fresh breeze, its half-filled sides luffing, the balloon scooted just over the treetops. The basket crashed into pine boughs and began to spin.

"Aunt Lizzy! Help me!"

Hattie Lee's head appeared over the rail. She waved her arms frantically, then thrust one leg over the rim. She was going to jump.

"No!" Lizzy screamed.

Louis DeCoeur's huge red face appeared beside Hattie Lee. Grabbing the child by one braid, he slung her back into the basket out of sight. He could be heard laughing and shouting, "My beauty! She is all mine! All mine at last!"

"Hattie Lee!" Lizzy started to run after the balloon, but La Peña cocked the pistol and commanded her to stay. Rafe dragged her behind him and held on to her wrists.

"He's taken your precious diamond, La Peña, and he'll kill the child!" Rafe said. "By the sacred thunder, you don't think he ever intended to let you take it back to Mexico, did you?"

La Peña threw an anxious glance heavenward. Then he took careful aim at the balloon.

"No! Don't shoot!" Lizzy said. "You'll blow it up— it's full of hydrogen!"

The Mexican's hand shook. His eyes full of agony,

he stared at his enemies and then at the balloon. Abruptly he changed his grip on the pistol and extended it to Rafe. "Go after her, Major. Save the little girl. I do not care what happens to the diamond anymore."

Rafe seized the gun and leaped onto La Peña's horse. "Stay with him, Eliza!"

"I'm coming with you!"

Geraud's horse stood close by. Lizzy ran to catch the bridle, then glanced at La Peña. His head bowed, he stood leaning on his saber. The bloodstain on his jacket was larger. Lizzy hesitated for an instant, then, with a sharp gasp of despair, ran to him and began to remove his uniform jacket. "We must dress your wound!"

She worked quickly, but by the time she finished Rafe was long gone. Taking Geraud's horse, she raced after him at breakneck speed.

Don't shoot, Rafe. No matter what, remember the hydrogen.

Hattie Lee clung tightly to the basket and scowled at DeCoeur. The big man was around the bend over that diamond—she could tell by the way he kept talking to it and kissing it.

He didn't seem to realize the danger they were in from the trees, either. The balloon didn't have enough lift to carry them over the taller ones; the gondola went crashing through the limbs. Any second now, they'd turn over and splatter all across the state of Tennessee.

Before long, they reached a narrow, grassy valley slashed down the middle by a river. The balloon dropped even closer to earth, less than fifty feet, but at least there were fewer trees. If they lost a little more height, Hattie Lee figured she'd jump into the river.

"This old balloon ain't got long to live," she said.

"Eh? And why does the girl-child say such things,

when the greatest scientific mind in all the world knows it is not so?''

'' 'Cause my granddaddy made this balloon, and he didn't design it to go wallowing through the trees like a drunk hog. We can't get over the mountains in this thing.''

''She will take us where we need to go.''

''And where's that?''

''To Washington,'' he said. ''To Mr. Lincoln.''

''Pshaw! Don't know why anybody'd want to see that ol' frock coat!''

''*He* wishes to see *me*.'' DeCoeur held the diamond to the light and turned it to and fro. ''For what I would show him, he will give me a Cabinet position.''

''You need to be stuffed in a cabinet,'' Hattie Lee said under her breath. DeCoeur gave her one of his nasty smiles. ''You gonna show him your diamond?''

''*Oui*. And the bomb technology to go with it.''

''You got a bomb?''

''In here.'' He tapped the side of his head with the diamond; shards of crimson and blue pricked his face. ''For what I know, Lincoln will lay the world at my feet.''

''That Yankee ain't got the world to give.''

''Then I will take it!'' DeCoeur's voice soared high. ''Into its breast I will burn my name—I will write upon it with my beautiful white phosphorus! The people will burn, yes, every one!''

Hattie Lee rose to her feet. She felt very peculiar. The horrible man was talking about destroying the world; he was *really* crazy!

''What are you staring at?'' DeCoeur looked at her out of strangely innocent eyes.

Hattie Lee stretched even taller. ''That's what I'm trying to figure out. Looks to me like your stern wheel's short one paddle."

DeCoeur's face underwent a hideous transformation. His eyes seemed to sink back into his skull, his lips disappeared, and every muscle in his face convulsed. Stretching out a huge paw, he stepped toward her.

Hattie Lee climbed up the basket and into the sheets. As DeCoeur stumbled toward her, the gondola swayed violently. He fell to one knee.

Clinging to the lines, Hattie Lee walked the basket rail to stay clear of him. DeCoeur plunged toward her, his shifting weight canting the basket. Losing her footing, Hattie Lee swung out over the earth. In that terrifying instant she saw Rafe gallop out of the trees two hundred yards behind them.

DeCoeur saw the rider, too. Growling like a bear, he snatched Hattie Lee's foot and tried to yank her off the lines. Instead, her shoe came off in his hand. She clambered up the line to get out of reach.

"Let go!" DeCoeur said. "I must make the balloon lighter! Let go!"

"No!" Hattie Lee pulled herself up another few inches. Feeling DeCoeur's fingers on her ankle, she kicked as hard as she could.

"You are nothing!" DeCoeur said. "One little child, you mean nothing compared to the beautiful fire I would bring the world! Throw yourself off!"

Sobbing, clinging to the line with all her strength, Hattie Lee pulled her feet up close under her. As the balloon turned in the air, she saw another rider emerge from the trees. It was Aunt Lizzy, but she and Rafe seemed too far away to help.

"Lighten the load!" DeCoeur screamed, drawing his pistol. "You will sacrifice for me!"

The pistol cracked, thunder in her ears. Hattie Lee's

right hand slipped from the line. She looked down at DeCoeur. Holding the smoking pistol in one hand, the diamond in the other, he stared intently at a point above her head.

Hattie Lee heard a muffled whoosh. She looked where DeCoeur was looking. The balloon was on fire! Flames curled like bright orange ribbons around the upper part of the envelope. Oddly, the bottom half remained intact; the blue silk still curved like a bowl over her head.

Hattie Lee slid down the line and dropped into the basket. Screaming and laughing, DeCoeur held the diamond to the firelight. Ten thousand burning balloons seemed reflected in its crystal walls.

"My beauty will destroy this ugly world!"

"We got to jump!" Hattie Lee shouted. Flinging the rope ladder overboard, she thrust one leg over the side. "Come on, Mr. DeCoeur! You're gonna burn up!"

But he did not hear her. Eaten by flames of gold, the balloon began to disappear. Pieces of burning silk fell onto his head, mixing red hair and flames into a burning crown.

"My beauty!" DeCoeur screamed above the noise.

The diamond became a ball of red fire in his hand. The spirit of the diamond shone into the madman's face. Then the jewel sizzled and became too slippery to hold. Hattie Lee saw his eyes fly wide with horror as the stone flew from his grasp. Over and over it turned, lancing the air with self-generated fire.

Uttering an agonized shriek, DeCoeur hurled himself after it. The diamond hovered just below his outstretched hands. Then, heated as it was, suffused by its unnatural energy, the precious stone struck a boulder and disintegrated into a million points of light.

"My beauty!" DeCoeur screamed just before he hit

the boulder. Diamond dust settled over his shattered body.

Rafe galloped past him without a glance. He was fifteen feet behind the balloon now, spurring his horse with his bare heels. Hattie Lee dangled out of reach on the ladder. In no time at all the burning canopy would crash down on top of her.

Lashing the horse with the reins, he closed the gap. Reaching precariously out over his horse's head, Rafe caught the end of the ladder just as the horse veered away in terror. Fiery debris rained down on him as he climbed the ladder toward the child.

He could hear Lizzy screaming from behind him, "Keep climbing down! Don't stop! Go to Rafe!"

But the balloon was collapsing across the earth like a dying comet. Hattie Lee stopped climbing and froze on the ladder. She was still twenty feet off the ground.

"Hattie Lee! Go to Mr. Rafe! Go!"

"Come on, honey, climb down to me!"

"Jump, Hattie Lee!" Lizzy shouted.

The little girl let go. Rafe lunged to catch her, and together they fell ten feet to the ground. Rafe corkscrewed to land on his back with the child on top of him.

Two seconds later, the gondola plowed into an oak and hung there. The balloon crumpled into the tree and exploded in a gigantic fireball.

Lizzy jumped from her horse and ran. "Rafe! Hattie Lee! Oh, dear God, are you alive?"

Rafe pulled Hattie Lee up beside him. Heat from the fire licked at them. Lizzy urged them away from the danger zone before she allowed them to drop to the ground again. Kneeling, she held Hattie Lee's shoulders and searched her eyes.

"Thank the good Lord you're all right!" she said.

"Course we are, Aunt Lizzy," Hattie Lee said, and began to cry.

Rafe pulled Lizzy and the child against him. "Eliza McCord, I doubt we'll do any more flying for a while," he said in her ear. "Sorry about your balloon."

"We won't be chasing any more diamonds for a while, either, so I don't care." Wiping her tears on her sleeve, she smiled up at him. In a shaky voice she asked, "What shall we do for our next adventure?"

"Let's go steal a train, honey," he said with a dazzling smile.

Lizzy blinked. "And go where?"

"Why, to Richmond."

"But the diamond's gone, Rafe. We don't have anything to offer Richmond."

His handsome face lit with playful seriousness. "No, but Richmond has something to offer us. A church . . . and a preacher to marry us."

There wasn't anything to do but kiss him.

Epilogue

"You're home! Praise God, you're home at last!" Grace Fairlove shouted from an upstairs window. The curtains fluttered as she disappeared back into the house.

Hattie Lee took off at a run, leaving Rafe and Lizzy on the creek bridge. When Lizzy started to race after her, Rafe caught her hand and made her walk beside him.

"Not so fast, honey," he said. "We've been gone a long time; you can spare one more minute to let them get the crying out of the way."

"But I want to see Grace!"

"And so you will, but all things in their proper order."

Relenting, Lizzy reached up to touch his face. "What proper order, darling?"

"First we do this." He escorted her through the gate

and hurried her along the front walk. "And then we do this."

He swept her into his arms and bore her up the steps to the open front door. Then, smiling down at her, he carried her across the threshold.

"Welcome home, Mrs. Laffite," he said, and kissed her.

FOREVER & A DAY

VICTORIA CHANCELLOR

When Linda O'Rourke returns to her grandmother's South Carolina beach house, it is for a quiet summer of tying up loose ends. And although the lovely dwelling charms her, she can't help but remember the evil presence that threatened her there so many years ago. Plagued by her fear, and tormented by visions of a virile Englishman tempting her with his every caress, she is unprepared for reality in the form of the mysterious and handsome Gifford Knight. His kisses evoke memories of the man in her dreams, but his sensual demands are all too real. Linda longs to surrender to Giff's masterful touch, but is it a safe haven she finds in his arms, or the beginning of her worst nightmare?

_52063-X $5.50 US/$7.50 CAN

Bestselling Author Of *Blind Fortune*

Wealthy and handsome, Reese Ashburn is the most eligible bachelor in Mobile, Alabama. And although every young debutante dreams of becoming the lady of Bonne Chance—Reese's elegant bayside plantation—none believes that its master will ever finish sowing his wild oats. Then one night Reese's carousing ends in tragedy and shame: His gambling partner, James Bentley, is brutally murdered while Reese is too drunk to save him.

Entrusted with the care of James's daughter, Reese knows that he is hardly the model guardian. And fiery Patience Bentley's stubborn pride and irresistible beauty are sure to make her a difficult ward. Still, driven by guilt, Reese is bound and determined to honor Bentley's dying wish—as well as exact revenge on his friend's killers. But can he resist Patience's enticing advances long enough to win back his pride and his reputation?

_3943-5 $4.99 US/$6.99 CAN

BESTSELLING AUTHOR OF
BLAZE

Kane Roemer heads up into the Wyoming mountains hell-bent on fulfilling his heart's desire. There the rugged horseman falls in love with a white stallion that has no equal anywhere in the West. But Kane has to use his considerable charms to gentle a beautiful spitfire who claims the animal as her own. Jade Farrow will be damned if she'll give up her beloved horse without a fight. But then a sudden blizzard traps Jade with her sworn enemy, and she discovers that the only way to true bliss is to rope, corral, and brand Kane with her unbridled passion.

___4310-6 $5.99 US/$6.99 CAN

DREAM WEAVER

MARTI JONES

Bestselling Author Of *Time's Healing Heart*

Brandy Ashton peddles homemade remedies to treat every disease from ague to gout. Yet no tonic can save her reputation as far as Sheriff Adam McCullough is concerned. Despite his threats to lock her up if she doesn't move on, Brandy is torn between offering him a fatal dose of poison—or an even more lethal helping of love.

When Brandy arrives in Charming, Oklahoma, McCullough is convinced she is a smooth-talking drifter out to cheat his good neighbors. And he isn't about to let her sell snake oil in his town. But one stolen kiss makes him forget the larceny he thinks is on Brandy's mind—and yearn to sample the innocence he knows is in her heart.

_3641-X $4.50 US/$5.50 CAN

BLIND FORTUNE

MARTI JONES

Young and carefree bachelors Garreth Armstrong and Sebastian Avery make a reckless bet: The first to succumb to the velvet bonds of matrimony will forfeit his inheritance to the other. Shipping baron Garreth never anticipates that one day he will be in desperate need of a fortune—or that the only way to get it will be to find Sebastian a wife.

Determined to save her family's Alabama estate, Lacey Webster is the perfect belle for Garreth's plans. To gain Armstrong's share of the winnings, the beguiling blonde agrees to seduce his adversary. But the more she tries to lure Sebastian with her feminine wiles, the more she longs for Garreth's warm embrace.

Playing at love is a dangerous game, and soon the passion between Garreth and Lacey burns hotter than the summer sun. But the stakes are higher than either realizes: a lifetime of wealth or a love no money can buy.

_3866-8 $4.99 US/$6.99 CAN

SEDUCED
CATHERINE LANIGAN

"Catherine Lanigan is in a class by herself: unequaled and simply fabulous!"

—*Affaire de Coeur*

Even amid the spectacle and splendor of the carnival in Venice, the masked rogue is brazen, reckless, and dangerously risqué. As he steals Valentine St. James away from the costume ball at which her betrothal to a complete stranger is to be announced, the exquisite beauty revels in the illicit thrill of his touch, the tender passion in his kiss. But Valentine learns that illusion rules the festival when, at the stroke of midnight, her mysterious suitor reveals he is Lord Hawkeston, the very man she is to wed. Convinced her intended is an unrepentant scoundrel, Valentine wants to deny her maddening attraction for him, only to keep finding herself in his heated embrace. Yet is she truly losing her heart to the dashing peer—or is she being ruthlessly seduced?

_3942-7 $5.50 US/$7.50 CAN

Forsaking All Others

GAIL LINK

"Gail Link was born to write romance!"
—Jayne Ann Krentz

Anthony Chambers will inherit half of his Great Uncle Cedric's sprawling Australian homestead on one condition: He must leave England behind and spend a year living at the homestead with his uncle's live-in companion, Annie Ross. Certain the young American is his uncle's mistress, he sets out for Camelot Station eager to meet the scheming tart clever enough to bleed the old man dry, and foolish enough to have a child out of wedlock. But what he finds waiting for him is a softer, gentler woman, a natural beauty who is not intimidated by his arrogant, upper-crust ways. Stubbornly independent, she certainly doesn't fit Tony's idea of the perfect woman—someone he can mold to what he wants. Instead, with her proud spirit and sweet kisses, Annie makes him lose all control, and he wonders if he has the courage to forsake all others and surrender to a love as untamed as the wild Australian landscape.

_4151-0 $5.50 US/$6.50 CAN